Amy Andrews and Ros Baxter are sisters who are as close as they are different. Amy married the first boy she ever loved. Ros tried to remember the name of her first love the other day and gave up and had a chocolate bar instead. Amy thinks everything will work out. Ros thinks everything will get found out. But for all their differences they are fiercely close and desperately proud of each other. Nothing feels real until it has been spoken aloud to the other. They both love to talk, laugh and write, preferably over a bottle of bubbly and something coated in chocolate.

Numbered

AMY ANDREWS & ROS BAXTER

HARLEQUIN® MIRA®

First Published 2016
First Australian Paperback Edition 2016
ISBN 978 148923741 5

NUMBERED
© 2016 by Amy Andrews and Ros Baxter
Australian Copyright 2016
New Zealand Copyright 2016

Published by
Harlequin Mira
An imprint of Harlequin Enterprises (Australia) Pty Ltd.
Level 13, 201 Elizabeth St
SYDNEY NSW 2000
AUSTRALIA

* and TM are trademarks of Harlequin Enterprises Limited or its corporate affiliates. Trademarks indicated with * are registered in Australia, New Zealand and in other countries.

Cataloguing-in-Publication details are available from the National Library of Australia
www.librariesaustralia.nla.gov.au

MIX
Paper from
responsible sources
FSC
www.fsc.org   FSC® C009448

To our father, Noel Baxter, who taught us every day that fatherhood isn't about the big and flashy but about being there and showing up. We are proud to call you our dad.

Chapter One

Quentin Carmody didn't do early mornings, heights or bossy women. So as he peered out of the tiny plane at the breaking dawn and then back towards the tawny-brown eyes of the woman viciously punching her iPhone, the last thing he wanted to do was jump.

But Quentin had made a promise. *I'll go first.*

It had seemed like a good idea at the time, a sure-fire way to impress this girl, who was as cute as hell but wound tighter than one of his father's antique clocks.

Sure, I'll jump out of a plane with you. No problems. I'll even go first.

To tell the truth, jumping out of a plane hadn't exactly been what he'd had in mind as he'd looked across the counter at five-feet-two of pointy sexiness. Kind of like a young Anjelica Huston. With curly hair. It hadn't exactly been what he'd meant when he'd handed over her cheese-and-tomato sandwich on wholegrain (not wholemeal), cut into four triangles. When he'd looked right into those feline eyes, held onto the plastic plate a few seconds too long, while she'd tugged at it, and he'd said: 'You look like a girl who needs to take some risks.'

What he'd had in mind had involved a lot less equipment than jumping out of a plane required. Fewer clothes in general, really.

He sighed. A guy had to start somewhere.

He'd been snookered, of course. Because he'd seen the challenge in those intriguing eyes as she'd pushed those ridiculous glasses back up her nose. He'd seen her look him up and down and try to find the easiest way to blow him off. That quirky mouth that looked like it was about to make some wisecrack had opened intriguingly. He'd felt something stir south of his belt buckle as she'd spoken.

'Take a risk? Sure. Come jump out of a plane with me. Tomorrow.'

Now here they were. He watched his instructor adjust their straps and check their packs, and thought again how this was just not his kind of sport. Too much equipment, too much hassle. Leaving aside how altogether weird it was to be strapped to another dude, even if it was in a purely functional kind of way. He momentarily wished he could be surfing, if he had to be up this early at all. Why waste a beautiful sunrise on this madness?

Quentin flicked a quick glance back at her again. Poppy. This girl had the wrong name. She should have been Rose. Great face, lots of prickles. She was sitting on the pint-sized bench behind him, studying her iPhone like it held the secrets to the universe. He already knew what was making her look so intent. He'd sneaked a peek at the phone when she'd gone to the bathroom for the sixth time back at the hangar. It was a list, detailed in one of those clever apps that help busy people organise themselves.

Quentin never needed lists. He believed in keeping life simple. But he chuckled as he recalled this particular list.

Dawn skydive from small plane (with propeller but also backup engines).

Rappel down cliff face on significant mountain (at least 2000 metres above sea level).

Take some form of hallucinogenic drug (ensuring pre-testing for purity).

And so on.

Man, this chick was specific.

He hadn't had time to read the entire catalogue, but he'd had long enough to notice it seemed to go on in a similar vein up to item number twenty.

His instructor and partner-in-nylon, Calvin, flashed the two-minute signal on calloused fingers. The guy looked like he'd been on seven hundred tours of Iraq. Kind of like Jack Nicholson in *A Few Good Men*. Which was exactly what you wanted in a parachute professional. He had more tattoos than Quentin's drummer. And this guy's tattoos were a lot more badass, too. Quentin had told Spike that inking 'percussion' across your knuckles was kind of lame. It takes more than ten letters to make a badass knuckle tattoo. That was the problem with drummers. They didn't listen. But they always seemed to get laid anyway.

Quentin looked over again at the diminutive figure concentrating intently on her list as she sat swathed in nylon and rope. Even under all that gear she still looked tiny. Her pointy little chin rose slightly when she glanced up and eyeballed him back. She looked kind of green, but her golden-brown eyes flashed in a way that was a bit disconcerting. It made him feel annoyed but sort of tingly at the same time.

He figured this was the time to offer the bossy minx some words. A bit of the old Q charm. No doubt she was anxious. Time to drive home his advantage. Demonstrate what an evolved guy he was. But also tough, you know. Cool. Problem was, he didn't necessarily feel so cool. In fact, he felt rather sick.

Not afraid, he quickly assured himself. Probably just the unusual early morning and lack of breakfast. He laced his hands together, stretched his long arms over his head and winced. And possibly the tiniest shred of a hangover. Occupational hazard. It was important to have a drink with the manager after the gig.

He shook his head. Time was a-wastin'. What should he say to her before he turned to jump? Some words of comfort. He searched his considerable bank of classic movie quotes for the right piece of advice. Something that would tell her she had nothing to worry about. That this was gonna be a piece of cake.

Maybe Lauren Bacall? *You know how to whistle, don't you, Steve? You just put your lips together and blow.* Hmmm. She might not get it.

He frowned. She might even think he was being lewd.

Here's lookin' at you kid? Everyone knew that one, right? Too clichéd?

Just as he prevaricated, Calvin gave him the signal that he was about to count down from five on that big fist. And Quentin had it. As he made for the door, ignoring the thrumming in his blood, he turned his head towards her and performed his signature move, flicking his overlong dirty-blond fringe out of his eyes.

The engine noise was so loud he had to yell.

'May the force be with you!'

As Quentin's body connected with the first cold rush of air, he heard her throaty chuckle follow him down. Down, down, down.

* * *

The petite body hurled itself at him, hard enough for him to register, even through his shock and all those layers of nylon, that although she might look small she was all woman. 'That was fucking amazing!' Her face was lit up like someone had shone a torch into one of her ears. 'Wasn't it?'

Poppy had just landed, crashing with a kind of clumsy elegance into a patch of grass. As soon as she had detached from her instructor, she'd hurtled over to him.

'Oh my god! I feel like I just died!' She was still hugging him fiercely around the waist and squealing into his chest, surprisingly strong for such a small woman. Her grip on him was ferocious. He got it. The thump of adrenaline was still making his skin tingle and heart gallop as well. But he couldn't find the words to explain that while she was pressing so closely against him. Instead, he cradled her heart-shaped face and lifted it up to look at his. *There was something about this girl.*

'Let's get a drink.'

* * *

Poppy arched above him like a wild thing. Her skin was flushed down her neck and across her chest and he was mesmerised by the shadow play on her breasts. It was late afternoon and they'd been in bed for seven hours.

Quentin's whole body was on fire. Again. He pushed himself harder up into her, wanting to see if he could get her to make that noise again, the one that sounded like a cross between a gurgle and a squeal. He scraped rough hands down the long expanse of her, from throat to thigh, amazed again that such a tiny package could hold so much power. And passion.

As he reached her thigh, her face changed. It became intense, concentrated. She raised her arms to pull sticky hair off the back of her neck. The unconscious move elevated her breasts and framed her face in a way that tipped him over the edge. He yanked her down beside him and drove into her. She slammed herself back against him, tilting her hips and pulling on his in an effort to bring him deeper into her. Finally, he heard it again. That gurgly squeal.

It was like the voice of angels.

As they lay pulsing and confused in the March heat, he became dimly aware of his surroundings again. The old ceiling fan in his bedroom fought against its better judgement to make another lazy revolution. His big wooden bed made its cranky settling sound. The framed Nirvana poster on his wall seemed to wink at him – 1994, Le Zenith, Paris. They'd been on top of the world at that gig.

The way he felt right now.

As an ex-footballer, sometimes surfer and wannabe rock star, Quentin had been fucked by cheerleaders, surfer girls and group-ies, but he had never, ever been fucked like that. He thought about James Cagney in *Yankee Doodle Dandy*. "My mother thanks you. My father thanks you. My sister thanks you. And I thank you."

And yet nothing about this girl made him feel like using a line anyone else had ever used before.

He wanted to mark the moment. He wanted to turn over, kiss this girl one more time and tell her how amazing it had been. And as soon as he could move again, he was going to do just that. But for now, he planned to lie there, sniffing her chocolatey-smelling hair and continuing to pat this really smooth piece of skin in the middle of her back.

Trust a girl to upset the plan.

He felt her drawing away from him, rolling out of bed and scrabbling on the floor. *Oh no. Not yet.* 'Where you going?' His voice sounded strange and hoarse, or maybe it was because his ears weren't working properly yet. They had that underwater quality often brought on by really loud gigs and outrageously good orgasms.

'Nowhere.' She was back, propped on one elbow, glasses perched on her nose.

Every one of his cells yelled with joy. Until they saw she had company.

She was holding that damn iPhone, and viciously punching buttons again, a frown of concentration creasing the smooth spot between her lush eyebrows.

How could she even work her fingers? The girl must be a genius. His felt like his would never function again.

Quentin moved to lean lazily onto one elbow as well, trying to make it look effortless, but still struggling to coordinate basic movement. 'What is it? You gotta be somewhere?'

'Hmmmm?' Poppy didn't look up from her work on the phone.

He nudged her and motioned to the phone. 'Looking at your schedule?'

'What?' She focused on him at last and he was relieved to see that she continued to look flushed and strung out. Whatever she needed to check must be important.

'Oh, no, sorry. It's nothing.' She had the good grace to look abashed. 'I just …'

'Good, then.' Quentin laughed, plucking the phone from her small hands and holding it at a stretch above his head. Hoping she might come fetch.

'I was just … er … crossing you off my list.'

'Your … list?' A vague memory stirred in a part of Quentin's brain. A part that had been pushed way back by the hours of ridiculously good sex. Oh yeah. The list. On the app on the phone. Some kind of 'things I wanna do' list.

Poppy gazed down at her fingernails, and the flush that Quentin was pretty sure had been caused by hours of passion started to deepen. She looked suspiciously like she was flushing from embarrassment. Or guilt? She looked up at him slowly as she spoke. 'Surely you don't think I do this all the time?'

Quentin wasn't stupid, despite living what his father called 'a lifestyle unworthy of yourself'. But he really did not have the faintest idea what she meant. Summoning a superhuman effort, he commanded his brain to work.

What the hell was she asking him again? Oh, that's right. Did he think she did this all the time? He wasn't normally this vague – what was this witch doing to him?

He shook his head at her question. Did women really think men cared about that stuff? Did he care if she did this all the time? Definitely, definitely not. He could honestly say he did not give a flying fuck whether this girl dragged guys home every other day to have her way with them for seven hours. He was just glad as hell she'd decided to do it with him. Today. And hopefully maybe again. Sometime. Now. How to find a way to say that.

As the possible word combinations formed in his head, he became aware that he was walking on dangerous ground. Women were notoriously crazy and unpredictable when it came to matters of how men perceived them, and he was completely sure he'd never been able to work out why.

He was pretty sure *I guess you do* wasn't the right answer.

He rejected *I couldn't care less* as well, quickly followed by *Let's go again and I'll tell you what I think afterwards.*

Eventually, he decided it might be one of those cases where actions speak louder than words. He held up the phone and took a quick picture of himself before handing it back to her and sneaking in for a kiss while he was close. Mmm, mmmm. Yep, he hadn't been imagining it. She definitely smelled like chocolate but tasted like watermelon. Now how the hell did she accomplish that?

Satisfied, he leaned back into one of his super-soft pillows. A man needed a good pillow when life could be so trying. And women so confusing.

But she was looking at him expectantly. 'Well?'

Was this some kind of test? Oh no. He'd never been much good at those. 'We-ell?' He drew the word out, hoping for a hint.

'*Do* you think I do this all the time?'

Play it safe. 'No,' he said, finally making a decision. 'Definitely not. I'm assuming it was the—' He studied her face carefully for signs of wrong-stepping. 'Post-skydive adrenaline?'

That sardonic smile curved up on one side. He almost cheered. He'd got it right. For once. Time to bring this baby home. 'Hey,' he whispered to her, reaching up to stroke the side of her face. 'You should definitely skydive more.'

She laughed, and he liked it. It sounded like the way men laughed, or kids. Full and throaty and without any artifice. 'Well, I definitely don't. Do this all the time. In fact, I'm only doing this because of my list.'

It was Quentin's turn to frown. Surely he hadn't heard right. 'That list again?'

She nodded.

'You mean crossing the skydive off, right?' He didn't want to sound precious but somehow diminishing what they'd just done to an item on a list made him feel terrible.

She shook her head slowly, wrinkling her cute nose like a muddled guinea pig. 'Er, no.' She gave him a small smile. It looked extra small because he'd seen the really, really big one many times over the last seven hours. 'I meant the ...'

'The …?' He prompted her with his eyes. Come on. You're a big girl. Fess up. No way was he gonna help her tell him he was an item on some list.

'The … whoopee.'

'The *whoopee?*'

She nodded again, encouragingly, like a mum when a kid starts to get the answer right.

He took his hands and placed them firmly on her shoulders. She looked into his eyes with her big serious brown ones. 'Okay, first. No-one calls it whoopee. Anymore. If they ever did. And second, what the hell …?'

Quentin's head suddenly hurt a lot. He played lead guitar in a band for chrissakes. He understood one-off experiences. There'd been times, lots of times, hell maybe most times, when he'd been looking for exactly that. And other times when some girl was looking for it, too. He was totally cool with that. That's what people did, sometimes at least. And hey, if getting crossed off some list meant getting hot sex off a gorgeous almost-stranger he was down with that.

Or was he?

The strange girl called Poppy grabbed his hands and held them to her chest like a supplicant nun. 'Come on now, don't be like that, Quentin. Please.' She waved her iPhone in the air as if it held all the answers.

He glanced down at his hands in hers. She was sitting cross-legged, tangled up in his navy-blue sheets, and she looked tiny and almost innocent. Well, apart from the post-orgasm flush that lingered around her shoulders and neck. His hands seemed enormous compared to hers. He knew they were big anyway. Big hands helped in his line of work. Lines of work. But grasped in hers they appeared huge.

He felt clumsy, like an ape trying to woo a fairy.

'Okay,' he breathed, willing himself to be cool. He gave himself a bit of a pep talk. *You're a man, man. Men dream about this shit. Being used for their bodies.* 'Can I see it, then?'

'See what?' She flicked her eyes to the side. *She damn well knew what.*

'The list.' Quentin allowed his voice to deepen. 'Please.'

Poppy took a deep breath, and Quentin tried not to get distracted by the rise and fall of that pretty chest as she did. 'Sure, why not? I mean, of course. You're on it, after all.' She held out her hand and passed the phone to him, touching it lightly on the transfer so the screen would stay lit.

As she handed it over, their fingers connected and a zing of something wicked snaked between them. Quentin tried to focus on the screen. It was hard to make sense of the words with that wicked feeling crowding up his breathing room.

'Number ten,' she contributed, pointing at the screen with her finger.

And there it was. Underneath nine. *Buy a pet snake. Keep and feed for at least a month (check with Biology department re appropriate sub-species).*

He was definitely number ten.

'Sex with a stranger?' He felt somewhat light-headed reading it. And he also felt surprised. Surprised to see how low on details this item seemed to be compared with the rest of the list, at least the parts he'd read. He wondered why. This seemed to be a girl who planned everything. 'You were planning this?' He gestured south, somewhere in the direction of the action.

'Oh no.' Poppy's hand flew to her mouth and she reached out to pat his shoulder. Her fingers felt cool and soft. 'Of course not. That's so … clinical. No, some of them, some of the items I mean, they need a lot of planning. Like the skydive this morning. Others I'm just sort of … going with the flow.'

He took a deep breath. *Sex with a stranger.* 'Hey, Poppy. I'm not exactly a stranger, y'know. I mean we did meet yesterday. At the cafeteria.'

She raised an eyebrow.

He shrugged. She was right. It was a technicality.

Sex with a stranger. 'I notice you didn't call it whoopee on your list.'

She nodded, head to the side. 'No,' she agreed. 'Probably because it's a formal document, you know? Like a … deed, I guess.'

A horrible thought abruptly occurred to him. My god, was she going to try this with other almost-complete strangers?

'So, er … Is the plan …? I mean … Do you only do each item once?'

Why did he care? Why did he care if she planned to do item ten over and over again? While the thought that she might have done this a hundred times before hadn't disturbed him at all, the thought that she might do it again, with someone other than him, unexpectedly did disturb him. Very much.

She snorted. 'Of course not. What do I look like?'

He studied her: medium-length curly brown hair falling over one creamy shoulder. Black square glasses perched on her nose. Cat-like eyes watching him watching her. Half-smile playing around those strange, exquisite lips that were all tight and thin one moment and then scrumptious and kissable the next.

'Gorgeous,' he said. 'Absolutely gorgeous.'

She shrugged and snorted again. 'Please. We've already done the sex. You don't need to say all that.'

'All what?'

'All the empty-flattery-to-sleep-with-me stuff.'

He laughed, and he felt the tension ooze from shoulders that had worked really, really hard for the last seven hours. It was good to do something that felt effortless again. 'Okay.' He sighed. 'No problem.'

She started to shift in the bed and Quentin could feel the Leaving Speech coming. Quentin knew the Leaving Speech by heart. In fact, he liked to think he'd written some of its best lines. He knew it had to happen. It served an important function at this delicate juncture. He just didn't want it to happen yet.

Not quite yet.

'So,' he started again. 'Tell me some more about the list.'

Poppy shrugged and studied her fingernails again. Quentin noticed they were short and ragged. 'Not so interesting. Bucket list.'

'Huh?' It was so difficult to follow what she was saying when her mouth looked so good every time it moved.

She twitched her nose and flapped a hand at him. 'Bucket list. You know, like the movie. Like the things you need to do before you kick the bucket list.'

Quentin just could not stop looking at this strange creature. Every time she talked her face was in motion, like it had a tough time containing itself when it needed to be polite and stay still. This girl must play a really crap hand of poker. He was about to laugh out loud again when he remembered where they'd met.

The hospital.

Bucket list.

Oh crap.

He touched her hand, gently, in case she could break. He felt himself start to redden thinking about how he'd been throwing her around all day.

Something dark and nasty curled its fingers around his heart.
Bucket list.

'Oh, Poppy, I'm so sorry. What is it?'

'Pardon?'

'What's wrong with you? I'm so sorry, I didn't even realise. I mean, I didn't really connect the …' He willed himself to stop blathering. 'Oh fuck. You're dying?'

She laughed, but it was a pale echo of the squealy gurgle he'd tried so earnestly to inspire earlier. 'Nah.' She paused. 'At least not that I know of. But I had to go have some tests. Yesterday. You fixed me that sandwich at the café after.'

'What kind of tests?' Quentin didn't know why he was finding it so strenuous to catch his breath. But he did know enough about hospitals to understand that your garden-variety tests usually happened elsewhere.

'Breast.' Poppy traced a finger over her chest in a mesmerising figure eight, on top of the navy sheet.

Quentin tried with all his might to remember that they were discussing potentially life-threatening medical issues. He willed himself not to get his usual reaction to any woman, let alone this beautiful one, touching herself.

She was talking again and he tried to zone in through the thrumming in his ears. 'Breast *cancer*, I guess. It's not that, though, right? Not yet, okay? Just a weird lump. Just a test. I should know the results by now, but of course I had to schedule the tests for yesterday. Bloody Friday. I had to pick a bloody Friday. Gotta wait till Monday to find out for sure.'

'But why now? Why'd you write the bucket list now? You're probably fine. It's probably nothing. One of those … what do they call them? Cyst. A cyst.'

She laughed again. 'Oh, I didn't write the list just now, silly. I've had it for years. My best friend Julia and I wrote them a few years back. It's important to be prepared. When I found out I needed the tests on Wednesday, I just dusted it off. Figured I might as well get a headstart. You know, just in case. Just in case I am going to …' She paused. 'Die.'

'Yeah, right, just in case.' Quentin moved closer, dragging in the chocolatey smell of her and stroking the underside of one wrist with a long index finger.

Her face changed, took on a dark and flushed look. 'What are you doing?'

Quentin moved closer still, so that he could feel his own breath bouncing back at him after it skimmed her cheek. 'I'm … checking.'

She frowned and narrowed her eyes. 'Checking for what?'

'Any signs that you're gonna die.'

Quentin went slowly, tracing fingers calloused from guitar strings across baby-soft skin. Burying his head in that hair that smelled like sunlight and chocolate. Nibbling slightly on those watermelon lips.

It took a huge effort of will to pull away and not push her back down on the bed under some lame guise of needing a more intimate examination.

Finally, heroically, he drew back. 'Nope.'

Poppy looked messy and flustered. 'Nope what?'

'Nope, definitely not dying. You can take my word for it. I have a nose for these things.'

She raised that cute eyebrow at him again.

'Hey, I work in a hospital.'

'You work in a hospital *cafeteria*,' she corrected him.

'Details,' he murmured, winking at her. 'Know this, Poppy Devine. I am very many things. Lots of 'em bad. But I am never, ever wrong.'

He liked the sound of her full name rolling around in his mouth. As he finished his diagnosis, she swatted him on the bicep, then trailed a finger down his arm. Something thick and unmoving sat in the air between them. He watched her eyes darken and flick down to his lips. He eyeballed her from under his long fringe and blasted her with what his drummer, Spike, called The Look That Asks The Question.

He obviously did it wrong.

'I've got to go.' Poppy started to move away.

Really?

'You sure?' Not yet, Poppy Devine. Not quite yet.

'Yep,' she said, smiling as she began to detach herself from the bed.

He was losing her.

'Okay.' Time for the trump card. 'But man, I am ravenous.'

It was true. Quentin was almost always ravenous. With a six-foot-six frame to feed, life truly was one long picnic. It was the reason he'd learned to cook so well in the first place. Survival.

'Tell you what. Why don't I come with you and we go work on number twelve?'

Poppy's brow puckered.

'Don't tell me you don't remember,' he chided gently. 'Number twelve? *Eat a Mexican meal.*' He made the inverted commas sign with his fingers. '"At an authentic Mexican restaurant".' He smiled at her slowly and wiggled his fingers once again. '"Definitely, definitely no Tex Mex."'

Poppy blushed. 'Okay, so I know it's kind of lame.'

'Kind of lame? Poppy.' Quentin used his entire lower register as he scolded her. 'It's almost unforgiveable. I don't know anyone who's never eaten Mexican.'

Poppy shrugged, that pointy, delicate chin lifting defiantly. 'Yeah, well, I'm not just anyone,' she declared. 'There are things about me. Historical things.' She wriggled her eyebrows dramatically. 'Family things. Things you do not know.'

'Amen to that.' Quentin chuckled. With women, that was generally just how he liked it. 'Come on, get your coat.'

'I can't.' Poppy bit her lip and stayed firmly wrapped in the navy-blue sheets.

Quentin studied her. He had the strangest feeling that nothing would ever be easy with this girl.

'Can't what? Can't eat Mexican yet? Need to take a hallucinogenic drug first? Because if you're going to try to tell me it's an ordering problem, let me tell you, girl, that I know better. I happen to know for a fact that you skipped from number one right on through to number ten when it suited you.'

Poppy chuckled. 'No, it's not the order. It's … well, I suppose it's … you.'

'Me?' This was confusing. She seemed pretty happy to be with him the last seven and a half hours. What the hell could be wrong with him? Women loved Quentin, at least at this stage of the relationship. He tried not to think about other lists, the very long ones all his ex-girlfriends had composed about all the reasons he was a crap boyfriend. Partner. Potential husband.

And really, it had never worried him. But the idea that he somehow wasn't good enough to eat Mexican with? Man, he'd eaten Mexican food with all kinds of unsavoury characters. Didn't this girl get it? Mexican was *anything goes* food.

'Well, not you exactly. Obviously, you're …' Her eyes skittered over his broad, naked chest in what he could have sworn was an appreciative manner. 'It's just that you're not my type.'

He raised his eyebrows and she blushed some more.

'I mean, for dating, you know.'

Oh, that. Well, of course he wasn't. About time a woman was clever enough to realise it. 'Okay, so no worries.' He grinned in what he hoped was a charming, boyish way. Chicks liked that. 'So let's not call it a date. Let's call it additional bucket-list ticking.'

She rested her chin on her finger and studied his face.

He waited while he watched her ponder his proposal. It was hard. He just wasn't the patient type.

He tried another tack. 'Okay, so tell you what. While you're thinking about that terrifying idea, tell me. Who exactly is your type?'

The question seemed to perplex her even more than his Mexican-food proposal. She reached over to the rickety coffee table beside his bed and punched the red button on the remote. The television flickered to life. The news. The US president saying something to a bunch of journalists.

'Him.' She pointed a chewed finger at the box.

'Obama?'

She nodded.

He nodded at the television. 'Obama is your type?'

She nodded again.

'Don't you think he's a little …'

'Are you going to say black?' She was almost out of the bed before he registered what she meant. She was like quicksilver.

'No.' And it was true. 'I wasn't going to say black. I was going to say don't you think he's a little serious. And presidenty. And you know, kind of ... married? Pretty happily, too, by the looks of things.'

Poppy nodded earnestly. 'Yeah,' she agreed. 'But I'm also serious,' she said quietly, sitting cross-legged on the bed.

He eyed her in disbelief.

She met his gaze dead on. 'I am. I'll prove it. See if you can guess my job.'

He groaned inwardly. *Oh, goody.* Games. Girls love games. Almost as much as the *what are you thinking* conversation. But on the other hand, he wasn't quite ready for her to leave. Not quite. So maybe he could tolerate a game. A short one.

'Okay, great.' At least it might keep her here a while longer. 'Let's see.' He rubbed his chin and scratched his head. 'How many guesses do I get?'

She cocked her head to the side. 'Three.' This was one girl who knew her mind. Heaven help the guy who crossed her.

'Okay, here goes. Accountant?'

She shook that curly hair emphatically.

'Lawyer?'

Another shake, this time with an accompanying droop to that pretty mouth.

He stretched for something serious yet sexier sounding. He could tell the first two guesses weren't making her happy. 'Cellist?'

She seemed to brighten at this. 'No. No, no, no. You lose. Maths lecturer.'

'Maths lecturer?' Quentin could feel his jaw hanging open in a most unmanly fashion so he scooped it up again. 'Aren't you like ... twenty-five?'

'Twenty-nine,' she countered. 'And I was kind of in a hurry. How old are you?'

Quentin swallowed. Was she going to freak out? 'Twenty-two.'

Poppy shrugged. 'Hmmm,' she mused. 'You look older.'

'Okay,' he went on quickly, still trying to join the dots. 'So you can't eat Mexican with me because you're a maths professor. Hey, that's cool.' He shrugged. 'We'll always have Paris.' Was she a *Casablanca* fan?

'It's not that,' she scolded, punching him on the arm. 'It's just that I can tell we're not compatible. So what's the point? Why start dating at all?'

'How can you tell we're not compatible?' He wasn't arguing. Truth to tell, he was pretty sure he'd never met a woman he'd been compatible with. Leastways there didn't seem to be that many who liked old movies, late-night guitar gigs in smoky pubs, and surfing. And none who didn't want to change him, set him up with a real job, make him respectable. So yeah, he wasn't arguing on the compatibility front. Merely curious.

'I'm an expert.'

'Yeah, you said that, Ms Maths Lecturer.'

'Doctor Maths Lecturer to you.'

Man, she was cute. He tried to work out how to tell her that without sounding patronising. But she was too quick for him again.

'No, I mean my field is human connection. Well, the algorithms of internet dating, actually. Whether they can help you find your perfect match. I'm doing some research right now. Let me tell you, I've done thousands of hours of research in this field and …'

She was starting to speak really fast, and as she did he noticed the tiniest shred of a lisp start to creep in on a very occasional word.

But he needed to stop her. This was not right. 'Hang on, that's your field of maths? Internet dating? 'Cause that doesn't sound really serious to me.'

At least not serious enough to stop you eating Mexican with me.

'Oh, you have no idea. That's why I've been fast-tracked. There's huge, literally huge, money in it.'

He looked her over, up and down. She sure was cute, but it had been clear from the first moment they'd tumbled into this big old bed of his that she did not do this a lot. She was too … skittish. Which begged the question …

'So. This romance expertise of yours. How's it working for you?'

'What?'

'All this expertise. How is it working for,' he paused emphatically, 'you?'

Poppy blushed again, and then narrowed those eyes at him. 'You sure Julia didn't set you up with me?'

'Julia?'

'My best friend, Julia. The bucket list, remember?' She flapped a hand at him. 'Anyway, enough about me. What about you? You're a chef?'

He laughed. 'Kind of a grand title. No. I do days at the Royal, short-order cook. Nights I do …' He motioned towards a six-string leaning on the bookshelf.

'Oh. You're a musician.' Before he could open his mouth for a shrugging-off remark, she reached up and pulled his face close to hers. 'Play me something.'

Quentin took in her shiny eyes and half-open mouth. He grinned.

Oh yeah, baby. She might be a maths professor and all, but she's still a girl. He could almost smell the tacos.

Chapter Two

'God, do you think they nicked these chairs from Guantanamo?' Julia Shrewsbury asked, adjusting her bottom on the solid plastic.

Julia had grown up not only with a silver spoon in her mouth, but with opulent furnishings beneath her backside. And she may have rejected all that trust-fund crap and the strings with which it came, but, much like the princess who had issues with that pesky pea, her lower vertebrae remembered luxury.

'Mmm,' Poppy said noncommittally.

'I mean really, this whole place is seriously fucking depressing,' she continued, her eyes roaming around the impersonal hospital waiting room with its garish orange-and-green decor. It looked like a relic from the disco era. 'Why don't they just put up a sign pronouncing Abandon Hope All Ye Who Enter Here? It could do with a good interior designer.' She paused, chewing her lip. 'Missy Althrop. She'd be perfect.'

Poppy shuddered. 'It would look like a fairy had thrown up by the time Missy was done with it. Besides, I don't think public-hospital budgets run to that kind of extravagance.'

Julia sighed. She supposed that was true. 'Even so, it wouldn't take much. Change the curtains, rip up the carpet, some neutral colours and a bit of modern art on the walls.'

'Modern art is not going to stop me thinking about dying.'

Julia felt the same hot fist of fear from yesterday afternoon, when she'd first learned about Poppy's scare, slug her square in the solar plexus. She gripped her best friend's hand with ferocious determination. 'You are not going to die. I won't let you,' she whispered fiercely. 'You are twenty-nine with no family history of breast cancer. And anyway,' she continued, her grip easing up at Poppy's wince, forcing her voice to be less maniacal, 'they wouldn't let you wait out here for almost two fucking hours if you had cancer, would they?'

'I suppose not,' Poppy muttered.

Julia hugged her then. A hard, life-affirming hug. She could feel the slightness of Poppy's frame and the hot fist burrowed an inch deeper under her diaphragm. She'd always felt like an Amazon next to Poppy, but that simple fact suddenly felt sinister instead of just part of some wildly unfair genetic lottery.

'Why didn't you ring me straightaway on Friday?' she said, pulling away. 'I could've stayed with you over the weekend.'

She'd known Poppy since they'd both found themselves at a boarding school where neither of them had wanted to be. Julia's parents had thought the freeform curriculum at the expensive Montessori school would give their spirited daughter room to express herself *and* develop self-discipline – they'd been wrong. Poppy's mother Scarlett, a single mother who'd always been hazy on the identity of Poppy's father, embraced the alternate education philosophy as if she herself had come up with the concept. She'd hoped it would encourage her quiet, serious daughter to look beyond her narrow world of numbers – she'd been wrong, too.

At the age of eleven Julia and Poppy were standing next to each other on the morning of their first assembly when Julia turned to her and said, 'Bloody hell. I think we joined the circus.' Poppy had laughed and they'd been BFFs ever since. Told each other *everything*, no matter how intimate.

Like Poppy's first experience with a rather frightening-looking vibrator called the Orgasmatron. Or Julia's blow-by-blow retelling of her sexual encounter with a man who'd wanted to be slapped across his backside with a paddle while she yelled at him for being a naughty boy.

They hadn't kept *anything* from each other.

'Sorry,' Poppy said, pushing her glasses up her nose. 'I needed to … think for a bit. And,' she said, removing her phone from her bag, 'I also took some time to knock a couple of items off my bucket list.'

Julia felt sick at the mention of the list they'd compiled several years ago after the movie had first come out. It had seemed like a fun, crazy thing to do at the time, but today it was coming back to bite them in the arse. 'No, I won't have you talking that way, do you hear?' she said, coming over all Mama Bear again as her heart raced in her chest. 'I simply refuse to believe—'

She was cut short by Poppy pushing the phone at her. 'Meet Number Ten.'

Julia automatically grabbed the phone as she looked down at it but it took a few seconds to compute the image as her brain grappled with the potential of her best friend having cancer. 'Whoa,' she said as she examined the shirtless guy with the dirty-blond fringe staring into the camera with a very content look.

Julia knew that look. She rather fancied she had a particular penchant for producing just that look on many a man's face. The I've-had-the-life-shagged-out-of-me look.

'His name's Quentin. And I jumped out of a plane with him on Saturday morning and then had hot, dirty, stranger sex with him for pretty much the rest of the day.'

Julia blinked at the image and then at Poppy. Poppy, who never did anything that could be classified as wild or impulsive. 'You jumped out of a plane?'

Poppy rolled her eyes. 'Trust you to be more shocked by the jump than the stranger sex!'

Julia shrugged. Poppy sighed. 'Number one on the list, remember?'

'I know, but …' Julia was lost for words for a second or two. 'A plane?'

'You're always telling me I should take a risk so … I took a risk.'

That was true. Julia's entire life philosophy consisted of the three-word mantra *take a risk*. She'd built up her highly success-ful events-management company with nothing but a couple of contacts and the ample seat of her pants.

But that was her …

'Well look at you.' Julia smiled. 'And was I right, or was I right?'

Poppy gave her a huge smile and Julia tried to remember the last time her friend had ever smiled this big. Maybe when Julia had dragged her on the Wild Mouse roller coaster at Luna Park a few months ago and it had been so beautiful with the night lights of the harbour below them. They'd both screamed as the coaster had seemed destined to fling itself and its passengers right off the rails and plunge them into the cold black water before whipping them around at the last minute and plunging them down, down, down into the belly of the next loop.

'Let's do it again,' Poppy had said as the ride had ended. Maybe she was a closet adrenaline junkie?

It wasn't that Poppy wasn't a happy person. She was. God knew Julia had never laughed so hard over the years than she had when she was with Poppy. It was just that her friend was generally a more considered type. Poppy brought the quiet maths professor. Julia brought the brash and loud.

'That good, huh?'

'The jump or the sex?'

Julia laughed. 'The sex, of course.'

'Oh, god.' Poppy shook her head as she took back her phone and looked at Quentin. 'It was like … a smorgasbord.'

Julia laughed again. 'There's a reason why the first six letters of smorgasbord are an anagram for orgasm, you know.'

'Hah, so they are.' Poppy grinned.

'So come on, spill,' Julia demanded. 'If I have to sit here getting a numb bum and possibly,' she added as a man across from them coughed fit to hack up a lung without covering his mouth, 'a communicable disease, I might as well be titillated. Titillate me, woman.'

'Don't,' Poppy groaned, closing down the image on her phone. 'I picked a bad time to blot my copybook. He's twenty-two. I'm going to hell for sure.'

Julia laughed a little too loudly, ignoring the reference to mortality. 'Way to go, girlfriend! I'm seriously impressed.'

'You're a terrible friend,' Poppy said, though she was smiling. 'You should be lecturing me on acting my age.'

'Hah! As if.' Julia shuddered. 'I say you should fuck as many twenty-two-years-olds as your heart desires.'

'Thanks.' Poppy found the image in her phone album again and traced the floppy fringe. 'I think I'll just stick with the one.'

'So this Quentin, was he the skydive instructor?'

Poppy shook her head. 'Nope. He's a cook here at the hospital canteen. I met him on Friday and he was flirting with me and I thought what the hell. So I asked him to come with me.'

Julia blinked. 'Oh. That was …'

'Risky?' Poppy said, lifting an eyebrow at the irony.

'No.' Julia rolled her eyes. 'Unexpected.'

And also, Julia admitted, a tiny bit hurtful. Why hadn't her best friend of eighteen years asked *her* to go along for the skydive? She'd have been up for it – more than up for it. And Poppy knew that. They did everything together. *Everything.*

Poppy shrugged. 'It was an impulse. I was taking *your* advice.'

Julia smiled, kicking the green-eyed monster to the curb. Poppy was doing something she'd urged her to do for years – she couldn't be angry or jealous about it. Particularly today. 'About bloody time,' she said.

'Thank you,' Poppy said, and Julia felt a hitch somewhere in the vicinity of her heart at the gratitude she could hear in her friend's voice. Maybe Poppy had been worried that Julia would feel left out?

'So you scratched off number one and number ten in a day,' Julia mused. 'I think you might need to pace yourself.'

'Actually, we also crossed off number twelve.'

Julia tried to remember her friend's list but all she could think of apart from the skydiving and sex with a stranger was how specific it had been. Actually, posing for a life-art class had also been involved if her memory served her correctly. But god knew what number it was on the extensive list. Julia's list had consisted of three items: *Find a soul mate. Keep a journal. Paint something.*

So far she was zero for three.

Poppy had been puzzled at the simplicity and staidness of it considering Julia's usual flamboyance. But Julia knew that when it got down to it, she lived her life in fast forward most days and there were few things she'd have left to regret.

'Remind me what number twelve was again?'

'Eating Mexican.'

Julia nodded as it came back to her. 'The real deal. No Tex Mex.'

'Absolute blow-your-head-off real deal.'

'Where'd you go?'

'Nowhere.' Poppy's smile was dreamy and for a moment Julia wondered if she'd been possessed. 'He cooked it for me.'

'Ah,' Julia said, puzzled at the strange look on her friend's face. 'He *is* a cook though, right?'

'And a musician. He's the lead singer in a band.'

Julia gritted her teeth. 'Of course he is.'

'You'll have to meet him. You'll love him. He does old-movie quotes, too.'

Crap. *Houston, we have a problem.* 'Isn't the purpose of having sex with a stranger to … you know … keep him a stranger?'

Poppy dropped her head to one aside, and with her black-rimmed glasses perched imperiously on her nose she looked exactly like a maths professor contemplating a particularly difficult equation. 'No,' she said, slowly scrunching her brow in concentration. 'I don't think so. I think it counts as long as you didn't really know them when you hit the sheets.'

Julia sighed. Trust Poppy to want to befriend Number Ten. She opened her mouth to explain the etiquette of stranger sex, but a rather severely groomed nurse who could have given Nurse Ratched a run for her money called, 'Poppy Devine,' and everything seized inside Julia. The fist was back, worming its way right through to her middle.

'Okay, babe,' she said, taking her friend's hand and hauling her up. 'It's going to be fine. Let's go kick cancer's arse.'

The walk across the floor seemed to take forever. A young guy in a blue uniform pushing an elderly man in a wheelchair almost ran into the wall checking Julia out. Julia was used to men looking at her. She had an honest-to-god, old-fashioned hourglass figure and from the age of thirteen, when her breasts had grown rapidly to a double D, she'd been the object of the copulatory gaze. And she'd worked out early that if she truly had to be lumbered with one of those classic fifties movie-star bodies instead of the petite package that Poppy came in, then she might as well dress like one. She had a bottom and thighs and boobs and she'd been alive long enough and had a good enough eye for fashion to know how to dress them up or dress them down.

But right now it just didn't seem appropriate for anyone to be noticing that and she wanted to hiss at the orderly to fuck off. Nurse Ratched looked Julia over as they got closer, in a much less flattering light than the orderly had done. Like she could tell, through one narrowed gaze, that Julia was going to be trouble.

The room they were ushered into suffered the same sense of decay and lack of style as the rest of the department, but the doctor who sat in the chair behind the desk looked comfortingly middle-aged and experienced, and his smile as they entered was encouraging. He had thick, dark wavy hair that was turning grey and a don't-scare-the-horses look on his face. He introduced himself as Richard Bradshaw, an oncologist, and there were a brief few minutes with banal pleasantries before he got down to it.

Julia instantly nicknamed him Dr Dick. Because that's what she always did when faced with authority – mentally belittled it.

She'd made a habit out of it as a child when she'd encountered endless rounds of boring adults, friends of her parents, who'd talked down to her as if she was of no consequence.

Dr Dick folded his hands on a chart in front of him as he surveyed them both, making sure to meet their eyes, and Julia absently noticed he had a piano-player's hands. 'Poppy, I have the results from your biopsy here.' His voice was low and calm and Julia felt soothed and less worried suddenly. 'I'm sorry to tell you that the lump is malignant and, as is often the case in younger women, quite aggressive.'

A strange noise came out of Poppy's mouth and Julia turned to her and grabbed her hand. It was cold and her face looked frozen. 'It's going to be fine, just fine. Stay calm.' She smoothed Poppy's hand gently, before turning serenely back to the doctor and taking a deep breath. 'What the fuck do you mean it's cancerous, it's aggressive?' she demanded. 'She's only twenty-fucking-nine! She has no family history!'

Julia had been angry most of her life. She may have grown up in wealth and privilege but she'd had to fight to be heard and seen. To be validated. To be something other than a piece to be moved around her parents' Monopoly board. Rage had given her a voice against their manipulations and the guts to walk away. But it had also become ingrained.

There were times when she'd contemplated therapy for it. Right now, she was pleased she hadn't.

If anything could kill this cancer it would be the weight of Julia's wrath.

Dr Dick, obviously used to the gamut of emotions playing out in his office day after day, nodded calmly and said, 'Yes, that's right.'

After that, Julia didn't hear a lot. Something about scans and hormone receptors and surgery and margins and nodes and chemo and radiation. Options. Taking it one step at a time. Needing more information.

Blah, blah-de-fucking-blah.

None of it could get past the overwhelming sense that this shit couldn't possibly be happening to Poppy. One glance at Poppy's face told Julia that Poppy wasn't taking in a whole hell of a lot either.

And then before they knew it, Poppy was being whisked off for a combined CT/PET scan – whatever the hell that was – leaving Julia to pace the floor of the X-ray waiting room. She couldn't decide if she wanted to spraypaint *Cancer Sucks* on the walls of yet another department with depressing decor or throw up.

At least this looked like a place that knew what to do with vomit should the urge to lose her stomach contents come to pass. The last place she'd barfed had been in a pot plant at her cousin Freya's daughter's first birthday party. Freya had certainly not known what to do at the sight of her cousin hurling in front of twenty-two toddlers and their horrified mothers. But in her defence Julia had learned long ago that one had to be drunk to get through any party thrown by Freya. Ridiculous extravagance combined with large amounts of prissy were hard to deal with sober.

Julia looked at her watch for the twentieth time. What the fuck was taking so long?

She paced some more, oblivious to the way it stretched her Betty Page skirt across her Betty Boop derrière and the gawping of every male with a pulse in the near vicinity.

This couldn't be right. It couldn't be happening.

Poppy Devine did not deserve cancer. Poppy was sweet and industrious and careful and measured and always, always did the right thing. If anyone deserved cancer it was Julia. Julia was loud and opinionated and disagreeable. Rude, some might even say. She went out with bad men, took unnecessary risks, pushed people to their limits, swore like a sailor and flipped the bird more than any female in the history of the world.

It should be her number coming up in the cancer lottery.

And all the time she paced, the lyrics of 'Only the Good Die Young' played louder and faster in her head.

Poppy should have been badder. Why hadn't she been badder? Why, why, why?

And then the door opened and Poppy wandered out looking tiny and lost and like someone or something had just punched her in the gut, and Julia wanted to yell at that insidious lump inside her, 'Get away from her, you bitch,' like some crazy Ripley wannabe.

And as she crossed the room and pulled Poppy into her arms, Julia knew she'd do anything – *anything* – to help Poppy through this. With the strained relationship that existed between Julia and her upper-class parents and Poppy's disconnect with her own mother, it had always felt a bit like the two of them against the world anyway.

But now it was for real.

Cancer was the enemy and she was putting it on notice. If it wanted a tug of war, it was going to get one, because she wasn't going to sit idly by and let it take her best friend away.

'The doctor wants to see me again,' Poppy said and her voice sounded muffled and so small Julia wanted to punch the wall.

They went back to the office and waited. 'Well one thing's for sure,' Julia said as she sat in another uncomfortable chair. 'You're abso-fucking-lutely not having any treatment done here. You'd probably have some paint chip peeling off the ceiling drop into your wound and get septicaemia.'

Julia watched as Poppy absently reached for a plastic mould sitting on the desk. It was a spinal column that looked like someone had taken a hammer to it; it also sported the name of a well-known, over-the-counter analgesic. Julia figured the person owning that back bone was going to need something way more heavy duty than that – crack cocaine possibly.

'It's fine,' Poppy said, not looking up from the macabre drug-company toy.

'It looks like it's about to come down around our ears.'

Poppy turned and looked at her and Julia's breath caught in her throat at the lacklustre flatness inside her usually vibrant tawny gaze. 'It's fine, Julia. It may be a little worn around the edge but the hospital's reputation is second to none. I did some online research last night. Their stats are impressive.'

Julia's anger dissolved in a heartbeat. Poppy always had been a balm to her fiery temper. The door opened and Dr Dick entered the room. She knew by his sombre look that the news wasn't good. The man should *never, ever* gamble!

He didn't bother with the pleasantries this time. 'I'm sorry, Poppy, but the scans have shown us that the cancer is grade four, which means it's invasive. It's spread to the lymph nodes under your arm and there's a spot on one of your ribs and your left hip that is most certainly metastatic growth.'

Julia had no words this time as she groped for her friend's hand. Poppy managed, 'I see.'

Dr Dick glanced at Julia, obviously expecting another emotional outburst with frequent use of the *f* word, but the fear that had been gnawing at her since yesterday afternoon had moved from her chest to her throat, threatening to strangle her. When it became obvious that neither of them was going to say anything, he filled up the stunned silence by explaining what the hell it all meant and where to go from here.

It took ages for Julia's brain to come back online. When it did, she shuffled her chair closer to Poppy and snaked her arm around her friend's shoulders. 'I want a second opinion,' she demanded, desperation making her bold and bolshie as she interrupted him. The thought that maybe Dr Dick had got it terribly wrong had taken hold and she seized it with both hands.

Maybe Dr Dick was just a dick?

'Julia ...'

Julia squeezed Poppy's shoulder. 'It's going to be fine, you'll see,' she told her. 'There's been a terrible mistake.'

'You are of course most welcome to get a second opinion,' Dr Dick said, his voice a soothing baritone. 'I could arrange for another oncologist from here to see you or you could see one of your own choosing privately and I would forward all the scans and tests to them.'

And that's when Julia knew it was real. And that Dr Dick was telling the truth. She could see it in his crap-at-poker face.

Poppy must have seen it too because she shook her head. 'No, it's fine. I don't need a second opinion.'

Dr Dick nodded. 'I know you've had a lot dumped in your lap today, but I'd like to schedule you for the mastectomy we talked about as soon as possible and then get straight on with the chemo. I can get you on the theatre list the day after tomorrow,' he said.

Julia blinked at the rapidity of it, but now that it was happening, she didn't want Poppy to be lumbered with a cancerous breast. She wanted it off, gone, along with that prick of a lump inside blinking away like the freaking mother ship, spreading its poison. No longer able to do any more damage.

'She'll take it,' Julia said.

'No.'

Julia blinked at the vehement word coming from Poppy's throat. It was loud in the small room. 'Babe, we can't muck around with this,' she said, squeezing Poppy's stiff shoulder. 'The sooner you start treatment, the better the outcome, right D ... er, Richard?' she said, turning to Dr Dick for confirmation.

'It's always better to get on to these situations right away,' he agreed in that calm, quiet way of his.

'I can go a few days, surely?' Poppy implored.

'Babe, no,' Julia said, jumping in ahead of Dr Dick, whose mouth was opening. 'How can you even want it inside you for any longer than you have to? Is this a body-image problem? Because Richard mentioned reconstructive surgery and in the meantime we can fake it. God knows I've been tutoring you in that since the seventh grade.'

There was a pain behind Julia's eyeballs which came purely from the pressure of words building in her brain. Sharp, sane, persuasive words. She hoped she was being coherent because she needed to convince Poppy to follow the doctor's orders. 'You know I'll love you no matter how many boobs you have, right?'

Poppy didn't look at her as she addressed Dr Dick. 'I just need to ... think about some stuff. Absorb it all.'

Dr Dick nodded. 'Of course,' he said gently and smiled at Poppy. 'Take whatever time you need. It's important to feel confident in your choices.' He lifted a card from the holder on his desk. 'Ring me if you need to know anything else. And when you're ready, we'll go from there.'

Julia shook her head. *What the fuck?* 'Poppy.'

It was Poppy's turn to squeeze her hand now and Julia felt the squeeze wrap its fingers right around her heart. 'Julia ... I need some time ...'

Julia swallowed. Hard. She was used to being the one in charge of the twosome. Boldly leading on, Poppy happy to follow. But when Poppy gave her *that look*, it was All Over Red Rover. Her best friend of eighteen years was asking her to back off and she knew she had to respect that. 'Okay.' She forced a smile. 'Sure. A few days isn't going to hurt, right?'

She turned back to Dr Dick, her eyes fiery, silently pleading with him to contradict her even though he'd already said it was fine. Julia couldn't go against *that look* but Dr Dick sure as hell could. For god's sake, the man had a medical degree. And a PhD in calm.

Instead, he smiled at her in that reassuring way and said, 'It's not going to hurt. Poppy's been dealt a huge whammy. It's perfectly fine to take some time to consider it all.'

She glanced at Poppy, who looked like an inflatable toy that had sprung a leak and was deflating at a rate of knots. 'Right, then,' Julia said briskly as her nose prickled with emotions and her tear ducts felt like a red-hot needle had been jammed into both of them simultaneously. She pulled Poppy into her side and gave her a fierce hug. 'We'll have a think. And get back to you.'

A minute later they were outside, mute and confused like they'd just emerged from years of darkness into the bright sunshine. Like Gollum from *Lord of the Rings*. Julia could feel a rising urge to shake her fist at the sky. How dare it be so fucking bright and gorgeous on such an ugly day? They didn't say anything as they made their way to where Julia had parked her cute Beetle so many hours ago.

They climbed inside and the fake flower near the steering wheel mocked her. Julia grabbed it, crushed it in her hand and tossed it in the back seat.

Silence reigned as they both stared out though the windscreen at the sweltering parking lot. Julia turned to face her friend, her friend who had a fucking horrible disease that she'd read about and heard about on the news but which had never personally touched her. Until now. Tears burned hot in her eyes.

'Don't,' Poppy said, her voice strong and commanding. 'Don't you cry. Don't you dare cry. You are my rock. You have always been my rock. You've been the buffer between me and the world since I was eleven. You are the one who's going to get me through this. I'm sorry, but if you lose it now, I'll never come back from that.'

Julia heaved in a breath. *Aggressive, invasive cancer. Aggressive, invasive cancer.* She wanted to cry hysterically. She wanted to take a knife to the beautiful leather seats in her beautiful car – bought with the very first hefty paycheque she'd earned from her business – and slash great big gashes in them. Like the gash that was in her heart.

But she didn't. She sucked in a deep, deep breath. She had to be who Poppy needed her to be. She had to be that rock. Poppy needed Julia's anger to propel them through this. Not her tears. 'Where to?' she asked.

Poppy shrugged as she stared out of the windscreen again and she looked so lost Julia had to bite her tongue to stop the first tear from falling. Because if that leaked out – she was never going to stop. 'I don't know,' she whispered.

Julia thought for a second. 'I do. Give me your phone.'

Poppy frowned. 'What?'

Julia held out her hand. 'Your phone.'

Poppy handed it over and Julia quickly scrolled to the app she knew held the bloody stupid bucket list she'd insisted they do years ago. A list she hated almost as much as she hated cancer right at this moment.

Trust Poppy to have it all neat and organised and readily available like a freaking shopping list. Julia had made out her own list on paper sourced from some women's cooperative in Ethiopia. Scarlett, Poppy's mother, had given the paper to Julia for her eighteenth birthday. Julia had then stashed the list in a box with shells glued to the outside. Julia and Poppy had made the boxes under Scarlett's watchful eye when they'd camped at Byron Bay the Easter they'd been in grade nine.

Bloody hell – did she even know where that freaking box was now?

Julia's fingers scrolled through Poppy's precise list, searching for the right number. There it was.

Number six. *Tell boss (whoever it may be at the time) to go fuck him/herself and shove the job where the sun don't shine (note – ensure other job already in place).*

'This,' Julia said, passing the phone back and starting the engine.

Poppy consulted the list. She raised a ragged nail to her lips and gnawed on it. 'Really?'

'Fucking A,' Julia said. 'Damned if you're going to waste your time researching losers in love who need some computer algorithm to be happy when we have a dragon to slay.' She paused. 'And how many times have you told me how much you hate that lecherous old plagiarist you work for?'

* * *

Several hours later, in the weird way that the world often serves up, Julia found herself following Poppy into a dingy alley to an even dingier doorway guarded by a dubious-looking dude with a webbed neck and tree-trunk legs who looked them up and down like they may possibly be dinner for him later should he run out of regular, everyday food. His official-looking nametag proclaimed him to be Charles, but Julia couldn't help but think he'd be right at home performing the haka for his bikie homeboys.

'What decent club even opens on a Monday night?' Julia bitched as Charles grunted his approval and the door closed behind them.

They were immediately plunged into an eerie neon glow and Julia half expected to see illegal Asian prostitutes lined up against the corridor asking them if they'd like a bit of girl-on-girl. It was only the heavy bass beat thudding around them that gave her any confidence that they might actually be in the right place.

She was relieved when the corridor opened out into a relatively normal bar area and her gaze skimmed immediately to the band playing on the small narrow stage. The room was only half full, but the scantily dressed women at the front were gyrating in a most unseemly fashion, reaching out their hands, trying to grab at the lead singer's legs. Someone really needed to explain to them the principles of playing hard to get.

And there he was. Number Ten. A tall string of energy, flicking his dirty-blond fringe away with a casual toss of the head that increased the screaming up front another notch or two. His eyes were shut as his fingers flew across the frets during a garishly loud guitar solo that hissed and squealed in an almighty frenzy.

Julia stared open-mouthed.

'Isn't he amazing?' Poppy murmured.

He was something, alright. Julia had a feeling she was going to need some kind of animal book to figure out just what.

Julia had been surprised when Poppy had wanted to come here. It hadn't been a surprise when Poppy had chickened out of ringing her boss, but this … this was unexpected. Julia had wanted to spend the night strategising and web surfing together or at least getting messy drunk, but Poppy, who'd been texting Number Ten for most of the day, had said, 'Let's go to his gig. You're going to love him, Julia. He's a movie nut like you.'

And it wasn't a day to deny Poppy anything.

So here they were and, mercifully, the solo drew to a close with another flick of the fringe and spray of sweat over the audience, and Julia could actually hear herself think enough to come up with a suitable adjective for the guy who was so unlike Poppy's usual type he may as well have been Prince Harry.

But then Poppy was waving at him and he spied her through the girls swarming around him at the front and the tacky disco lighting and he jumped off the stage, pushing through his groupies to get to her. Julia blinked as Poppy ran the last few steps into his arms and burst into tears.

What the fuck?

She watched as his big hands stroked Poppy's hair, and he murmured words in Poppy's ear, obviously giving her the comfort that Julia had wanted to give Poppy all afternoon but had been firmly rebuffed.

Eventually, this stranger who was taking her place looked at her and gave her a suave nod of his head. 'Hey,' he said. 'You must be Jules.'

Julia shuddered at the bastardisation of her name. 'And you must be Number Ten.'

She hated him already.

Chapter Three

Quentin studied the two women carefully, trying to remember a time when he had felt so unsure of himself. It was two in the morning, and instead of reviewing the high points of the gig with his band over two or three or seven beers, or enjoying the affections of one of the enthusiastic music lovers in tight jeans from the front row, he was making Italian hot chocolate for a tiny woman he hadn't been able to get out of his mind for two days, and her very drunk, and even more terrifying, best friend.

As he melted Swiss chocolate the right way – in a glass dish over a saucepan of water – he tried to work out what the two women were saying to each other as they were seated on flat cushions at his coffee table. The petite brunette was gesticulating wildly, her fascinating lips moving as quickly as lightning. The tall redhead, with the kind of body that would normally make Quentin want to write a song about the sweetness of life, was slumped down, forearms on the table, head resting on them. Occasionally, she would lift her head to mutter something at Poppy. It was clear, even from the vantage point of the kitchen, that whatever they were arguing about, Poppy was winning.

Quentin poured melted chocolate over warm milk, stirred several marshmallows into each mug, and shook powdered chocolate over the top. He settled each mug on a matching plate, and reached up to retrieve a Tupperware container from the top cupboard. He extracted several sticky-date-and-caramel cookies, and arranged one on each plate. Then he sashayed back into the living room, such as it was, with the kind of dramatic flourish for which lead singers and guitarists were known, and arranged his features to receive some praise. As he did, he caught the tail end of the conversation between the two women.

'Don't you dare,' Poppy was hissing into the untidy clump of hair that was her best friend. She poked her shoulder viciously as she said it. 'I mean it.'

Julia grunted from under the hair, her face flat against the coffee table. 'Whatever,' she mumbled. 'But I think you're wrong.'

Quentin would have been curious about what the women were discussing, except that the sight of Poppy, all flustered and red-cheeked, had a disturbing way of making him lose his train of thought. She was sitting cross-legged like a sweet, compact Buddha. Her brown curly hair was tied up in some kind of fascinating pigtail, tantalising tendrils of the stuff he knew smelled like chocolate escaping from the hair tie. Her fine hands were clasped Zen-like on the coffee table in front of her, and her nose was wrinkled with the remnants of her snarl at Julia. Her lips were painted a really pretty shade of pink, and the mascara she was wearing made her lashes look incredibly long.

Quentin realised Poppy hadn't been wearing makeup the last two times they had met. The effect with makeup was different – a cross between sexy and something like a kid playing dress-up. He decided he liked her better without it. Which was weird, for him. He loved makeup – all that pretty colour and glittery yumminess and good smells. Makeup took women, who were already puzzling and amazing and kind of scrumptious, and made them into altogether magical creatures. Except this one, he decided. The makeup looked good on her, sure. But she didn't need it. There was something plain old magical about her without it.

Quentin cleared his throat, deposited his offerings on the table in front of the two women, and waited (again) for the adulation. After all, not every guy knew how to make Italian hot chocolate. The proper way. Let alone sticky-date-and-caramel cookies. From scratch.

The gentle noise drew Poppy's attention and she finally looked at him. 'Oh,' she said, smiling at him in a way that used her whole face – eyes, lips, teeth, and even those pretty round cheeks – and made him forget how to breathe. 'Ta.' She wrapped her hands around the mug and nudged the bundle of hair that was Julia. 'Drink, Juju?'

She said it way more sweetly than she'd said *don't you dare*, and Quentin wondered again what that was all about. He never brought drunk best friends home along with the girl he was interested in, so he wasn't sure if this was how they always behaved. He wasn't even sure how this had happened. One minute Poppy had been wrapped around him dancing, her body all small and soft and relaxed, giggling and asking muffled questions into his chest about what it felt like to have groupies, the next they had all been out on the street in the dark, and Poppy had looked like she was planning to head home. With Julia. Without him. And well, a man had to do something about that, even if it meant bringing the mountain to Mohammed. So to speak. So he'd suggested they head back to his for hot chocolates.

Julia had shot him a look that suggested she'd had more appealing invitations to go for a pap smear, but Poppy had stopped dead, right there in the alley, and nailed her friend with a pleading look, and it had been all over. Julia had grumbled and bitched, broken a heel on her shoe as she'd fallen into the cab, and generally been a pain in the arse. But she'd capitulated to Poppy's wishes and come along for the ride. And, more importantly and as a direct result, so had Poppy. Which, Quentin reflected as he watched Julia's head snap up from her drunken reverie facedown on the coffee table, was kind of a weird situation. Especially as he couldn't seem to tear his eyes off the ball of manic energy that was Poppy, but he felt that if he looked at Julia too long or the wrong way she might actually bare some fangs and rip out his throat.

Quentin had no idea exactly what he had done to make Julia so angry, but he sure did hope the hot chocolate would go some way to compensate. The last thing he needed was a cranky best friend cramping his style.

He parked himself on the floor on the opposite side of the coffee table to the two women, and manoeuvred himself so his long legs were pointing sideways, rather than fighting for space under the table with Julia. Quentin knew how challenging it could be to find enough space for your body when you were as tall as Julia. He didn't want to accidentally offend her any further. As Julia looked up from her Cousin It position, Quentin almost felt sorry for her. She really was well and truly plastered, and she was going to have one hell of a hangover tomorrow. He wondered what had made her hit it so hard on a Monday night. Then he remembered.

'Oh.' He grinned, raising his mug. 'So here's to near misses, hey?'

Poppy frowned delicately at him and Julia raised one elegant eyebrow and twisted her mouth into a snarl. 'What fucking near miss?' Julia's voice had not got any less posh as she had become more and more inebriated. In fact, if anything, she was articulating more slowly and carefully. Quentin was sure he'd never heard another woman swear so profanely with that much panache.

Quentin tipped his mug towards Poppy. 'The results,' he said, frowning back at the two of them. 'Today.' He thought about Poppy crying with joy at the club, and nodded at Julia. 'Poppy told me she got the all-clear.' He smiled, unnerved by Julia's can-I-castrate-you-now-or-should-I-finish-the-hot-chocolate-first stare. 'Didn't I tell you I have a nose for these things?' He winked at Poppy. 'And I'm never wrong.'

'You sure did,' Poppy agreed, reaching across and squeezing his hand quickly. 'So awesome, huh?'

'So you can put your bucket list away for a while yet, right?' He closed his eyes and tried not to think about his ongoing concern that she was going to try number ten a few more times for good measure.

He didn't care, he didn't care, he didn't care.

He opened his eyes and Poppy was staring at him curiously, her pretty mouth full and her lips parted, her head on the side tipping that enticing pigtail lopsided, and her eyes dancing with curiosity.

Who was he kidding? He cared alright. The thought of this mystifying little firecracker having the sort of wild sex she'd had with him on Saturday with someone else sat like a fat stone, hard and heavy, in his stomach. The thought of her making that gurgly squeal with someone else, sitting on another man like a wanton cowgirl, lifting her hair ... He shut his eyes again. Man, this chick was getting into his head. He needed to think about something else.

'So,' he tried again. 'How are the chocolates?' He realised neither woman had tried them yet so he gestured for them to drink up.

Poppy brought hers to her lips experimentally, her pink tongue darting out to lick some froth, chocolate powder and marshmallow oozing from the top before she took her first sip. She closed her eyes like she was praying as she sipped. Her eyes fluttered open as the stuff hit her tastebuds, and her gaze was all dreamy and sensual. 'Oh my god,' she whispered reverentially.

He realised he normally wanted to be alone at confusing times like this. Except now he didn't. He wanted to be alone with Poppy. He wanted to lick that errant smudge of froth from her top lip and see if it tasted anywhere near as good and chocolatey and sinful as she did.

'I'm sure that's what all the girls he drags home say to him,' Julia snapped, taking a long swig from her own mug, and allowing only a small widening of her eyes to give away the pleasure assault her mouth had just experienced. 'Not bad,' she conceded haughtily, ruining the effect with an ill-timed hiccup.

Quentin felt obliged to defend himself. He didn't want Poppy thinking he was some kind of sleaze because he played guitar and sang in a rock band. Because there may have been some girls in the audience tonight who may have been hoping to get a bit friendly after the show. Because any other time that might have seemed like a grand idea.

'Hey, Julia,' he drawled, shrugging sassily and fixing her with his best little-boy, wide-eyed smile. 'I'm not bad, I'm just drawn that way.'

Poppy clapped in delight but Julia's eyes narrowed. '*Who framed Roger Rabbit?*' She was almost snarling. 'You're really going to quote Jessica Rabbit to me?' She stood up quickly, knocking her knees unpleasantly on the coffee table as she rose and drew herself up to her full five feet eleven inches. 'I *am* Jessica Rabbit,' she declared, poking at her substantial bosom.

She sure was some woman, Quentin thought, watching her unfurl the elegant length of her body. She was built like some old-time goddess – tall and long and endowed with more than her fair share of dangerous curves. The kind of woman Quentin adored. Tall as they came, even shoeless. Ballsy and sharp and at the top of her game. She was the kind of woman who knew the score and took no prisoners. And with her long red hair and perfect skin, she was someone's idea of heaven on a stick.

Just not his. Not anymore.

He blinked as the thought settled in his brain. Holy crap, where had that come from? He flicked a quick glance over at Poppy, staring adoringly up at Julia.

'Isn't she something else?' Poppy asked, tugging on her friend's hand to encourage her to sit again. Julia lurched drunkenly downwards, tucking herself with great logistical difficulty back under the coffee table and making short work of her hot chocolate.

'She certainly is,' Quentin agreed, watching the way Poppy's lips stretched right up into her cheeks when she smiled and liberated these two tiny adorable dimples which were somehow higher than dimples were on most other people. He wanted to stick his pinkie in one of them and see if it was for real. But he needed to deal with this whole Quentin's-a-bad-influence vibe he was getting from Julia. 'Look, *Jessica*,' he started, grinning in what he felt was a pretty winning way.

'Ms Rabbit to you,' Julia huffed.

'Ms Rabbit,' he said, working hard on a smile but feeling strangely and unfortunately that he possibly came off as looking somewhat constipated. 'I'm not a bad guy. You shouldn't get the wrong idea. Just 'cause of the … y'know.' He shrugged and tried for the little-boy smile again. Even though it hadn't been so successful the last time. 'The rock-band thing.'

Julia pursed her lips and gestured at the surfboard hanging prominently on one of the walls. 'And the surfer thing.'

'Uh-huh,' he agreed, spreading his hands open as though to say, *exactly.*

Julia gestured to the trophy cabinet that could be seen in the next room, bulging with faux-gold statues of various sizes, most featuring an image of a man with a football. 'And the football thing.'

'Yeah,' Quentin agreed hurriedly, suddenly feeling like perhaps he was losing the advantage. 'Anyway,' he squeezed Poppy's hand, 'they're stereotypes, all that stuff about what certain …' He fought to find the right words. 'Certain kinds of people might get up to in their spare time.'

Poppy nodded at him sympathetically and took a huge swallow of her drink.

Julia, who still looked kind of hazy around the eyes, seemed to be sharpening up by the minute. 'So you're not,' she said, drumming her red-painted fingernails on the table, 'the kind of guy who sleeps with women all the time.'

He shook his head and examined his fingers delicately as if to say: *these callouses really are a guitarist's curse.*

'Or the kind of guy who makes sure women get really interested in him, then ditches them when the next best thing comes along.'

He shook his head again, this time making a manful effort to meet Julia's eyes and look sincere. 'No way.' Well, not usually. Not for the most part.

Julia kept drumming, tapping the table so hard Quentin expected to see the tired old glass shatter under her attentions. Man, something was really eating this chick tonight; was she always like this? She plugged on. 'You don't take drugs; consort with undesirables; go to the wrong kind of parties; make plans you don't keep; or leave jobs to take off to Southeast Asia just because the mood strikes you?'

Holy shit, that was more words in one sentence than Quentin usually said in a whole day. And was she only guessing here, or did she have some weird clairvoyance trick going on?

But Poppy saved him from answering. 'Juju,' she protested, placing a restraining hand on the arm with the drumming fingers. 'You do all those things.'

'So?' Julia shook her head furiously, like she was finally losing her grip on her fragile self-control. 'So? So? Soooo? What I do …' She stabbed the table. 'What I do,' she repeated. 'Is not the point. The point is you don't, Poppy. You don't do them. You don't hang around people who do those things. So what I am trying to ascertain here is whether Mr-Rock-God-Surfer-Boy-Football-Legend does them. Because let me tell you.' Julia spat out each of the last four words as though they tasted nasty. 'I can't help but feel that the two of you aren't compatible. That this whole …' She made a circling motion to encompass the two of them. 'This whole thing simply isn't going to work.'

Content she had made her point, Julia slumped down against the coffee table again, eyeing Quentin as though she dared him to disagree.

Quentin chewed his lip, looking at the wild redhead, who seemed really worried about what kind of influence he was going to be on her best girl. He thought about all the women, and their mothers, fathers and brothers, who had thought he was no good over the years. All the times he had heard some version of this particular speech. And he for one had always heartily agreed with them. But right now a plaintive voice rose up inside him in protest.

A valiant voice said: *You're wrong, Jessica Rabbit; this is different.*

But how to find the words for that, on the basis of the last two days, and with this terrifying woman cross-examining him? But in the end, and yet again, he didn't need to find the words at all. Because Poppy started laughing.

She smacked Julia playfully on the arm. 'Of course we aren't compatible. Jeez Louise, I could've told you that without you being so mean to the guy who only a few minutes ago made us these sensational hot chocolates. I wouldn't even need to develop a basic algorithm to work it out.' She screwed up her nose in a friendly but assessing way at Quentin. 'I wouldn't even need to run a sampling questionnaire with him.'

Quentin felt compelled to protest, but he wasn't sure at what exactly. 'Italian hot chocolates,' he said instead, somewhat weakly.

What the hell was with this woman? Why was she here, lounging on his coffee table, confusing him with her chocolatey hair and her whole sexy Buddha thing, if she didn't think they were compatible? They had felt pretty damned compatible on Saturday, as they'd lost the afternoon and a good part of the evening together. And wasn't compatibility at the heart of it? Wasn't it what all girls were after?

'I'm not interested in compatibility,' Poppy sniffed, wriggling around to Quentin's side of the coffee table and inserting herself into his lap. He could hardly believe the confidence (or was it cluelessness?) of this girl. That she could sit there and baldly say that they weren't compatible, and then come over for a cuddle, like some outrageous cat. He should tip her off him. He should stand up and start cleaning mugs, giving both of these unreasonable, befuddling, rule-breaking creatures the cue to leave. He should clear his throat and speak up and defend himself.

He should, but the problem was that Poppy had started wriggling around in his lap, trying to scrape the last dregs out of the mug with her index finger, and it was fuzzing his brain and constraining his capacity to act rationally. She was just so compact but curvy, and she smelled so good, and his poor, tired, musician-surfer-footballer brain simply couldn't keep up whenever she was around, but he still liked watching the play of her clever mind through the open windows of her eyes.

'Oh ho,' Julia snorted in Poppy's direction.

Quentin could feel Poppy tense on his lap as she twisted her body towards Julia. 'Oh ho what?'

It was a challenge. He wasn't sure how, or why, but he could feel it thickening the air. If there had been a main street and a couple of cowboy outlaws, this would be the showdown.

'Oh ho, you don't care about compatibility. You've made a life on compatibility.' Julia was speaking quietly but deliberately, her face scrunched as she looked over at Poppy on Quentin's lap. 'Your study, your career.'

Poppy flicked her hair dramatically and it whacked Quentin in the face. He didn't care, as long as she kept sitting on his lap. 'And how's that working for me, Juju?'

Julia grimaced. 'There's the perfect person for you, waiting out there.' Her voice was deathly quiet now, and there was something in her eyes that Quentin couldn't quite understand.

How had this got so damn serious? Some booze, followed by some excellent (if he did say so himself) hot chocolate. Julia looked like she was pleading with Poppy. And quite frankly, he was getting kind of offended. And it took a lot to offend Quentin. Most things just didn't seem like they were worth the effort.

'Really?' Now Poppy's voice was quiet, too, and damn if there wasn't some undertone that Quentin couldn't grab onto. 'You really think so, Julia? Now?' She put this queer emphasis on *now* and Quentin felt something stir to life inside him. What was going on between these two? What was the conversation they weren't having in front of him?

Before Julia could answer, Poppy flicked her hair again and changed speed. 'Anyway, like I said, screw compatibility. I want some fun.' And again, Quentin felt like he should somehow be offended to be referred to as the fun, when fun was being juxta-posed with compatibility. But once more the offence didn't seem to want to show its face, with Poppy moving the way she was so intimately against him. All he felt was a warm glow and some bewilderment at the way this woman seemed to fit exactly right into the hollow of his body.

Goddamn it, he sure hoped he didn't have to get up anytime soon.

'Tell you what,' he said, trying to keep his tone low like he used to when he worked with horses at his father's stables. 'How about this, Jessica? Let's make a game of it.' Julia shot him another one of those laser-force stares, but he ploughed on. 'You like games?' He was almost sure she did, because he saw her eyes twinkle slightly. But she'd rather chow down on a razor blade than admit it right now.

'Sometimes,' she purred.

'Well, I tell you what, Jessica. How about you get to ask me three questions. Any three questions you like. To make sure I'm not an axe murderer or stealer-of-virtue. And I promise you I'll answer honestly.' It was a gamble, but Quentin understood gambling. And he understood games.

Julia nodded, and Poppy squeaked enthusiastically from his lap. Quentin was (almost) relieved when she shimmied off his legs and went back to sit next to Julia. At least he might be able to fire up some synapses with her over there. Except now he found himself confronted across the table by both Julia's shrewd (and increasingly sober) gaze, and Poppy's frank one.

'Okayyy …' Julia began, starting up that irritating drumming with her fingers again. She paused, and Quentin could have sworn she was just working the build-up of tension. 'Have you ever had a threesome?'

He laughed. 'That the best you got, Ms Rabbit?'

She opened her palms towards him as if to say: *Well, you gonna answer or not?* And he couldn't help but notice that Poppy looked really, really interested.

'A foursome,' he said, keeping his voice even and deep. 'If you count my guitar. But, you see—'

Poppy interrupted. 'Were they both girls? The other two, apart from your guitar?'

'Is that one of the three questions?' Quentin smiled lazily at her.

'Yes,' Poppy said.

'No,' Julia overruled her. 'They're my questions. Quentin said. And that one's a waste.'

'To you, maybe,' Poppy mumbled.

Julia waved her hand at Poppy. 'Listen, hon. I can guarantee you that boy—' and she pointed at Quentin like he was an old man perusing pornography in a service station, '—has never been with a boy. He likes girls.'

'Women,' Quentin corrected her. And it was true. He did like women. Far, far more than girls. Especially, he thought, looking over at Poppy's flushed cheeks and bright eyes, that one over there. 'So.' He eyeballed Julia, placing his palms flat towards her this time. 'What else you got in the tank, sister?'

Julia was like quicksilver. 'What's the longest relationship you've ever had?'

Quentin fired back. 'Define relationship.'

Julia groaned. 'Something where you both agreed you were together, monogamously.' She chewed her lush bottom lip then added, 'For longer than a night.'

Quentin stared into the air, making quick calculations. 'Seven weeks,' he said finally, feeling pretty impressed with himself that he'd managed to remember the German yoga instructor. Of course, she'd only been in town for eight days during those seven weeks. But still.

Poppy's pretty face wrinkled in disbelief. 'Oh my god, seven weeks. That's all? Who was she?'

Quentin shrugged and grinned at her. 'Is that your last question?'

'Yes,' Poppy said quickly.

'No,' Julia overruled her again, placing a restraining hand on her arm. Something sly and rather scary slid over Julia's features then. 'It's not.'

'Shoot,' Quentin said, shrugging his shoulders like the interrogation meant nothing and he wasn't at all worried by what she was going to ask next.

Julia eyeballed him critically. 'What was your leaving score?'

Quentin frowned. *Really?* 'My high-school leaving score?'

'Uh-huh,' Julia almost purred.

Oh no, not this. Quentin hated this bit. He'd had enough of this from his father, his teachers and everyone else who had ever tried to tell him what to do. Did he really need to pass some intelligence test to date this woman? He considered telling Julia to go jump, then he glanced at Poppy, and she looked some-how so nervous and vulnerable. She was biting her lip, and she reached out and squeezed his hand.

'Don't worry,' she said quickly, not meeting his eyes. 'It doesn't matter, we don't need to know. I don't need to know.' Then she dragged her eyes up to his. 'Honestly.' She repeated herself for emphasis. 'I honestly don't care.'

But he could see it, in her face.

She'd made him as a high-school dropout. Her little chin was jutting out and she was valiantly playing the *I don't care* card, but it was bullshit. And normally he wouldn't have cared less. Hav-ing women think he was some deadshit was all part and parcel of the offering and the escape route. It suited him fine. Just fine.

'One,' he said finally, leaning back against the sofa behind him and stretching his hands above his head.

'One?' Julia repeated the word like a jumbled parrot. 'One, the top score? One, the highest? One?'

He nodded. 'The very One.'

Julia looked like she wanted to break something. Preferably his face.

* * *

Quentin looked down at Poppy, sleeping all twisted up in his sheets. Her hair was loose now, released from the confin-ing shackles of that lopsided pigtail. Her shoulders were bare – milky-smooth. He traced a finger along her collarbone, amazed that something so small and fragile could hold such power. Because, if possible, tonight had been even better than Saturday. Shorter, sure, but it was actually sweeter. It was like some demon was driving Poppy. Like she wanted to screw up all her power and passion into a ball and hurl it at him.

She'd left him breathless and all the more baffled.

Maybe he should tell girls his school leaving score more often.

Poppy's irritating black iPhone buzzed and blinked on his bedside table. He looked over and considered throwing it across the room. How dare it interrupt his appreciation of her? But as he glanced at it, something caught his eye. It was a message, from Julia. All in caps.

DON'T FORGET, YOU PROMISED. I DON'T TELL HIM, BUT YOU AGREE TO HAVE THE OP. IT'S ALL GOING TO BE OK. XX

Chapter Four

Julia couldn't breathe. The ticking of the clock was like clashing cymbals keeping time with Poppy's shallow breaths in the silent room. She was so still and pale – Poppy who was usually so tanned and vital. She seemed to blend in with the white sheets and the white blanket pulled up to her chest. She looked alien, foreign, this strange, motionless creature without glasses, and Julia's diaphragm refused to cooperate. Refused to lift itself under the weight of crushing fear.

Julia hadn't thought she could be any more scared than when they'd wheeled Poppy's bed into the operating theatre. She'd been wrong. She *really* needed to stop underestimating what a scary bitch cancer could be.

Drops of clear fluid plopped into a burette that fed into a drip in the back of Poppy's right hand, and, on the left side a large tube protruded from underneath Poppy's awful blue hospital-issue gown.

Seriously, who designed those things? Julia understood their purpose was to be functional, but did that mean they had to be ugly, too? Jesus, why didn't they just stamp 'property of the state' on them and be done with it?

The tube led to a drainage bag where a small amount of blood had already collected.

Poppy's blood.

Julia's gaze was drawn to it again and again, and as she watched the slow ooze of Poppy's life force, the fear left her and anger took over and built, a perfect accompaniment to the swelling of her rage. It flooded Julia, building like a crescendo until she could taste it in her mouth, thick and metallic.

Tears welled in Julia's eyes and she fought them back. She wouldn't cry. Poppy needed her to be brave and she hadn't given in to tears yet.

Being someone's rock sucked.

She glanced across the bed instead and her fury found a different focus.

Number Ten.

His head was bowed over Poppy's right hand, so all she could see was his dirty-blond hair. Why she was looking at a twenty-two-year-old rocker/footballer/surfer/interloper who had known Poppy for less than a week, she didn't know.

Why was he here? What did Poppy see in him? Why did Julia have to *play nice* with him? She grabbed hold of the questions and let them simmer in the cauldron of seething emotions that had taken up residence in her gut, preferring them to other, bigger questions.

Like *why.*

Why Poppy? Why now? Why cancer?

With his head bowed so that he looked like he was praying it took all Julia's willpower not to demand he cease and desist. If he wanted to pray to a god that gave twenty-nine-year-old women aggressive breast cancer, that was his affair. But he couldn't do it in front of her. Because she'd shove all that power and glory crap in a place it was never going to shine.

Play nice.

They were the words Poppy had used this morning. And Julia had promised she would. But as she watched Poppy's blood oozing into the drain, it was killing her. She wanted to reach across the bed, yank him up by his silly rock-star hair and hiss at him to leave. More than that, she wanted to *hurt* him. To make *him* pay. Slash her crimson nails across his rock-god face and watch *him* bleed.

Number Ten. *Not* Poppy.

'Ah, here you are!'

The harried yet still somehow melodic interruption startled Julia out of her murderous daydream and Number Ten out of whatever the hell it was he was doing.

He stared at the older, less conservative version of Poppy as she jangled into the room, drowning out the noise inside Julia's head with the gentle tinkle of bangles and anklets.

She leaned down and swept Julia into a warm embrace where she sat. 'How you ever put up with this traffic, I'll never know.'

Julia sagged into the hug. 'Scarlett.'

That was it, just the one word, because Julia knew if she said any more right now she was going to burst into tears. Being hugged by Poppy's mother was like being wrapped in a cloud of incense and summer rain. Unlike her own mother, who smelled like old money and the calm before the storm.

'How's my girl doing?' Scarlett said as she pulled out of the embrace and searched around in her voluminous hemp bag for something.

'She's only been back for about twenty minutes. We haven't seen the surgeon yet. Apart from opening her eyes briefly, she's been sleeping. She's very groggy.'

'Sleep is good,' Scarlett said, her entire head practically inside the bag now.

Julia nodded, her relief at having Poppy's mother here already starting to wane. Growing up, Julia had found Scarlett utterly enchanting with her dreamy expression and funky, veggie-growing, additive-free, organic lifestyle. It had been a far cry from her own dress-circle existence.

But the second Scarlett plucked a crystal out of her bag exclaiming, 'Aha!', Julia realised she'd made a mistake and Poppy was going to kill her. Poppy had vetoed her mother being here today, insisting she'd let Scarlett know after the operation. And Julia had agreed. But last night she'd caved. And now here Scarlett was. With a crystal and god knew what else. For sure there were homeopathic drops somewhere in that bag. She could feel the heavy glare coming from Number Ten already.

'I'll pop this under her pillow,' Scarlett said, leaning forward to do just that, dropping a light kiss on Poppy's forehead as she did. 'This will protect you, my darling,' she whispered.

Julia was relieved that Poppy was too zonked to see it. Poppy believed in numbers and science and facts. She had no patience with crystals. Julia, however, was prepared to use whatever the fuck might work from both modern and woo-woo medicine in any and all combinations.

'Well hello there and who are you?'

Ten rose from his seat. 'I'm Quentin, Mrs Devine,' he said, flicking his hair back as he stretched out his hand across the bed. 'Pleased to meet you.'

'Ms,' Julia hissed.

'Delighted.' Scarlett smiled as if Julia hadn't just sprouted snakes from her hair. 'Are you a friend of Poppy's?'

He glanced at Julia, clearly unsure of what to say, before he looked back at Scarlett. 'Yes.'

'Recent,' Julia clarified stiffly.

Scarlett smiled again. 'Lovely.'

Oh yes. *Lovely.* Like a cyanide pill.

Julia stood and dragged over an empty chair propped against a faded cream wall and they all sat again, their eyes returning to Poppy.

Still asleep. Still bleeding. Still looking small and pale.

'I'm going to get a coffee from the cafeteria,' Ten announced a few minutes later. He stood. 'Anyone want one?'

'No thank you, Quentin, I try not to put any toxins in my body.'

Ten looked confounded that anyone would consider the world's most slavishly adored hot beverage in such a way. Julia felt momentarily sorry for him. He seemed like a guy who'd had it all figured out – join a band and get himself laid every night of the week. *Living the dream.*

He had no fucking clue what was ahead of him. And that was without Scarlett and what Poppy liked to call her Hogwarts hogwash.

'Probably a good idea,' he said finally. 'They do serve a fairly toxic brew down there. Jules?'

Julia stiffened at the horrible name and the even worse familiarity. *She and Ten needed to talk.* 'No thank you.' She rose from her chair. 'But I'll come for a walk and stretch my legs.'

He placed a kiss on Poppy's hand and Julia suppressed the urge to ask the nearest nurse for some anti-bacterial foam. God alone knew what dive bars and their skanky inhabitants he usually frequented, but given that he'd been spreading his germs all over Poppy for days now, she was probably immune. 'We won't be long,' she assured Scarlett, who gave her one of her beatific smiles.

She followed Ten's lanky stride out of the room and down the corridor. There was something urgent in his gait today. No loose-hipped, rock-god swagger about him at all.

'You called her mother?' he demanded as he stabbed the lift button. 'Poppy expressly asked you not to.'

Julia glared. *What the ever-loving fuck?* All her fear and rage and unshed tears welled inside and built with all the menace of a tornado. She drew herself up to her full six feet. Most men would have cowered. At six-foot-six, Ten didn't blink an eyelid.

'This is none of your business,' she said, her voice low and ominous. The voice she kept for men with wandering hands and recalcitrant contractors – often the same beast. '*You* don't know her. *You* don't know what she wants.'

He crossed his arms and Julia caught a glimpse of maturity. Of the man he might be one day. If he ever got himself a haircut and a proper job.

'Maybe I know her better than you think?'

Julia stared at him. He had to be kidding. He'd known her for less than a week. She couldn't decide whether she should laugh or have the men in white coats come for him. If it hadn't felt so serious, so *gladiatorial*, she'd have chosen laughter. Here they were in the hospital of the damned, marking their territory.

The lift arrived and the doors opened. He gestured for her to precede him. If he tried to lift his leg on her in here she was going to neuter him.

She walked to the back and turned to face him as the door slid shut, stuffing all the anger and grief back down inside. It was time for a different tack. 'Listen, Ten …'

He laughed then, a harsh noise that echoed around the confines of the metal box that seemed too flimsy to contain their antagonism. 'Are you seriously going to call me Ten?'

'Are you *seriously* going to call me Jules?'

He shrugged. 'It suits you.'

It was Julia's turn to laugh. If her mother was here she'd be reaching for her Xanax.

'In a *Pulp Fiction* kind of way.'

'I'm a black hit man to you?'

He rested his butt against the back wall. 'You're the most terrifying white woman I've ever known.'

A grudging kind of smile tugged at the corner of Julia's mouth. *Good.* Now that he was sufficiently scared of her, it was time for her to employ the first part of speak softly and carry a big stick.

'Look,' she said, sidling a little closer to him in the lift. 'I understand this wasn't what you bargained for when some cute girl at the café dared you to jump out of a plane with her. You were in it for thrills and sex and you got breast-cancer girl, her terrifying friend and her flaky mother. That's above and beyond. And I totally get you're here because you'd feel like some louse if you left her now, but it's okay, she's going to be fine, *I'm* going to take good care of her. And … if you're short on cash at the moment, maybe I can help you out with that?'

The lift dinged and bounced slightly as it touched down on the ground floor. 'You're trying to *pay me off*?' he said incredulously as the doors opened.

Julia grimaced in the same way she'd seen her mother do a hundred times when anyone was vulgar enough to mention money out loud. 'No, no,' she said. 'Think of it as a kind of thank you for helping Poppy out with some of her list.'

He stared at her for a few seconds. 'Please do not be offended when I tell you this, but—' he pushed off the back wall, '—fuck off, Jules.'

Unoffended, Julia scurried out of the lift after him. 'The longest relationship you had was seven weeks. I was there when you said it. And while I may have been resoundingly drunk, even then I thought you were being economical with the truth. Do you think she needs her heart broken while she's trying to fight this?'

'I think she needs to be loved.'

'Oh. You *love* her now?' Julia scoffed. 'After a *week?*'

His step faltered. 'I meant that in a generic sense,' he clarified. 'I think she's going to need all the support, all the *love* she can get, Jules.'

Julia felt the hot scald of tears again. She didn't need him to tell her about what Poppy did and didn't need. 'Oh I'll just bet you do.'

Ten paused mid-stride. 'Because you have her best interests at heart, I'm going to pretend you didn't imply I'm only in this for the sex.'

He took off again and Julia followed. Her father used to say she was like a dog with a bone. But today she was ten times worse. Today she was Mamma Bear with a bone.

'So you're up for all this, are you? For Poppy only having one breast and the pain and recovery and the body-image crap that's sure to go with it? For when she's throwing up from chemo and losing her hair and too damn weary to lift her head off the pillow let alone service *your* needs. You don't get to *love* and leave this girl. She's not one of your groupies and I swear to god,' Julia grabbed his arm and they halted in the middle of the foyer. 'You break her heart and that band of yours will be looking for a new lead because you'll only be singing soprano.'

'Noted,' he said and jerked out of her grasp.

* * *

Half an hour later Scarlett stood up from her seat. 'I'm going to get some air,' she announced. 'All this tension and sickness is messing with my chi.'

Julia, used to such pronouncements, barely acknowledged the statement. Ten looked like he was going to say something but nodded politely instead.

As Scarlett swept out two nurses entered. 'Goodness, you're both still here,' one of them said. She was a tall, willowy bottle-blonde in her mid-twenties, who had introduced herself earlier as Nina.

Her comment seemed more an accusation than a statement of fact.

Where else would they be?

The shorter, older one smiled at them. 'Just going to do some obs and give her some antibiotics,' she said almost apologetically in a soothing Irish lilt.

Julia was relieved that Scarlett had already left. She didn't have the wherewithal to endure a lecture on the evils of *unnatural chemicals*. Maybe her chi had sensed the impending doom.

They checked Poppy's armband together with Poppy barely stirring.

'Do you think … Is she okay?' Julia asked. 'She hasn't moved.'

'She's just had a major operation,' Blondie said, peering down her nose at them. Then she checked her watch and said, 'We have strict visiting hours here and they finish in five minutes.'

Julia was so gobsmacked at the distinct lack of caring in the nurse's voice she was rendered speechless. She must have been out pulling wings off flies the day they'd taught bedside manner.

There was nothing warm and fuzzy about her. By the time Julia had roused herself enough to tell Blondie there was no way she was leaving this hospital unless it was on the inside of a paddy wagon, visiting hours or not, the nurse was out the door.

Julia stared after her, mouth open.

A hand slid onto her shoulder and gave a little squeeze. 'It's alright,' the soothing Irish voice crooned. 'We don't like her much either and she's off in a jiffy.'

Julia, her eyes glassy from the sting of such casual heartlessness at a time when she'd never felt so frightened and so in need of assurance, gave a half-laugh. 'I think she needs to get laid.'

'Ooh no. I'm pretty sure she only gives the fellas five minutes, too.'

Julia laughed genuinely this time and the nurse, who introduced herself as Siobhan, joined in. 'I'll shut the door on the way out.' Another squeeze to the shoulder. 'Give you all some privacy. Just push the buzzer if you need anything.'

She left then, closing them in as promised, and Julia felt relieved knowing that Siobhan was in Poppy's corner.

'You okay?'

Julia glanced across the bed. They hadn't spoken since Ten had pulled away from her. 'Fine. Thank you.'

They lapsed back into silence, Ten taking up his meditative state over Poppy's hand. It wasn't until Poppy moved her other hand a few moments later that Julia became aware she was awake. 'Poppy?'

Ten looked up then he stood. 'Poppy?'

Poppy ignored both of them. The flat of her hand slowly moved up her body over the top of the bedding until it reached the place her breast had been since she hit puberty. It groped the empty space as if searching for it.

A muted sob filled the heavy silence as Poppy shut her eyes. Tears spilled out from behind her closed lids and she made a low keening noise.

It sounded like an animal in pain and clawed at Julia's gut with hot talons.

'Poppy,' she whispered.

'Are you in pain?' Ten asked.

Poppy didn't answer, just shook her head from side to side, more tears escaping.

Julia also stood. 'What can I do?' she asked – *begged* was closer to the mark. In this instant Julia knew she'd do whatever she could to ease Poppy's distress.

'I want you to make it stop,' Poppy moaned.

Julia struggled to keep the fear and panic out of her voice. Make what stop? 'The pain? You're in pain?'

Poppy hiccupped as she continued to sob. '*It*,' she said. 'I want you to make *it* stop.'

Julia sat down again, defeated before she'd even begun. She couldn't do that. With access to a veritable fortune she could probably get anything Poppy wanted. Sure, she'd refused to touch it, but there were always exceptions to pride and principle and Poppy was it.

But she couldn't buy what Poppy wanted.

'Shh, baby, shh,' Ten said, pressing his forehead to hers, cupping her cheek in his hand, his thumb stroking over Poppy's closed eye. 'Shh now.'

Julia watched as the deep, low timbre of Ten's voice and the rhythmic brush of his thumb slowly quietened Poppy and she drifted back to sleep.

She'd never felt helpless before but she did now. And she hated it.

'Pass me her phone,' Julia said, sitting higher in the chair. It was on top of the bedside table right next to Ten.

He handed it over. 'I think it's locked.'

Julia took it and quickly tapped in Poppy's pin code. Her thumb flew across the screen as she searched for the app among the crowded screens.

'What are you looking for?' he asked.

Julia ignored him as she continued the search, finally locating the bucket list app and opening it up. There *had* to be something in here she could do for Poppy. Now. Right now.

Julia's thumb got busy again as she flicked through the list.

So much active stuff. Stuff Poppy wouldn't be up to for a while. Then number nine jumped out at her. *Buy a pet snake – keep and feed for at least a month (check with Biology department re appropriate sub-species).*

Perfect. There were some things she couldn't fix but she could get Poppy number nine.

She glanced across the bed. Or Number Ten could anyway.

'Can you get me a snake?'

To give Ten his due, he didn't bat an eyelid. 'A snake?'

Julia leaned forward to give him the phone. 'Number nine.'

He read it. 'What kind of snake?'

'I don't care,' she dismissed. 'One that will make her happy.'

'So no pressure, then …'

Julia thought further about the care and feeding a snake might require and shuddered. 'Not too big. Something friendly and … vegetarian would be good.'

'I think vegetarian snake is an oxymoron.'

It killed Julia that with Ten's apparent smarts (if his leaving score was indeed real and he hadn't paid some sad geek chick to write the answers to his finals all up her leg) she couldn't make some quip about *him* being the only moron in the room.

He looked at her and his lips quirked, as if he knew exactly what she was thinking. 'And *I'm* sourcing this snake because …?'

Julia shrugged. 'You wouldn't be the first lead singer to have a pet snake. Use your rock connections.'

'Do I look like Alice fucking Cooper to you?'

'You look more like Alice than I look like Samuel L. Jackson,' she retorted.

Honestly, what was the good of having a rocker at your disposal if he couldn't find a small, friendly, vegetarian snake when you wanted one?

Poppy stirred again, mumbling something, and Julia watched as Ten stood and gently stroked his thumb across her cheekbone until she settled.

A lump rose in Julia's throat.

He glanced at her, and she saw the hollow feeling in her gut reflected in his eyes. 'Leave it with me.'

* * *

Three days later they were home and Poppy was the proud owner of a three-metre albino Darwin Carpet Python. It looked kind of like a yellow zebra with freaky white eyes. 'I'm calling her Madam Curie,' Poppy announced as they gazed at the huge reptile sleeping under a heat lamp in its enormous glass tank.

'Do we know it's a she?' Julia asked. She was fairly certain Ten hadn't been so bothered with checking important points like sub-species or sex.

'Oh come on, look at her,' Poppy said. 'Have you seen anything more girly in your life?'

Julia shook her head. All Madam Curie needed was a set of fake eyelashes and she'd be all set.

'I love her,' Poppy sighed, staring through the glass. She glanced at Julia. 'Thank you.'

'Now we just have to keep the damn thing alive.'

'Do we have food?'

Julia nodded, although she preferred not to think about it. There was a ziplock bag full of dead baby rodents in the freezer – not the gourmet fare she usually stashed there.

Ten had said he'd do the feeding. So at least he was going to be of some use.

Julia slid her arms around Poppy's shoulders and gave them a gentle squeeze. She could feel bones. She'd never been aware of Poppy's bones before. 'You should sit.'

Poppy squeezed her back hard, belying the fragility that was scaring the bejesus out of Julia. 'I'm not going to break.'

'I know. But you should sit anyway.'

'Julia …'

'Humour me. I'll pull up a chair right near this macabre reptile tank.' Madam Curie's tongue flicked out in seeming approval.

'Okay, fine.'

Julia gave a whoop as she dragged over the brand-new recliner she'd bought yesterday. She'd bought two actually, not wanting Poppy to feel conspicuous. They'd always joked about living together when they were old and grey, two spinsters with matching old-lady chairs. Looked like they were getting a headstart.

Julia fussed around settling Poppy into it, grateful that she'd agreed to move out of her flat and move into Julia's. It made sense. Julia's apartment was bigger and closer to the hospital and Dr Dick had lectured Poppy on the necessity of live-in support.

'Okay, here's the deal,' Ten said, emerging from the kitchen where he'd been rummaging around for the last half-hour. 'We're going to stay up late, swap some manly stories and in the morning,' he said, pulling out an appliance from behind his back, 'I'm making waffles.'

Poppy laughed. 'Oh goody. I love waffles.'

Ten bowed slightly. 'As you wish.' He glanced at Julia. '*Great* kitchen by the way. I could die in there and go quite happily.'

And then he was off again, like an excited puppy with a new chew toy, oblivious to the blow he'd delivered to Julia's solar plexus with his faux pas. That *will* do, Donkey! She stared after him, her breath stuck in her throat.

'It's fine, Julia,' Poppy said. 'He didn't mean anything by it.'

'I know,' she said, fixing a smile on a face that felt as frozen as the air in her lungs. And she did know logically that had Ten been thinking properly – *thinking at all* – he'd never have chosen those words. He'd been at Poppy's side all day for three whole days, for which Julia, grudgingly, had admired him.

That didn't mean she didn't want to help him on his way to that happy ending right about now. And not the good kind dished out by dubious massage parlours.

'Come on,' Poppy insisted. 'Sit with me.'

Julia sat and seethed. Luckily Scarlett came along to distract her. 'Julia,' she said. 'You don't mind if I make some changes around here, do you?'

'Changes? Like redecorating?' Julia liked the kitsch retro feel of her place. It was cool and hip and suited her Betty Boop vibe.

'Oh no, I mean—' she waved her hand around in the air '—shift some items around. The feng shui in this apartment is all wrong. Poppy needs some good feng shui.'

Julia glanced at Poppy, who was rolling her eyes. 'Okay … sure.' If by some whacky miracle good feng shui gave Poppy an edge then Julia couldn't care less what Scarlett did. It was all just stuff. Although god alone knew what dead baby mice did to feng shui.

'Ah, Quentin dear …' Scarlett's voice faded as she trailed into the kitchen.

'Are you *still* sure it was a good idea to get Mum involved at this point?'

'I'm sorry, Pop. I know you're mad. I know you and your mum aren't close and she'll flit around and be trivial, but …' She shrugged. 'She's your *mother*.'

'I was going to tell her in a few days.'

'I know. But she'd have been so hurt when she realised you'd waited so long to tell her and then, *I know you*, you'd feel guilty about it, and at the risk of sounding like Scarlett, you don't need that kind of negativity in your life.'

Poppy sighed. 'You *do* know me.'

'We're going to need plants.' Scarlett's voice became louder again as she entered the room with Ten in tow. He smiled at Poppy. 'Write this down, Quentin,' she said as she wandered around the large open living area inspecting it more thoroughly than the pest inspector who'd been last week.

Julia smiled. Only Scarlett, who carried her journal every-where, would expect somebody to have a pen and paper at the ready. But Ten followed her patiently, pulling out his phone.

'So … is she moving in?' Poppy asked.

'No.' Julia frowned. At least she hoped not. 'I think she's plan-ning on … coming and going.'

Poppy gave a soft snort. 'Imagine my surprise.'

'Lush, green plants,' Scarlett said as she continued her assess-ment. 'And take down these venetians to let the light in … maybe some gauzy green fabric at the window instead that can billow with the breeze … how are you with a screwdriver?'

Ten opened his mouth to reply but Scarlett had moved on. 'A water feature over here,' she said, tapping her finger to her mouth. 'We'll make a wellness altar, I think … have some incense burning, fresh flowers every day and string some lights around it …'

Poppy rolled her head to the side. 'Still think it's a good idea?'

Julia blanched at the tackiness of a wellness altar with fairy lights and a water feature, but what the hell, she already had a three-metre girly snake ruining the ambience. 'Sure,' she said. If it made Scarlett happy.

Poppy laughed. 'I'm going to remind you of this conversation when your apartment looks like a Chinese brothel.'

Chapter Five

Quentin rolled over and looked at the woman his arm was pinned underneath. Even sleeping deeply and snoring slightly she was cute. She looked different now, in the couple of weeks since the operation, and since she'd decided to cut her hair, but she was still cute as hell. From the moment he'd met her, there had been something about her quirky smile, sharp tongue and brown eyes that had captivated him. Now, with that young Sinead O'Connor buzz cut, she was all eyes and smile. And let's face it, he'd always held a candle for Sinead. But Poppy was even more delicious. She had a tiny and completely preoccupying dip above her top lip. He found himself constantly wanting to put his little finger there. She joked that she felt like she had a semi-permanent moustache, the amount he'd been doing it.

He squinted as the early-evening light winked in through the window. He had thought she might not be as interested in lazing around in bed with him after the operation, but he'd been wrong. And boy, he had never been so glad to be wrong. Being in bed with Poppy was fast moving to the top of his list of favourite things. It was even bumping out the Sunday-afternoon session of *Australia's Next Top Model*. And that was some achievement.

Quentin didn't want to get out of bed, but he had made the band a promise that he wouldn't miss this gig. And he had an ulterior motive for wanting to make sure he got there on time today. But he sure hated waking her.

He tried to extract his arm very carefully, wriggling it inch by inch from under Poppy, and breathing very quietly so as not to disturb her.

It didn't work; she was awake in a heartbeat.

'Ugh, you cruel bugger,' she moaned, rolling onto her side. 'Even before I was dying I hated waking up. Where's your heart?'

Quentin smiled because he was pretty sure his heart was wherever this woman wanted it to be right now. Even the miserable sentence she'd just uttered sounded like it had a wry, acerbic smile at its core. And that was why he couldn't get enough of her. She had the most fascinating, confusing brain.

And it kept getting even better, seemingly unaffected by the indignities her body was experiencing. Like last night (or had it been this morning?) when they'd lain in bed for hours playing Poppy's favourite game: Queen for a Day. Like all things with Poppy, the game had rules. A lot of rules. But they only served to make the game more interesting. In Queen for a Day, you got to say three things you would change in the world if you were in charge for a day. But they weren't allowed to be system-changing things. You couldn't vastly re-create the world. After all, that wouldn't be right, given you only had it for a day. So, no. You could only make minor tweaks that made life better in marginal ways for the inhabitants of your world. And you couldn't do things that were clearly magical. For example, Poppy had been very clear that 'no more cancer' was intellectually lazy and not in the spirit of the game. It had to be a change that could be legislated or decreed by the hand of humans, not gods. This was real life, after all. Sort of.

Oh, and you couldn't be king. That was another rule: queen or nothing.

Quentin had found himself becoming quite addicted to the game, much as he was addicted to Poppy's smell. And her skin. And the taste of her lips. This morning he had pleased Poppy enormously by coming up with three fixes that she'd found acceptable. They'd met all her rules and she'd even declared them clever. Especially the one about bouncers at bars and nightclubs being required to do a conflict-resolution course before being licensed. If there was anything Quentin loved more than listening to Poppy's ideas it was being told she liked his. What a sap he was becoming.

'I already told you,' he chastised her, tickling her in that sweet spot just under her ribs. 'You aren't dying, remember? I know all about these things. I work at a hospital.' He knew she loved him squeezing and tickling her, even though she feigned outrage. She had expressly forbidden him from being gentle with her.

Just because I have cancer doesn't mean you can treat me like a geriatric.

Lucky, because he couldn't keep his hands off her.

Quentin also knew that Julia hated all his arse-pinching, hugging and physical play with Poppy, but he didn't give a fuck. For two reasons. Firstly, Julia was a damn killjoy, and he would do almost anything he could to annoy the hell out of her just for the satisfaction of seeing that irritated look cross her smug face. Secondly, Poppy liked it. He knew she liked it, because she squealed and yelled at him, which she always did when she liked something but didn't really want to let on. He could see it in her eyes. It made her feel like she was still alive. Julia loved her, but all her cotton-wool wrapping made Poppy feel like the end was nigh and Julia was just trying to keep it at bay a few more days. It made her crazy.

'Café,' Poppy reminded him, sitting up in bed groggily before groaning and lying quickly back down. She shielded her eyes from the sunlight with an arm. 'Is that where you're off to now?'

'No,' Quentin said, frowning. He'd already told her this. 'The gig at the Jubilee, remember?'

He leaned over to kiss her as he pushed off the bed, and breathed in the now familiar but still maddening smells of her. He felt her wriggle herself into a slightly different position as he kissed her, so that her chest was turned from him. He grimaced as he realised what she was doing. He wanted to tear that damn pyjama top off her, and get rid of the weird binding bra thingy she'd taken to wearing everywhere, even bed. He wanted to touch her, all of her, and make her feel good. He wanted to show her that while her body might feel different to her, he didn't feel any differently about it. He was sad for her that she had lost her breast but he still wanted her with an urgency that made him feel like that gauche fifteen-year-old boy shamelessly chasing Helen Harper around the school. He sighed. This wasn't the time. But later, that damn bra contraption was meeting its maker. And he knew just the ticket to help him with that objective. Which reminded him, he needed to get going.

'Bye, sweet one,' he said, wanting to say more.

But she held a finger up to his lips. 'Uh-uh,' she said, shaking her head. 'You gotta remember the rules. You don't remember the rules, you're not allowed to come round here anymore.'

He smiled. He loved that she absolutely knew she held the upper hand in this affair of theirs, despite the cancer, where other girls would perhaps be afraid he might leave and become clingy and afraid. She was so brave. It made him hard as hell.

She frowned at him, those interesting eyes narrowing. 'You remember, right?'

He nodded. 'No lovey-dovey talk.'

She clapped her hands like he was a slightly dense pupil who'd managed to get his times tables right. 'Good boy,' she said, rewarding him by leaning forward for another kiss.

'Not until after you're better,' he reminded her darkly.

'Mm,' she agreed shortly. 'Now get the hell to work. You think you're going to be my toy boy?'

'No, ma'am,' he said, standing up and getting into his jeans. He was pretty sure she was copping an eyeful from the bed, so he exaggerated his movements, making his arse wiggle cheekily as he pulled them on. He was nothing if not a showman.

Then he turned back to her. 'Now remember, we have a date tonight.'

She nodded gravely. 'Number six,' she agreed. 'What time?'

'Should be home by two am,' he said, reaching for his wallet and keys.

She frowned, and the effect was so pretty he wondered if he was going mad. Why did he find this cranky, kooky woman so damned appealing? He knew for a fact he could go out tonight and drag home some hot, willing chick who would stroke his ego and never argue with him about anything. He closed his eyes and remembered just how good that felt. Willing women; god bless them. Then he opened them and realised he was a goner. She was blowing him a kiss and he wanted to blow the whole thing off, stand his band-mates up yet again and get back into bed with her. But there was the other thing. He needed to go tonight. And he needed to get a move on.

Before he left, he tuned back in to what Poppy was frowning about. 'You don't think that's kind of inappropriate?' she asked, sitting up and looking like a fallen angel with the buzz cut highlighting her delicate features and the purple pyjamas hanging off one shoulder. 'Calling her at that hour of night?'

Quentin made a show of considering the question. 'We-ell,' he answered finally, rubbing his chin. 'I think the whole deal is kinda mad, really. I'm not sure the time of day changes that much either way.'

One of his groupies might take that as a sign that he disagreed with a proposed course of action, and take steps to remedy the situation. Steps to make him happy; make him approve. Poppy just nodded. 'Excellent,' she said, lying back down and flapping a hand at him. 'If it makes no real difference to the outcome, let's do it tonight.' She yawned loudly and snuggled back under her covers. 'It's a date.'

Quentin grinned and strode from the room, finding Scarlett plucking his guitar in one of the recliners in front of Madam Curie.

Shit. He'd never been good with mothers, and earth mothers were proving to be no exception.

'I didn't know you played,' he said, wondering how he could quickly extract Jerry Hall from her without seeming too rude. He had other guitars, but tonight was a big gig, and Jerry was his best girl. And truth to tell, Scarlett's plucking was pretty horrible, at least to his well-trained ears. It seemed to be some kind of childish version of 'By the Rivers of Babylon'.

'Oh, just a little,' Scarlett said, staring into Madam Curie's cage. 'Magnificent creature, isn't she?'

For a millisecond, Quentin had a horrible feeling that Scarlett was referring to her daughter, and wondered if she knew the indecent things he had done to that magnificent creature since he'd met her. But then he realised she was talking about the snake. 'Never much went in for reptiles,' he said, his fingers itching to wrap themselves around Jerry's delicate neck.

Scarlett eyeballed him, and he was disconcerted by how much she looked like Poppy. An older, taller, more buxom version.

'She isn't talking to me much,' Scarlett said sadly.

Uh-oh. Just because Quentin was dating a girl with cancer, it didn't mean he was comfortable getting into some screwy family situation. And he knew, from the snippets Poppy had given him, that things with her ma were pretty darned screwy indeed.

He was still a bloke, for fuck's sake. So he decided to feign ignorance. He was pretty sure they all thought he was stupid anyway. 'Must be the cold blood,' he said, motioning to the snake and hoping she might believe he thought she had been referring to Madame Curie. 'Doesn't make them very conversational.'

Scarlett nodded, and for a fleeting moment he caught a glimmer of Poppy's shrewdness in those familiar brown eyes. 'Very well, Quentin,' she said, passing him the guitar. 'I understand.'

He got it; she knew he was obfuscating. And he was pretty sure her pointed message was his cue to ask some more about how Scarlett was feeling regarding her strained relationship with Poppy, and 'fess up that he had got her drift the first time. On the other hand, it also gave him just enough of an out to allow him to make some polite noises, grab hold of Jerry Hall like he was eloping, and scoot out of there.

It was no competition.

With any luck, he might still be able to do what he needed to before the gig.

* * *

'What the fuck time do you call this?' Spike was young, hot, an unbelievable drummer, and bad in a punk kind of way. But he wasn't known for his subtlety.

Quentin was tired, and he needed to get this over with quickly so he could still conduct his business before the gig started. So he pressed a rock-star smile onto his face and punched the air. 'Time to rock'n'roll,' he yelled, to a chorus of agreement from the other two band members, sculling last drinks in the sticky green room.

Spike narrowed his eyes at Quentin and adjusted his black singlet top to better show off the dragon tattoo that climbed his neck and decorated most of one shoulder. 'Fifteen minutes till go, Q,' he said, his British accent still discernible, even after seven years in the land of sun. 'We need to tune up. You know that, bruvva.'

'Fair cop,' Quentin placated, starting the process with his strings. He smiled at his best mate. 'But y'think we could do it quickly?'

Spike rolled his eyes. 'Got somewhere else to be?' He picked up his drumsticks and rapped them on Quentin's head. 'Yoko calling?'

It was Quentin's turn to roll his eyes. 'That's not even clever,' he said darkly.

Spike dragged Quentin into the corner, one arm around his neck in a semi-joking headlock. 'Look, my darlin',' he crooned, releasing Quentin from the lock but turning to face him, his hands on his shoulders. 'I know shit's going on for you, but I'm worried about ya. You gettin' in over yer head?'

Quentin tried not to think about the answer to that. Instead, he winked. 'No pain, no gain, baby.'

Spike hesitated, then grinned at him. 'She must be some fuckin' girl,' he said, smacking Quentin hard in the middle of the back. Then he frowned. 'So wotcha got going down then, before the show?'

'Mate,' Quentin said, reaching out and squeezing his friend's shoulder. 'I gotta meet someone, real quick.'

Spike's eyes lit up, and Quentin knew what he was thinking: *That's more like our Quentin, reliably slutty.*

'Nothing like that,' he said quickly. 'I gotta do a deal. And it's special. I gotta meet them before the show.'

Spike frowned and swore. 'I didn't know you were using, you daft—'

Quentin interrupted him. 'It's okay, mate,' he assured him, leading him back to the others. 'Just trust me. You guys get ready. I'll be back in five.'

* * *

The girl was exactly the kind he loved. Young, blonde and built like a swimsuit model. She kept pressing up against him in the alley, despite the fact that there was plenty of room for both of them.

He was straight to the point. Spike was going to kill him if he was late for the gig. 'Have you got it?'

The girl pouted prettily. 'Of course, baby,' she said, running a finger along his arm. 'But you need to say please.'

'Please, sweetie,' he cajoled, trying for the old Q winning grin but feeling like a terrible fraud. He just needed what she had. He didn't want whatever else she was selling.

'Okay, then,' she agreed, reaching into her handbag and extracting a small alfoil package. 'But this is serious shit. You sure you up for this?'

'Is it good?' Quentin fixed her with his eyes. 'The guys swore that you're the one to go to; you wouldn't steer me wrong, would you?'

'I told you,' the girl said, rolling her eyes and suddenly seeming older and harder. 'For what you want, mushrooms are the best bet. Anything chemical and you could get tricky interactions.'

'Great.' Quentin tried smiling at her again as he handed over the hundred-dollar bill.

She tucked it into her bra, at the front, drawing his eyes again to her impressive cleavage.

She clocked him noticing. 'You want something else, baby?' she asked breathily, pressing closer once more. 'I saw you guys perform two weeks ago, and you were a-mazing!'

She grinned, showing big white teeth. Somehow, everything about her seemed too big – her teeth, her smile, even her boobs. And nothing about her seemed real, including (he'd be almost willing to bet) those gorgeous boobs.

'Ta, darlin',' he said, winking at her. 'That sure is nice to hear.'

Her face closed down as she realised she was being blown off. 'Fuck you,' she snapped, walking off down the alley.

'No thanks,' Quentin breathed to himself, following her at a run so he could make the gig.

* * *

'How was it?' Poppy felt small and warm as he crawled back into bed with her six hours later. She smelled like peaches and pure heaven after the heaving mass of rock'n'roll-fuelled bodies he had needed to push his way through to make it back to her after the gig finished.

'Loud,' he said, relishing the silence of her soft breathing.

'You old fogey,' she chastised, punching him lightly in the darkness. 'Are you ready for this?'

'Are you?' he asked, lifting her up easily and setting her on top of his chest carefully, lest he hurt her. 'You don't need to, you know. Just 'cause you made a damn bucket list, doesn't mean you gotta stick to it. I told you, remember?' He grabbed hold of her arse, loving the feeling of her soft skin in his palms. Was there something wrong with him that she turned him on like this all the time?

He pushed the thought away. Who gave a shit? If he was sick, at least they had that in common, too.

'You only need a bucket list if you're dying.'

'No,' Poppy clucked, determination written so large in her voice he didn't even need to see her face – he could imagine how it looked. Pointy and determined. 'I need to be prepared. These things can come on you quickly. Anyway.' She sighed and it was so unlike her that he immediately took notice. 'Being sick makes you think about things.' She paused and he listened to her take a few deep breaths in the darkness. 'It makes you think about how you live. And whether I live or die, I want to do the things on that list.'

He still wasn't convinced. 'I thought you liked your job. You don't need to do this just because it's number six.'

She laughed; god, he loved that sound. 'I know that, silly,' she said. 'And yeah, I like my job well enough. But I don't love it as much as … say … diving with sharks, or doing a cooking class in Tuscany, or …'

'I get it,' Quentin said, smiling. No-one ever needed to convince him of the rightness of living for the moment. He thought about his father, half-dead with overwork even though he could buy the world many times over. Quentin had worked out long ago that life was for the taking, and if something didn't raise your blood pressure, it probably wasn't worth the trouble. 'Okay,' he said, handing her the phone. 'You ready?'

'Uh-huh,' she purred, her voice high with excitement.

'You got your lines planned?'

She hit him with the phone. 'What do you think, Bozo?'

Fair point. 'Then go forth and do the deed, Ms Poppy. In a few minutes you'll be a free woman.'

He listened to her tapping the numbers on the touch screen. Whatever happened now, he was glad he was here.

So. Fucking. Glad.

'Bob? It's Poppy. No, no I'm fine.' She paused, and grabbed Quentin's hand under the covers. He could feel the tremor in hers. 'Oh you are sweet, but no, honestly, I'm fine.' She paused again. 'Okay, yeah, a bit sore still, after the op, but listen I do have to tell you something.'

Here it goes. Quentin found he was nervous for her. Why the hell was that? He'd never even had a boss, not a real one. Why did he care what she did with hers?

Problem was, he seemed to care about everything she did.

'You see, Bob, I just don't think I want to do it anymore.' A few beats. 'The job. My job, that is.' More pause. 'Well, yeah, sure it's the cancer, but—'

Quentin couldn't believe how frustrated he was by not being able to hear Bob's side of the conversation. Even worse, he couldn't believe that he hadn't thought to insist that Poppy put the phone on speaker.

'You're kind,' she went on, starting to sound quite irritated, and raising her voice. 'You know what, Bob? It's really not the cancer. It's just …' She elbowed Quentin to let him know this bit was important. 'It's just like I told a friend. It's more the clarifying effect of cancer. I don't really want to work anymore. Not really. I want to …' She paused, and he swore he could hear her chewing her lip in the soft light of the lamp, or maybe she just did that so often he was projecting. 'I just want to do exactly what I want to do, every day. For me.'

He felt like punching the air in a victory salute. Holy shit, was he actually turning into a girl? How was this happening? Was he really identifying so much with Poppy's feelings, with her pain and needs and triumphs, that he was feeling her nerves and her small victories in this ridiculous conversation with her boss at two am?

And if he was, what did that mean? Was he going to start being one of those guys who wore those weird man bags and watched *The Notebook*? And cried?

He tuned back in. Oh dear, he'd missed something during his rare moment of furious introspection. Poppy was pissed.

'Why thank you, Bob,' she hissed with sweet sarcasm. 'I, and all the other cancer victims of the world truly appreciate your largess. But no fucking thank you. You know what?'

Quentin was pretty sure Bob said 'what?' at this point, because the pause was briefer than it had been before.

'I'd rather shoot myself in the face than work for you again. Yeah, sure, I loved my job. But you are a patronising, unoriginal bureaucrat who always took credit for everyone else's work.' She sucked in a breath, and Quentin could feel she was gathering for a final assault.

Oh dear. *Oh dear oh dear oh dear.*

'Your shirts are too small. You chair a bad meeting. I hate how you always pick a hot personal assistant. And …' Poppy drew out this last word quite dramatically. 'You need to get some help for your halitosis. Goodbye.'

Quentin felt her muscles flex as she made to throw the phone across the room and ducked just in time.

He waited, trying to decide if she was happy or sad or mad.

She didn't make him wait long. 'Woooeeeee,' she screamed. 'That felt un-fucking-believable!'

He hugged her tightly, but oh-so-carefully, worried about hurting her. 'Just don't get addicted to that particular brand of honesty,' he whispered in her ear. 'I really don't need to know about my halitosis.'

Poppy jumped up and started bouncing on her bed. Her exhilaration was contagious. Quentin leapt up and bounced right alongside, hoping they didn't break the bed. He'd meant it when he'd said Julia was the scariest white woman he'd ever met. After a few more bounces, he caught Poppy in his arms. 'Wanna knock another one off tonight?' he asked, kissing her neck.

'Off the list?' She was breathless with the high of number six.

'Yep,' he said, feeling her smile against his face.

'Which one?'

'Do you know them by number?'

She smacked him, hard, in the stomach as she stopped bouncing. 'Do you really need to ask?'

He laughed, caught in her exuberance. 'Number three?'

'Really?' Her voice was full of wonder. 'You mean …?'

'*Take some form of hallucinogenic drug. Ensuring pre-testing for purity.*'

She wrapped her arms around him and squeezed softly. 'Really? Are you sure? I thought you said you couldn't help me with that one.' She pulled a face so he would remember how disbelieving she had been. "Cause you're the only rock'n'roller in the whole world who doesn't do drugs.'

Was he sure? No, he was scared as hell; he'd seen what drugs did to people. Good people. Talented people. But she had made it very clear what she wanted and he had done his research on this one.

'Wee-ell,' he said slowly. 'I got mushrooms. I looked into it. I wanted to pick something that wasn't manufactured in a lab.'

Poppy kissed him. 'Good idea,' she said. 'I'm going to have enough of that when I start chemo in a few days.' She kissed him again, softly, and whispered against his cheek. 'I like you. I really like you.'

'I don't,' he said as she snuggled against him. 'I don't like you at all.'

'Good boy,' she said, patting his cheek and then sinking back onto the bed. 'Now, where are they and how do we get this done?'

* * *

Four hours later, Quentin was floating in a lovely, blissful bubble. The wild hallucinogenic effects had started to abate, and the crazy ride he and Poppy had been on together was subsiding.

She leaned over and kissed him hard. 'I will never, ever forget that,' she whispered against his face.

'And I will never, ever forget you,' he said, his voice suddenly tight in his throat as he wrapped his arms around her and squeezed. But he wasn't quite done.

He rolled her on top of him, and she sat up, as she liked to do. He touched her pyjama top, with the constraining bra underneath. 'This is coming off,' he said, softly lest he scare her. 'Now.'

'Okay.' She nodded. And he could hear how afraid she was.

As he removed it, Poppy covered her chest with her hands.

'Drop them,' he commanded, and at that moment he wanted her to listen to him more than he ever remembered wanting anything.

'Uh-uh,' she said, folding her arms across her chest.

He frowned at her, tugging at her arms in protest. 'I'm stronger than you,' he said, begging her with his eyes. 'Don't make me get all Tarzan on you.'

She shook her head again.

It was his turn to suck in a breath. 'Poppy,' he said, stroking her crossed arms lightly. 'I want to see you. All of you. I want to touch you. All of you.'

She crunched her face up at him. 'Is that a lyric? Did you really just use a cheesy lyric on me?'

He considered the question. *Did he?*

'Er, maybe,' he conceded. He did know a lot of lyrics. 'But it doesn't mean I didn't mean it.'

Her face softened, and this time when he tugged at her arms gently she relaxed and let him move them away.

'You're beautiful,' he whispered, looking at her in the early-morning light that filtered in through the window. 'Perfect.' He reached up and ran the flat of his hands across her chest. All of it – the bumpy scar, the soft skin, the slight indent where her breast had been. 'I don't ever want you to hide from me.'

She leaned down to kiss him, and that was the last thing he said for a long time.

Chapter Six

Five months later

Lights flared and music thrashed around Julia as she smiled mechanically at Poppy, who was gyrating on the dance floor with Ten in some godforsaken grunge pub to some god-awful grunge band. He had his hands firmly planted on Poppy's behind and it took all Julia's willpower not to march over and hiss *gentle* at him.

But Poppy would *kill* her.

Throughout the last five months of chemo Poppy had insisted she didn't want to be treated with kid gloves. And Julia had tried really, *really* hard, but Poppy had been so sick there for a while as the doctors had chopped and changed treatments, trying to wrest her sprinting cancer under control, that even Ten had gone easy.

Although no-one would guess by looking at Poppy's energetic, vibrant display on the dance floor tonight just what she'd been through. Sure, she was thinner and the funky turbanesque scarf that covered the wispy regrowth of her hair was a dead giveaway, but two weeks off chemo had totally recharged Poppy's batteries and she was making the most of it.

Poppy turned her back to Ten, waving her arms in the air, clicking her fingers to the beat. His hands snaked onto her hips, drawing her in close to his chest, one hand gliding onto her belly as he moved behind her. His frame dwarfed hers and she was clearly revelling in it.

Poppy was living like she was dying and Julia could barely breathe for the fear of it.

Tomorrow they would know for sure. The scans would tell them whether the last desperate attempts from the oncologist had been the magic bullet they'd all been hoping for. Whether it had halted the galloping progress of the disease. Given Poppy hadn't caught one single break, Julia wasn't at all confident.

Poppy, on the other hand, was dancing.

How could she *dance?* Julia wanted to throw up. Or smash things. Both, preferably.

Someone sat on the bar stool beside her and said, 'Dance wiv me, sugar doll?'

Julia rolled her eyes at the thick British accent as she came face to face with an elaborate dragon tattoo. 'Spike, how often have you asked me that these last five months?'

'Pretty much every time we've been at a club togever.'

'And how many times have I said yes?'

He grinned at her in his infectious, unabashed way. 'None. But I live in hope.'

She blocked him with a sardonic eyebrow lift. 'Never going to happen.'

Sure, Spike was a good-looking guy. Hot, she supposed if you were into grungy, high-cheekboned, ratty-haired, earring-wearing, tattooed, rock-star types. Julia wasn't.

She liked well-groomed men with bare earlobes who changed their clothes at least once a day and smelled like anything from

Calvin Klein. Spike smelled like beer nuts and hair gel. And he *never* seemed to change his clothes. Every time she'd seen him (and that had been way too many times as far as she was concerned) he'd been wearing some version of tatty jeans and black singlet. Sure, the style showed off his great biceps and the impressive tattoo so popular with his band of hardcore groupies, but there was no excuse for an unoriginal wardrobe.

Now *she* could dress him like a rock god.

'Why not? You know I'm just gonna wear you down.'

Julia laughed at his complete and utter brashness. She'd never met someone so young who was so damn cocky. Most twenty-year-old guys she knew were either gauche or monosyllabic in her presence, but not Spike. There was a directness, a confidence in his inky-blue eyes that a lot of *men* never mastered.

Cleary Spike was getting laid far too easily.

But Julia didn't let any guy call the shots. Growing up as nothing much more than a *marriageable* commodity to her father, she'd learned to take charge real quick. She said who and when and where. Men didn't wear her down.

'Not even in a million years.'

'Okay.' He folded his arms across his chest, a move she was sure was designed to draw her gaze to those biceps. Julia didn't fall for it. 'Give me one good reason and I'll stop botherin' ya.'

'I'll give you three,' she said briskly and held up three fingers to emphasise her points. 'Number one. You're *twenty* years old, Spike. Number two. You're called *Spike* for fuck's sake. Number three. You're a *drummer*.'

He grinned. 'So was Ringo, baby.'

Julia rolled her eyes. 'I rest my case.'

His grin broadened. 'It's just a dance, sugar doll.'

Julia raised another finger. 'Number four. Sugar doll? It might work with the groupies but I'm neither sweet nor am I a doll.'

He laughed then and a spurt of irritation crinkled her brow.

'Oh I bet you're *sweet as* under all that posh.'

And he looked at her in a way that left her in no doubt that he wasn't talking about the way she might move on the dance floor. If he mentioned honey pots she was going to pour her vodka shot over him. 'You'll never know,' she said as she returned her gaze to the dance floor.

Poppy was laughing at Ten as he whispered in her ear and Julia watched as he grabbed her hand and spun her out from him. Poppy's short skirt flared and she laughed heartily, jubilantly almost. Spike said something then but Poppy stumbled (she'd done that a bit the last few days) and Julia didn't hear him as Ten grabbed her just before she hit the floor. Julia's blood ran cold.

'Right, that's it!' she announced, leaping off the stool and marching into the gyrating mass of bodies. 'We're going home,' she barked.

Julia's blood practically snap-froze when a suddenly frail-looking Poppy meekly agreed.

* * *

'I'm sorry.'

Poppy's hand was clammy in Julia's as Dr Dick, who had pulled up a chair next to Poppy's bed, looked at them with that empathetic gaze they knew so well. Julia decided if she heard those two words coming out of one more doctor's mouth she was going to freaking raze the hospital to the ground. Five months of *I'm sorry* was more than enough.

I'm sorry you have aggressive metastatic cancer. *I'm sorry* each treatment cycle failed to produce results. *I'm sorry* the next therapy didn't help. *I'm sorry* we brought out the big guns and they didn't work either.

I'm sorry wasn't good enough. They needed to *fix* it.

But that was what he was saying. He couldn't fix it. Poppy's recent headaches and the stumbling … The scan and the lumbar puncture this morning confirmed the cancer cells had spread to the meninges of the brain.

Poor prognosis. Two to four months. Maybe longer with whole-brain radiation. And something else about therapies to prolong and improve quality of life.

Julia's heart punched into her ribcage with every beat.

'Any questions?'

Poppy raised herself up on her elbows. She'd been lying flat since her lumbar puncture a few hours ago. 'So that's it?' She didn't say it loudly or in any kind of accusatory way, just in that methodical way of hers.

'No. Definitely not.' His words were gentle. Kind. As always. 'Like I said, there are options … for example, intrathecal chemotherapy is recommended. It has good short-term effects on neurological symptoms and can buy you some more time.'

More time. That's what they were looking at now. There was no more talk of hope. On one hand Julia was grateful there was such a thing, on the other she couldn't even start to comprehend the implications.

It was madness.

Six months ago Poppy had been vibrant and alive and now her life was down to months.

'There have been some successes,' the doctor added to fill the weighty space in the room. 'I can show you some studies where—'

'But it's palliative, right?' Poppy interrupted.

Her voice was even, her posture easy, her hands relaxed. She looked the epitome of calm considering the news she'd just been delivered. But Poppy *never* interrupted.

'I'm dying, that's what you're saying. *Really* dying. No matter what you do, I'm not going to survive this.'

It wasn't a question. He shook his head. 'No.'

Poppy stared at him with her big eyes, even bigger now that her eyelashes and eyebrows were non-existent. There was something about the twin ridges of eyebrows that made a face a face. That framed and defined it. Poppy's face seemed to go on forever, melding into the baldness of her scalp.

Poppy didn't say anything for long moments. Tears shimmered in her eyes and Julia waited for them to spill, for her to erupt. It didn't happen. She merely swallowed hard and said, 'Right,' then eased herself back down again.

Julia stared at her. Was that it?

'Julia?' Dr Dick looked at her as the silence in the room stretched. 'You're quiet.'

Julia dragged her gaze away from Poppy to glare at the oncologist. He gave her a half-smile. 'You've always got *something* to say.'

Yeah. She did. And now wasn't any different. Poppy may be taking this lying down but there was no way Julia was. She stood. 'That's it? You're going to sit there and tell me that all the billions of dollars of government money, *my*—' Julia stabbed a finger at her chest, 'tax money, that goes into cancer research and you can't cure a twenty-nine-year-old woman yet? Did you get your medical degree in a fucking cornflakes packet?'

She started to pace then, her mind flying in a hundred different directions at a hundred miles an hour as the cold harsh reality of Poppy's condition sank its teeth into her neck and sucked hard. 'You can give a bunch of middle-aged men erections that last for freaking days but you can't figure out how to kill a lousy cancer cell? You know what?'

She stopped and stabbed the oncologist with a murderous glare, furiously wiping at a tear she hadn't been aware had formed. 'I bet if cancer of the penis was more prevalent there'd be a cure for this fucker. I bet if dicks were being amputated or dropping off left, right and centre there'd have been a cure decades ago. There'd be a whole fucking government dick department dedicated to it.'

The doctor just nodded empathetically and patiently at her like he always did when she ranted at him, and god knew Julia had done that a lot over the last five months. But, as ever, he seemed impervious to insult.

His quiet acceptance of her vitriol shamed her into silence. Poor bastard – what a terrible job. Julia had to give him kudos. He looked like he had all the time in the world to sit there and take her insults when she knew for a fact after five months of seeing way too much of him that his days were crazy busy.

Julia sat on Poppy's bed, suddenly depleted. Defeated. She glanced at Poppy, lying there so still and rigid, her fingers gripping the sheet like she might somehow fall out of the bed. Her gaze flicked to him as she repeated the phrase she must have thrown at him dozens of times over their short acquaintance. 'She's twenty-fucking-nine.'

He nodded. 'I know. I'm sorry.'

Julia gave a snort that bordered on the hysterical. They were back to that again.

'Poppy?' he said after several long beats of silence. 'Would you like to hear some more about your options?'

'No.' Poppy shook her head. 'Not now. Could you please just … go? Thank you for coming to talk to me and for being so honest, but I really need to wrap my head around this for a second.'

'Of course. You can go home anytime you're feeling up to it, it's been four hours since the LP so that should be fine. Make an appointment to come back and talk to me in the next few days, okay?'

Poppy nodded but Julia could tell that she hadn't taken any of it in. So could Dr Dick. He looked at Julia for confirmation. 'Okay?'

Julia nodded. 'Yep.'

He left and Julia watched the spot where he disappeared out the door and listened to the squeak of his expensive shoes down the linoleum corridor. She watched it long after he was gone and strained to listen until she couldn't hear him anymore. It was the easier thing to do. Easier than looking at Poppy. Her best friend. Who had cancer. *In her brain.*

Who was terminal. Dying. *Really freaking soon.*

Poppy's hand found hers. 'Julia?'

Julia shut her eyes briefly against the tide of threatening tears as she engulfed Poppy's icy hand in both of hers. Poppy was going to tell her not to cry and she wasn't sure she could do that.

Poppy curled on her side, tucking Julia's hand against her abdomen. 'I don't want to die,' she whispered.

A lump of Titanic proportions wedged in Julia's throat as she blinked away her tears and looked at her friend. 'I don't want you to die either.'

'This … sucks.'

Julia felt like a knife was being slid between her ribs at the utter despair in Poppy's voice. She squeezed Poppy's hand tight. 'We'll get a second opinion.'

Poppy didn't say anything for a few minutes. 'Where's my phone? I need to talk to Quentin.'

Despite his devotion to Poppy these last months, Julia, self-ishly, didn't want Ten in this moment, but she was too gutted to argue. And besides, while neither she (nor *any* of the medical profession apparently) could cure Poppy's cancer, Julia *could* rattle up Ten for her. The band had an audition this morning then a practice session that Poppy had insisted he go to. Julia had been relieved – she hadn't wanted him here anyway.

With her free hand she reached into Poppy's bag, which had been placed in the bedside table, and pulled out her mobile, passing it over. Poppy didn't let go of Julia's hand as her thumb swiped across the screen and she put the phone to her ear. Julia smiled at Poppy encouragingly and squeezed her hand, even though her insides felt like they were being ground up in a blender.

A tiny frown appeared on Poppy's bald forehead as the phone rang and rang. 'Not answering,' she muttered as she tried again.

It almost killed Julia to keep her smile in place.

What. The. Fuck.

Surely when your girlfriend *who had cancer* rang you on the day she was *finding out her fate*, you answered the fucking phone?

The anger she'd vented at the oncologist earlier spewed up inside her again like a cloud of hot brimstone, searing her chest on the inside and, once again, Ten unwittingly became the focus of her rage.

He'd been a good distraction for Poppy and Julia had humoured that, but shit just got serious.

Poppy texted then rang again. 'Here, let me text him,' Julia offered and Poppy handed over the phone. 'Be nice,' she said.

Julia smiled and nodded as her fingers flew across the keyboard.

Ten! Where the fuck r u? V bad news. Poppy needs u now! Pick up ph or I swear next time I c u I will insert it so far up your arse you'll have ringtones where your bowel sounds should b!

'Julia.'

Julia smiled again and nodded reassuringly at the warning note in Poppy's voice. 'All done,' she said brightly, hitting the send button.

Poppy didn't look convinced. 'Here,' she said, 'let me try him again.'

Julia watched the sadness and disappointment deepen on Poppy's face when he still didn't answer. 'He's at practice.' Julia shrugged, even though it killed her to defend him. 'He probably hasn't even heard the phone.'

Poppy nodded miserably as two tears squeezed out of her eyes and trekked down her cheeks. Poppy hadn't cried – not that Julia knew of anyway – since the day of her mastectomy. Not through any of the horror she'd been through. Not when her hair had fallen out or when she'd been spewing her guts up or when she had bleeding mouth ulcers the size of Alaska. Not even ten minutes ago when she'd been told she had only months to live.

And Julia couldn't bear it. 'You know they all get lost in that crap they call music.'

Poppy drew in a hiccupy breath. 'I kn-know.'

And that was enough for Julia. She couldn't bear to see Poppy like this. Rage – at cancer *and* at Ten – drove her to her feet. 'I'll go and get him. It's not far from here.'

'C-could you?' Poppy whispered.

Julia was picking up her bag. 'Absolutely,' she said briskly. If she stopped, if she cracked, she'd be useless. 'I'll have him back here in twenty minutes and then we'll all go home, okay?'

Poppy nodded and shut her eyes, more tears squeezing out. 'Thank you.'

Julia didn't want to leave her like this, and she certainly didn't want to have to deal with Ten. But today was a game changer.

She suddenly realised they'd only been rolling the dice these last months. As of today, Poppy's days were officially numbered. And by god if Poppy wanted Ten then she was getting Ten.

* * *

By the time Julia arrived at the suburban community hall where the band practised, she'd had twelve minutes to play out the last tragic months of Poppy's life *and* her funeral in full technicolour detail and she was a sodden mess. She'd deliberately chosen her poppy dress this morning not just because of the symbolism but because she wanted to exude a bright, cheery confidence, and the big red poppies crowding out their black background were perfect.

So much for that.

Not even the capped sleeves, the sweetheart neckline with its cute strategic bow or the retro flared skirt she adored so much were enough to give her a lift now or hide the fact that she'd spent the last twelve minutes alternating between extreme rage and ugly snot crying. When she screeched to a halt in the car park and thought about Ten and *where the hell he was that was more important than Poppy*, the rage cranked up another notch.

She didn't even bother checking herself out in the rear-view mirror. She didn't care what kind of hell she looked like when Poppy was in *actual* hell.

She could hear the muffled crash of drums as she slammed the car door and marched across the concrete car park, the tap of her patent cherry slingbacks an ominous portent. She wanted to scream, yell and kick something, and Ten was looking like a pretty good target right now.

She burst through the door, wishing she could pop Ten's head open as easily. The reverb of a drum solo blasted like bullets into her chest, stopping her in her tracks. It was loud and trashy, just like the shirtless drummer beating it out.

Spike stopped abruptly as their gazes meshed and Julia almost dropped to the floor at the sudden cessation of the buoyant bass. He stood and she couldn't help but notice the top button of his fly was undone.

'Are you okay?'

Julia ignored the question. She was breathing hard, like she'd walked up a hill to get here instead of ten metres across a car park, and she was annoyed that somewhere in the broiling churn of fury she noticed that damn button. 'Is Ten here?' she demanded.

Spike shook his head. 'He looked at his phone about five minutes ago, said *holy fuck I have to go* and left.'

Julia's knees almost gave way for a second time as relief, sharp and hot, flooded through her. Ten would be almost at the hospital by now. But she was still pissed at him. 'Why didn't he bloody pick up?'

'It was on vibrate because he can't hear it ring over the noise anyway, and then our manager came with some other geezer to chat about some possible support gig so he left it on charge and stepped outside for ten minutes.'

Julia realised the explanation was perfectly reasonable, but she wasn't very rational right now. She looked around the hall, realising Spike was the only one there. 'Where's everybody else?'

'They left earlier.'

She nodded absently. 'I'm sorry … I … didn't mean to interrupt your practice.'

Which was a lie. She didn't give a damn whether she interrupted him or not. All she really cared about was getting back to Poppy. But another, perverse, part of her wanted to run away to a place where she didn't have to watch her best friend fade and die.

And for now, that was here.

Plus, she figured Poppy and Ten would probably appreciate some time together.

He gave a dismissive shrug of his shoulders. 'Are you okay?' he asked again.

'No.' Julia wasn't sure why she'd answered. She didn't *want* Spike to know her stuff. She didn't want his pity or his brashness.

'What can I do?'

Rage, sharp and molten, rose in her again. Do? As if he could *do* anything. What, just because he thought he was god's gift to the universe he thought he could also cure cancer? 'Cause *that's* what she needed.

Cocky bastard.

Julia didn't mean to laugh. And even if she had she certainly wouldn't have meant for it to sound quite so maniacal. 'Nothing.'

'I lost my muvver to breast cancer,' he said. 'I was twelve.'

Julia recoiled at the news, a spurt of hot tears scalding the back of her eyes. The thought was horrifying. She couldn't bear thinking about him at twelve, all gangly and pubescent, losing his anchor. She couldn't bear the thought of any of it.

She just didn't want to think.

Her brain ached from the thinking.

'Can you play?' she asked, not really conscious of where she was going with it. 'Loud?'

He shrugged those magnificent shoulders and the dragon danced. 'How loud?'

'*Really* loud. Loud enough that I can't hear myself think.'

He looked at her for a few beats, then, without saying a word, he sat down on his stool and started to play.

The first notes hit her as she'd hoped they would. They thudded into her chest hard enough that she wished she was wearing

Kevlar, and reverberated through her cerebral cortex with enough oomph to disrupt her clashing thoughts. For long minutes she stood there, eyes shut, and absorbed the crash and boom. She let it shake through her thighs, throb through her belly and vibrate through her grey matter.

She looked around the rickety old hall and found a stash of folding chairs. She grabbed one and sat in the middle of the empty space and let the noise consume her, tapping her cherry slingback shoe to the beat.

Tears came and she let them fall like rain. She watched him watch her as they fell and she didn't care. Her brain was full of rage and bass meshing together into one blinding blast that left no room for anything else. The beat was intense, angry almost, and Julia revelled in it. Revelled in its vigour and its gut-wrenching emotion.

Anger. Her old friend.

She felt good suddenly. Good to have the noise in every cell of her being, to have no room for anything other than the furious beat.

Julia didn't know how long it went on. All she knew was that at some stage Spike shut his eyes and went to another plain. She wasn't sure then who he was playing for. Her? Ten? Poppy? His mother maybe? But he sure was working up a sweat.

She could see him perspiring from a good ten metres away. He flicked his head to the beat and the sun slanting through the high window behind him caught the droplets as they sprayed from his hair. There was a dewy sheen to his smooth pecs and she could see moisture gathering in the hollow at the base of his throat.

Her nostrils flared as the salty aroma of fresh sweat wafted towards her. It filled her head and swirled with the earthy masculine beat, pulling at her, potent and real, and she wondered how that hollow would taste.

Suddenly something more than the beat filled her head. Suddenly *Spike* filled her head.

And that just made her madder.

She stood, angry and repulsed that she could be thinking of sweaty drummers when Poppy, *her best friend*, was dying. The chair fell back with a clatter and he opened his eyes. His gaze pierced her to the spot. He looked at her like he knew.

Everything.

A small smile passed over his mouth before he tossed his head again and his eyes drifted shut and Julia felt her blood pressure skyrocket.

How freaking dare he? Did his cockiness know no bounds?

She stalked up to the stage, taking the stairs two at a time until she was standing in front of him, breathing erratically. The noise was deafening up here, hitting her in the chest like grenade blasts, the cacophony feeding her fury.

She watched him, utterly mesmerised by the show. His biceps flexing. His forearms straining as he belted the drums like he was possessed, like he was playing for his soul, the tattooed letters on his fingers and the sticks a blur of movement.

He was someplace else. Totally in the moment. And she wanted that. She wanted to be someplace else, too. In *his* moment.

Far the hell away from hers.

Julia moved closer until she was standing beside him. Close enough to touch him. Close enough to see him breathing hard at what was obviously quite a physical workout. To see the wink of his diamond stud and the sweat on his chest. To see that damn popped button.

And he didn't smell like beer nuts and hair gel now. He smelled like rock-and-freaking-roll.

He stopped abruptly and his eyes flashed open, capturing hers. For long seconds neither of them did or said anything and only the wild tempo of their breathing broke the deafening silence.

Then she was lifting her skirt. Straddling him. Sliding her hands onto the bare smoothness of his shoulders up into his hair, twisting her fingers brutally into the shaggy locks.

He kissed her then. Not tentative. Not polite.

This was no first-kiss kiss. It was demanding. Dirty. And it went on and on. Deep, open-mouthed, head-twisting, tongue-fucking, rock'n'roll kissing.

His hands were everywhere. On her arse, her back, her breasts. Gliding up her legs, sliding under her skirt, stroking up the insides of her thighs.

Pushing into her underwear.

She gasped against his mouth as his finger swept aside the scrap of lace and found exactly the right spot to completely obliterate the events of the day.

'Condom,' she panted as her hands untwined from his hair, groping between them for his fly, making short work of it.

'*Fuuuuck*,' he groaned against her mouth when she reached inside his underwear and freed his cock. It was long and thick in her hand, but that wasn't where she wanted him.

He produced a condom and she snatched it off him, his wallet falling to the ground as she tore at the wrapper with her teeth then rolled it on him in one smooth movement. Normally she would have done a thorough quality-control check.

But this was no normal day.

Then he was dirty-kissing her again – deep and wet – as he lifted her onto him and she kissed him deep and wet right back, grabbing his shoulders for stability as she flexed her hips and sank down on him in one swift move. She threw her head back, a gasp wrenched from her throat at the utter totality of it.

'*Jesus*. You feel good,' he panted into her neck.

Julia sucked in a ragged breath. Good didn't even begin to describe it.

He fucked as dirty as he kissed. It wasn't slow and gentle. It wasn't *nice*. He didn't *make love*. He *screwed*. Hard and fast. Bucking and thrusting deep, finding the right spot quickly and angling himself to hit it over and over and over.

And it was *exactly* what Julia needed as her hips rose and fell to meet every demand of his. Stroke after stroke. Annihilating *all* thought. No room in her head for *anything*.

No Poppy. No Ten. No anger.

No *cancer*.

Just the harsh suck of her breath and the drum of her pulse as pleasure spiralled inside, sharp and sweet.

And Spike.

The deep, hard thrust of him and the low, raspy growl of his, '*Fuuuuuuuck*,' as he came, turning up the intensity of her own release.

That was the way you fucked cancer.

Chapter Seven

Port Lincoln, South Australia

Quentin did not want them to lower the cage.

He looked at Poppy, tiny and bright-eyed, that mischievous face peeking out through the diving mask, and he wanted to yell at the big South African working the pulley to just take a breath. Because the thought of watching her slip under the waves, where sharks were already circling, was wrong. So wrong.

For fuck's sake, Poppy was already dying. He got it. They'd told him. Over and over and freakin' over. Like they thought he was too slow to understand. But why the hell was she so determined to tempt the fates by doing all manner of life-threatening things? Like swimming with sharks. Wasn't cancer enough of a mother-fucking shark for her?

Speaking of sharks, Julia and Scarlett circled behind him, saying the most unbelievably facile things as Poppy gave them all the thumbs up. 'Go get 'em, baby.' (Julia.) 'Remember to breathe.' (Scarlett.)

Remember to freakin' *breathe?* Was that actually something you could forget? Although, now that he thought about it, Quentin was having a hard time recalling the delicate procedure of in/out, in/out himself. The apparatus started to make a metallic whine as the big South African yelled final instructions at Poppy. Her eyes locked on Quentin's and in them he saw all the things they had avoided talking about over the last months.

Impending death. Fear. And her out-of-this-world determination.

Quentin had known some guys who fancied themselves really hard men. Surfers. Footballers. Guys who worked some truly mean nightclubs for a living. But he had never, ever met anyone as brave, or desperately foolhardy, as Poppy.

Poppy shot Quentin the thumbs up as she gave the South African the signal, and Quentin signalled her back weakly as the water started to lap at her feet.

He tried to be rational. There was a cage, right? It was all triple-checked and made to withstand a nuclear blast, yadda yadda yadda. But there were still going to be big, nasty predators eyeballing Poppy. His Poppy. And she was going to be all alone, exactly as she'd wanted it. He'd told her that he could dive. He'd got the certificates back when he'd been seeing a Swedish back-packer. In the end, he'd liked the reef more than the leggy blonde and there was only so much you could accomplish with a wetsuit on. But when he'd told Poppy he could go with her, she'd just smiled that particular smile that meant she had already made up her mind and nothing he said was going to make a blind bit of difference. It was so frustrating, like being a lion thwarted by a kitten. She was so small, and looked so fragile, especially now, but man, she had a will of steel, and she'd got it into her head that this particular item of bucket-list ticking was happening solo. She was killing him.

The cage was descending slowly, the water at her knees now, and the South African was singing along to the AC/DC tune they were using to attract the sharks. Singing along badly. Quentin wanted to turn around and punch the guy square on his Bear Grylls jaw, but he couldn't decide if it was because of his bad vocals or the fact that he was cranking Poppy down into the ocean to get headbutted by some great whites.

A little of both, he decided.

But he couldn't punch him, because that would mean breaking eye contact with Poppy as she descended. And he couldn't do that.

He couldn't speak, couldn't move, couldn't join Julia and Scarlett in their last-minute cheerleading efforts. A terribly unevolved, caveman part of his brain was screaming at him that he might not be able to wield a club to fight off the cancer that was eating Poppy up, but he could sure as hell stop her from playing with predators.

He had never felt so conflicted. His fingers itched to lean over and pull back the lever that was sending her relentlessly downwards, but in his heart he knew that if he did it she might never forgive him. And never would suck, because in Poppy's case there would be no second chances.

Quentin's stomach rolled and bitched as he watched the cage fill with water, now up to her waist. All he needed was a sign. One tiny sign from Poppy and he would call a halt to this ridiculous charade.

Fuck number sixteen, and the wild monstrous great white it rode in on.

And then he got his sign. The slightest wrinkle formed between Poppy's spectacular brown eyes; he could see the slightest hesitation in those intense eyes, even through the mask.

Game on.

'Stop!' Quentin yelled, turning to glare at the big South African. 'Stop the winch!'

The guy hesitated, frowning at Quentin through greasy dreadlocks that partly hid his pretty-boy blue eyes. Quentin had an enormous amount of respect for Rastas, some of whom he'd played with in a reggae band when he was seventeen. This guy's white-boy wannabe Rasta dreads just gave Quentin another reason to hate him, added to the fact that he was lowering Poppy to the sharks, and regardless of the fact that Poppy had not only signed up, but paid big bucks for this particular experience.

The cage paused, as Dr Dreads stared at Quentin. He must have read something in Quentin's face that gave him pause, because he glanced over at Poppy. 'Lady's choice,' he said, in a thick Joburg grunt. 'She's paying.'

Quentin summoned the courage to look back at Poppy, waist-deep in seawater. Her brown eyes flashed fury at him and her slender hands were balled into fists.

Shit, he was going to have to think quickly to get out of this one.

'What the hell?' she said, removing her mouthpiece so she could be heard.

Quentin looked around at Julia and Scarlett, who were facing him, arms folded across their chests like the twin gargoyles of hell. Then he spread his hands and appealed to Poppy. 'I just forgot,' he started, making it up as he went along. 'I've always wanted to swim with sharks, too. I want to come with you.'

Poppy pushed her mask back and her face was stone-cold judgement. 'You never said that,' she said, her mouth a thin line that tore at his heart. He preferred that mouth all sweet and mobile and pouty and interesting. He preferred it pressed against his, making him crazy with all those little kisses and moans that ...

Shit, he was really going mad. He shook his head and tuned back in to what she was saying.

'In fact,' she went on. 'As I recall, when you read number sixteen on my list you said I was,' she made inverted commas with her hands, '"batshit crazy".' She raised her eyebrows, which had started to grow back recently. 'You said,' she continued, like she was cataloguing his sins, 'sharks were dangerous and that surfers knew they were not to be fucked with.'

It was true. He didn't hate sharks, he admired them. He respected their awesome power and their prehistoric beauty. But there was a good reason why those fuckers were one of the very few creatures left on earth that had shared it with the dinosaurs. They were sly, impressive survivors, and Quentin for one was scared shitless of the things they could do to the human body. He'd seen it more than once on surf sites and televisions shows. A great white could take a chunk out of a human that was the size of Poppy's whole body.

Surfers had a healthy respect for creatures that could kill you out in the ocean. They didn't go right up to them and attempt to irritate them with raw meat or loud music.

As she stared him down, Poppy's eyes were huge and luminous, pared back by illness and hair loss. A month of intrathecal chemotherapy had worked, giving her a reprieve of wellness they all knew was going to be short-lived, but she remained somehow a more concentrated version of the self she had been before – tiny, powerful, radiant.

She slayed him.

'Yeah,' he agreed, trying to give her his best smoky grin but feeling a touch uncertain because she usually spotted any attempt to play her a mile off and it tended to kind of cramp his style. 'I did say that, but then remember, you reminded me they don't chuck meat at them here at Neptune Islands. It's all vibrations. Music.' He shrugged. 'Now music I totally get.'

Her mouth turned down unhappily, but she didn't say anything.

He remembered that moment of hesitation as the water had lapped at her waist and decided that maybe a tiny bit of her was freaked out by doing this, too.

Maybe that tiny bit of her wanted to be rescued, or at least provided with some company as she did this wild thing. He just needed to find the right words to convince her that she should let him come, the words that would allow her to save some face. 'In fact,' he said, marshalling his argument. 'As I stand here listening to the fine tunes of my good friends Malcolm and Angus Young, I'm actually thinking that if you deny me this chance, you might really be compromising my ability to grow as a musician.'

Behind him, Julia groaned and he just knew she wanted to kick him. But Poppy's mouth twitched.

Dr Dreads was losing patience. 'Let's make a decision here, broos,' he barked.

Quentin worked hard to bring it home. 'Poppy love, I know you want to do this alone.' He put on his best puppy-dog face. 'I know you feel like you need to do this alone. And I get why. But maybe …' He shrugged his shoulders, like he was just piecing it all together as he spoke. 'Maybe this is like another thing you need to do – help me towards a higher level of musical development.' He swallowed with difficulty. 'Help me realise my full potential.'

Oh, god, he hoped like hell that she could not hear the bullshit in this, because otherwise he was going to have to wrestle her out of that cage and he was almost certain that Dr Dreads, Scarlett and Julia would get in his way. He was pretty sure he could take the poser South African and the old lady, but Julia was likely as not to kick him in the balls and throw him to the sharks. He just knew, now, that he absolutely could not let her go down there alone. There was no way in hell he could be up here while she was down there, tiny and alone.

And dying, his brain snarled at him.

Fuck off, he snarled back.

Letting her go would be pure torture.

Quentin figured he had put up with a lot, holding Poppy's hand while they stuck all manner of pointy instruments and bad chemicals into her. He'd seen her sick and crying and even bleeding. He'd sung to her, made jokes and stayed strong and positive while she'd cried on his shoulder. But for fuck's sake, a man had his limits. Feeding her to the sharks was a bridge too far.

'Tell you what,' Quentin said, his mind hitting on the perfect solution. 'How about we play a game? You win, you go be shark meat solo. I win, I get to come.'

Poppy's eyes narrowed. *Oh this was good.* Poppy loved a game. He could almost smell her competitive juices starting to flow.

'What game?'

The South African groaned. 'I don't have time for this shit.'

To Quentin's surprise, Julia stalked over to the guy working the controls. None of them had failed to notice how impressed

Dr Dreads had been by the buxom redhead's retro black-and-white spotted bikini. Dreads smiled appreciatively as she made her way over.

But she wasn't headed his way for any flirtation.

'Listen, arsehole,' she spat at him. 'Mind your own business, right? You're being paid a ridiculous amount of money for this shit – whether she dives, he dives, or we decide to hold a naked dance party on your boat instead.'

Dr Dreads' eyes widened like he was hopeful such a spectacle might eventuate.

'You are not the boss here,' she said, making sure he understood the pecking order. 'I—'

She stopped, checking herself, and then stabbed a long red fingernail in the direction of Poppy. 'She is the boss. She wants to play a game, she plays a fuckin' game. She wants the whole fuckin' lot of us to go down in that cage with her, we do it. She wants shark fuckin' soup for dinner, she gets it. Do we understand each other?'

Dr Dreads nodded his agreement, but Quentin was sure he remained more interested in the contents of Julia's bikini top than the content of her monologue. He made some incomprehensible noise that sounded suspiciously like a drool.

Poppy grinned wider. 'What game?' she repeated.

'Queen for a Day,' he said, issuing a challenge with his eyes.

Hers narrowed even further. 'Who judges?'

Quentin took a gamble. He knew they were firmly in Poppy's camp, but he hoped they might cut him a break with this. Surely they didn't really want her to swim with the sharks all alone either? 'Them,' he said, motioning at Scarlett and Julia.

Poppy chewed her lip. 'And him,' she said, gesturing towards Dr Dreads.

Quentin almost swore. That guy hadn't liked him from the start. He was too used to being the eye candy; he didn't like another young guy along for the ride.

Damn Poppy; she was trying to stack the jury.

'Okay,' he agreed, knowing she'd snookered him, like she always did. He was going to have to play really hard.

'Good,' she sniffed, motioning to Dr Dreads to raise the cage. 'You remember the rules?'

'Of course,' Quentin breathed, relief flooding his system as he hauled her out of the cage and onto the deck.

She was safe, for now. As safe as a woman with brain cancer living on borrowed time got, anyway.

'Three things you would change if you were in charge for a day,' he said. 'Just tweaks, no magic.'

Poppy gave him a smile that lit her up from the inside and he almost swooned. She was so beautiful with her mask framing her perfect face. All that black – the wetsuit, the tank, flippers – only underlined the fragility and paleness of her. He felt like he'd passed some kind of test. Like he always felt with her. It should annoy him, but every time he passed, he felt like punching the air in victory. It never stopped amazing him. She saw something in him, something beyond the flash and glitter, the guitar and the voice. She really liked him.

'Good,' she said.

'Ladies first,' he said, inclining his head to her.

'Okay.' Poppy sank down onto a small crate and began to chew her lip again. Man, Quentin loved watching this girl think. She was beautiful, like a custom-made Washburn 22 series Hawk. Compact, smart and operating on a whole other vibration.

Scarlett, Julia and Dr Dreads pulled up crates in front of Poppy and Quentin. He had the most terrible feeling he was going to

Amy Andrews & Ros Baxter

get creamed. Oh well, if that happened, he'd try another tactic. For now, all that mattered was that she was out of that cage. And he wasn't going down without a fight.

'Right,' Poppy said, holding up one finger. 'Number one. Politicians who are found to have misled parliament have to stand on a street corner cleaning people's windscreens. Double-time sentence if they lied to or about poor people.'

Scarlett and Poppy clapped. Dr Dreads grunted his agreement.

'Second,' Poppy continued, extending her next finger. 'Condoms, lubricant, contraceptive pills and sex toys should be available free to all men who can pass a simple test about the location and correct use of the clitoris.'

The audience laughed and Dr Dreads whistled. Quentin didn't even want to think about the South African near anybody's clitoris, but he started to feel worried. The tiny smile on Poppy's face was her tell. She was sure she had him on the ropes.

'Three,' she said, shooting him a *wait for it* look. 'Terminally ill people should have free access to flights, hotels and attractions for a two-month window.'

All was silent on the boat. Two *months*. That was the very longest Dr Dick had thought the intrathecal therapy could give Poppy.

'After all,' she went on like she was explaining an algorithm, 'I can afford a proper bucket-list assault, but lots of people couldn't.' Then she assembled her features into a sad little smile, and Quentin felt like he could hear the hearts of everyone on the boat break cleanly in two.

Damn her, she was totally playing them. Poppy hadn't spent a single moment of what was left to her in self-pity or dwelling on what was coming. This was pure theatre.

She leaned over and pressed a gentle kiss on his cheek, whispering in his ear as she did, 'Now you're fucked.'

Quentin knew she would expect big things, so he marshalled his resources and consulted Lead Singer 101. Make every single member of the audience feel like you're performing for them alone.

Three answers; three audience members. He was going to bring this baby home.

'Okay,' he drawled, regarding Scarlett intensely. He'd learned a lot about Poppy's hippy mother over the last six months, so he went straight for the jugular. 'Number one, CEOs of companies that test products on animals should be required to test the products on themselves first.' He looked beseechingly at Scarlett from under his long fringe. 'That shit is just unacceptable.'

Scarlett sighed and applauded wildly. The other two remained unmoved. The South African may even have mumbled something about big game being fair game.

Poppy scowled at Quentin. 'No scruples,' she muttered under her breath.

'Next,' Quentin said, settling into the game and deepening his voice as he caught Dr Dreads in his practised audience-hypnotising gaze. 'The government should recognise that tourism is the sustainable backbone of this country and grant tax-free status to sole operators, as well as residence and citizenship rights to foreign nationals who come here to help grow the industry.'

Dr Dreads whooped in appreciation.

Quentin turned to Julia, who he already knew would be his toughest critic.

'And finally,' he said, being careful not to do what Julia called his rock-star eyes, of which she was deeply suspicious. 'In recognition of the critically important role played by best friends, there should be a national Best Friends' Day, on which best friends who have displayed superhuman loyalty, strength, and,' he smiled at Julia, 'tolerance of irritating boyfriends, are recognised in a national Hall of Fame.'

Poppy swore and Julia inclined her head towards Quentin, her eyes twinkling. Like she knew she'd been played but she didn't care.

* * *

Poppy had requested they change the recording, even though Dr Dreads had insisted the great whites went mad for AC/DC.

Poppy said she thought Rachmaninoff's Piano concerto no. 3 in D minor was the most fitting. She had, of course, brought her own copy. Poppy was nothing if not prepared. For his part, Quentin was sure she was trying to undo him. Poppy had introduced him to the Russian composer recently, and now it was impossible to hear it without thinking of her naked, which had to be ten kinds of inappropriate floating about in a cage waiting to be headbutted by some trained killers.

The concerto started slowly, flirting with them as the cage lowered. Quentin squeezed Poppy's hand and worked hard not to let his utter terror show through his mask. He made a supreme effort to unclench each contorted muscle group, one by excruciating one. Poppy grinned at him through her mask.

He was right; she was glad to have company down here.

As the water covered them over and the music took on a different, more magical quality, Quentin couldn't keep his eyes off her. She floated and played in the cage, and she looked like a mermaid – her slender body skittering about, her selkie-like deep-brown eyes darting around, watching for the things she wanted to see.

Quentin consoled himself with the thought that they might not come. After all, the South African had said they preferred hardcore rock'n'roll. He decided to sit back and enjoy it for the time being – the relative quiet, the precious solitude (he had never imagined a bucket-list trip could be so damn crowded with best friends and mothers and various support crew), and the music that wrapped him up in Russian passion. And, of course, Poppy. It was romantic. If you could screen out the cage and the cancer.

Quentin motioned to Poppy and as she drew closer he grasped her shoulders. He just wanted to stay still for a second so that he could look at her. She smiled as he did it, but it was an impatient smile, like she was eager for what was about to come.

It frustrated him. He just wanted to look at her. To underline his point, he grasped her shoulders more firmly and tried to communicate with his eyes that he needed a minute. She settled under his hands and looked back at him.

Man, there were things he wanted to tell her, but it was so tricky to unravel them all. This girl – this spirited, brilliant, unpredictable girl – he'd never met anyone like her and he never wanted to again. He just wanted to wrap her in his arms and run away – somewhere so far and so safe nothing bad could touch them. He wanted to watch her face while she talked, and hold her hand and kiss those expressive, mobile lips for the rest of their lives. As the thought landed in his brain, Rachmaninoff kicked up his angst another notch and the bottom fell out of Quentin's stomach. The rest of their lives. Some fuckin' joke. He felt like screaming at the universe, asking whether this whole deal was some sick joke, or worse, some divine retribution for all the girls he had so casually known, dated, loved and moved on from. A lesson to teach him the brutal possibilities of human emotion.

What did he want to tell her, looking at her like this? He saw a flash of something in her eyes, and she gestured quickly to him. A finger wag – a clear message.

Nothing mushy, you know the drill.

He didn't get it. She was dying. Surely when you were dying you wanted people to tell you how they felt about you? He felt like doing it anyway; like signing it with his hands. But then her eyes widened, and it was game on.

He swivelled in the direction she was facing and the first hunter was upon them. Quentin wrapped his arms around Poppy and prepared for the impact. He had seen the videos, he knew that the sharks could become curious, or frightened, or angry at the intrusion into their domain, and start to attack the cage in a desperate attempt to get at what was inside. So he squeezed her tightly, waiting for the first assault.

But the creature swam closer, its tail moving minimally, the whole machine imbued with clinical grace. It slid past, and neither Quentin nor Poppy breathed as it stared at them before sliding away again to regard them from a little further ahead. Quentin's skin tingled in his wetsuit and the urge to cover Poppy with his body was so strong he was afraid he might suffocate her. She wriggled uncomfortably in his grasp and he forced himself to release her from his arms. It was very difficult to do.

But this was her moment.

As she danced over to the edge of the cage, two more predators joined the first and performed the same lazy reconnaissance of the cage. Quentin's heart thudded painfully, every sense on high alert. The three sharks circled the cage, tails keeping time like metronomes as they motored effortlessly through the deep.

Several times they swam very close. Quentin forced himself to join Poppy at the cage's edge, and after a while he settled somewhat. The creatures were joined by two more, then three. But whether it was the music or what was going on, they didn't seem to see Quentin and Poppy as a threat. They simply circled them in an elegant ballet, sometimes brushing curiously against the cage's edge, sometimes zeroing in to check out their human visitors.

And, Quentin had to admit to himself, this was pretty magical. There was something altogether clarifying about being deep underwater with only each other and half a dozen ancient beasts for company. The creatures were so huge, their jaws wide and wild and lined with long teeth, their bodies slick and elegant. It made Quentin feel small and vulnerable, and also bizarrely connected to the life surrounding them.

Poppy seemed particularly taken with them. It was as if she could not get close enough to the cage's edge. She stared out at them, fixated, and Quentin wished he knew what she was thinking.

In the end, he just wrapped an arm around her and watched, the music and the moving sharks drumming his humanness and vulnerability into his brain.

He knew he would never forget this moment – these creatures, the music, and this altogether confusing, surprising and brave girl in his arms.

* * *

'So,' Poppy said, rolling in the bed and landing pressed against his chest. 'Did you have a musical epiphany?'

Quentin grinned, relishing the softness of her skin against his chest as he leaned forward to breathe in her chocolatey goodness. 'I'm thinking that concerto would sound awesome on a six-string.' He paused. 'Parts of it, at least.'

Poppy sighed against his chest like a delicate being he wanted to capture and press into a scrapbook. Things had been different since their cage had been dragged up. There was a new closeness between them, and he wanted to give it a voice.

'Poppy.'

'Shh.' She pressed a finger to his lips. 'There's no need.'

'Why not?' He tried to keep the accusation from his voice. She didn't owe him anything, but it still hurt. Couldn't she see what this was doing to him?

'What's it going to achieve?' There was a clinical detachment to her voice that he couldn't bear. He knew that tone. It was the one she adopted when she was standing back, looking at a problem, examining its various edges and features. Looking for a solution. It was her mathematician's voice.

Well screw her; he was not a problem to be solved.

'Why does it have to achieve anything?' He rolled away from her, staring out of the window at the lights of Port Lincoln. She couldn't have it all. She couldn't have his warmth and his comfort and his utter fucking devotion, and not let him say the words he wanted to say.

When she spoke, the mathematician was gone. 'I feel responsible,' she said quietly.

He rolled back to her, relieved to return to the zone of chocolate and watermelon and smooth skin and Poppy goodness. Any separation was miserable. 'You feel responsible for me?'

He felt her nod in the darkness, and trace a finger over the pointy bone of his shoulder. He shivered.

'It's bad enough that we're doing all of this, with what's going to happen to me. If we talk about …' She trailed off. 'If we say the words …'

He grasped her face, the outline of which he could just see in the darkness, and pressed a firm kiss against those watermelon lips. 'It doesn't matter,' he breathed against her skin. 'Whether we say them or not, I'm going to be fucked either way.'

She made a strangled noise and tried to move away, but he held her tight.

'It's true, Poppy, and so what? I'd still rather have known you than not. Sure, when you …' He swallowed hard, and his spit tasted like acid and bitter rage. 'When you go, I'll be ruined. But it doesn't matter. Because I'd do it again. I'd do it a thousand times over. And you know what?'

She shook her head.

'I wish I could.'

She pressed her face against his chest and he ran his hand across her cheek, feeling the tears there. There was more that he needed to say.

'Whatever happens, Poppy, I just know I'm going to be better after this. And it's because of you.'

It came out sounding so trite he felt like Jack Nicholson in *As Good as it Gets*: "You make me want to be a better man". He almost vomited in his own mouth.

But she didn't seem disgusted. She didn't recoil in horror. In fact, she wriggled closer. 'In that case,' she said, squeezing his bicep. 'Let me go first. Quentin Carmody …'

She paused, dragging in a breath as he held his.

'I really dig you.'

Chapter Eight

'I think I'm going to throw up,' Poppy yelled over the noise of the band as she slammed back her third tequila shot.

'You're going to be fine,' Julia yelled back. She didn't see any point in stating the bleeding obvious – the tequila probably wasn't helping – she just lined up another one. If Poppy wanted to spend the last of her days on earth on a permanent tequila buzz, that was fine by Julia.

God knew, Julia had started drinking at breakfast just to face the day. How Poppy managed to function she had no idea.

'I don't know … I've thrown up a lot in the last six months. I'm pretty familiar with how it feels.'

'That was chemo,' Julia dismissed. 'Stage fright is a walk in the park compared to that toxic shit.'

Poppy threw back another one and wiped her hand across her mouth. It trembled slightly. 'I can't believe I'm going to do this.'

Julia couldn't believe that someone who had stared down a pack of great whites two days ago without blinking could be wigging out over number four – the least harrowing item on Poppy's bucket list as far as Julia was concerned. She could still hear the creepy notes of *Jaws* playing in her head.

'It's only a song. And you're queen of karaoke, remember.'

'This is different,' she said, shaking her head. 'This is a proper band.'

Julia glanced at Ten up on the stage, his dirty-blond hair flicking as his electric guitar hissed out a heavy-metal solo that sounded like nothing but noise to her. They may be a band, but the jury was out on whether there was anything proper about them.

* * *

'How do I look?'

A sudden rush of hot tears scalded the back of Julia's eyes as Poppy's question hit her in the big, spongy bruise that had formed right in her centre from Dr Dick's very first *I'm sorry*. Poppy had been asking Julia that question for as long as she'd known her in that same hesitant, unsure way.

Only it wasn't the same anymore.

Poppy wasn't the same anymore.

She was being ravaged by an evil, mother-fucking disease, and try as she might, Julia couldn't see beyond it. With something so ugly and brutal inside her best friend, eating her from the inside out, it was hard to see anything else.

Others could see her. Those who didn't know. But every time Julia looked at Poppy *all* she could see was the black stain of cancer spreading beneath her skin like silent death, choking everything in its path.

But Poppy didn't need to hear that from her tonight. She didn't need to hear Julia say, *I can see it eating you*. She was *living* that shit.

Julia smiled at the person who was more precious to her than anyone else in the world. 'You look amazing, Pop.'

Because she did – objectively. If you looked no further than the veneer, Poppy was shining like a disco ball. She'd knocked herself out tonight to look stunning. She was wearing a platinum-blonde wig cut in a sharp, chic bob that made her cheekbones and eyes look enormous. The perfectly arched eyebrows Julia had drawn on added to the glamorous ensemble.

A tight, strapless, silver lame top clung to her chest. A pair of skinny black jeans tucked into black lace-up, knee-high boots with a chunky eight-inch platform heel gave her a crazy cowgirl kind of look. On anyone else the clash of disco and boot-scootin' would have been plain wrong. But Poppy's particular brand of fragility wore it well. She looked like she could shatter *and* fly at the same time.

She touched her eyebrows self-consciously. 'Are you sure? It's not too … weird? I don't look too …'

Julia hugged her before Poppy could use the adjective she couldn't bear to hear – sick. 'I'm positive.' Julia had never been surer of anything. 'You look dazzling.'

'Yeah, but look at them,' Poppy said, breaking out of Julia's embrace and nodding her head at the gaggle of late teens/early twenty-somethings lining the edge of the stage, all shaking their booties and batting their eyelashes at Ten, in their boob tubes and miniscule miniskirts.

'They're so young and hot and curvy and—'

'No!' Julia was afraid Poppy was going to say *alive*, and damn it, she wasn't dead yet! She was going to get up on stage and sing. And that's all she needed to be thinking about now.

'Don't look at them, Pop. Look at *him*. Look at Ten.' Poppy glanced up and Ten was gazing at her as if the rest of the room didn't exist, as if he was playing for her alone. He grinned at her, giving her the one-minute sign.

For the first time since she'd met him, Julia wanted to smack a big kiss right on his mouth. 'He's only got eyes for you, Pop.'

Poppy grinned back then turned to Julia and grinned at her, too, before throwing her arms around her. With those chunky platform heels, diminutive Poppy was almost Julia's height and Julia hugged her back fiercely. She hugged her long and hard, refusing to let go until the song ended.

They pulled apart as the usual avalanche of ecstatic applause and female screaming rang around the bar. Ten waited for the noise to settle before moving in close to the microphone, gaze fixed on Poppy as he announced, 'This is going to be our last gig for a while, so this one's for Poppy.'

Girls' heads swivelled as they tried to track where he was looking, but then the watery notes of a familiar guitar riff filled the room and all eyes were back on him. Spike came in with the drums and the two of them played the iconic opening notes as he nodded at Poppy to join him.

She turned to Julia, grabbing her arm, the blunt edge of her bob swinging. 'I'm terrified.'

Julia blinked. Poppy was dying and *this* terrified her? 'You're going to be great,' she enthused.

Poppy shook her head. 'What if I … screw it up?'

'You could sing this song backwards, Poppy.'

'No, I mean … I don't want to let Quentin down. I don't want to … embarrass him in front of his fans.'

Julia looked over Poppy's shoulder. Ten and Spike were keeping the riff going but the natives were getting restless. 'You won't,' she said. 'This is *your* moment, babe.'

Ten raised an eyebrow and Julia gave a helpless shrug of her shoulders as Poppy chewed nervously on her lip. 'This isn't just about me tonight,' she said, turning to look at the crowd clapping and cheering, urging the band to launch head-first into the Nirvana classic.

'Don't look at them,' Julia said. 'Look at him.'

Poppy looked at Ten, who smiled at her, pressed his lips to the microphone and crooned, 'Come, as you are ...'

It sounded so husky and dirty that Julia was pretty damn sure every woman in the first three rows just came as they were.

'Go,' Julia urged, giving Poppy a gentle push. 'Break a leg.'

Poppy took her first tentative steps towards the stage in those ridiculously high boots and Julia knew *she'd* be the one throwing up if Poppy actually did break her leg in the damn things. Dr Dick had told them all the illnesses Poppy was now susceptible to, and the very long list still rang in her ears.

Ten's gaze locked tight on Poppy as he sang to her. Julia watched as he drew Poppy closer and closer, trance-like, with the power of his vocals and the moody pull of the beat. The crowd seemed to part as Poppy walked into it and then suddenly dozens of hands were lifting her onto the stage and a microphone was being thrust into her hand and she was singing.

Julia's arms broke out in goosebumps as Poppy's shy, hesitant vibrato added a touch of innocence to the lyric. Ten smiled at her encouragingly, his lips pressed to the mic as he joined her and their voices blended into something sweet and dirty all at once.

By the end of the song Poppy and Ten held the crowd in the palm of their hands and it wasn't until the music had crashed to a halt that Julia realised she'd been holding her breath. She sucked in huge lungfuls of oxygen as the audience went wild. Poppy grinned crazily in the spotlight, launching herself at Ten, who quickly pushed his guitar out of the way to accommodate her, lifting her high, her bent knees digging in to straddle his waist. He looked up into Poppy's excited face and laughed, then twirled them around and around, Poppy's chic platinum bob swishing sexily in the spotlight.

Julia turned back to the bar, needing something to hold her upright as relief washed through her. She pressed her hand to her face, feeling flushed from the rush. Her face was wet and Julia realised she'd been crying.

Unexpectedly, a shot glass appeared in front of her and she glanced up to find Owen, the bar owner, brandishing a tissue and a bottle of tequila. She took the tissue and dabbed at her face as he poured. 'Get that into you. On the house.'

Julia, who'd been too busy feeding alcohol to Poppy before the show to indulge in a stiff drink herself, didn't argue. The band had a regular Saturday-night gig here and she'd got to know Owen. He was one of those strong silent types. She wasn't sure how much he knew but she was damn sure he knew a shit-load more than he ever let on.

'Thanks.'

'No worries. Here—' He poured another. 'The hordes are about to descend. No telling when I'll get back to you.'

Owen was right. Swiftly, with the band taking a break, bodies pressed in all around her. She threw back the shot, feeling it join the other and ooze through her system, mellowing her out somewhat now that Poppy's big performance was out of the way.

Julia eased out of the ever-thickening bar crowd, looking around for her best friend. She and Ten were on the stage being all kissy-kissy and Julia rolled her eyes. She wanted to sit with Poppy and analyse the performance late into the night like they'd analysed everything they'd ever done together, but it didn't look like that was going to happen anytime soon.

'Oh please, get a room,' a curvy brunette muttered to her friend as they brushed past Julia to stand in the queue. Julia smiled.

'Yeah,' her equally curvy blonde friend commiserated. 'What does he want to be with that skinny bitch for anyway? Looks like he could snap her in two.'

The smile died on Julia's lips.

'She's not even very pretty,' the blonde continued. 'She's got no tits and those eyebrows are freaky. And she seriously needs to spend some time on a tanning bed. She looks like a corpse.'

The colour drained from Julia's face. *Then she saw red.* She turned around, reached past two other people who'd just joined the line and grabbed the blonde by the shoulder.

'Hey!' she protested as Julia spun her around.

Julia stuck her face right up into Blondie's. Her pulse whooshed through her ears, beating like one of Spike's drums in her head. 'Why don't you shut the fuck up, you ignorant imbecile,' she growled.

There was an audible gasp from the friend. 'I beg your pardon?'

'You heard me,' Julia snapped, switching her attention to the other woman, her pulse roaring like a cyclone now as her brain fought against images of Poppy's corpse. 'Why don't you tell Trailer Park Barbie here to watch her mouth?'

Blondie let out a strangled noise from the back of her throat. 'Oh fuck off, you big ranga bitch.' The blonde stepped back, pushing both of her flattened hands in the direction of Julia's chest.

Julia braced herself for the contact, reaching out her hands to yank at the blonde's pretty up-do, but the push never landed and the blonde's hair slipped through her fingers as Julia found herself being lifted away from the confrontation, her legs running in mid-air, her hands still grabbing for flesh and bone.

'*Oh-kay*, ladies, let's not fight.'

The curvy short blonde pouted. 'Tell that to that mad fucking bitch, Spike. I was just minding my own business.'

Spike? Julia turned her head to find herself staring into the eyes of a dragon and the red mist grew even thicker.

He was supposed to be on her fucking side.

'Let me go, you bloody great oaf,' Julia spat, struggling against the thick band of arm muscle clamped around her waist as she tried to launch herself at the smug blonde and her equally smug friend.

'Whoa!' His arm tightened around her as he dragged her back further. 'Time to cool down, sugar doll.'

Julia's temper went from seething to explosive as she struggled some more. 'Don't tell me to cool down, you sexist Neanderthal.'

'Okay.' His sigh ruffled the hair at her temple. 'I didn't want to do this.'

Without warning Julia was upside down, staring at the ground as Spike threw her over his shoulder like a sack of potatoes. Julia was no delicate flower. She was tall and strong, but the hand clamped across the backs of her legs wasn't giving an inch, no matter how much she kicked and struggled. 'Spike! *Put. Me. Down.*'

He didn't put her down. In fact, he didn't answer at all. Just strode out of the bar area with her squirming and protesting all the way, her hands clinging to the damp singlet covering his rib-cage for purchase as she lolled from side to side with every stride.

'I swear to god, Spike, if you don't let me down this instant, I will tell every girl at this bar that you have a bad case of the clap.'

She felt the vibrations of his laughter through the palms of her hands. 'Good luck finding any chick in this demographic who even knows what that is,' he said, as they turned a corner.

The noise of the crowd and the backing track receded, and Julia recognised the more subdued lighting of the corridor that led to the restrooms and beyond to the alley out the back door of the bar. If he took her out there he wouldn't need to worry about sexually transmitted infections because she was going to injure him so badly he'd never be able to get it up again.

'*Spike!*'

'Yeah, yeah. Don't get your panties in a wad.' He stopped and dumped her against the wall, pinning her there with his big body, one arm pressed into the wall near her head, one lanky denim thigh thrust between hers. 'Jeez,' he said, stretching out his back. 'You're feistier than a sack full of cats.'

Julia struggled against him. He didn't budge. 'Get off me,' she seethed through gritted teeth.

'Nope. Not while you're still this pissed.'

'Do you have any idea what that blonde bitch said?' she demanded.

He nodded calmly. 'I heard what she said.'

Julia pushed hard against his chest, wriggling her hips to try to dislodge the thick wedge of his thigh. 'So let me smack her a little.'

'You want to get bounced out of here for fighting on Poppy's big night?'

Julia considered it for a moment. 'Just the once, then.'

'Jesus.' Spike grinned. 'How old are you?'

She moved her hands down to his hips. The denim of his low-rider jeans was rough on her palms as she hooked her fingers through two belt loops for purchase as she bucked her pelvis, trying to displace him. 'Old enough to know I could take her.'

He chuckled and it oozed into the spaces between them, soothing and irritating all at once. She glared at him. 'You don't think I could take her?'

'I think you can do whatever you put your mind to.'

'Except, *apparently*, get you off me,' she snapped.

He grinned, slow and lazy. 'But you should really keep trying, sugar doll,' he murmured. 'You're taking me to my happy place.'

Julia's hands stilled on his hips as his meaning slapped her in the face. 'Oh my god.' Her hands dropped from his belt loops as she became very aware of the thrust of his thigh and the bulk of his bare bicep on the wall beside her head. 'Are you … are you getting a hard on?'

'Well I *am* just a guy and you *are* rubbing yourself against me.'

'I am not *rubbing* myself against you.' She smacked a bicep then shoved a hand on his chest to keep as much distance between them as possible. 'I'm trying to *get away from you*, you pervert!'

He shrugged. 'You say po-ta-to, I say po-tar-to.'

'Oh my god.' Julia couldn't believe what she was hearing. She snorted. 'You don't seriously think I'm going to fuck you again, do you?'

If she insulted him by her scathing tone it slid easily off his broad tattooed shoulders. 'I think you need to burn off some anger and I'm more than happy to oblige.'

Ordinarily his audacity would have a blood vessel rupturing in Julia's brain, but instead of an eruption, Julia was surprised by a sudden spurt of hot tears. Spike's easy acceptance of her mood completely undid her. Her body sagged against the wall as the last of her fight drained away. She looked at Spike, a massive lump in her throat. 'She said Poppy looked like a corpse.'

He nodded slowly. 'Yes.'

A tear rolled down Julia's cheek and she didn't bother to check it. 'I dream about that. About her … death.'

'I know.'

Julia frowned. 'You do?'

'Yep. I used to dream the same thing about my mum.'

'Did it stop?'

'Yes. After …'

'I've never seen a dead person.'

He shrugged. 'They look the same. They're just not there anymore.'

The lump swelled and threatened to choke Julia as she ducked her head. She didn't want to look at Poppy and Poppy not be there anymore.

She placed her cheek on his chest and shut her eyes, and she was conscious of his hand at her nape, stroking rhythmically as she struggled for control.

She pulled back after long moments and straightened. 'I'm okay now,' she said because she couldn't stay here forever and she couldn't break down either.

Julia was relieved when Spike stepped back. 'You're not going to smack anyone?'

She smiled. 'I'll give Blondie a wide berth. I promise.'

He laughed. 'Okay, then.'

'Thank you,' Julia said.

Spike shrugged. 'Anytime you want a shoulder to lean on or a drummer to screw, I'm your man.'

Julia laughed. 'You'll be top of my list.' And just because she knew he was watching, she put some extra swing in her hip as she walked away.

* * *

Two hours later they were home, and Poppy was on such a high it was easy to forget for a heartbeat that she had a terminal disease. The band had given her a microphone and a stand and she'd sung backup for all of their last set and she was high and humming as Julia slid the key into the lock. Her eyes shone and her skin glowed and it was easy to imagine in that moment before they stepped through the door that they were all normal twenty-somethings coming home from a club, buzzed on music and tequila and absolutely ravenous.

Apart from the fact that it was barely ten because it was vital that Poppy got adequate rest.

'I want salt-and-vinegar popcorn and marshmallows,' Poppy announced as she danced through the door into the hallway.

'Your wish is my command,' Ten said, following close behind. He'd been a permanent fixture at Julia's since a few weeks into Poppy's chemo. He hadn't exactly been invited, he just hadn't gone home one night.

'You hear that, Madam Curie?' Poppy called as Ten headed for the kitchen and she shimmied into the lounge room with Julia in tow. 'We're having a party.'

But Scarlett sitting on the lounge with two bags at her feet brought Poppy to an instant standstill. 'Mum?' she said, her fake eyebrows crinkling together in her bald forehead.

Scarlett crossed to Poppy and gave her a hug. 'You look like you had a great time, darling.'

Julia looked at the bags then at Scarlett then at Poppy as something hard and heavy sank in her stomach. *Not now, Scarlett, not now.* 'Poppy was da bomb,' she said, keeping her voice peppy. 'She looked like a country go-go dancer with her bob and the silver lame. You'd have loved it, Scarlett and—'

'Where are you going?' Poppy interrupted in a flat, toneless voice. 'We don't leave for Italy until *tomorrow* night.'

'I've decided I'll catch you up later in the trip. In Paris. I have to attend to a situation that's arisen—'

'You're going to India,' Poppy interrupted again.

It wasn't a question. It was a statement. Actually, it sounded pretty much like an accusation to Julia's ears.

'Yes.'

Poppy crossed to the nearest lounge chair, all the glitter and glow fading from her face. She looked pale and thin again. Ravaged. 'To the orphanage.'

'Yes. Well not *just* there, but … yes.'

'I thought you wanted to spend this time with *me?*'

Scarlett shrugged and her bangles tinkled. 'I've been to Italy before and you'll have much more fun without me anyway.'

Poppy didn't say anything for a long time, just stared at her fake liquid-silver fingernails. Finally she looked up at Scarlett. 'Why do you always chose India over me?'

Julia shut her eyes as the plaintive question, which she knew came from deep inside Poppy's heart, punched her square in the gut. All through their friendship Poppy had asked the same question. Had wondered why a bunch of orphans on another continent were more important than her school recitals, her broken collarbone, her birthday.

And Scarlett was doing it again? *Now?*

Julia wanted to shake Scarlett. But right now Poppy needed her more. She crossed to the lounge and sat beside Poppy, grabbing her hands.

'Don't be silly, darling,' Scarlett said, taking a few paces towards her daughter. 'I'm not. I need to do something there. It's very important.'

'More important than me *dying?*' Poppy demanded. 'Do you think it could wait till *after* that?'

'No. Stop it.' Scarlett stomped her foot and glared at Poppy. 'I won't hear you say that. I *won't*. You're *not* dying.'

Julia gaped at the bald statement. She knew Scarlett had struggled to accept Poppy's conventional-medicine path and then her terminal status. But this was more than that. *This was denial.*

Poppy looked at her mother in disbelief. She reached for her wig and tore it off. The overhead light shone off Poppy's bald head, belying Scarlett's assertion. Scarlett looked away.

'Look at me,' Poppy said, and when Scarlett didn't she stood and yelled, '*Look* at me.'

Julia stood, too, sliding her hand into Poppy's, as Scarlett turned, her face ashen, tears rolling down her cheeks. 'I'm *dying*, Mum. Don't you get it?'

Scarlett shook her head vehemently. 'No.'

Poppy nodded hers just as vehemently. '*Yes*. If I'm lucky I have two or three months and let's face it,' she snorted, 'I've been shit out of luck for months now so it's probably going to be more like weeks.'

Scarlett shook her head again, the metal bangles jangling as she wiped angrily at her tears. 'Unless we try something different, Poppy? I've sat and I've watched them stick needles in your arms and reservoirs in your head and pump you full of toxic chemicals and you've refused to do it any other way. But there *are* other ways.'

'Oh, god, not this again. I'm done, Mum. *It's over.*' Poppy's voice cracked and Julia squeezed her hand. 'And I want to spend what time I have left with the people who mean the most to me. Strangely enough, I thought that included you.'

'It does.' Scarlett wrung her hands. 'But I just have to do this first, darling. You'll see why. India is such a special place and I need to go there now more than ever. I've lived my whole life following my gut, and the universe is telling me I *need* to do this.'

'Well hey,' Poppy said, her lips twisting. 'Why didn't you say so? If the *universe* is telling you, then that makes all the difference.'

Scarlett made a distressed noise at the back of her throat at Poppy's sarcasm. No matter how much Julia wanted to bash some sense into Scarlett right now, she also felt sorry for her. Scarlett's huge humanitarian heart made her very good at seeing the big picture but lousy at seeing what was right in front of her.

'Poppy … *please* …'

Scarlett's plea clawed at Julia's gut. It wasn't fair of Scarlett to do this, to ask her dying daughter to understand. But then nothing about this situation was fair.

Poppy stared at her mother for long minutes and Julia could feel the steel in Poppy's frame as she vibrated with the kind of resentment born from years of disappointment. She waited for Poppy to finally tell her mother to fuck off – something she'd never done despite considerable provocation. But she didn't. She just sagged and Julia guided her gently back down to the couch.

'I guess you've gotta do what you've gotta do, Mum,' Poppy said, and she sounded so weary, so *old*, Julia was frightened she was going to die on the spot. 'You always have.'

'Poppy …' Scarlett knelt in front of her daughter, putting her hands on Poppy's bony knees. 'Come and see it,' she pleaded. 'After Tuscany, come to India. Come to the orphanage. You'll love it there, too, I know you will. You'll get it then.'

A blaring horn blasted into the silence that followed. 'That's my taxi,' Scarlett announced, squeezing Poppy's knees. 'Think about it, darling?' she murmured.

Poppy shot her mother a weak smile and Julia admired the hell out of her for it. Even at the close of her life as Scarlett deserted her yet again, Poppy knew and somehow accepted that Scarlett was never going to be a conventional mother. 'I'll think about it,' she whispered.

Scarlett leaned forward and gathered Poppy into a hug. 'I love you, darling and I'll see you soon.'

Poppy nodded. 'Yes.'

To Julia it sounded completely non-committal, but it seemed to satisfy Scarlett, who kissed Poppy on the forehead before standing and sweeping out of the room, followed by a bewildered Ten, who had just joined them and had no idea what was going on but helped her out with her bags anyway.

The front door clicked shut and Julia hugged Poppy into her side as she gathered herself to do what she'd always done – make excuses for Scarlett.

'She does love you. In her own way.'

'I know.'

The acceptance in Poppy's voice yanked at Julia's heartstrings and she held Poppy tighter, feeling the individual ruts of her friend's ribs beneath her hand. 'She's in denial.'

'I know.'

'Maybe India will help her with that?'

'Maybe.'

'Maybe … maybe she just can't …'

A lump in Julia's throat stopped her from going any further. Stopped her from saying *maybe your mother can't watch you die.* But Poppy didn't need her to complete the sentence. She merely nodded, a tear falling down her cheek. 'I know.'

Julia pressed her temple against Poppy's and squeezed her eyes shut. She didn't want to have to watch it either.

The difference was she'd never *not* be there for Poppy.

Chapter Nine

Quentin poked the tomatoes and breathed in garlic and basil, feeling all the cells of his body roll over and sigh contentedly, the way they always did when he had a wooden spoon in his hand. He grinned at Poppy over the huge pot, as she brushed yet another smear of flour across her face, a determined little frown creasing her forehead. She and Julia were wrestling with the pasta maker. He wanted to go over and help, but he knew better. If Signora Rosa didn't bust his balls for trying to take over her class, Julia was sure to shoot him one of her *fuck you* glares. And even for someone with an ego as healthy as Quentin's, those glares were becoming a bit much.

He was finding himself increasingly fond of the incendiary redhead over the last month, but the feeling was most definitely not reciprocated. It seemed to Quentin that his presence was like a splinter in Julia's heel – what had been a minor irritant at first was rapidly deepening to an unbearable agony. She was working hard to pin on a brave face, making sure her irritation didn't peek through when Poppy was watching. But Quentin wasn't entirely sure he could take one more of her martyred sighs without snapping and spitting at her to get down off her crucifix.

A noble man would have bowed out, given the two women some alone time in Poppy's final weeks. But the last time Quentin had been anywhere near nobility was a gig in Sydney when he'd played support for a hot new band from the US and they'd given him a Duane Noble custom hand-built acoustic to play.

Julia scowled at him now as she caught him watching them with the pasta machine. She poked her tongue out at him, and he raised an eyebrow back at her.

Really?

This was a whole new level of juvenile, even for Julia, and his face flushed. Juvenile was usually his department. His father had once told him he deserved an honorary doctorate in juvenile. If there was one thing Quentin resented more than anything else right now (and god knew he was resenting a helluva lot), it was being out-juveniled. Lately, he'd been having the most horrible creeping feeling that this whole thing, this thing with Poppy (and Julia), was some sick experiential learning gig set up by a whacko god to teach him to grow up. Talk about overkill.

Before he could poke his tongue back at Julia, Poppy looked up, flicking a glance over them both, and Julia blew him a kiss. 'How's it going over there, Ten?' she asked sweetly. 'That ragu going to be good enough to grace our perfect pasta?'

Quentin forced a smile onto his face and let out a long whistle. 'I think so, Ms Julia. Question is, will your pasta be man enough for the job?'

He'd chosen his words deliberately, knowing Julia's sensitive radar for sexism. To divert attention from his needling, he leaned forward and scooped some ragu onto a spoon, breathing on it to cool it a bit before tasting its rich sweetness. But when he looked up again, all innocence, Poppy was facing him, hands on her hips. She was wearing a simple turquoise headscarf today, turban-style. It set off her brown eyes and lent her a strange grandeur. Poppy was fearsome generally, but over the last month she had assumed a whole other level of don't-fuck-with-me.

'Cut it out, you two,' she hissed. 'You're like children. So competitive over every little thing. Grow up.'

'Competitive?' Julia arched a perfect eyebrow and swept her fierce gaze over Quentin. 'That's ridiculous, Poppy. For me to be competitive, Ten would have to represent some competition.'

Poppy flashed Julia a hard glare.

Quentin gritted his teeth and nodded. 'No competitiveness here, Pop.'

* * *

Quentin gripped the spoon firmly. He was going to whip Julia's arse if it was the last thing he ever did. She would be eating his dust in about thirty seconds.

'Isn't this a great idea?' Poppy's eyes were bright, and twin spots of colour burned in her cheeks. 'I reckon it's a fabulous way for you two to have some fun together. Signora Rosa is the best, isn't she?'

Quentin nodded and forced a smile. *Just swell.*

Poppy and her bloody games. The only reason he was getting involved in this ridiculous charade was so he could teach Julia a lesson. If Julia was a guy, they could have settled this the easy way, with a minor dust-up and a beer afterwards. But it didn't matter. Quentin knew public failure would be far worse for the superior redhead. And if it took an egg-and-spoon race for Quentin to put Julia in her place, well so be it. He'd lowered himself further than this for far smaller prizes.

As if she could read his mind, Poppy squeezed Quentin's arm then looped her other arm through Julia's. The redhead was sporting a Rambo-like black sweatband on her forehead and a look of determination that would have felled a lesser man. 'Now you two know this is just for fun, right? You're not taking it too seriously?'

'Of course not.' Quentin and Julia spoke simultaneously, giving Poppy matching wide-eyed smiles. But once she turned away and sauntered back to assume her spot on the picnic rug, Julia muttered under her breath. 'Eat my dust, pretty boy.'

'Not if it tastes as bad as your focaccia,' he hissed back.

'Ha,' Julia returned. 'Just remember: you can't beat me, and you know it.' She shot him an evil smile. 'You can't win because you can't commit to anything, you wannabe rock-star dropout. No grit.'

Even though she sounded like she didn't really believe it anymore, like she was just rehearsing some line that made her world make sense, Quentin still wanted to reach over and throttle her. But as Signora Rosa ambled up to the starting line with her brightly coloured horn, he did something that he knew would irritate her far more. He made a huge deal of reaching over and shaking her hand with a big grin, in a deliberate show of 'may the best man win'. He glanced back to check that Poppy had clocked his good sportsmanship. She gave him a warm smile.

Julia swore under her breath and pulled Quentin into a friendly hug. 'I see your fake nice and raise you one,' she muttered into his ear, thumping him roughly on the back and earning a matching smile from Poppy.

Quentin could hardly breathe after the assault.

The little Italian woman with the big voice and magical way with tomatoes interrupted them. 'Enough with ze wishing each other well, bambinos,' she said, shooting them a shrewd look. She hadn't missed a second of their rivalry in the kitchen and her heavily accented English didn't mask her irony. 'Time to race.'

Quentin dug his heels into the soft grass and gently adjusted the spoon in his right hand, feeling its weight and balance. He shot a last sideways glance at Julia as he surveyed the terrain in front of him. She was entirely focused on the course as well, her lips pursed, her eyes narrowed. The race would not be long, but it was perilous for those holding a raw egg balanced on a spoon. It required contestants to skirt two large trees and wade through a shallow pond to reach the finishing line.

Quentin briefly surveyed the other contenders. It was a small field. Most of the tourists doing the Two Days in Tuscany cooking course were lolling on blankets, revelling in their post-pasta glow. It was a perfect day, still warm; the grass was the impossible green of story books. Pitchers of fresh sangria stood invitingly on a long picnic table. And the smell of freshly baked bread wafted over the scene, coating them in an all's-well-with-the-world dozy sort of peace.

But five fools had taken up Signora Rosa's challenge: Quentin, Julia, a set of blonde Californian twins, and one older bloke who looked like his arteries weren't up to the challenge of heaving his considerable girth up Signora Rosa's winding stairs, let alone facing off the rest of the field. Sizing them up, Quentin decided that while the two blondes looked fit enough, Julia was his only real competition. They didn't seem to have her killer instinct. And they certainly wouldn't have her motivation.

Quentin just knew that Julia wanted to grind him into the Tuscan dust and work out the angst she had been building up over the last few weeks – the angst that seemed to have become almost solely focused on him. And if she could manage victory while also causing him some kind of injury as a bonus prize, he had no doubt she would.

Rosa raised her megaphone and recapped the rules. 'Drop ze egg, disqualified,' she said, drawing out the last word theatrically. 'Any body contact, disqualified,' she continued, with the same flourish on the last word. 'Any shortcuts, disqualified.'

Okay, they got the picture. Quentin had no doubt the little Italian would be watching them like hawks. She didn't tolerate miscreants on her watch.

'May ze best cook win,' she finished, blasting the horn and stepping away from the line.

Every synapse in Quentin's brain and every nerve ending in his body leapt to life as he charged forward as quickly as the delicately balanced egg would permit. This was not an egg-and-spoon race. This was not some bit of fun dreamt up by an Italian mama who had spent too many summers at British picnics. This was not an idle sunny-afternoon pursuit to pass the time while the pasta boiled.

This was war.

From the moment Quentin had met Poppy, Julia had been in his way, with her facetious superiority, her high-handed dismissals, and her over-protective suffocating of his girlfriend. It was as clear as it could be that she considered Quentin not good enough for Poppy. Not smart enough, not trustworthy enough, not worthy enough in general. And, worse, she considered him a waste of Poppy's precious last days. In spite of the fact that Poppy had been pretty clear that she wanted Quentin around.

No grit, she said? Well, today Quentin would show her just what he had in the tank. She had no idea the kind of grit it had taken to defy his father consistently and creatively for the last ten years. Not many men had it in them to stand up to Ray

Carmody – his money, his power and his bullish determination. If Julia thought she was going to sashay over the finish line in front of him with that egg in her hand, she had no idea who she was dealing with. Just like if she thought he was going to bow out, drop out of Poppy's life when she needed him most, to never see her again, she was completely deluded.

Quentin grinned as he realised he had leapt to the front of the pack. The portly gent had already dropped his egg, retreating to clean sticky yolk off an expensive loafer. He heard Poppy squealing and cheering in delight and registered the two blondes, neck and neck in his peripheral vision, making good time behind him as he closed on the first tree. He couldn't see Julia and was determined not to take his eye off the egg. That was exactly the kind of amateur mistake Julia would expect him to make. *No grit.* As he reached the tree, his foot connected with a large root, and he stumbled, the egg rolling precariously towards the edge of the spoon. He was forced to stop to right its path, and behind him one of the blondes let out a very bad word as she also ran foul of the root but without the same luck. Her egg smashed messily and she retreated in tears. Too much sangria.

Quentin regained his balance, but the delay had been costly. Julia scooted past him, bumping him viciously with her hip as she rounded the tree, sheltered from the hawk-like gaze of Signora Rosa by the second blonde. Quentin wanted to call foul as his egg rolled perilously again, but he clamped down on his tongue. He'd show her grit. If that was how she wanted to play it, he'd take it right up to her.

The next obstacle was the shallow pond and Quentin reached it a second behind the two women. He smiled to himself, realising his long legs gave him a natural advantage in the knee-high muck. Summoning every ounce of his surfer's balance, he streaked through the pond, carefully skirting both women, who had slowed considerably in the murky water, and made it to the other side a whisker ahead of them. As he stepped up onto the opposite bank, he kicked back strongly with his other leg, sending Julia a face full of muddy water.

He thought the shock might have been enough to unbalance her and make her lose her egg, but no such luck. Julia swore under her breath but she didn't appeal to the umpire either. This was the Colosseum, not kindergarten, and neither of them was a crybaby. As the final tree came into sight, Quentin felt both women gaining on him on the firmer ground. He picked up speed, and they matched his stride. He could almost feel their breath on his neck as Poppy screamed encouragement to both him and Julia. He sped up further, and the new pace was too much for the second blonde, who matched her sister's profanity as she stumbled and her egg bit the dust.

Now it was only the two of them.

The final tree was ringed by a stand of bushes, and as Quentin and Julia entered its sheltered circle, side by side, Julia trod maliciously on his foot. He gritted his teeth and made to shove her with his elbow, but she was already a heartbeat in front of him, rounding the huge tree.

Knowing they couldn't be seen, he took a chance and reached out to tug her ponytail. She grunted in shock and stopped to right her egg. By the time she recovered, he was out of the bushes and powering down the home stretch Signora Rosa had slung a red ribbon between two trees back near the main group, and it looked to Quentin like a victory beacon. He lengthened his stride, almost tasting triumph in his mouth. He allowed a grin to slip onto his face as he saw Poppy, standing near the finish line, her face alight with excitement, dancing on the spot.

But he had underestimated Julia's will to win. From god-knows-where, she produced a last desperate burst of speed. He lengthened his stride again, but she matched him, and he knew he couldn't risk going any faster, lest he lose the precious egg. He basically had to hope she might stumble, or lose steam.

No cigar.

They crashed through the red ribbon together to Poppy's excited screech of 'Tie!' It hurt, but not as badly as the look on Poppy's face as Julia plucked her egg from her spoon, took aim, and threw it right at Quentin, smiling like a mad person as sticky yellow yolk dribbled down his face.

It should have felt like a consolation prize. After all, Poppy's expression of stunned horror as she regarded Julia made it pretty clear who the loser was. But it didn't. It just hurt, some place high and awkward in Quentin's chest. He wanted to wipe away Poppy's wounded look. He wanted to tell her it was okay, all part of the fun. He took a breath to summon the right words, but Poppy had already turned and fled in the direction of the villa. Julia stood open-mouthed and red-faced for a second before she dashed after her. 'Oh dear,' Signora Rosa said, putting a restraining hand on his arm as he made to follow them. 'I zink zis one is for zem to sort out, *sì*?'

* * *

Quentin waited an hour before he sought Poppy out. It was a very long hour. His inclination was to run after her, find a way to make her happy again. Shame filled him as he did penance in the kitchen, helping Rosa wash up all the big pots from lunch. The suds were therapeutic, and he even offered to mop the floor for her afterwards. She rewarded him by promising her cannoli recipe, but even that didn't make him feel better. Sure, a lot of this had been Julia's fault, but he was equally to blame. Poppy had just wanted them to get along, have some fun, and they'd turned it into a pissing contest, like primary schoolers fighting over a best friend. He swallowed nervously as he ran through all the ways he could make it right.

The problem was, everything seemed so important when it came to Poppy, and he was having a bloody hard time working out why. Try as he might to be objective, he kept drawing a blank. Why *this* girl? Why had *this* girl crawled right under his skin and made an uncomfortable home there? Why did he want to make things good for her, to see her smile, to make her face and her voice make all those interesting shapes and noises? Why did he want to stay up late with her when he knew she should be sleeping, just to hear her talk about maths and politics and the state of the world?

This was not Quentin. Quentin did not like skinny girls. He didn't like serious girls. And he really hated bossy girls. Quentin loved curvy, fun, uncomplicated girls; girls who laughed at his jokes and took off their bras when they danced on tables. If they wore bras at all. Yet here he was, washing up and mopping and feeling like five kinds of an arsehole over hurting the feelings of some skinny, serious, bossy girl. It wasn't like they had a future. He wouldn't be marrying her; he wouldn't be having babies with her. As that thought landed, something horrible poked into his brain. Was that what this was about? A sudden chill skittered down his spine.

Was this some kind of sick want-her-because-I-can't-have-her problem?

Oh fuck.

Quentin's father had accused him of being a screw-up, and maybe he really was. Maybe everything he'd ever really wanted had come so easily to him – girls, music, more girls – that this one was the most desirable because he knew he could never have her, not really.

He stood in the middle of Rosa's kitchen, looking out over the valley spread out below her big picture window, and examined the thought, checking its provenance. He thought about how he had felt when Poppy had stood in his line at the cafeteria and asked for that ridiculous sandwich. He remembered the way his heart had raced as she had launched herself at him after the sky-dive. And then he recalled how he had heard the voices of angels after the first time she had come like some kind of ancient goddess in his bed a few hours later.

No, this had nothing to do with hard-to-get. Goddammit, it was all to do with the mysterious bundle of energy and whimsical creature that was Poppy Devine. Even her name made him shiver. She was some kind of witch, and it was time to go find her and make it right.

He hurried to their room in the villa.

Even the sight of her door made him feel better. It meant that in a short moment he would be talking to her, explaining, saying sorry. His skin itched to be in there as he raised his hand to knock.

But then he heard Julia's voice.

'I know, Pop, I do.' Quentin had never heard the redhead sound so contrite. 'And I've been able to hack all of it. Well, you know …' Quentin heard the petulance in her voice and could imagine the mulish look on her face. 'A bit, anyway.'

There was a pause, and Quentin was decent enough to realise he should go.

And curious enough to stay rooted to the spot.

Julia went on. 'But the trip to the Dalai Lama?'

Poppy mumbled something Quentin couldn't quite make out.

'I know, Poppy, but that's our gig. It's always been our gig, remember? It was on your list but we always said we'd go together.' Julia's voice took on a reciting quality. 'I can still remember you writing that: *Sit at the feet of Dalai Lama in Dharamsala and work out what the fuck it's all about.*' Julia paused again. 'Remember?'

This time Quentin did hear Poppy's reply, and her voice sounded so small and sad Quentin wanted to bash the door down and scoop her out of there. 'I remember.'

'Well,' Julia went on. 'I get that you wanted him at the cooking class. I'll admit he can cook, okay?'

Poppy laughed at the grudging concession. 'And play guitar,' she said.

Julia grunted.

'And sing,' Poppy went on.

'Okay, okay, enough,' Julia said loudly. 'I've already said sorry about the egg incident; don't make me start singing his praises.'

Poppy mumbled something and Quentin pressed his ear closer to the door, knowing he should be ashamed of himself and also knowing there was no way he was stopping now. In for a penny ...

'And the northern lights, okay. Fine to both of those. But, Pop,' Julia's tone turned from petulant to pleading, 'not Dharamsala.'

When Poppy spoke, her voice was so clear but so sad it almost burned Quentin's eavesdropping ear. 'I'm sorry, Juju. I love you, you know that. To the moon and back.' She paused. 'But he's coming. Or I'm not.'

Quentin's insides jumped up and did a victory dance. He hadn't known exactly what the plan was; Poppy had been pretty secretive about it all. More games. And he hadn't really cared. She had just said they were going on a trip and he had said *yes I'm in*. But to hear her stand up to the indomitable Julia, for him. It took his breath away. He knew right then that he did not want to be away from her for a second of whatever was to come over the next few weeks.

And now he knew she felt the same.

She hadn't said it to him, she never said it to him, but he had heard it. He had heard her saying it to her very best friend.

He didn't deserve it after the performance he and Julia had put on during the race, and after all the hopeless and screwy things he'd done in his life to date. But the gods were somehow smiling on him anyway. Poppy wanted him with her. And he wanted to be with her. The knowledge of how badly he wanted to be there for her settled in his bones like the chorus of a well-known and much-loved song. Something slow and sexy.

And he knew in that moment that he was in deep, deep trouble.

* * *

Quentin licked his fingers decadently, and clucked his tongue at Poppy.

'Is there anything you can't do?'

Poppy grinned over her tiramisu. 'It was pretty good, wasn't it?'

There was a chorus of agreement from around the table. 'Top marks, I'd say,' the portly guy from the egg-and-spoon race said, scraping his spoon against his plate.

All around the long antique table diners scraped and licked in the candlelight. Quentin looked around at them all. The tiramisu was good, for sure. Poppy was a quick study and she had hung from Signora Rosa's skirts like an avid schoolgirl, not wanting to miss a trick. But this was more than that, and Quentin knew it. He saw the way the assembled students lavished attention on Poppy. They knew she was sick, but they also loved her already. One by one she had laughed with them, tasted their goodies, made jokes about her situation, asked about their kids, and gradually wormed her way into each of their hearts. Like she had into his.

Like he said, she was a magician.

But right now, he noticed, glancing over at her, she looked like one very tired magician. A hot poker of guilt stabbed at him as he thought about how tumultuous the day had been for her – the stupid race and the scene with Julia, on top of her illness.

'You two go for a walk,' one of the blonde Californians said, standing up to gather plates. 'It's a gorgeous night out there. We'll do the dishes.' The girl appealed to her fellow gluttons, rolling around in their chairs on a coffee-and-chocolate high. 'Won't we?' They all murmured agreement. Julia hadn't showed for dinner, and Quentin hadn't asked. But he needed to talk to Poppy now.

'Well, okay,' he said, greedily taking the chance to walk in the warm night with Poppy. 'I'll take you good people up on that.' He stood, pushed back his chair, bowed grandly to all of them, and stood behind Poppy. She blushed sweetly as he pulled her chair back. He leaned down and scooped her out of her chair. 'Someone who can cook tiramisu that well should never have to walk,' he joked.

Poppy began to protest but then sagged against him, and he realised just how tired she must be. 'Okay, then,' she agreed, nestling against his chest. 'You're right, a master chef like me deserves a free ride.'

He squeezed her in his arms. There was less of her every day; it was as if he could feel her slipping through his fingers. 'Onward, to the moonlight,' he joked to the others as they left the room.

And then, to her, 'But hang on a tic. I have to organise something.'

'Something' was his guitar. Jerry Hall had a job to do tonight. And he had to get a blanket. He had stashed them earlier and now he needed to quickly set up.

Five minutes later, Quentin had settled a sleepy Poppy on a blanket under an old olive tree a short distance from the villa, down by the sparkling blue pool. She was bathed in moonlight, her beautiful face turned up to him expectantly. 'Well?'

She always knew when he was a man on a mission.

He cleared his throat. 'I wanted to say sorry,' he started, feeling his way. 'About today.' He stopped, watching for a signal, but she was waiting, those brown eyes urging him on. No way would she give him a free pass. 'For all of it really, with Julia. We've—' He shut his eyes momentarily, realising he needed to do better than that. 'What I mean is, *I've* been childish.'

She nodded. 'Yes.' A slight pause. 'This is hard for her. Not just the cancer. The sharing. Julia's not used to sharing me. Not with anyone, really.' Poppy patted the place next to her on the blanket and Quentin eased himself down, picking up her hand. His always felt so much better when hers was nestled inside it. 'We're all each other ever had, really.'

Quentin nodded. He knew by now that there had been a few boyfriends for Poppy – but no-one serious. She had been too busy, and (he suspected) too different. 'You're lucky,' he said, squeezing her hand. 'She loves you so much.' He had avoided asking; it never seemed like Poppy really wanted to discuss it, and god knew Quentin was almost positive he wouldn't know what to say if she decided she did want to. But now seemed like the right time; the right opening. 'What happened, Poppy? Between you and your ma?'

Poppy snorted, wrinkling her delicate nose and wriggling her body down to stretch out like a kitten on the blanket. 'Nothing ever had a chance to happen,' she said. 'She wasn't there. I was in boarding school, and she was in India.'

Quentin tried to work out the right words to say. He knew it hurt Poppy, the stuff with her mother, but on the other hand, it didn't seem as if she liked her very much when she was around. 'How old were you when you started boarding school?'

'Eleven.' Poppy sighed, and something about the noise tugged at his heart. 'And from then on, it's been Julia and me.'

Quentin murmured something non-committal while he thought it through. Scarlett sure seemed interested in Poppy now. 'What was it like, before that?' He wriggled down next to her on the blanket and she hauled herself up somewhat on one elbow and lay her head on his chest. He could smell wild basil and rich earth and the ever-enticing smells of Poppy – chocolate and watermelon. They were having a serious discussion, but his senses leapt to life as she trailed a hand across his tummy.

'Hard,' she said, fiddling with his belt buckle in a way that made it difficult to decide if he wanted her to stop or keep going. 'She never really liked me.'

Quentin laughed, thinking about the people around the table tonight. He imagined how much more appealing Poppy would be if she was your kid. 'Now that's impossible,' he said, rubbing his hand across the scalp she had shaved bald of its wispy regrowth that morning. The skin was soft and smooth, and already his fingers had found a new favourite place. 'Everyone loves you.'

'Oh she loves me well enough,' Poppy agreed, lifting his t-shirt so she could trace the outer lip of his belly button. 'She just doesn't like me very much. Different issue.'

Quentin sucked in a breath and tried to focus. 'Why not?'

Poppy's face got all businesslike as she sat up and ignored his question. He had the sudden feeling there was something he needed to know, but the look on her face said she was done talking. 'So why did Jerry Hall come along for the ride?'

Quentin really liked how Poppy always gave his guitar her full name. It always seemed kind of impertinent when people took the liberty of calling her Jerry. Like they knew her as intimately as he did. He reached over and picked up his guitar, stroking her silky skin. 'Ah,' he said, shifting up so he was kneeling and flicking the strap over his shoulder. 'I'm glad you asked that.'

Poppy's mouth twitched. 'You been writing a new song?'

'Uh-huh,' he confirmed, removing a pick from his pocket and tuning up. 'It's called "Poppy".'

Poppy smiled but she also got that guarded look he'd got used to when she suspected he was going to get serious.

He smiled back, knowing this was a sure thing, and started.

The melody was slow and dark, sweet Southern-style riffs wrapped in a bluesy rhythm. 'Poppy,' he started singing, stretching her name out to match the melody and trying to inject into the word all the things she wouldn't let him say. He'd let the music do the job instead, just like he always had. 'Ohhh, Poppy.' The tune had been written to match the cadence and perfection of her name. 'Ohhh, my Poppy,' he crooned.

He knew it was good. The tune had come to him on the flight from Australia, and it had been almost torture to try to keep it in his head until he got his guitar back in his hands and could play it in privacy.

It was an ode to her. His beautiful girlfriend. It didn't need any more words, only the notes he'd composed.

By the time he finished the final 'my Poppy' and played the last few notes, she was entranced, her head on the side, eyes glistening and face flushed.

'That was beautiful,' she said, reaching up to trace the line of his cheek and stroke the small scar that made a punctuation mark over one eyebrow. 'And you know what I want now?'

Quentin put Jerry Hall down, hoping what she wanted was to kiss him really hard and lay back down on this blanket with him.

'I want to go for a swim,' she said, standing up and stepping out of her summer dress in one quick move, before yanking down her underwear and waltzing over to the pool.

Quentin felt relieved that everyone had retired for the night as he watched her move, her slender body outlined by moonlight, the back of her neck a sultry line dissolving into her fragile back, the delicate curve of her right breast tantalising him as she turned to beckon him to follow.

He had never moved so fast in his life.

Chapter Ten

No matter how exhausted Julia was at this moment – and she was, which meant Poppy had to be utterly shattered – she knew that the sight of glass domes nestled into thick snow and fringed by towering, white-capped pines would stay with her forever.

Suddenly the drive to Rome, then the delayed flight to Helsinki, and the even more delayed flight to Ivalo, followed by another car trip to the Kakslauttanen Arctic Resort, faded away to nothing. In the future, when she thought back to this time – when she could eventually bear to think about this time again – it wouldn't be about the delays or about the hours it took to get here, or fretting about how tiring it was for Poppy.

It would be about standing in the twilight hush on the edge of this amazing wilderness, the cold air burning her lungs, feeling utterly primal.

'Oh … it's so beautiful,' Poppy whispered.

Ten's hand slid onto her shoulder. 'It is,' he whispered back.

It was precisely the kind of place people whispered lest they disturb the reverence of it all – like a cathedral. And, like a cathedral, it was a place to feel small and insignificant in the presence of a greater power. And that power was nature. It ruled supreme here, looming large all around them, mocking human attempts to contain it.

Julia breathed out and it misted in the cold air. 'Oh look, dragon breath,' Poppy said with a smile.

Julia could see Ten quirk his eyebrow above Poppy's head and she could tell he was dying to make some crack to do with dragons. And her. But he simply smiled and she found herself smiling back, grudgingly admiring his restraint. They hadn't really talked since she'd impulsively – *stupidly* – egged him in Tuscany. She had been very careful since Poppy had laid down her cards where Ten was concerned. Julia had promised her best friend she'd make an effort, and she fully intended to.

For Poppy.

And that probably needed to start with an apology. Sure, she'd apologised to Poppy, but it had been two days since the egging and she hadn't yet uttered the words to him. And she really did need to do that.

Because whether she liked it or not, Ten was here for the duration and this whole thing wasn't about her and her feelings.

It was about Poppy.

'Are you warm enough?' Julia asked.

They'd come from an Italy enjoying an extended Indian summer to Lapland, which was having an early start to winter and had received a foot of snow over the last few days.

Poppy nodded. 'I could do with a nap though, before dinner.'

'Of course,' Julia murmured, glancing at Ten as a cold hand clutched her heart. How much had the weather-related delays on their journey today taken out of Poppy's reserves? She had precious few as it was.

'Let's go find our digs,' Ten said as the night fell rapidly around them.

They easily located their home for the next three nights, walking into the glorious warmth of their glass-domed igloo, which was constructed from a special thermal glass to insulate the interior and keep it warm and cosy. They gasped in awe as all three of them cast their eyes to the night sky. Poppy flopped on the nearest bed and pointed.

'Look at those stars.'

Julia looked. They were utterly magnificent. A billion pricks of light, gleaming down as if especially for them. As if they were the only people on earth. And it wasn't even fully dark yet. She went to join Poppy on the bed, to lie with her and take in the display, but Ten was climbing in beside her and a hot needle of jealousy slid into her chest. Poppy threaded her hand through his and Julia felt superfluous.

Worse than that, *it hurt*.

And what kind of a friend did that make her? Poppy was dying and Ten made her happy. What kind of a *friend* was she to be jealous of that?

'Think I'll go grab a drink—' *or three* '—at the bar,' she said, turning away to throw her overnight bag on her bed, unzipping it and fussing aimlessly in it for no good reason. 'Do you want me to wake you at seven-thirty?'

'I'll wake her.'

Julia gritted her teeth. Of course he would. She turned and forced a smile on her face. Ten's big hand lay flat on Poppy's belly. When they'd talked about seeing the northern lights as teenagers, there'd been no big male hands involved.

'Okay, I'll see you then,' she said.

But Poppy's eyes were already drifting closed and Ten barely acknowledged her as he gazed out of the glass ceiling.

Julia sighed. She hoped they had a well-stocked bar.

* * *

'I think you would make very sexy dog-sled handler. Not enough woman on the dog sleds.'

Julia gave an internal groan. She really didn't want company. But the second she'd peeled off her fleecy parka in deference to the toasty-warm bar, sat down and ordered a martini, she'd had a procession of men all trying their luck. Most of them had taken the hint immediately.

Not so dog-sled man.

Julia had always found an accent, Russian in particular, incredibly attractive, but there was no way she was joining him and his Siberian huskies for a one-on-one lesson tonight or any other night.

'I think I'm a little …' she looked down at the guy, who was a good head shorter than her and good deal slighter '… hefty for a bunch of poor dogs to be dragging around.'

His gaze dropped to the cleavage of her snug-fitting shirt. 'Dog-sled work needs a strong woman.'

He stared at her breasts. Julia didn't think he was measuring them for what they might be able to bench press. 'I'm not great with the cold.'

He grinned big and she noticed he was missing one of his front teeth. 'We have vays,' he wiggled his eyebrows, 'of keeping warm.'

Oh crap. Julia just bet he did. He looked like he'd volunteer to un-freeze her nipples with his tongue any chance he got.

'Hello.' Ten's voice said from behind. Julia stiffened as his hand slid onto her shoulder. 'Here you are, *darl*, I woke up and you were gone.'

Dog-sled man's face dropped. He looked from Ten to Julia then back to Ten, who towered over him. 'You no tell me you had a man.'

Julia figured she had two options. She could shrug off Ten's hand and deny it, an option the bitchy part of her was voting for. Or she could take the life raft Ten was offering and be rid of dog-sled man and the next guy and the next guy. A busty redhead alone at a bar seemed to be an open invitation to proposition in deepest, darkest Lapland.

'You no ask me,' Julia replied.

He eyed her suspiciously, threw back his vodka and vacated the chair. Ten laughed, low and quiet, as the other man walked away. 'Well played.'

'What can I say?' Julia muttered. 'You had me at hello.' He chuckled as she waved the barman over. 'Poppy still sleeping?'

'Yes.'

'Another martini,' she requested as the bartender approached.

'Let me guess. Shaken, not stirred?' Ten asked.

Julia looked at him. 'Dirty.'

He grinned. 'Make that two,' he said to the barman.

They watched in silence as their drinks were made in front of them, which suited Julia just fine. She was trying to find the right words for the apology she knew she had to give but it stuck in her craw. Sure, she'd behaved like a spoiled brat, but Ten counted as extreme provocation as far as she was concerned.

'So …' Ten said as he took a sip of his martini and still somehow managed to appear blokey. 'Are we going to need a bigger igloo, Jules?'

Julia sighed, ignoring his irritating nickname for her. He was right – they had to share digs here, and it was churlish of her to keep baiting him, provocation or not. 'No, look, I'm sorry. Okay? I apologise unreservedly for smashing the egg in your face, and also for not apologising for it sooner. It was … impetuous and childish.'

'Okay,' he said.

Julia blinked. She'd expected him to make her squirm for a lot longer. 'Okay … just like that?'

'Sure.' He shrugged. 'I don't want to fight with you, Jules. I like you.'

Now *that* she hadn't expected. 'You do? Why on earth do you like me?'

'Because of the way you love Poppy.'

His words were soft but they struck her hard in the chest and Julia felt absurdly like bursting into tears. She *did* love Poppy. She couldn't have loved her more had they been sisters. And this entire awful situation was killing her.

'But I love her, too, Jules. And I know you think I can't commit and I lack grit, but you're wrong. I'm still here, and, as I told you that day at the hospital, I'm not going anywhere.'

'You *love* her?' It came out as not much more than a squeak. *Crap.* It was worse than she thought.

'Of course.'

'Have you told *her* that?' Poppy hadn't said anything to Julia about the L-word and that was something she *knew* her best friend would have confided in her. They'd been telling each other their L-word stories forever.

Ten stared into his martini, his face grim. 'She doesn't want to hear it. She thinks she's protecting me from the inevitable fallout if I don't say it.'

Julia nodded. Sounded like Poppy. All logical and mathematical. The way she'd been her whole life because it was easier to live with Scarlett's choices if she attached a logical rather than an emotional reason to them.

'Don't take it personally. She's built a wall of logic around herself over the years to protect her from the illogic that is Scarlett.'

'Yeah. I figured.' He fiddled with the stem of his glass. 'What happened with them?'

Julia shook her head. 'Oh no.' Just because he'd rescued her from being press-ganged into a dog-sled team and they were drinking dirty martinis together, did not mean she was going to talk out of school. 'Sorry. It's not up to me to say.' Poppy would talk about it when she was ready. Or maybe she never would. Whatever. It wasn't Julia's story to tell. Still, she felt sorry for Ten, who'd always come across as being so damn sure of himself but suddenly didn't seem anything of the sort. Actually, he appeared rather diminished. 'Look, it wasn't any one issue or event, okay?'

He looked like he was going to push more but he took a slug of his martini instead. He stuck out his hand. 'Let's call a truce.'

Julia looked down at his extended hand then back up at him. *Truce?* She could do that for Poppy.

Was she ever going to really *like* Ten in the way he'd professed to like her? She doubted it. In fact, she was pretty damn sure she'd go right back to hating him the very first groupie he screwed after Poppy was in the ground.

He'd be out there quickly, she guessed, drowning his sorrows in heavy metal and easy women. Women who screamed at him from the mosh pit every time he played and would be more than willing to help him with his grief.

And for damn sure, she'd be watching him. See how much he *liked* her after she cock-blocked him at every move.

But for now he was right, he *wasn't* going anywhere whether she liked it or not, so she could give a truce a red-hot whirl.

For Poppy.

'Okay.' She slid her hand into his. 'Truce.'

He narrowed his eyes at her easy capitulation as they shook. 'I mean it, Jules. I'd like us to be friends.'

Julia was prepared to play nice for Poppy's sake, to put aside her less-than-charitable feelings and her tendency towards anger, mistrust and sarcasm, and try really hard to get along with Ten. Which wouldn't be too difficult, she acknowledged grudgingly. He was a funny, friendly guy who, had they met in different circumstances, she might actually have got along with. But she thought friendship might be pushing the realms of plausibility.

'Well, let's just take it one step at a time,' she hedged, slipping her hand out of his.

'Okay.' He nodded. 'Fine. But I am going to win you over, you'll see. I have it on good authority that I'm charming.'

Julia snorted into her drink. 'Oh yes, from your mother?'

'My father. Although I do believe his actual words were *charming wastrel*.'

Sounded like her father and Ten's father would get on like a house on fire. 'Poor Ten,' she mocked playfully.

He grinned at her then threw down the last of his drink. 'I'll go wake Poppy. Grab us a table.'

And he was gone before the sarcastic side of her could snap to attention and mutter *Aye, aye, Sir*.

This *truce* was not going to be easy …

* * *

They dined on traditional Lapland fare of moose, reindeer and lingonberries, and listened to Poppy chat excitedly about the northern lights. There was no iron-clad promise they'd see them in the three nights and the weather forecast was for more snow, which would virtually guarantee that they wouldn't, but Poppy refused to be deterred. Julia had no idea where she got her positivity from, considering the deep shit she was in. This was what people called making the most of a bad situation, she supposed. But it just made Julia want to curl up into a ball and rock.

It was so freaking *unfair*.

Ten scraped up the last remaining morsel from his fourth course and burped as he pushed it aside. 'As God is my witness, I'll never be hungry again.'

'Ha!' Poppy said, sliding her hand into his. 'Vivien Leigh, *Gone With the Wind*.'

Julia rolled her eyes. Knowing what she knew about him, Ten would be hungry again in no time. He would have died of starvation within two hours of the civil war *starting*. Where he put all the stuff he crammed into his mouth Julia had no idea. If Julia ate like that her curves would be more soft edges than the dangerous variety.

Poppy yawned and that familiar cold hand squeezed a bit harder. It wasn't quite nine pm and Poppy had not long woken from her nap. Plus she was a night owl. The cold hand crept up higher to Julia's throat. She glanced at Ten, whose brow was creased in concern.

'You want to head back, babe?' he asked.

Poppy nodded. 'Yep. I'm beat.'

'Let's go,' Julia said, pushing her chair back as she stood. 'We're probably missing aurora borealis anyway.'

Unfortunately, the stars were nowhere to be seen and it was snowing lightly when they stepped outside. Julia wanted to shake her fist at the sky and bellow at the elements, but Poppy's smile and her soft, delighted 'Oh' at the gently falling flakes calmed her down.

'Don't see this back home,' she said.

'Nope,' Julia agreed. It never snowed in Brisbane. And it was a stunningly beautiful sight as it floated silently around them.

'I want to make a snow angel tomorrow,' Poppy said.

'Sure thing,' Julia said as she swallowed against the firm grip of the cold hand. Where they came from, sand angels were the only option. But right now, she didn't want to think about angels at all.

They hurried into the igloo and shut out the cold behind them, shrugging out of their heavy coats as the warmth enveloped them. Ten pulled back the covers and Poppy collapsed onto the bed immediately, in her jeans, fleecy jumper and beanie. Julia followed suit, kicking out of her warm boots as Ten removed Poppy's.

He switched off the lights inside their cocoon and they lay and watched fat white flakes drift down towards them. They swirled in the cold night air, fell gracefully onto the glass then slid off.

'No northern lights tonight,' Poppy sighed.

Julia glanced over but Poppy's eyes were already fluttering shut. She sounded accepting and the hand around Julia's heart clamped tighter. 'Two more nights, Pop,' she said.

Part of Julia wanted to stay for as long as it took. The advice from tourist organisations was to stay for two weeks in the area to be sure. But Poppy didn't have two weeks to spare. Not if they were going to fit in the Dalai Lama and Paris. And *maybe* India.

How much time *had* Dr Dick bought her?

A smile touched Poppy's lips. 'I know. Tomorrow night,' she murmured, snuggling into Ten's side. 'I can feel it in my bones.'

Ten turned his head to face Julia, crossing his fingers at her. But Julia needed more than dubious gestures. She needed guarantees. And for that she was even willing to throw a prayer out there into the universe, which felt especially close at the moment.

She didn't have a good relationship with God. Any god. In fact, she didn't really believe in any of that stuff. But tonight she'd shaken on a truce with Ten – so clearly she'd crossed into no-man's-land.

So here went nothing.

Okay, if you're up there, I mean really *up there … well firstly, you can go to hell because seriously, dude, giving a twenty-nine-year-old cancer is just plain mean. But seeing as how you did see fit to do so then maybe you can make amends by sending us some clear weather and some goddamn northern lights. I don't think that's too much to ask seeing as how you're* God *and all. And it's not like I'm asking you for something every bloody night, right? I didn't even ask you to cure Poppy. In fact, I haven't asked you for anything since I asked you to bring Scarlett home so she could see Poppy being awarded the maths prize in grade eight. But I'm willing to give this one last shot. A chance to prove yourself. Yes, I know I'm not supposed to ask you to prove your existence, but I'm sorry … the more grandiose the claim, the more proof I require.*

So just … please. Please. *She's dying. And I love her and I don't know what else to do. Please help me give her this. Amen.*

Julia lay looking out at the drifting snow for a long time, waiting for the igloo to explode in one huge, divine, kick-ass smoting for her less-than-reverent prayer.

It didn't.

So maybe there was hope for the northern lights yet.

* * *

The weather did not cooperate the next night, with more snow falling, but Poppy's belief that it would happen was infectious and the weather forecast for the third night was for more favourable conditions. In the meantime, they went on a reindeer safari, made snow angels and snowmen and had snowball fights with the other tourists. They ate and drank and strangely, despite the circumstances, they were merry.

A kind of fatalistic sense surrounded them and all three were determined to embrace everything that this magical place had to offer. Julia fretted about Poppy being warm enough, but the cold put welcome colour in Poppy's cheeks and she couldn't remember a time in the last six months when Poppy had looked so healthy.

The irony was not lost on Julia.

On their last night in Lapland they shared a meal and too much ouzo with a group of tourists from Greece. A couple of them had guitars and there was an impromptu, internationally flavoured jam session with Ten. Poppy beamed through it, her cheeks glowing, her eyes sparkling. Julia got two offers to spend the night in other igloos. Tempting offers as well. Good-looking men with Mediterranean tans who clearly looked after themselves. At any other time Julia would most definitely have been interested. But she had her whole life to get laid by good-looking Greek men.

Tonight was special. Tonight was the night the northern lights *would* come and she only wanted to share that with Poppy.

And Ten, of course ...

* * *

Snuggled into their igloo just before midnight, three sets of eyes were cast to the brilliantly clear sky, and Julia could feel herself getting more and more pissed off. An hour had passed, the ouzo had long worn off and not even the breathtaking celestial display was enough to dampen her ire.

'Come the fuck on,' she huffed at the glass ceiling. Poppy hadn't made nine the last two nights – midnight was pushing it.

Poppy laughed. 'Patience, grasshopper. It'll happen. A watched pot never boils et cetera.'

'Yep,' Julia said, forcing a positivity she didn't feel into her voice, not wanting to be a buzz kill when Poppy was so chirpy and very much awake still. 'Definitely. Absolutely. It's going to happen. Of course it will. I prayed for it so it'll happen.'

'*You* prayed?' Poppy laughed, raising herself up on her elbow to look over Ten at Julia. 'Bloody hell, it's a wonder the igloo wasn't struck by lightning.'

'There's still time.'

Poppy laughed some more, collapsing back on the bed, disappearing behind Ten's long, lanky frame, and Julia felt a pang of jealousy. This wasn't how she'd imagined they'd see the lights together. Without Ten, *she* and Poppy would be lying side by side in the dark, staring up into the night. Whispering excitedly, waiting for the moment.

The thought brought tears to her eyes and she blinked rapidly to push them back. 'There's no moon,' she said in an attempt to distract herself from the push and pull of her roiling emotions.

'Oh Jerry, don't let's ask for the moon. We have the stars,' Ten murmured.

Julia shut her eyes, tears threatening again. Bette Davis always did get the best lines.

'There!'

Julia's eyes flew open at Poppy's exclamation and followed her pointed finger, just catching the faint green glow as it disappeared.

She sat up abruptly in her bed. 'Oh my god.' She grinned and looked at Poppy. The night sky lit up again as if a green genie, newly released from the lamp, was hovering above them. 'Oh my god,' she whispered. 'It's beautiful.'

Poppy grinned back as the glow flared once more. 'It's awesome.' She held out her hand. 'Come lie with us.'

Julia's breath caught at the request. She glanced at Ten. He looked very cosy there with Poppy plastered to his side, their hands interlinked. But he nodded and said, 'Come on, Jules.'

Fighting back more stupid tears, feeling needier than she ever had, Julia crossed round to Poppy's side of the bed and climbed in next to her. The beds were big enough for three, but Ten and Poppy shuffled over to make room for her anyway.

Poppy threaded her fingers through Julia's as soon as she'd settled and squeezed her hand. Julia squeezed back. This was how she'd always imagined it would be.

For the next half-hour none of them really said anything; they just lay there holding hands, Poppy in the middle, gasping in awe as the sky became the cathedral – its massive stained-glass windows dancing and swirling with light and colour that was completely other-worldly.

'Isn't it amazing, Julia?' Poppy sighed eventually.

Julia nodded. 'Stunning.'

'I wish Mum was here. She'd *love* this.'

Julia squeezed Poppy's hand, the wistfulness in her voice heartbreaking. 'Yes. She would.'

Julia wished she could say something that would ease this one last hurt for Poppy. Erase it from her mind in a time when she should be allowed to be thinking only of herself. But there wasn't anything to say. Scarlett *would* have loved this very much – it was, after all, utterly spiritual. But she'd made her choice. Julia could only hope that when the time came Scarlett would finally step up and be the mother that Poppy had always yearned for.

'We're all under the same sky, Pop,' Julia whispered. 'She's here with us in spirit.'

But she doubted Poppy heard her; a snuffly noise alerted Julia to the fact that Poppy had finally succumbed to sleep. Given it was almost one in the morning, she wasn't surprised.

Julia lifted her head off the bed to look at Ten. 'I should go,' she mouthed.

He shook his head and mouthed, 'Stay,' sincerity blazing in his eyes.

Julia hesitated, torn between wanting to stay and feeling like she didn't belong here with them. But the pull of Poppy won out. 'Thank you,' she mouthed, sinking back down again and returning her gaze to the heavens.

They watched the rest of the display together in silence as the most precious person in the world, to both of them, slept between them.

Julia never wanted the night to end.

Chapter Eleven

Quentin couldn't believe there wasn't another way to get to where they needed to go. He looked up the almost vertical stone path that disappeared into the morning mist, then longingly down at Kashmir Cottage, and then back at Poppy and Julia.

Poppy looked fragile and pale, velvety-brown eyes huge now in her face, dark circles ringing them. She was wearing simple yoga pants and a flowing white cotton top with a warm purple wrap around her shoulders in deference to the early-morning chill. She seemed different here – quieter and gentler, like she felt she didn't need to put on a show anymore. There was no more hiding it – she was dying, and anyone who looked could see it in her face and the fragility of her body. The monks they had passed in the airport and on the streets the days before had stopped as they had taken her in, pausing before bowing their heads and sometimes muttering a prayer over her. Quentin wanted to shoo them away, knowing they would make her feel conspicuous, and that she would hate it.

Julia's chin was thrust stubbornly forward, one foot poised on the first stone as she waited for Poppy to catch her breath. Julia was wearing what was no doubt her version of hippy chilled – tight black pants and a clingy black skivvy that had caused more than one passing tourist to have a dangerous trip on the stones. She caught Quentin's eyes and there was a warning look in hers: *Don't mess with the plan.*

But Quentin had experience with far more effective bullies than Julia trying to silence him. He thrust out his own chin and stared her down, before focusing on Poppy. 'We don't need to go up there, Pop.' He fixed her with what he hoped was his most earnest gaze as he pointed skyward. 'The teachings are in McLeod Ganj. We'll get our tickets here, in the town, later today. You won't get to see Himself up there today.' He gestured up the steep incline.

Poppy smiled at him. 'Does the going look too tough for you, city boy?'

Quentin sighed again, then smiled. 'Race you to the top.'

But he didn't, of course. He took her right arm, and Julia took the other one, and they started the ascent like they were taking a country stroll; like they weren't bodily supporting another human between them; like it was easy to manage the punishing climb with another person in tow. Nimble monks and impressively muscled tourists in yoga pants clambered past them like goats, sometimes stopping to ask if they could help, all determinedly climbing upwards, their eyes on the prize.

The climb was so hard, and Quentin was so worried about how the altitude and ascent were affecting Poppy, that he barely noticed the view. She was his sole focus during their pit stops. He plied her with water, massaged her feet, and checked how she was going. Finally, she put a restraining hand on his arm. 'Stop,' she said, motioning to the blanket beside her for him to sit. She pointed to the vista before them. 'Just look.'

Quentin did as he was told. The place they had chosen to rest was about halfway between the guesthouse owned by the Dalai Lama's brother, and the Dalai Lama's own home further up the 2000-metre peak. It was so early the sun was still a thin buttery ooze through the pine trees, outlining them all golden. A cowbell tinkled from somewhere higher up the path. And Quentin had to admit – the view was like nothing he had ever seen. The white-tipped mountains of the Dhauladhar poked their heads into the sky, as eagles surfed the currents around their peaks. Below, the plains of the Kangra Valley spread out like something you might see from the top of the beanstalk. He could make out the curving tiled roofs of some of the higher dwellings, yoga retreats and monasteries, and there was a grace and peace to the whole scene that touched Quentin in some peculiar way he couldn't quite put his finger on.

The whole thing made him feel simultaneously big and majestic himself, godlike, and small and afraid, utterly human. He shook his head and rolled his shoulders to try to dislodge the unsettling feelings, but they lingered. This was a place to remind you of your limited humanity against the vast splendour of the universe, but also to bring home the awesome wonder of your physical state. A fluttering, snapping sound drifted up to him on the thin morning air, and he frowned.

'Prayer flags,' Poppy said, watching his face with a small smile on hers. 'Thousands of them, all over the valley. Picking up the breeze.'

Quentin studied her as she took in the scene below them. He had been right; there was something different about her here. And he realised the same was true of Julia, who seemed less hurried, less certain, as she, too, surveyed the scene around them. Perhaps there was something different about him as well.

It was this place.

The world had seemed different from the moment they had arrived at the airport, eighteen clicks from lower Dharamsala. Kinder, somehow. Sure, white taxis still honked their horns in the larger town, tourists jostled and Instagrammed themselves, and the streets were crowded with internet cafés and souvenir shops. But the whole thing had a slower, gentler quality. The people they had come across looked at them, into them, like they were trying to discern their story. They asked after them – their families, their health. They checked what their guests required in a way that seemed far more genuine than something learned in a school of hospitality. Quentin felt as if they were among friends, held in some bubble where the normal rules of cut and thrust seemed somehow vulgar. He wondered if he was just reading too much into the whole thing because of the proximity of the world's most famous spiritual leader.

Quentin leaned back, feeling the cool earth under the blanket, and deciding he could probably just about handle resting here a while. Surprisingly, it was Poppy who rose to move first. 'Time's a-wastin',' she said, rising, brushing herself off and clapping her hands. 'Let's get this show on the road.' Quentin and Julia jumped to their feet, and each took an arm as they hit the path again.

By the time they reached the top, Quentin's lungs were screaming like he'd just finished a three-hour set covering AC/DC. Julia was red in the face and her hair clung stickily to her forehead. But Poppy still looked like she had some reserves in the tank, despite her overall pallor and frailty. Maybe it was because they had mostly carried her up the hill. Once they rounded the last bend, they found themselves going down a slope that met a path snaking around the leader's compound. A number of monks and others were circling the path.

'It's the kora, a walking meditation,' Poppy said in a small voice, nodding to the path around the buildings. 'Let's do it.'

'Really?' Quentin was glad it was Julia who voiced her exhaustion and lack of enthusiasm aloud and not him. Poppy's disgusted 'city boy' from earlier still rang in his ears. 'Can't we go grab a Coke first?'

Quentin frowned. 'Do they even drink Coke here?'

Poppy considered the two of them, her head to the side, and then looked back at the path, watching orange-robed monks turning a series of large drums. 'It's about the marriage of wisdom with compassion,' she started, and Quentin steeled himself for some more walking. After all, wisdom and compassion were pretty hard to argue with right now. God knew he could use a fat dose of both. But Poppy smiled at them. 'Maybe I need to use some compassion of my own and give us all a rest.'

'Hallelujah,' Julia sighed, finding a renewed burst of energy as she headed for the area outside the open-air temple, where monks and tourists mingled and did business.

While Julia went off to source drinks, Quentin settled Poppy on a small rise, overlooking the scene. 'We can go see the temple soon,' he promised, taking her hand. 'And then do the kora. Okay?'

She smiled and nodded, and he decided to take advantage of their unexpected alone time to talk to her about what had been bugging him.

'Pop,' he started, and she turned to look at him, dark eyes wary.

'Mmmm …?'

'Why this?' It troubled him, dammit. He didn't want her to need to go on a Buddhist pilgrimage to find her peace. He wanted her to know she was enough, perfect, without anyone else telling her. 'Why Dharamsala? Why this guy?'

Poppy shrugged, and looked back over the scene. Quentin saw her eyes follow Julia as she was stopped by a young guy with an iPhone. He assumed the guy wanted Julia to take his picture, until he lined Julia up in front of the temple and started snapping her instead. 'Shameless,' she sniffed.

'Poppy,' he growled. He wouldn't be distracted. He knew all her tricks now.

She sighed, and rolled her body towards him on the blanket. 'I just always wanted it,' she said, pulling off her beanie and running her hands over her smooth scalp. 'From the first time I saw a documentary about him, I've been fascinated. He always looks so happy.'

'But you're happy,' Quentin insisted. He wanted it to be true. She nodded, but he felt it in her. There was something within her that wasn't happy. There was a part of her that felt sad, and not just because of what was happening to her now. He had sensed it from the first time he had met her.

She was a contradiction. On the one hand, she was so assured, so methodical and controlled. On the other hand, she was awkward and afraid. She had never let anyone too close, apart from Julia, and he wondered why. He wanted to grab her thin shoulders and shake her, make her tell him. Or demand it from her, sulk and stomp and say he'd earned the right to know. But something about this place – the climb and now looking out over this scene of serene buzz before them – made it seem somehow profane. He needed to wait. She had to want to tell him.

She touched his arm lightly and gestured at the scene. 'Take me to the window. Let me look at the moors with you once more, my darling. Once more.'

His heart pounded at its confines in his chest as he looked at her, small and pale and so ridiculously beautiful, like a dandelion, clinging determinedly to its stem, but at danger any minute of blowing away into the breeze if you got too close, if you blew too hard. '*Wuthering Heights*,' he said quietly.

'Can't let you have all the good lines.' She smiled at him.

He waited. There was more in her face.

'I told you my mother didn't like me when I was growing up.' Her voice was clear but detached, like she was reciting multiplication tables.

He nodded, looking at her but not wanting to speak in case he broke the spell.

'Well.' Poppy picked up his hand and placed her own over the top of it, tracing the outline where hers ended with her other index finger. Her hand was so small and cool in his that Quentin wanted to close his into a fist and cover it, protect it, keep it safe there forever. But he forced himself to keep it flat, let her continue her abstracted doodling as she spoke. 'It was my father, you see.'

'You never say much about him.' Quentin's voice sounded odd, even to his own ears.

They hadn't talked about their family stuff; he suspected they had deliberately avoided it, especially once they knew Poppy was sick. What was the point? They both knew they had family issues. What was it Spike said? *Family problems are like arseholes; everyone has one, and no-one wants to hear about yours.*

But Quentin did want to know now. He wanted to know everything about Poppy, and he wanted to tell her everything about him. There was so little time, and he wanted to hear it from her, not from Julia after they put her in the ground. He was greedy for it; he wanted to know her story, know why she was the way she was. If she told him things, it might mean she really trusted him, wanted to really know him. He wanted to tell her everything, especially the one thing that was on the tip of his tongue every time they were alone together.

'It's not that interesting,' Poppy said, continuing to trace his palm. 'Boy meets hopelessly incompatible girl, they fall in love. He falls out of love, moves on. And girl never quite gets over it.'

'Oh.' It surprised Quentin. Scarlett didn't seem like the heart-break type.

Poppy pulled her hands away, and buried them inside her wrap. 'But you see, problem is, I reminded her of him. So it was always tough for her, to look at me, to be near me, without seeing him. At least that's what I think the problem was.' She paused, shrugged a little and dropped her chin. 'I was certainly never anything like her. Like I said, she loved me, but she didn't like me. It was easier for her to be away.'

Black rage rose hot and ugly in Quentin. He tried to imagine Poppy as a child, wanting Scarlett's attentions, feeling deserted. He wanted to rail at Scarlett for getting it so badly wrong back then and again now, for taking off to India when she had one last chance to actually show Poppy how she felt. He wanted to shake the woman and make her see what she had done.

Quentin thought about young Poppy, feeling the rejection but then piecing it all together, puzzling it out in her mathematician's brain. Making sense of things, the way Poppy did. But knowing that she had always been so alone, it made things fall into place. No wonder Poppy and Julia had bonded so fiercely.

Then he thought about what Poppy did for a living – her work on attraction and compatibility.

'Is that why you chose your field?' He tried to sound casual, but it mattered. It suddenly seemed very important. She was a serious intellect, fascinated by pure mathematics, who dedicated herself to the science of human attraction and working out what made relationships work.

He expected her to prevaricate, give him some line, but she just picked at the edge of the blanket. 'I think so,' she said, keeping her face down. 'People don't realise what they can do if they choose recklessly. They think it doesn't matter, they think it's their life. But ...' She shrugged again, and her eyes finally swept up to meet his. 'But it does matter, because sometimes, because of how they love, they get other people involved, particularly children.'

The truth hit Quentin like a punch to the gut. 'You would never have gone out with me, would you? Slept with me, and the rest of it? If not for the cancer?'

Poppy continued to hold his eyes, and he held his breath. 'No,' she said, leaning forward with both hands and cupping his face as she said the word. 'I don't think so. I've always thought that compatibility matters. And everything I know ...' She pulled her hands away and gestured at him, a frantic, fluttery move-ment. 'Everything I know tells me that you and me, we don't have enough basic domains in common.'

Quentin was finding it hard to breathe. He'd always thought it was probably the case, but hearing it was difficult. Everything had changed for him over the last months. And the thought that they might not have was too impossible to consider.

'But you didn't know when you asked me to go skydiving,' he said, needing to understand more. 'You didn't know about the cancer then. Or when we slept together that first time.'

Tears pooled in Poppy's eyes. 'I think I knew from the moment they booked me in for the test. Things felt very, very wrong. That's why I got the list out, even before I got the results.' Poppy reached up and stroked the side of his face, running a fingernail across the scratchy stubble. 'So I'm lucky,' she said, as a single tear started to track down each cheek. 'I'm lucky I got it. It made me do something different.'

He reached out and cupped her face the way she had been cupping his, using his thumbs to brush away the tears. Watching her cry turned his stomach to water.

Lucky. She thought she was lucky? He thought she had been handed the shittiest deal of anyone ever. Except maybe him.

But she wasn't done. 'You're right, Q. I would never have dated you. Some guy flipping burgers at the hospital café. Some guy seven years younger than me. Some guy in a band. Surfer. Footballer.' She reached up and placed her hands over his on her face. 'That's why I'm lucky. Because I never would have known how good it could be. How much I could laugh, and feel cherished.' She grinned. 'And come.'

He started to talk but she shushed him.

'I'm not done. I'm not sorry I got it, you know. I'm sad but not sorry. Because I know – I really know – that if I hadn't, if this hadn't happened, I would have kept doing the same things, with the same kind of guys, over and over. You and I—' Her voice broke, before she swallowed and kept going. 'We might not be compatible, but we're beautiful.'

Quentin dropped his hands from her face so he could fold her into his arms. It didn't matter how tiny she was; the press of her against him filled him up. She was exactly the right shape for him; for him, she was bigger than anyone he'd ever known. He drew her into his lap, and turned her to face the crowd. '*You're* beautiful,' he said.

She settled into his arms as they watched the scene before them, and he decided this was the moment. The words had been on his tongue for weeks, but she always stopped him from saying them. Not today. He was sure the conversation they had just been having signalled a shift. He was sure she could bear to hear it.

But she spoke first. 'So how about you? What happened with your father? And your mum?'

Quentin's body tensed the way it always did when anyone mentioned his family. But he wrapped his arms more tightly around her. She had opened up to him, and he wanted her to know how it felt. 'Same same but different,' he said, picking his way through how to tell it. 'In my case, it was just me and Dad.' He hesitated fleetingly, wondering if he should tell her his father's name. But it was time. 'My mum's dead. My father's Ray Carmody.'

Poppy whistled. 'Holy shit.'

'Yes he is,' he agreed. 'And a very rich shit.'

She laughed, and it felt good to hold her while she did. 'No. I didn't mean—'

'I know what you meant,' he assured her, squeezing her as closely as he dared. 'But you know that stuff you see on the telly? He really is like that. Except even more of a bastard. He was pretty keen on me becoming the bastard in training, too, but …'

How to find the words for that part of the story?

'But you weren't interested in learning the gentle art of bastardry?'

He smiled and breathed in the smell of her skin, rubbing his cheek against her smooth scalp. 'There's nothing gentle about him.' His voice broke, and he hurried on. 'I didn't want to be like him.' He drew in a breath. 'And I didn't want to be near him.'

She rubbed his arms with her small hands as they watched Julia making her way towards them, carrying three cold drinks. 'How did that go down?'

Quentin grunted. 'He said he hadn't paid to put me through some of the best schools in the state so I could surf, play football and screw girls.'

Poppy laughed again. 'What did you say to that?'

Quentin closed his eyes at the million memories of his bullish, angry father; his red face, his quick fists. 'I told him he forgot about playing guitar.' He watched Julia making her way over to them and knew the moment was about to pass. He could say it now, but he didn't want to rush it. There was so much he had to say.

'I'm sorry,' Poppy said quietly. 'You deserved better than that.'

'We both did,' Quentin said, wriggling over to make space for Julia.

'No-one deserves parents who don't like them,' Poppy mumbled. 'Lucky we like each other.'

Quentin wanted to tell her it wasn't true, that he was sure Scarlett did like Poppy, even if the sight of her had sometimes hurt. But instead other words came tumbling out, unbidden. 'I more than like you.'

Julia flopped onto the blanket beside them, handing out long drinks. 'No Cokes.' She pouted. 'Have a bhang lassi.'

Quentin and Poppy raised their eyebrows at her. 'Not a literal bang, please,' she said, sucking her smoothie enthusiastically. 'There are delicate eyes present.'

Quentin and Poppy both laughed, and the moment that had sat heavy between them skittered away in the thin morning air.

'So,' Julia said, tying her hair back into a ponytail. 'Anyone for a kora?'

* * *

The pilgrimage around the compound was slow and deliberate. Quentin found himself lulled by the ritual of the prayer wheels – the large drums they turned each time they came upon one, saying the words about the lotus and the jewel. Or maybe it was the after-effects of the conversation he had just had with Poppy that were filling him with serenity and general good vibes.

Quentin knew this much: it had felt good to tell Poppy a bit about his father, and to hear some more about her situation. It reinforced the feelings that had been growing inside him, that it didn't matter what was to come; all that mattered was that he tell her how he was feeling, what he wanted. To date, she had been adamant in not allowing him to talk about feelings, to make commitments, but hadn't all that changed today? Things had been different, sitting on that blanket at the top of the world, and Quentin felt a new peace as he joined the other pilgrims in the kora.

Tomorrow they were due to see the Dalai Lama himself, and even though Quentin wasn't exactly a believer, he sure admired the old guy. All that Zen couldn't have been easy to come by, after all he and his people had endured. Quentin found himself hoping he might get some kind of signal, a message from the universe that it was okay to open up fully to Poppy, tell her what he wanted.

Otherwise he was just going to have to wing it.

* * *

'What do you want to get from him?'

Poppy wrinkled her nose at him like he'd made a rude remark. 'What do you mean, get from him? He's not Santa Claus.'

They were sitting on their mats and Quentin thought he had more right than most to ask the question. He was, after all, the one who had lined up half of yesterday to register the three of them, and then to claim their spaces in the quadrangle. He liked to think he'd done pretty well, too. They were, if not right at the front, at least forward of the centre. And in the shade as well. And he hadn't even had to elbow his way through to get them, although he would have, if required.

It had all been very neat and orderly, if a bit slow.

Then he had lined up again for the translation radios. Things had apparently got tricky after a few security incidents, so you needed to have only the approved radios, and man, that line had been long. So, all in all, Quentin figured he had, at the very least, earned the right to ask what Poppy was hoping to get from today. They had been waiting for hours, and Julia had moved off to buy some more drinks. The crowd was getting restless, but was still peaceful, and a certain frisson was building as the appointed hour came closer.

'I know that,' he said, wriggling around uneasily on the thin mat. How the hell did Poppy look so comfortable, sitting back on her haunches and studying the assorted life crowded around them? 'But you must have some ideas about what you're hoping for?' He grinned. 'And I don't mean a new bike or a PlayStation.'

Poppy blew out her breath, and fanned her simple white cotton shirt. 'I'm sorry,' she said, reaching out to rub his arm. 'I'm just tired today.'

Quentin was suddenly on high alert. Poppy never complained. 'Should we go?'

'Are you serious?' Poppy whacked him on the arm. Hard. 'We've come to Dharamsala for this.'

'Come for what exactly?' He wasn't letting it go.

Poppy closed her eyes. 'I'm scared,' she said, wriggling closer to him and leaning into his shoulder. 'That's not why he was on my list, not to start with. Like I said, he was so happy, and I always figured, when I was younger, I'd like to see him before I died and work out how he managed it. But things are different now.' She pulled away from his shoulder and met his gaze. 'I am happy.'

'So what, then?' Quentin held up his palms to her in question.

'Now I'm scared.' She looked at him very carefully, and then flicked her eyes around the quadrangle, and Quentin was sure that she was checking to make sure that Julia wasn't near. Once she was satisfied, she leaned into him again, like she wanted his strength but couldn't bear to meet his eyes. 'It's close now, Q, I know it. And I'm scared. Not of dying, but of how I'm going to feel at the end. What if I panic?'

He pulled her close, wishing he could press her flesh into his, wishing he could take away the fear. 'I won't let you panic,' he said.

She jerked away from him, staring at him. 'You won't be there,' she said, a look of incredulity on her face. 'No-one will be.'

Okayyy. They had never discussed this before, and Quentin had a flash of insight that this patch of cement was not the place to have the discussion now. But Ms Poppy Devine could be sure that the conversation's time was coming, just as surely and relentlessly as hers was. 'Er ... let's park that for now, huh?'

Her face screwed up mutinously and he aimed for a distraction. 'So what is the little guy gonna say to us today, do you think?'

Poppy swallowed, and Quentin watched her face do war with itself. She wanted to argue the point now, about the end.

He shut his face down. *No, not here. I won't let you.*

Something changed in her eyes, like she was letting it go. For the time being.

'I want two things,' she said eventually.

Of course she did. So Poppy. Definite. And numbered.

He nodded at her to spill.

'I want to know what to think about, when it ends, I want a word or an image that I can focus on. Something to stop me from panicking. Something to make the moment easier. Is that cowardly?'

Quentin just shook his head because there was a lump the size of Texas in his throat. Poppy rescued him from having to respond. 'And I want to know what to do next.'

Quentin recovered enough to croak out 'Next?'

'After Dharamsala,' Poppy said, touching her scalp lightly. 'Especially whether I should go see Mum. We're not far from her here. But I just don't know. I'm angry with her, and I …'

She turned away and waved at Julia, who was coming towards them as the crowd around them started to hum with excitement. 'I just don't know.'

Quentin wrapped Poppy in a quick hug as Julia rejoined them. 'Game on,' the redhead pronounced as the leader's entourage shuffled onto the platform from which he would be teaching.

Quentin's heart thudded in his chest as the unassuming man walked to the front of the platform and smiled out at all of them.

* * *

It was very dark in the small room. Julia had taken up an offer to go and look at the stars on the mountain, and Quentin had stayed with Poppy, knowing she was exhausted from the day. He suspected Julia was trying to give them some space, and he reminded himself that he needed to do the same for her tomorrow.

None of them had spoken much after the teachings had finished. It was as though each was processing the experience.

Quentin rolled Poppy closer to him in the narrow bed, revelling in the feel of her warmth and the sweetness of her skin. A small glass pane offered them a window onto the night, the stars so close Quentin felt he could reach out and pluck them down for the woman he lay beside, just to make her smile.

'So,' he said finally, as she nuzzled into him. 'Did you get what you were after?'

She shook her head against his chest. 'Half of it,' she said.

He breathed out slowly, trying to keep a grip on it all, thinking about her words from earlier in the day: *I want to know what to think about; something to make the moment easier.* 'Which half?'

'Mum,' Poppy sighed, pulling away enough to allow her to look at him in the moonlight.

Quentin nodded. 'What did he say?'

Poppy trailed a hand across his naked chest and he shivered.

'If you want others to be happy, practice compassion. If you want to be happy, practice compassion.' Poppy paused. 'I can do compassion. Mum needs it.'

A day ago, Quentin might have argued the toss. He was so damn angry with Scarlett. But now ... Well, the little guy had a way of making you see things differently. He made you think about how all the things you wanted mightn't be all there is, and how you can create your own happiness no matter what's going on.

'What about you?' Poppy nudged with her knee. 'Get anything out of it?'

'Yep.' Quentin took a breath.

Here we go.

But his heart juddered and his breath caught. He didn't know how she might respond.

'So? You gonna leave a dying girl in suspense? I haven't got forever, you know. What did he say?'

Quentin reached out and put his arms all the way around her, pulling her close. 'He said the purpose of life is to be happy,' he whispered against her neck.

She sighed against his chest, and it gave him goosebumps. 'You make me happy.'

'I want to make you happy for all the time you have, Poppy,' he said, cupping her face, which was ethereal and perfect in the moonlight. 'The way you make me happy. There is no happiness without you. I don't care about what's next. I love you.'

He squeezed her hard as she froze in his arms.

'Marry me.'

* * *

The dawn was breaking as the old bus sputtered up the hill and lurched towards the stop. Quentin looked up and watched pink colour the sky over the guesthouse. He hoped she was sleeping. He hoped she understood, that the note he'd left her had made sense. He couldn't stay if she wouldn't let him in. She had been very clear. She was happy, she enjoyed being with him, but she didn't want what he was offering.

She just didn't see the point. And she didn't want to hurt him.

Quentin picked up his bag and his guitar case and stood up as the bus shuddered to a halt in front of him. His eyes were sore and scratchy from lack of sleep and his mind was a disordered mess of pain and fear. He had never, ever imagined that a girl could get to him the way Poppy Devine had. Everything about her undid him. Even the sight of her face, cold and brittle, as she'd told him she wouldn't marry him. Her eyes had been so dark, her little chin so defiant.

He kept replaying the scene in his mind – his chest filling with panic, his brain screaming at him that he shouldn't have said it, that he should take it back, somehow take it back, pretend it was a joke. Make it better.

But it was over, really over. Poppy was gone from his life, and soon she would be gone from everything. She didn't want him as her husband, and she didn't want him there at the end.

'Delhi,' he said to the small driver wearing a simple brown shift, handing over some notes.

Chapter Twelve

Julia clung to the old-fashioned strap that hung from above the window in the ancient, rattly taxi as it careened around yet another rocky, mountainous hairpin bend. Hand straps like this hadn't been around for decades because they were as antiquated as the cars that bore them, and frankly, plain unstylish, but she thanked all the gods and angels and even the freaking Dalai Lama for it right now. If it was her lot to have chosen the world's oldest taxi cab at least it was still in mint condition.

And if she got any more freaked out she could turn her head and bite down on the strap like they did in the movies when someone needed a bullet removed or a leg amputated. Come to think of it, they usually had whisky, too.

Whisky would also be handy about now.

The car fishtailed on the rocky surface as it negotiated another corner and Julia seriously contemplated biting the strap but chose her lip instead. She'd told the driver to go as fast as he could so she could barely complain when he was following her edict to the letter. The chickens in a wire coop on the back seat, however, didn't feel the need for such restraint. They squawked indignantly at every death-defying twist and turn that threw their flimsy cage from one side of the bench seat to the other.

Whatever eggs they laid for the next few days were going to come well and truly pre-scrambled.

Another car approached in the distance and Julia's heart rate ratcheted up. She wasn't even sure what side of the road they drove on over here but then neither, apparently, did the driver, who completely ignored such conventions, preferring to drive straight up the middle of the unsealed road.

Although road was probably generous. Track was more like it. Goat track.

The approaching car beeped its horn but her driver was not deterred from his path and Julia thought: *This is it, I don't have to worry about watching Poppy die because we're going to plunge down the side of this mountain and I am going to die right here, right now. I'm going to go to the next life accompanied by an ancient taxi driver with yellow teeth and seven pissed-off chickens.*

She shut her eyes and gripped the strap hard, her driver swerving at the last second, beeping his horn and yelling something she assumed was local for *fuck you* out the window at the other driver.

Julia opened her eyes, her pulse drumming in her ears, breathing hard. A rush of relief temporarily dampened the spike of adrenaline before nausea threatened. She swallowed it down. The inside of the taxi already smelled like chicken poop, feathers and cigarettes, it didn't need vomit added to the mix.

The driver nodded and smiled at her, his nicotine-stained teeth flashing. 'I go fast.' He grinned. 'I go fast.'

Julia nodded weakly. At least he was enjoying himself. All of her life she'd wanted to get into a taxi and say 'follow that cab' like they did in the movies, only to discover the experience was completely overrated.

And it was all Ten's fault.

Thoughts of her impending death or disability *with chickens by her side* had kept her mind off her reason for rattling along a bumpy, windy road in the middle of Buttfuck, Nowhere (she didn't care how freaking majestic it was, it was still the arse end of the earth), in an ancient Volvo with a yellow-toothed man, but suddenly it seemed like a far more economical use of her time.

The precise way to castrate a man with bare hands did, after all, require some planning. Because that's exactly what she planned to do to Ten when she finally caught up with his bus.

Julia had woken with a start when Poppy had slid into bed with her less than an hour ago with tears sliding down her face.

'What's wrong?' Julia had asked.

'He's gone,' she'd whispered and handed Julia the note.

And Julia had been furious. Beyond furious. She'd been white-hot-rage, blood-boiling incensed. *I'm not going anywhere.* Ten had told her that twice. *Assured* her of it. She'd shaken on a truce with him because of it.

But when things hadn't gone his way, when Poppy had turned him down, he'd just walked away?

Not on her watch, he didn't.

'I'll bring him back,' Julia had said as she'd leapt out of bed, reaching for the first set of clothes she could find. 'You stay right here. I'll find him.' She'd stuck her legs into the jeans she'd worn yesterday, thrown on a hoodie over the flannelette shirt she'd been sleeping in and was stuffing her feet into her Ugg boots because they were closest when a thought had occurred to her. 'Wait …' she'd said, stopping her frantic dressing for a beat. 'You *do* want him back?'

A girl could dream, right?

And that was when Poppy's face had crumpled and she'd curled into that ball. 'I ... love ... him,' she'd cried.

Julia's heart had temporarily seized in her chest both at the size of the admission and at the anguish with which it was delivered. It was wrung out of Poppy, all strangled and broken. They'd always whispered these things to each other, like they were afraid they'd jinx it if they said it too loudly.

And that had been enough for Julia. She hadn't looked at her face or brushed her hair. Hell, she hadn't even stopped to put on a bra.

'Stay right here,' she'd said again as she'd pulled the bed cover up over Poppy and tucked it around her. It had seemed to swallow her whole and Julia remembered how sick the sight had made her feel. 'He can't have got that far.'

And now she was here, courting death and contemplating violence in some fucked-up un-Buddha-like, unholy jumble in her head.

'Bus! Bus!'

Julia's heart leapt as she followed the direction of one thick gnarled finger to a beat-up old bus further ahead of them. That had to be it! The manager of the guesthouse had told her that Ten had caught the bus to Delhi fifteen minutes prior to her bursting in looking like the freaking yeti. And there wasn't another bus for three hours.

A beam of sunlight poking through the clouds behind them caught the bus in its path, setting the yellow paint job ablaze before it disappeared around a bend, and it was as if someone up there was sending Julia a sign.

Ten was on that bus. God was dobbing.

'I go faster?' the driver asked, smiling at her, his face breaking into a hundred deep ravines, excitement dancing in his keen, bright eyes.

Julia nodded and clutched the strap tighter.

* * *

In ten minutes they were up the backside of the bus, and the driver was merrily beeping his horn, gesturing out the window for the bus, which looked about the same vintage as the taxi, to pull over. It lumbered to a halt a minute later.

Julia opened her door. 'I wait?' the driver asked.

She nodded and smiled at him, despite her full bitch growling just beneath the surface. Her pulse was already accelerating, spoiling for a fight. 'Yes, thank you.'

She stalked out of the car and stormed down the side of the bus, conscious of faces staring at her from the windows. The driver opened the door and looked at her quizzically. She ignored him as she turned to face the rickety-looking vehicle. None of the faces looking at her belonged to Ten.

Probably cowering inside somewhere. Behind a *chicken* coop, no doubt.

'Ten!' she yelled. Julia had always possessed very good projection and it didn't let her down this time. It bounced straight off the side of the bus and Julia swore she could hear it echo through the valley below. 'Get your arse out here right this second.'

Everyone inside gaped at her, turning and looking at each other, shrugging and shaking their heads, talking quickly amongst themselves and gesturing to the crazy, white giant of a woman yelling almost loud enough to rock the entire bus.

Nothing happened for a minute and the driver looked increasingly worried. But then there was movement from inside and seconds later Ten was stepping down from the vehicle.

'Jules,' he nodded.

Julia did note, on some level, that Ten had the good grace to look ashamed. And also, to be fair, pretty damn wretched. But she was *beyond* worrying about him and his feelings. 'What the fuck do you think you're doing?' she hissed.

He held up his hands. 'It's over, Jules. You win, you get to have her all to yourself.'

Julia's rage grew exponentially. Did he have one single fucking clue just *how* much she'd wanted Poppy all to herself? How much she hadn't wanted his skinny football/surfer/rocker arse tagging along on *their* bucket-list trip? But he was here. Poppy wanted him here. *She freaking loved him!* And he was going to get his arse in that taxi and come back with her or she was seriously going to LOSE HER SHIT.

'You have got to be fucking kidding me. Do you think this is some kind of competition?'

He shot her an incredulous look. 'Hasn't it been? Hasn't this entire thing been you and me in a sick wrestling match over her affections?'

Julia's harsh laugh echoed around the mountains, giving it an almost demonic quality. 'Sweetie, your ego is writing cheques your body can't cash. This whole *thing* is about *Poppy*. About *Poppy* dying. Remember? The bald, fragile woman who is right now curled up in a foetal ball in my bed. And if you think for a second that I can't take you in a wrestling match for Poppy's affections or *any other damn thing I want*, then you clearly don't know a damn thing about me.'

Julia was breathing erratically. She wasn't entirely sure that statement was right anymore and she was damn sure arguing like this in the thin air wasn't very good for them. But hell, they'd been spoiling for this fight for such a long time she had a real buzz on.

It felt good to feel good. Even for this totally fucked-up reason.

'Fine,' he snapped. 'You win. You can take me in a wrestling match, Jules. Poppy loves you more than me. You win.' He clapped with feigned vigour. '*Bravo*. Give the woman a cigar.'

Julia nodded briskly, letting his sarcasm wash off her. She didn't care what frame of mind he was in – she just needed him to return with her. 'Excellent.' She zipped up her hoodie against the cold air. 'Now get in the damn taxi and go and crawl back to Poppy. Tell her what she needs to hear or not hear, do you understand? You do whatever it is *she* needs.'

He shook his head. 'No.'

Julia folded her arms. 'Yes.'

He walked over to the side of the road and stared down at the lush greenery in the valley below. 'No.'

'*Quentin.*'

Ten turned his head, obviously shocked at the use of his name, even if she did say it in the tone of voice usually reserved for mothers who are on their last nerve with a recalcitrant child. Which was kind of how she felt.

Unfortunately, not even the use of his real name dissuaded him. 'I can't do it anymore,' he said, turning away from her to face the vista.

Julia glared at his back and sucked in a breath, supressing the urge to tell him she was going to count to ten and he'd better be in the car or she was going to take his toys away. Sure, she could tell him that Poppy had said the L-word, but she wasn't their intermediary. They weren't in primary school passing love notes between desks.

It was Poppy's word to say and she had no idea if Poppy ever intended to say it to Ten at all. Just because she'd admitted it to Julia didn't mean she was going to break down and let Ten in on the secret. She'd been pretty damn adamant about *not* saying it, after all. Not *hearing* it.

But there was only one way he was going to find out and that involved him getting his arse back to the guesthouse.

'Right, I see,' she said, drawing on the strength that only yesterday His Holiness himself had told her she had in abundance, no matter how thinly stretched it felt right now. 'So when you said to me, *I'm not going anywhere, Julia* – twice,' she held up two fingers, 'what you meant to say was as long as Poppy plays the game my way.'

'Oh for fuck's sake,' he yelled, turning to glare at her, his dirty-blond hair flaring with the movement, his eyes flashing. 'When has she *ever* played the game *my* way? Don't say it, Q,' he mimicked. 'Don't say it. Don't talk about your feelings. Don't tell me how you feel. Don't say you …'

His voice cracked and his eyes were suddenly glassy and anguished as well as pissed off, packing an extra gut-wrenching punch.

'Don't say you *love* me, Q. Jump out of a plane with me, watch me dive with sharks, let me sing with you on stage but *don't* ask me to marry you. We don't need the words.' He raked a hand through his hair. 'Just don't say it, Q.'

Julia swallowed at the defeat in every line of his body. He was a tall guy and she was used to him swaggering around, but standing here in the majesty of the mountains, he looked small. Everyone did, she guessed, but this was different. He looked crushed. Completely and utterly beaten.

'Jesus, Ten,' she muttered. 'Does it really matter that freaking much?'

'Yes,' he yelled, the veins in his neck sticking out and it echoed around and around and around. 'Yes it *fucking* does. How would you like it if she didn't let you tell her? If she wouldn't accept your love? If she *rejected* it?'

Julia blinked at the force of his anger. They were several metres apart but it almost knocked her on her butt. His anguished questions tore at the very fabric of her heart.

She would hate it. To be rejected by Poppy in her final weeks on this earth would be gutting. One thing she'd always been able to count on since she was eleven years old was the depth of their devotion, the intensity of their friendship. And while neither of them went around spouting their love for each other every minute of the day, Julia doubted she'd ever recover if Poppy forbade her from expressing it at all.

'Look, you're right, it doesn't matter,' he said, his shoulders sagging, waving his hand at her dismissively. 'She doesn't need me anyway. She's got you.'

Julia's anger flared again. Yeah, Poppy had her. But she wanted *him*, too. Didn't the sonofabitch realise how privileged he was? Up until recently it had been Poppy and Julia against the world. Now he'd been allowed into the inner sanctum. And that was a one-way street. It had been since Dr Dick had looked across at them and said the C word. You didn't get to back out of the sanctum.

'Oh I see,' she retorted. 'We're getting to the pointy end now. That's it, isn't it? And this is just a convenient out so you don't have to be there at the end because while you're man enough to do the easy stuff, to tell her you love her and want to marry her, you're not man enough for the hard yards, you're not man enough to watch her die.'

'Oh you're kidding me?' he hissed. 'What the fuck do you think I've been doing these last eight months, Jules? We've *both* been watching her die.'

Hot tears burned the back of her eyes. Did he think she didn't know that? The thought of it had been like knives stabbing into her heart for every single day of it. 'That's been the easy bit,' she threw back at him. 'The hardest part will be being there for the moment she takes her *last* breath.'

Julia hated that fucking day already.

Ten gaped at her then his face twisted into a grotesque half-laugh, half-snort. He shook his head at her in what looked suspiciously like pity. 'Is that what you think? Oh no, Poppy has got plans for that day that don't not include me or *you*. You need to rethink that one, Jules, because she doesn't want *anyone* there for that.'

If Ten had reached across and slapped her, Julia could not have been more stunned. She looked at him, not quite able to even comprehend what he'd said. But the knowledge was out there now – thrown like a stone over the side of the mountain, freefalling in the abyss, as her brain scrambled to catch up.

It seemed to take forever to hit rock bottom.

'*What?*' she gasped finally. 'Don't be ridiculous.'

This time it was definitely pity she saw on his face. 'I'm sorry, Jules. Poppy told me yesterday, before she saw His Holiness. She's going solo on that one.'

Julia stared at him, her mouth agape. *What?* No.

No. No. No.

That couldn't be right. She searched his face for any signs of disingenuousness and found none. Only sad, hollow eyes.

'No.' She shook her head, breathing in and out quickly to try to dispel the notion with each expiration. 'She … can't. I won't … let her. What if she's s-scared?' Hot tears filled her eyes and spilled down her face. She couldn't *bear* the thought of Poppy all alone at the end. It was too … too *everything*. She breathed some more, pushing it away, trying to breathe the thought out of her body. 'What if she … panics? She needs to be surrounded by people who love her at the end. She needs to go knowing she was … l-loved.'

He took a step towards her. 'Jules.'

'No.' Julia scrubbed at the tears, holding up her hand in a stopping motion, dragging in oxygen, panting it out again. 'No. You're *wrong*.'

But she knew he was right. God knew she'd given Ten enough reason to want to hurt her, but he wasn't a callous person. He wouldn't say it if it wasn't true.

Why? Why had Poppy said that? Why would she want to be alone for that?

'Jules,' he said, taking another step towards her, his voice thick with concern. 'I'm sorry.'

Julia panted against the burn in her lungs and the pain in her chest as everything blurred in front of her, the tears flowing hot and acidic, burning a track down her cheeks. The mountains around them closed in on her and the ground beneath her wobbled precariously. Her hands shook, her vision greyed and narrowed.

The whole world seemed to tilt on its axis.

'Julia?' Strong arms grabbed her and pulled her in tight, and she struggled against their bonds, panicked. 'No.' She flailed her arms. 'No.'

'It's okay, I've got you, Jules,' he whispered. 'Breathe.'

Julia *was* breathing; she just couldn't seem to get any oxygen in. 'She can't d-do that,' she said, looking up at Ten even as she resisted, trying to shake him off.

'I know,' he said. 'I know.'

And suddenly the pain in her chest and the burn in her lungs gave in and the fight went out of her, and she was crying great racking, choking sobs, burying her face in his shirt, oblivious to the goggle-eyed spectators taking it all in behind them.

She cried like she hadn't cried since the beginning. Sobs that shredded her lungs, wrenched at her diaphragm, tore at her throat.

Loud, hiccupy crying. Messy, red-eyed, snotty-nosed crying.

Julia didn't know how long she went on for. She just knew it felt alternately good and horrid and one hundred percent necessary. Vital. The tears had been building for so long, hidden behind and coloured by a huge block of rage. Sure she'd let a few out from time to time, when she'd been alone, or fucking too-cocky, sweaty, slutty drummers. But not like this.

They'd been angry tears. Tears for Poppy and the heinous unfairness of it all. Not the-world-is-nigh tears. Not completely, utterly, helpless tears.

Tears for *Julia*.

And it felt *sooo* damn good she let every single one of the suckers out.

'I h-h-hate this,' she hiccuped into his shirt when the tears finally started to wane.

She felt his head nod against the top of hers. 'So do I.'

'It's ... it's so ... so fuck ... fucked up.'

His arms squeezed tighter. 'Yes.'

'She ca-can't do this, Ten. We c-can't le-let her.'

'I know.'

It was then that Julia realised he *did* know. That he was the only other person who *truly* knew. Not even Scarlett knew. Scarlett had chosen India. But Ten was here. And she *could* yell at him in the middle of a mountain range and then cry all over his shirt because he *knew* what she was going through.

And because he loved Poppy, too.

He may not have loved her for as long as she had, but that didn't diminish his feelings. He loved Poppy and he was *here*.

And when Julia put aside all her petty jealousy and anger at him over crashing her love-in with her best friend, she could see that he'd been good for Poppy. Finding her one great love at this time of her life had sucked so badly, but Poppy had lived more with Ten in the last eight months than she had the previous twenty-nine years of her existence.

He had gone fearlessly with her, supported her in everything, refused to treat her like she was dying, and given her a reason to keep going.

And he hadn't walked away – yet.

Poppy had needed him and he *had* stepped up to the mark.

But it was even more shocking for Julia to admit here in this barren, rocky place that *she* also needed him. *Because* he knew.

These last months had been rough. But it was going to get rougher and he was the one person she could turn to who understood that. Ten, alone, was always going to understand the toll of these last months. They'd forged a terrible, sacred bond.

Julia had always thought she was a strong person. Everyone in her life had told her so. But she wasn't strong enough for this. Glancing up at Ten now, looking miserable and wretched, she doubted he was strong enough either.

But together … maybe they could survive this together.

She pulled out of his grasp and he let go, stepping back. She scrubbed at her face, wiping god knows what on the sleeves of her hoodie. 'Please,' she said. 'Please come back. I know what I'm asking of you. I understand how hard it must be. But she needs you. And … so do I. I don't want to do this alone either.'

His face was unbearably bleak and Julia swore she saw something die in his eyes, but he nodded and said, 'Okay.'

More tears welled as she stepped back into his arms and hugged him. 'Thank you,' she whispered. 'Thank you.'

And an entire busload of people broke into applause.

* * *

Two and a half hours had passed by the time Julia and Ten arrived back. They'd barely talked on the much more sedate return taxi trip. But they hadn't needed to. What had happened on that mountain had been cathartic and they'd reached a kind of understanding that didn't need words.

'I'll leave you to have some time with her,' Julia said as they entered the guesthouse.

'No,' he said. 'I want you in there as well.'

Julia swallowed the lump in her throat and nodded as she unlocked the door to find Poppy in a ball in the middle of the bed.

'Q?' She lifted her head and her eyes were red-rimmed and her face was blotchy. But at least she was still alive. Julia had started to worry during the return journey that Poppy may have died from a broken heart while she'd waited.

'I'm here,' he said, striding over to her.

'I'm sorry, I'm so sorry,' Poppy said, her voice cracking.

Ten kicked off his shoes and climbed under the covers with her. 'Hey,' he said as he scooped her close. 'Shh.' He kissed her head. 'Love means never having to say you're sorry, remember?'

Julia smiled at the line. It should have been corny. It wasn't.

'Anyway,' he said. 'I'm sorry. I shouldn't have left like that. You're right, the words don't matter.'

Poppy pushed herself away from him. Julia was amazed at how strong she was sometimes despite outward appearances. 'No. I was wrong. They do matter. I do love you, Q. Of course I do.' She smiled tremulously, tracing his lips with her finger. 'I've loved you from the minute you said "may the force be with you" as we jumped out of that plane. And I think we should get married. I've been lying here trying to make some kind of logical sense out of getting married as I'm about to die, but then you came back and … love isn't about logic, is it?'

Ten smiled at her. 'It's logical to me.'

And then he raised his head and kissed Poppy and it was so tender Julia wanted to burst into tears all over again. The whole situation was poignant and wrenching. Achingly bittersweet. Screamingly tragic. But Julia doubted she'd ever witness anything this beautiful again.

She turned to go. She'd played her part and for this brief moment in time everything had turned out okay. They didn't need her now.

And after the emotional upheaval she could murder a decent cup of coffee. That strong shit they sold here in tiny cups. Failing that, she'd go for that whisky she'd been hankering for earlier. She was going to need something to get her through while she figured out the logistics of a quickie wedding.

She was almost out the door when Poppy called out to her. 'Julia?'

Julia turned. 'Yes?'

Poppy had snuggled back down onto Ten's shoulder, but she was holding out her hand. 'Come and join us.'

Julia didn't glance at Ten for his permission as she had in Lapland, and it didn't feel awkward to climb into bed with them. She just scooted in behind Poppy, feeling every notch of her spine as she spooned in close.

'I'm getting married,' Poppy whispered dreamily, lifting up her hand.

Julia smiled into Poppy's neck as she threaded her fingers through the proffered hand, like they'd done as kids. 'Yes.'

Poppy's arm flopped down and their joined hands rested on her bony hip. Then Ten slid his big warm hand over the tops of theirs and Julia looked at the three of them joined together.

Julia and Poppy and Ten against the world.

Chapter Thirteen

The skinny dog with no fur licked Poppy's hand and Quentin desperately wanted to reach for Julia's hand sanitiser. Except Poppy was watching and he didn't want her to think he was being uncool with the whole grotty vibe. After all, he'd told her about all the grungy shit he'd done over the last few years – all the scuzzy surfing holidays, all the dives he'd played for beer. It was just that he could only begin to imagine how many germs that skin-dog was carrying around on his drooling pink tongue, and he didn't want a single one of them near his terminally ill fiancée.

Fiancée. Even now the word made him smile, two days and god knows how many kilometres of train travel later. It made him smile, and then the unfairness of it made him want to cry. Or vomit. But he wouldn't think about that part.

Poppy turned to wave as her mother made her way towards them on the platform, hurrying along in a sari that some kindly Indian should tell her was really not the right look for a middle-aged white woman. Its voluminous fuchsia folds were decorated with gold-and-teal detailing and brilliant-purple splotches. Quentin understood the hold India had on some people; it was like a form of insanity. It seemed Scarlett was one of those with India fever. He groaned internally and turned to nudge the dog out of the way while Poppy wasn't looking.

'Shoo,' he hissed at it, but it just looked at him like a groupie – huge eyes, desperate smile, too-skinny legs. It started to make its way over to Poppy again, some doggy sixth sense telling it she was the soft touch of the group, but Quentin couldn't bear it. Every infection Poppy got was going to shorten her life. And when life was only measured in weeks, it couldn't afford to get any shorter.

He resorted to guerrilla tactics while Poppy, Julia and Scarlett hugged noisily, pulling a peanut-butter sandwich from his backpack and breaking off a piece. 'Here, boy,' he whispered, showing the morsel to the dog and earning grateful eyes and a lolling tongue in return, before turning and hurling it towards the latrines. 'Go get it, mate,' he urged. The dog had no need for second invitations, dragging its battered body towards the bathrooms to retrieve the prize.

'Scarlett.' Quentin greeted his soon-to-be-mother-in-law as heartily as he could. Which wasn't particularly heartily. The knowledge of how much she had hurt Poppy as a child still burned in him, and part of him wanted to pull her hair as he was wrapped into her diaphanous technicolour hug. But instead he used the opportunity afforded by the hug to pull her along with his arm around her, sure it was the best opportunity to break free of the attentions of the diseased canine. 'Come on, good women,' he enthused cheerily. 'Onward to the chariot.'

'What's the rush?'

Damn Scarlett. She was always buggering things up, even his quick getaway from the Dog of Death.

'I haven't seen you all for ages. Since you got engaged. Let me look at you.' She dragged Quentin to a halt in his forward momentum, and turned, making a big show of checking them all out. Except they all knew what she was really doing. Quentin looked over at Julia and realised she was mirroring his body language – arms folded, eyebrows raised at Poppy's mother. If bodies really did have language, they would be saying the same thing:

Do. Not. Say. It. Do not make a single comment about how sick she looks.

For once, Scarlett took the hint. 'Well,' she said with a huge, over-bright smile. 'You all look great. The lights and the Lama obviously agree with you.'

'Yeah, yeah,' Julia grumbled, rubbing her eyes blearily. 'Come on, let's blow this popsicle stand.'

Quentin couldn't have agreed more. 'Yeah. Quick sticks.'

Just as he was sure they were going to lose the skinny dog, it limped towards them, its face smeared in peanut butter and a whole new level of adoration reflected in its eyes as it made a beeline for Quentin. Poppy clapped her hands in delight, cooed adoringly and bent down to pat it. Quentin almost pushed her over in his hurry to keep the mangy creature away from her. 'Sorry, Pop.' He sighed, bending down to scoop it up. 'It's me the little champ's got a thing for, haven't you, mate?'

Poppy reached across to scratch its scabby nose and Quentin swung his body hard to the left so her fingers didn't connect. 'Er, I think I saw a lost dog owner over there.' He pointed far away from their group, and as he turned back Poppy and Scarlett were eyeing him suspiciously while Julia smirked in understanding. He dropped the dog onto the concrete of the railway platform and patted its butt. 'Be free, Fido,' he sang cheerily, tossing the rest of his sandwich as far as he could down the platform.

Poppy scowled at him as Julia winked and hustled them out of the station. As he caught up with her, she handed him the sanitiser. 'Nice job, Ten.'

* * *

Outside the station, the madness of the train and the platform seemed almost tranquil. The street was a teeming mass of people, animals and vehicles of every variety – from the downright ramshackle to the most luxurious – and it all pressed together on what should have been a road in a most disorganised and unseemly fashion. Julia looked like she was about to pass out. She leaned towards Quentin and whispered, 'Can you imagine how many germs there are in this cesspit?'

Quentin didn't even want to think about it, but Poppy, as ever, could read their minds and was determined to thwart their plans. She took one look at Quentin, longingly eyeing off a slick black Mercedes taxi, and turned towards the rickshaw stand. 'Now that's the way to travel,' she declared with an excited squeal.

Oh my god, she was trying to torture him. As a bony, smiley driver waved toothlessly at them, Quentin closed his eyes and visualised every perilous bump between here and the backwoods village to which they were headed. He imagined the sickening crunch of Poppy's fragile bones as they broke while she tried to hang on. Then he opened them and Poppy was looking at him with a challenge in her eyes.

'It sure is,' he said, summoning every ounce of the renowned cool that had somehow deserted him since his gorgeous girlfriend had become sick and he had somehow turned into the fun police. He nodded at Poppy and Julia. 'Why don't you ladies travel together; I'll ride with Scarlett.'

Poppy narrowed her eyes at him. 'Why?'

'Simple matter of weight distribution,' he bluffed, eyeing off the scrawny driver Julia was already haggling with. And there was something in that; after all, the best bullshit always contained a shard of truth. Julia and Quentin could have been brother and sister in that they were both giants compared to the smaller Scarlett and Poppy. Any shit-out-of-luck cycle-rickshaw driver who had to cart Julia and Quentin together was going to earn every rupee, and probably need to spend them and more on physiotherapy afterwards. Even the toothless grinner's megawatt smile had dimmed slightly as he had taken in Quentin's six-foot-six frame. 'There's no way you and your ma can travel together while Jules and I give some poor rickshaw driver a spinal injury. I'm almost positive these guys don't get WorkCover.'

Poppy didn't look convinced. 'Why don't you travel with me, then?' she asked archly, and Quentin could almost see her trying to sniff out a plot. As Quentin and Julia had become more devious and united in their attempts to protect her, so Poppy had become more adept at identifying and disrupting their schemes.

Quentin blasted her with what he hoped was his best version of the old Q charm. 'Thought you girls might like some alone time.'

Poppy still looked mutinous, but Julia flicked a puzzled glance his way and bundled her into the nearest rickshaw. The toothless one grinned in relief, took one last look at Quentin's gigantic frame, and shot the driver behind him a glance that clearly said: *Bad luck, sucker.*

Quentin gestured theatrically to the next rickshaw. 'After you, Scarlett.'

Scarlett regarded him just as suspiciously as Poppy had as she climbed aboard in a flurry of colourful sari, but Quentin didn't give a damn. He had things to say to this woman, and he was bloody well going to say them before she got a chance to hurt Poppy any more. And if it took being squashed against her in a rickshaw to achieve that goal, well, Quentin would suffer that for the woman he loved. His fiancée, he reminded himself, enjoying the warmth the thought of that label brought to him.

He waited until the rickshaw had cleared the mad noise of the city proper and was bumping nauseatingly along an unsealed road with rice fields on either side before he began. Scarlett was chattering away, pointing out various landmarks and explaining the activities of the people dotting the fields, when he did a careful reconnaissance to check Poppy and Julia's rickshaw was still safely attached to the road ahead of them and there were no signs that Poppy might jump out and catch him in what he was about to do. You could never be too sure with that woman. Once he was certain she was not in hearing distance, and he was safe to start, he interrupted her.

'Scarlett.'

It took a minute for her to notice his interruption, so intent was she on explaining the local attitudes to domestic violence. He nudged her with his elbow and tried again. 'Scarlett.'

'Hmmm?' She turned away from her musings in the direction of the rice fields, a preoccupied half-smile on her face. 'Ah,' she said, the smile dying as she registered the serious look on his face. 'I thought there was something. It's about Poppy, isn't it? How bad is it right now?'

'Bad,' he grunted, thinking about the meds he and Julia had injected her with that morning in the jarring heat of the train carriage. 'But that's not what I want to talk about.'

'Okay,' Scarlett said slowly, hands worrying at a silky edge of sari. 'Shoot.'

He would like to. He would like to shoot this selfish, careless woman, who had made Poppy feel unloved.

He stopped himself. No, worse than unloved. Un*liked*. As if there was something inside his lovely, funny, clever Poppy that had made it impossible for her mother to like her.

Because of what? Some man.

Quentin knew right then and there that if they ever had children, Poppy would never make them feel that way, no matter what happened between the two of them. Poppy had more love – more *like* – in her little finger than this woman had in her whole body. As quickly as he thought it, he remembered that there would never be any children with tawny-brown eyes and quick, clever brains. The resulting punch to his gut almost knocked him off course.

He drew in a breath and fought hard to remember why he was sharing this rickshaw with this selfish witch. Not only had she made Poppy feel unliked, she had abandoned her, at some school. She hadn't been there for the speech nights and the show-and-tells and all the rest of the crap that you signed on for when you made a person. And, worse, she had left Poppy again, now. When Poppy had asked her to come with them on the bucket-list trip, she had said no.

No. Because she had to go to freakin' *India*. To her freakin' *orphanage*. Even though her daughter, her only child, her beautiful, beautiful Poppy was dying.

So yeah, they needed to have some words.

'Don't let her down.' Quentin growled the words at Scarlett, turning in the crowded contraption to give her the full death-stare treatment.

Scarlett's eyes widened as she considered the set of his face and the clenched fists in his lap. 'Of course not,' she said lightly, smoothing her sari skirts. 'I never would, Quentin, you need to understand that. Poppy is my daughter and I—'

'Enough of the bullshit, okay?' Quentin had heard excuses and self-delusion too much in his life. He had no reason to play nice with this woman and he didn't intend to. 'You *have* hurt her. Her whole life you've hurt her, and please don't pretend like you don't know it. I don't know what it is with you and her, but I do know this. I love her, and she's dying, you get that? She's dying and I won't have her hurt, or let down, or disappointed, by you or by anyone. I don't care who you are, her mother or the Dalai Lama himself.'

Scarlett's chin set hard – so like Poppy. She folded her arms across her chest. 'And what are you going to do, if I do something you consider inappropriate?'

That was a very good question.

What would he do? Beating the hell out of her seemed extreme, and kind of wrong. Kind of. At least it would seem wrong to say it out loud. That he knew.

'I'll take her,' he said, meanly, because he wanted to hurt Scarlett, at least enough that she behaved herself. 'I'll take her away, for the end, and that will be it. You'll never have a chance to make up for everything.'

Scarlett's face crumpled and her voice was a low croak. 'You wouldn't.'

He studied the woman in the voluminous sari. Her chin was still thrust out Poppy-style, and her eyes had a hard gleam to them, but her bottom lip quivered slightly, and her hand shook where she pulled at her sari. He thought about her face when she had asked Poppy to come to India, way back in Brisbane, before Tuscany, and the lights, and Dharamsala. For some reason, she had wanted Poppy to come very much. There was something

Scarlett believed was going to come together because of Poppy coming here. She had to have seen how much it had hurt Poppy, how broken she had been when her mother had chosen India yet again.

'Understand this,' Quentin said, turning away from her slightly so she got the vibe that the discussion was over. 'I would do it in a heartbeat. And if you hurt her again, I will.'

By the time they arrived at the village, the atmosphere on the rickshaw was denser than a room full of drummers, and Quentin almost vaulted from his seat and threw the rupees at the driver in his eagerness to be away from Scarlett. It was a small place, not unlike the villages they had passed through on their way. A cluster of flimsy dwellings, some on stilts, some hugging the ground. Some slightly larger buildings, a clearing where a few women sat on the ground, deep in conversation.

It took a moment for Quentin's eyes to adjust to the differences as he made his way over to Poppy and Julia's rickshaw to help her down. It was like looking into a picture, rather than at it. First, he noticed that the villagers seemed rounder, sharper and altogether better fed and dressed than those raw-boned and hollow-eyed people in the towns they had passed through. Then he noticed that the dwellings, while flimsy, had a look of permanence to them that he had not seen in the other places. There he had looked at the buildings and wondered whether a stiff breeze might blow them over, Big Bad Wolf style. There were gardens, too, bordering the village and creeping out to where it met the rice fields.

He held out his arms to Poppy when he reached her rickshaw and she almost fell into them. 'You okay?' Her face was very pale, and her tawny-brown eyes were sharp and questioning.

'Never better,' he assured her, turning to where Scarlett was being greeted like royalty by the women who had been sitting chatting in the central clearing. 'Your ma and I had a grand chat.'

'Really?' Poppy looked unconvinced. 'What about?'

'Orphan stuff,' he said, looking around for something to assist him in a swift change of subject. He resisted the urge to go with 'Oh look, there's another mangy dog,' as one of them ambled over to Poppy and lolled ecstatically at her feet.

'For the love of god,' Julia exclaimed, folding herself out of the rickshaw and handing some cash to the driver. 'Someone call the RSPCA and get rid of all these disgusting mutts. We're going to catch the freakin' bubonic plague.'

'I think that was rats,' Quentin said, relieved not to be the only one troubled by the dogs.

'Wow,' Poppy breathed, staring in the direction of Scarlett. 'Check it out.'

Scarlett stood in the middle of a mob of women, touching their faces as though bestowing blessings. For their part, they touched her sari and pressed their faces hard against her fingers when she touched them.

'What the hell is that all about?' Julia rolled her eyes. 'Your mum never mentioned she was running a cult here.'

Scarlett floated towards them on her multi-coloured sari cloud and the crowd followed her like a bridal procession. She beamed, opening her hands to encompass the three of them and say something to the local people in their dialect. They all nodded enthusiastically. 'I'm merely explaining who you all are,' she said, as she turned back to speak to them again. 'I hadn't said much about it all before this.' She faltered, swallowed, then forced a smile on her face after a quick glance at Quentin. 'I wasn't sure if you could make it.'

'Wow,' Poppy said, watching the faces of the local people as they listened intently to her mother. 'They adore you.'

Scarlett shrugged. 'It's not any magic, really. It's just that we have to sweeten them up so they'll accept the kids.' She gestured off up the hill, into the distance. 'Orphans are bad luck, pretty much as low as it gets on the caste ladder here. No-one wants the place here, not really. So we can't only help them, we have to help the whole village.'

'That's good,' Julia said.

Scarlett shrugged again. 'It's practical. We made a lot of mistakes in the beginning. Before we realised this stuff, the kids used to get stoned on the way to school. The people couldn't face seeing them getting better fed, dressed and schooled than their own kids. This way, we bring them all along, and the kids get left alone.'

Quentin couldn't help but admire the approach.

He considered the incline and caught up to Poppy. 'Piggyback?'

Two days ago she would have refused in horror, but he was pretty sure the morning's illness, the train trip and the rickshaw ride had weakened her pride a little.

'Why the hell not?' She laughed, stopping and smiling at him in a way that looked very relieved. He turned around and crouched and she climbed onto his back. He'd learned that she preferred piggyback rides to him picking her up and carrying her in his arms; that made her feel like a baby, an invalid. Piggybacks, on the other hand, seemed fun and adventurous. She wrapped her arms around his neck and her legs around his waist and he held her under her thighs for further support. 'Giddyup.' She giggled as he galloped to catch up to Scarlett and Julia.

When they made it to the top of the hill, the sight that met them caused Quentin to stop suddenly, and momentarily lose his grip on Poppy. 'Holy shit,' he breathed.

'Holy shit indeed,' she echoed.

A series of low, long wooden huts on short stilts greeted them. They were simple and uniform but pleasing to the eye. Tall gardens overflowing with flowers ringed the buildings and what looked to be a central eating hall stood to one side. A squarer hut stood at the other end of the township. A modest sign at the entry declared, 'The Poppy Devine Home for Orphaned Children.'

'She named it after me?' Poppy's voice seemed caught in her throat.

Quentin resisted bitching that Scarlett might have been better off staying with her own daughter so she wouldn't feel like an orphan herself. But it didn't seem like the right moment.

As they watched, a sea of small children in neat school uniforms mobbed Scarlett and Julia. They were saying some word Quentin couldn't quite work out but it sounded something like 'Mama'. Scarlett had her arms wrapped around as many of the tiny people as possible, hugging and chattering to them, gesturing at Julia, who looked bewildered but was grinning at the contagious enthusiasm. Scarlett turned and gestured to Quentin and Poppy, and as she did the children surged forward.

'Poppydevine, Poppydevine,' they were all shouting, grabbing at her skirts playfully and kissing her hands. Quentin pulled her in hard against him, even though he could feel her happiness at this sea of irrepressible childish joy. He was worried she was going to be accidentally pulled over in the crush.

Scarlett and Julia pushed through. 'Fuck me,' Julia exclaimed, quickly covering her mouth as she realised she'd dropped the f-bomb in front of a sea of children, albeit ones who probably had no idea what she had said. 'Now I know how it feels to be a rock god, Ten.'

Poppy raised her palms towards Scarlett. 'How do they all know me?'

Scarlett smiled, tears pooling in her eyes. 'I have a lot of photos of you in my office.' She gestured to the square hut.

Poppy stood, leaning against Quentin like she was trying to make sense of it all. Scarlett stood in front of her, uncharacteristically quiet as the moment seemed to stretch, a collectively held breath while they all wondered whether something would happen to break the brittle distance between Poppy and her mother. Even the children seemed to comprehend that something strange and adult was at work. A sea of little faces seemed to flick from one to the other like they were watching a tennis game.

After a while, all the miniature bodies around them started to press in closer, like they wanted the two women to work this moment out, wrapping their arms around whichever piece of Scarlett or Poppy they could get their hands on. Quentin watched as a sea of small people fanned out from his fiancée and her mother like an exotic flower. Poppy started to sway towards her mother, who was watching Poppy with a silent appeal in her eyes. But at the last moment, she leaned back against Quentin again and cleared her throat, motioning that she should go somewhere and sit down.

Quentin felt churlishly glad. He didn't want Poppy to give in to Scarlett's need to make it all better right away. It wasn't selfishness, some desire to have her all to himself. He just worried that down that path lay more hurt for Poppy.

The children seemed to deflate as the moment passed, but they all remained fixated on Poppy and Scarlett; all but one. One little boy could not tear his hands or his eyes from Julia. He looked to be five or six, but it was hard to tell because he was terribly skinny and had a shaved head. He was so different from the others, who appeared robust and healthy, that Quentin assumed he was a new arrival. Whoever he was, he had developed a major and instant crush on Julia.

'So beautiful,' he was repeating in reverential tones as he stared solemnly up at her. He held out his arms to her and she picked him up, even though Quentin was sure the way his nose was running would be making Julia want to reach for her hand sanitiser. Once he drew level with Julia's face, the boy touched it softly with his skinny brown hand. 'Are you a giant?' he enunciated in perfect English.

Julia guffawed and wrapped him in a quick squeeze. 'No, pet,' she said, smiling so blindingly at him that he blinked as though dazzled. 'But I tell you what, while I'm here, you can be my special mate if you like.'

Eventually, Quentin was the one who had to break the spell. 'I'm sorry, guys.' He coughed awkwardly. 'But I really need to get Poppydevine inside to rest.'

They all chattered in agreement, unpeeling themselves from the women and grabbing whichever hand or piece of clothing of the newcomers they could reach.

Quentin caught snippets of their words as they were moved towards one of the low buildings.

'A dorm, Poppydevine.'

'Just for you, Poppydevine.'

'You will love it, Poppydevine.'

And they weren't wrong. The look on Poppy's face as she was ushered into the low building was like nothing Quentin had ever seen – not at the lights, not in Dharamsala, not even when he made love to her. As she looked around at the simple dorm that had been filled to the brim with a thousand kind of exotic flowers – garlands, streamers, bouquets – she looked, finally, as though she was utterly at peace.

'This is your room,' Julia's little fan declared. 'For Poppy-devine. And the giant ones.' He looked appealingly at Julia. 'But I can stay in here with you. If you wish. In case you are lonely.'

Julia burst out laughing and picked him up for another squeeze.

* * *

It was well past the children's bedtime, and Poppy, Julia and Scarlett were sitting on the small patio of Scarlett's office-cum-quarters, watching the outline of the orphanage in the light of the moon and listening as Quentin picked at the guitar, playing a sad song about a girl with red hair.

Julia smiled at him.

'It's nice to see you two liking each other,' Poppy murmured from her spot lying beside Quentin on the daybed.

'Nonsense,' Julia snorted. 'I only tolerate him for your sake. The minute you're gone, he's off my Christmas-card list.' She grinned, and wrapped a piece of hair around one finger. 'Spike, on the other hand, I may need to check in on occasionally. Purely for musical development purposes, of course.'

But she smiled at Quentin and he smiled back.

Poppy roused herself sleepily from the daybed, sat up and looked across at Scarlett, who was examining some papers, tapping her feet to the music. She caught her mother's eyes and raised her hands in appeal. 'Why, Mum?'

The cosy, sleepy vibe of the evening changed, and all the warm-blooded creatures that drowsed in the humid evening snapped to attention.

Quentin's hand closed protectively around Poppy's waist.

Scarlett looked over her bifocals and frowned in bewilderment.

Poppy gestured around her. 'Why all this? Why name it after me?'

Her mother dragged in a breath and stood up, pushing back her chair. She stepped towards Poppy and eyed Quentin carefully before she spoke. He had the distinct impression Scarlett was wary of what she might say, lest she violate the rules he had laid out in the rickshaw. But this time he knew the time had come, and it was not his fight to get in the middle of.

'I know I was no good, Poppy, my darling,' she said slowly. 'I was so young when I had you, and foolish. My heart was broken and I didn't know how to fix it. I wanted to reach out to you, but I was so damn bad at it.'

She eyed Quentin again and he nodded at her, as Julia watched on in hushed fascination.

Poppy's face was hard and closed, but she also nodded at her mother to go on.

'I came here and it felt like a way to atone.'

Poppy sighed, a slippery, disappointed gesture. She sagged back against Quentin and he wanted to scream at Scarlett to try harder, do better.

The older woman plugged on, stepping another foot closer. 'I never intended this.' She gestured around her in a slow sweep. 'It happened by accident, I swear. One by one. The first time I found a child who had been left at a train station, waiting for his family to come back.' She paused and stared into the distance as though remembering. 'They had told him to wait there, that they would return for him. He was still there six months later.'

Scarlett kneeled at Poppy's feet and reached out for her daughter's hand. Poppy hesitated, then sat forward in her seat, leaning away from Quentin, who felt the loss like a physical pain, as Poppy took her mother's hand.

'It felt like I couldn't fix us, but I could somehow change their circumstances for them.' She shrugged, and the tears spilled down onto her cheeks. 'I should have visited you more often; I should have tried harder. I should have made it work. But every time I did, I seemed to mess it up, and the gap grew wider and wider. Oh, Poppy …' She was openly crying now and Quentin's innate desire to comfort a woman in distress warred with his concern for his lover. Poppy said nothing, but she held onto her mother's hand and watched her face, as though Scarlett must say more, as though surely she had more to say.

Scarlett reached up to wipe away some tears, then brought Poppy's hand to her cheek. 'I am so sorry, my darling, darling girl. I can never make it up to you, what I did.' The tears spilled anew as she pressed Poppy's fingers to her tear-stained face. 'I don't deserve you coming here. I don't deserve another chance.'

Too bloody right, Quentin wanted to mutter. But he didn't, which just showed he was capable of evolving, despite what his father thought.

Scarlett gathered herself, sucking in a breath. 'But oh, I do love you, my Poppydevine.' There was a wonder and vulnerability in her voice that Quentin had never heard before. It hit him with ferocity in the stomach, because he recognised the feeling.

Scarlett wasn't done. 'What a beautiful woman you have become, Poppy. And it's all down to you. I don't deserve any compassion for how badly I messed everything up with you.' She tapped herself on the chest, close to her heart. 'But I'm here, asking for it anyway.'

Finally, Poppy's face changed. It was as though a light had gone on inside her. 'Shh.' Poppy stood and held out her arms and her mother stepped into them. After a few moments she pulled back, and her face, too, was wet with tears. 'What do you mean?' She spread her arms wide, gesturing at the place, the gardens and the buildings outlined in the moonlight. 'What do you mean, you don't deserve compassion?' She smiled, and Quentin remembered what Poppy had said about the Dalai Lama's words. *Compassion.*

Something seemed to click into place and Quentin had the strangest feeling that His Holiness had somehow engineered the entire event. His breath caught in his throat as he wondered how Poppy could be so magnanimous, after everything, after all the hurt. He blinked back tears and tuned to his fiancée, who was still reassuring her mother.

'Look at this place. All you have done here; all you've built, all the lives you've saved. And it has my name.' She smiled more broadly. 'Of course you deserve compassion, more compassion than I've ever been able to find for you.'

Poppy sat back down with a slight thump, and shuffled along closer to Quentin, patting the seat beside her. Scarlett sat next to her, and Poppy lay her head down in her mother's lap. Scarlett started to pat her hair, and Poppy's voice, when it came, was very soft, as though she was suddenly exhausted from the day and the emotion of the evening.

'We're good, Mum,' she murmured. 'We're all good. Everything's going to be fine.'

Chapter Fourteen

An hour later, Julia and Ten were trying to convince Poppy to have an early night. Scarlett had disappeared for a moment and Julia was worried that Poppy wouldn't last all day tomorrow – her wedding day – unless she had a good night's sleep.

Scarlett entered the dorm clasping an oddly shaped bottle. 'Before you go to bed, darling, I want you to have this,' she said and handed it to Poppy with a flourish. 'This is perhaps the biggest reason I wanted you to come to India.'

Poppy held the tiny green bottle up in the soft light. It seemed to be filled with some kind of liquid. 'What is it?'

'Sacred water,' Scarlett whispered. 'From the Ghudja Springs, high up in the mountains.' She lowered her voice still further. 'It has world-renowned healing properties. I trekked for three days to get it.'

Poppy sat there, open-mouthed, holding the bottle in her hands while a molten ball of rage exploded in Julia's chest. *She had to be kidding.* 'For fuck's sake,' she snapped. 'Get a grip, Scarlett.'

'Now don't be like that, Julia,' Scarlett pleaded as Ten and Poppy turned to look at Julia.

Ten's face was full of thunder, clearly pissed off with the sacred water bullshit, but Poppy's mouth formed a perfect surprised O at the outburst. Which Julia understood perfectly. All of their lives, Julia had been a staunch supporter of Scarlett's alternativeness, had been the one to shrug off the older woman's eccentricities and jolly Poppy along until she did, too.

God, how many times had she lain awake at night and wished Scarlett had been *her* mother? Scarlett, who had always seemed so at peace, so spiritual, who tinkled when she walked, smiled beatifically, spoke calmly and said deeply wise things like, *The quieter you become the more you can hear* and *If you wish to experience peace, provide peace for another.*

All her mother had ever said was, *Think of your reputation, Julia.* Which translated to 'think of the Shrewsbury reputation'. And, *Mr and Mrs Rich-Bastard are coming around for cocktails tonight, put on a pretty dress and smile at their son.*

In her own house she'd felt like some bargaining chip, a pawn to be moved around her father's chess board like something out of Victorian England. Useful but not necessary. A chattel. A belonging. Whereas in Scarlett's house she'd felt like she *belonged.* She'd felt *included.* Scarlett had always seemed genuinely interested in what Julia had to say, had *listened* and had talked in return about the world with wisdom and wonder in her eyes instead of dollar signs.

Scarlett's attention had felt like rain on parched skin.

Considering that Julia's mother holidayed in Paris, wrote faceless cheques to the latest fashionable charity and believed in accessorising with Tiffany, it had seemed terribly exotic and exciting for Poppy to have a mother who swanned off to an Indian orphanage, did good works with *her own two hands* and whose only accessories were tinny bangles and henna tattoos.

Yep, Julia had been utterly fascinated by Scarlett from the very first day they'd met. And that week she'd spent camping with Scarlett and Poppy on the beach at Byron Bay would always be in her top-ten memories.

But. Even through her adoration, Julia hadn't been blind. Scarlett just simply hadn't been around very much and that had hurt Poppy. Sure, *her* mother hadn't been around much either, but then she was rarely present even when she was right in front of her. At least when Scarlett had been around she made Julia feel like she was the centre of her universe.

And so Julia had made excuses for Scarlett, because despite all the woman's shortcomings, she'd liked her so damn much. And because she hadn't been able to bear Poppy's hurt and disappointment, Julia had taken on the role of chief mitigator. How many excuses had she made for Scarlett over the years? How many small white lies had she told to Poppy *and* herself, trying to make up for Scarlett's emotional neglect?

She wanted to come to your graduation, Pop, but hundreds of orphans depended on her during those dreadful floods.

She wanted to be there for the nationally televised Maths Mastermind, but being asked to Delhi to speak on child exploitation is a huge honour, Pop, something to be so proud of.

She loves you really, Pop, she's just trying to be a mother to so many who need her.

But there was no excuse for this. For freaking sacred water. Not when she knew how strongly Poppy – *her daughter who was dying* – felt about woo-woo medicine.

Scarlett's presentation of this supposed elixir flew in the face of what everyone knew – everyone except Scarlett, it seemed. Scarlett, who had insisted all along that Poppy would pull through this because some freaking voice up here in the mountains had told her she would.

Anyone who looked at Poppy could tell she wasn't long for this world. It had been clear to everybody who'd met her in recent weeks. And yet Scarlett, Poppy's *mother*, was so blinded by her convictions that she couldn't see what was right in front of her.

Julia was pleased and thankful that Poppy had decided to come to India and make it right with Scarlett. But Scarlett also had to make things right with Poppy. And this wasn't the way to go about it.

They *all* had to face that Poppy was dying. *It sucked*. But it was an inescapable truth.

Julia took a deep, ragged breath, reaching for a calm she didn't feel in a situation she didn't want. 'Scarlett, I love you,' she said, 'but this has got to stop.'

Scarlett shook her head. 'No.'

Julia was about to argue, but Poppy got in before her. 'Yes,' she said. 'Yes, Mum.'

Scarlett's head shook more definitively, her bangles tinkling with the movement. 'No,' she said firmly. 'No. I have watched you being put through the wringer for the last eight months with this … *conventional* medicine—'

If it hadn't been so deadly serious, Julia would have laughed at the comic way Scarlett's lip had curled and her face had screwed up as if she'd just had arsenic shoved on her tongue. She spoke about modern medicine as if it was some kind of satanic cult instead of an instrument of good that had saved billions of lives in one way or another.

'—this modern-medicine myth you were so gung-ho on. Watched week by week, month by month, as it did nothing. *Nothing*. As you got sicker and thinner and paler.'

She reached over and grabbed the bottle out of Poppy's hands. 'I have seen this work incredible miracles. I have witnessed amazing cures. I have watched as people afflicted with terrible conditions have bathed in it and been cleansed and healed. In the pool area, where the water flows into a natural warm spring, there are walking sticks and walking frames hanging from the trees all around like candy canes at Christmas time. It's inspiring.'

Poppy shook her head sadly. 'This isn't a dicky hip or leprosy, Mum. This is cancer.'

Scarlett looked around at all of them, her eyes pleading with them to understand, to not dismiss her. 'What have you got to lose, Poppy? You say it doesn't work. That there's no scientific basis for it. No double-blind study, no human trials. But every toxic chemical they pumped into your body had all that and none of it worked. I refuse to believe that you're going to die. I refuse to believe that any god would be so cruel as to take you from me. But if you truly believe that your death from this is inevitable, then I repeat, what have you got to lose?'

'Look at me, Mum,' Poppy said, her eyes huge above rail-like cheekbones, dark smudges defining the perimeter of her prominent eye sockets. 'Do you really think it's going to do any good? Now?'

Scarlett's eyes filled with tears. She grabbed Poppy's hands. 'If only you'd listened to me sooner. If it had been up to me, if you'd let me in enough, allowed me to help you with medical decisions, then you could have been benefiting from this much, much sooner.'

Ten took a step forward and a noise which Julia could best describe as a growl came from the back of his throat. 'You're not seriously going to unload an I-told-you-so on her now, are you?' he demanded.

Scarlett released Poppy's hands. 'No … of course not …'

'Of course not.' Ten nodded emphatically. 'Because if it's such a miracle cure then it's not going to matter when she gets it, is it?'

Julia winced at the blatant hostility in Ten's voice. Part of her, as usual, wanted to rise up in Scarlett's defence, tell Ten to shut his mouth, that he couldn't speak to Scarlett like that. But the other part knew that he was right – *miracles* weren't supposed to have expiration dates. And he had as much stake in this conversation as she did. He had as much right as she did to be pissed, to question *supposedly* sacred water.

'I … don't know, Quentin. Maybe. I hope not.'

'This means a lot to you, doesn't it?' Poppy asked quietly.

Scarlett looked at her daughter. 'You have no idea how much.'

Poppy gave a brittle half-laugh. 'Really? As much as five missed mother-and-daughter days? As much as an emergency appendectomy with only the school headmistress by my side? As much as an empty seat at my university graduation?'

Julia watched as a tear slid down Scarlett's cheek. 'I'm truly sorry, Poppy. I know I wasn't there for you. I know I screwed up. But I'm trying to be there for you now.'

It was on the tip of Julia's tongue to say but you *haven't* been there. You could have cooked pasta with her in Tuscany. You could have seen the northern lights with her. You could have sat at the feet of the Dalai Lama with her. You could have made lasting memories that would comfort you in the bleak days ahead.

But you were *here*. In India. Trekking for three days to collect dubious water from some freaking mountain spring with who knew what bacteria count floating around in it.

Poppy held out her hand for the water. 'Okay.'

'*What?*'

'*No!*'

Both Julia and Ten spoke at the same time as they made a beeline for the bottle exchanging hands. Poppy, startled at their reaction, blinked at them owlishly as they approached quickly from both sides, grabbing for the water. Ten was faster, plucking it out of Poppy's hands.

Scarlett looked at them both reproachfully. 'Do you think I would poison my own daughter?'

Julia remembered Poppy returning to school after a term break with an infected toenail and announcing that she thought Scarlett was trying to poison her. When Julia had asked her to explain, Poppy had kicked off her shoe to reveal a disgusting poultice made from god knew what. Apparently, it was from some ancient recipe an Indian shaman had given to Scarlett on one of her many travels. It had looked like lumpy vegemite and smelled like roadkill. They'd both decided on the spot it was better for Poppy to risk amputation than have to live with the twice-daily dressing requirements that Scarlett had handwritten for Julia to follow to the letter.

Scarlett lived by the (thankfully) ancient medical creed: *If it tastes awful and smells worse, it's probably good for you.*

Julia wasn't so sure about that. She lived by the edict: *If it tastes awful and smells worse, leave it the hell alone.* On the other hand, if it tasted good and smelled better, you either ate it, squirted it on your neck or fucked it.

It hadn't led her wrong so far.

'I'm not so sure her immune system is up to drinking unfiltered water,' Ten said much more tactfully this time, his tone conciliatory.

Julia nodded. They'd bought so much bottled water they could tip it into a hole in the ground and open their own damn spring.

'It'll be fine,' Poppy dismissed, pulling the bottle off a resisting Ten and twisting the lid.

'Wait.' Julia could hear the panic in her voice. 'I think Ten's right.'

He quirked his eyebrow at her. 'How'd that one taste going down?'

Julia smiled but continued. 'I really think we need to consider ...' She glanced at Scarlett, not wanting to offend her, her sacred water or her adopted country any more than they already had. But her duty of care was to Poppy. Ten's hot button had been mangy dogs. Julia wasn't comfortable with Poppy – with any of them – drinking *any* water that wasn't sealed in a nice clear plastic bottle with a label she could read. In English.

'What?' Scarlett enquired waspishly. 'What do we need to consider?'

Julia glanced at Ten. He nodded his head encouragingly. 'Well,' she began, 'just how many ... lepers have bathed in that sacred water, before we let Poppy drink it?'

'*Julia!*'

Scarlett's horrified voice had the desired shaming effect. 'I know, I know, it's not very PC of me,' Julia said, holding up her hand as Scarlett looked like she was about to launch into another spiel, 'and I'm sure I'll suffer some kind of karmic kick-back over it, but this is India, right? I mean, aren't there like dead cows floating in waterways everywhere?'

'I think,' Scarlett said stiffly, 'you're referring to the Ganges. It's about one thousand miles in that direction.' She pointed out her office door.

'Okay, no wait, to be fair, Scarlett, I see Julia's point,' Ten jumped in. 'I mean what collection method did you use? Did you just ... scoop it up randomly during or after opening hours when every person with a walking stick or a communicable disease in India had been to wallow in it or—'

'I collected it further upstream,' Scarlett interrupted, glaring at the two of them now. 'And yes,' she said, raising her finger in warning at Ten, who'd opened his mouth again, 'I checked it thoroughly for dead cows first.'

Poppy, whose head had been pinging back and forth between the three of them, laughed. She ran her hand up Ten's arm, patting it absently, and smiled at Julia. 'It's fine,' she said, nodding assuredly. 'Really. If this is important to Mum,' she looked at her mother, 'if this is what she needs to feel like she's done what she can to help, then I'm okay with that. And,' Poppy shrugged, 'she's right. What have I got to lose?'

Scarlett reached for her daughter's hands again. 'It would mean so much to me, darling.'

A spike of anger surged into Julia's bloodstream. Nothing like emotionally blackmailing your terminally ill daughter. She glared at Scarlett, but Scarlett only had eyes for her daughter, and the conviction that Julia saw there was powerful. Scarlett wasn't trying to control Poppy, she wasn't even being frustratingly obtuse for once. She clearly, honestly, truly believed that Poppy was going to be miraculously cured by the sacred water.

Poppy unscrewed the lid completely and pulled it off. Julia shot a helpless look at Ten. He shrugged slightly, but she could tell he was ready to leap into action should Poppy so much as breathe strangely afterwards.

'Here goes,' Poppy announced, winking at them. 'Bottoms up.'

As Poppy tipped back her head, Julia fought the urge to grab the bottle and at least wipe it over several times with her hand sanitiser. *Damn it, why hadn't she thought to do that?* She held her breath as Poppy swallowed, glugging it all down in one hit.

When she was done, she wiped her hand across her mouth and handed the bottle back to Scarlett.

Nobody moved for a long, pregnant moment. The three of them just stared at Poppy. Julia was waiting for Poppy to start salivating or break out in hives. Ten looked like he was pumped to give her the kiss of life should she suddenly succumb to some fucked-up mountain strain of dead-cow, leprosy-cum-Ebola.

But Scarlett was looking at Poppy as if her hair was going to suddenly grow back and she was going to gain the ten kilos she had lost over the past months.

'Okay, show's over, folks.' Poppy laughed. 'It's done now, so you can all quit looking at me like I'm going to either throw away my metaphorical crutches or go to Jesus.' She squeezed Julia's hand and kissed Ten lightly. 'Haven't we got a wedding to plan?'

* * *

A low mist hung over the silent mountain village early the next morning, draping a gossamer veil across the entire valley below. Julia couldn't help but think how very bridal it was as she stood on the wooden deck of the dorm and breathed in the sweet, clean air.

Poppy was getting married today.

She sucked in a deeper breath, refusing to let the hot ball of emotion rise from her belly to her throat – this was a happy day. But breaking down in front of Ten on that mountain pass seemed to have opened the floodgates and Julia was finding it harder and harder to block the emotion, to switch it off and put on her game face.

Maybe it was the sucker punch of Ten's revelation that had done the damage to her usually iron-clad emotional control. Learning that Poppy didn't want her – or Ten, or Scarlett – there at the end had been battering against her brain like a pair of insect's wings ever since. Quiet but deadly, always there, beating away incessantly, driving her slowly insane.

If she hadn't wanted her, if she'd only wanted Ten or even, peculiarly, just Scarlett, then Julia would have understood. She'd have *hated* it, but she'd have understood that Poppy was entitled to die as she'd lived – with her free will intact.

But with nobody?

It had killed her not to say anything. Not to yell and cry and demand that Poppy explain herself. To cajole and plead until Poppy changed her mind. But she'd made a promise to herself that she wouldn't say anything until *after* the wedding. Poppy was excited about it and that had been infectious. It wasn't, after all, every day that a girl got married. She hadn't wanted to rain on Poppy's parade or taint the lead-up. Poppy had so few days left, Julia didn't want to ruin the ones that should be extra special.

But after the wedding – they *were* going to have this out.

'Hey.'

Julia turned slightly to see Ten approaching with two steaming mugs of what she assumed was tea. There was no shortage of tea in India. 'Morning,' she said as she took hers, grateful for the warmth in the cool mountain air.

'You're up early,' he said as he joined her at the railing.

Julia blew on the hot brew. 'Couldn't sleep.'

She didn't have to ask to know he hadn't been able to sleep either. Between Poppy's deathbed edict, bittersweet thoughts of the approaching nuptials and worry over rabid, water-born amoeba multiplying in Poppy's gut, slumber had been elusive.

Thankfully, though, Poppy had slept. After her rough time on the train, it was good to see her relaxed and peaceful.

'It's beautiful here,' Ten said, staring out over the vista. 'I can see why Scarlett loves it so much.'

Julia nodded. It was very beautiful. She could imagine find-ing inner peace or nirvana or whatever kind of spiritual bullshit people craved in a place like this.

'What are you thinking about?' he asked.

'The wedding.' The lie slipped easily off her tongue. She didn't want to talk about Poppy's deathbed decision – it was, after all, Ten's wedding day, too, and she was sure he thought about it enough without her bringing it up again on the morning of his nuptials. 'About … how this is so far from the weddings we'd pictured having when we were kids.'

Because it most definitely was the polar opposite of what they'd whispered to each other in the dorm late at night.

'You pictured your weddings?'

Julia rolled her eyes at him. 'Of course.'

He shook his head. 'I never pictured you as being the marry-ing type.'

'What can I say? I was twelve. My illusions hadn't yet been shattered.'

'So India wasn't on the agenda then?'

'Absolutely not. I wanted to get married on a beach with a garland of shells in my hair, because even at twelve I figured that would annoy the crap out of my parents.'

He laughed. 'And Poppy?'

'Poppy wanted a full-on church wedding. The priest, the brides-maids, the meringue dress. Mendelssohn's Wedding March. Her father escorting her down the aisle. The whole shebang.'

'Because that would annoy the crap out of her mother?'

Julia smiled. 'I think that had a lot to do with it.'

'A priest though.' Ten blew on his tea. 'I find that hard to believe given Poppy's atheist tendencies?'

'It wasn't about God,' Julia said. 'Poppy's always craved … normalcy, and tradition. That's what it was about.'

They were both quiet for a while, contemplating the view. 'I could've given her that,' he murmured into the hush.

'What?'

'The whole white-wedding shebang.'

Julia shrugged. 'She was twelve years old. Trust me, she's moved on.'

'But still … here. This place,' he said. 'India – not a lot of happy memories for her here, are there?'

'No. But I think finally coming here has been good for that. I think she can see why Scarlett was drawn to this country so much, why she felt so … compelled. And I think there's a nice serendipitous feeling about it. Like she and Scarlett have come to a greater understanding, like they've come full circle.'

Ten nodded. 'I guess …' he said, taking a sip of his tea. 'It would've been nice to give her something traditional.'

'It would have. But then I don't think her being weeks away from death was on her agenda either, so as His Holiness said to me, you play with the cards you're dealt.'

Ten raised his eyebrows. 'The *Dalai Lama* told you that?'

'Well.' She grinned. 'I'm paraphrasing. And anyway, we can still add some tradition.'

'I don't think that's what Scarlett's got in mind. And, you know, we're in the middle of *India*.'

'Scarlett knows what Poppy wants. More than that, she knows weddings are all about *the bride*. This one even more so. Poppy wants traditional, Poppy gets traditional. Or as traditional as possible anyway in this faraway land.'

He looked at her for long moments then suddenly nodded. 'You're right.' He pulled out his phone and checked the clock.

'I've got time.' He tossed his tea over the edge. 'I'll be back. Don't start without me.'

Julia frowned at him but he was already walking away. 'Where are you going?'

'Trust me,' he threw over his shoulder. 'It's a surprise.'

Julia felt weirdly comforted by the fact that she did actually trust him as he pounded down the stairs and in the opposite direction to where his wedding was being held in a few short hours' time.

* * *

'How do I look?' Poppy asked five hours later as she appeared from a clutch of colourful saris and fussing brown arms. Julia drew in a ragged breath, pressing her hand to her chest as tears welled in her eyes. 'Poppy,' she whispered. 'You look …'

Julia glanced at the eager smiling faces all around waiting for her proclamation, but she just didn't have the words. Poppy had been transformed. She still looked fragile but it only added to the ethereal vision of her.

The bodice and the petticoat of the exquisite cream traditional dress were heavily beaded with deep garnet and creamy pearls. The beading was repeated in the diaphanous swathe of cream fabric that wrapped around the skirt and covered Poppy's shoulder, the trim of which was a heavy garnet brocade. Her arms, from wrist to elbows, were covered in multi-coloured thin bangles and a simply stunning choker of red and gold sat around Poppy's slender neck and draped beautifully onto her chest.

But the absolute pièce de résistance was the intricate henna tattooing that covered Poppy's bald head. Women from the village had come early to perform the ritual. Julia had sat and watched them in awe, barely even registering the shy young woman who had busily decorated her hands for the ceremony. And yes, Julia loved how her hands looked, but they had nothing on the breath-taking mastery of Poppy's tattooing.

There wasn't a spare centimetre of scalp on view as an intricate pattern of peacocks and marigolds all linked together in a kaleidoscope of light-brown swirls. The convoluted pattern dipped down onto Poppy's forehead like the scalloped edge of a veil, forming a radiant sun in the very centre.

And that was exactly how Poppy looked with this superb piece of art adorning her on this special day – she looked radiant. Julia didn't look at Poppy and think *she's dying* like she had for so long now. Instead, she thought *she's glowing*.

'Well?' Poppy prompted. 'I'm dying over here.' And then she grinned at her own joke. 'Compliment me already.'

Julia swallowed the gargantuan lump in her throat. 'You're … an absolute vision.' The dozen women all around broke out in smiles and nods. The whole village had come together to see that Poppy had a wedding to remember, and these amazing, artistic women were the tip of the iceberg.

Poppy grinned at her. 'I'm getting married. Like, now!'

A tear slid from Julia's eye as she nodded. 'It's really happening.'

'Oh no,' Poppy said, moving over to Julia and grabbing her hand. 'Remember what I said last night? *No tears*. Not today. Plenty of time for them. Whatever the circumstances of how we got here, it's my wedding day.'

'Oh, Pop,' Julia said, struggling for composure. 'It's got nothing to do with the circumstances.' Well, not *all* to do with them anyway. 'I would've cried on your wedding day regardless.'

Poppy squeezed her hand. 'And I on yours.'

Julia smiled, biting the inside of her lip hard to stop the sob sitting at the back of her throat from coming out. They both knew Poppy would never be there for Julia's big day.

'Well.' Julia cleared her throat and reached for every ounce of bluff she had left inside her. 'C'mon, then. Your mother and Ten are waiting. Let's go get you hitched.'

* * *

'Oh … it's so beautiful,' Poppy murmured to Julia as they walked the short distance to the clearing at the edge of the village that looked over the valley. The mist had lifted and the entire expanse of lush green foliage was laid out like a jewel in front of them.

Julia was pretty sure Poppy wasn't referring to the view, but rather to the gathering of the entire village. From the women who had fussed over Poppy today, to their elegant men, and the bright garlands around the necks of the children from the orphanage, it was a riot of vibrant colour. From the saris to the aisle the crowd had formed and strewn with marigold petals, it was like walking into a Bollywood rainbow.

Julia heard the excited 'Poppydevine, Poppydevine' whispers first. The children had formed a kind of guard of honour, and then everyone's head was turning and the entire village was beaming at both of them as they reached the start of the aisle.

Scarlett and Ten stood at the other end. Scarlett, like Julia, was wearing a sari. Ten was dressed in his usual jeans but, surprisingly, he also wore a white linen shirt with long, loose sleeves that looked a bit on the hippy side with a row of embroidered flowers along the rounded neckline and the cuffs. It wasn't something she'd seen him in thus far and certainly not one she'd have ever imagined him wearing – it wasn't very rock'n'roll.

It must have been what he was up to earlier.

Two garlands of yellow-and-orange marigolds were slung around his neck and Poppy leaned in and whispered, 'Huh.

Look at that. Who knew a man wearing flowers could be so damn sexy?' She smiled up at Julia. 'I'm a lucky girl.'

Julia forced another smile onto her face as she drew in a deep, slow breath. Poppy was the very definition of *un*lucky. 'Yep,' she agreed, reining in the roar of unfairness that was beating against her larynx. 'He's a hottie. Not too late to back out though. We could make a run for it?'

Poppy grinned. 'Take me to my husband.'

Julia and Poppy walked down the aisle, hundreds of petals soft and cool on their bare feet. When they got to the end, Ten held out his hand and Poppy took it as Julia stood to the other side of Scarlett.

'Ready?' Scarlett said to both of them.

'Yes,' they said in unison.

Scarlett smiled at them. 'Friends and family. We are gathered here today to witness the joining of Poppy Devine to Quentin Carmody. But first, I have to ask, who here gives Poppy to Quentin?'

Scarlett had been astonished last night when Poppy had discussed the fairly stock-standard, traditional way she wanted her mother to run the ceremony. Scarlett had been a celebrant for many years and Julia had heard enough of Scarlett's whacky wedding stories to know that she'd never been hired for her conventional style.

But Julia hadn't been surprised. And Poppy had been adamant with her mother. And, to give Scarlett her due, she was embracing it with her usual panache.

'I do,' Julia said, smiling at Poppy as that damn lump grew bigger in her throat.

'Thank you,' Ten murmured, and Julia glanced at him, their gazes locking for a shared moment of miserable solidarity.

Scarlett continued then, going through the usual stuff covered in a wedding service, and it was as if the whole mountain had fallen silent to bear witness to the sacred event. The only sounds that could be heard across the entire valley were the clear, crisp notes of Scarlett's voice. No birds called, no insects trilled, no restless babies or impatient children murmured in the gathering.

'Time for the vows,' Scarlett announced. 'Poppy? I think you wanted to go first?'

Julia braced herself as Poppy nodded and smiled at her mother. The vows were the one thing that Poppy had wanted to freeform and it didn't take a shrink to know that they were going to be difficult to hear.

Poppy turned to her fiancé, their hands clasped. 'Quentin … Q … my Number Ten.' She smiled and Ten smiled back. 'I wish I could promise you that things will be better and not worse. That your days will be richer from the get-go instead of poorer. That there will be health instead of sickness. I wish I could promise that there will be no death do us part for many, many years and that we're going to grow old together, but—'

A tear rolled down Ten's cheek and Poppy's voice broke off as a matching tear rolled down hers. Julia squeezed her eyes together tight as a ton of grief smacked her in the chest.

'But … I can't,' Poppy continued, her voice tremulous. 'I'm sorry, I know you got the rough end of the deal. But I give thanks every day for this cancer because—'

'No,' Ten whispered fiercely, interrupting her with a crack in his voice and tears flowing freely.

Julia almost choked on the sobs demanding to be given voice.

'Yes,' Poppy said, nodding her head vehemently. 'Yes. Because without it I would never have met you. I've lived more *with* you and *because* of you in the last months than I have in the last twenty-nine years of my life and I know I will leave this earth having known my one true love.'

'Poppy, no—' Ten's voice, thick with grief and anguish, broke on whatever it was he was going to say and it speared right into Julia's heart, piercing her resolve to hold it together. The tears came, a sob slipped out and she gave in to them both.

Poppy shook her head to silence him and she smiled up at him through glassy eyes. 'So this is my promise to you today. *My solemn vow.* I promise to love you for whatever time I have left and after that I promise to love you for all eternity.'

Then she reached up onto her tippy-toes and embraced him and they stood there in front of everyone, Ten quietly crying, Poppy letting him. Julia cried, Scarlett cried. Half the gathering, who were complete strangers, cried.

Poppy pulled back after a while, her cheeks damp as she reached up to wipe the tears from Ten's face. 'Now it's your turn,' she said.

'Yes,' Scarlett said, dabbing at her eyes and drawing in a shaky breath. 'Quentin?'

Julia couldn't even begin to imagine how brutal this must be for Ten. She'd wasted a lot of time and effort disliking him and now her insides were just one big squishy ball of hurt for him.

'Poppy.' He stopped and cleared his throat of the emotion that was clearly still threatening to crack it wide open. Then he smiled at her because Poppy hadn't wanted this to be a sad occasion and Julia could tell it cost him to do that – it cost him a lot. 'All my life I've been good with words. I could talk myself out of most situations. I've written stories and pick-up lines and limericks and angsty teenager poetry and, even if I do say so myself, some pretty damn good lyrics.'

Poppy laughed. 'Definitely.'

'But finding the right words for today, for the most important moment in my life, has completely eluded me. So I think I will stick to the tried and true. I, Quentin Arthur Carmody, take you,' he drew Poppy's hand to his mouth and pressed a kiss to her knuckles, 'Poppy Alice Devine, to be my wife. To have and to hold from this day forward, for better or for worse, for richer, for poorer, in sickness—'

Ten's voice fractured and for a second Julia thought he was going to lose it. But he took a shuddering breath and ploughed on. 'And in health. To love and to cherish, from this day forward until death do us part.'

Poppy smiled up at him, wiping away the tear that trekked down his face. 'An oldie but a goody.'

'Poppy, I've been called a lot of names in my life. A talented screw-up, a gifted cook, a crap surfer … but today I am taking the name I am most proud of. Today I take the name *husband*. And I promise to be there for every week, every day, every minute, every second of our time together.'

Julia scrubbed at her face as Ten finished and he and Poppy embraced again. The horrifying fact was that this was how Poppy's life was measured now. Weeks, days, minutes, seconds.

'Now for the exchange of rings,' Scarlett murmured once the almost-newlyweds parted.

'Oh no,' Poppy said, frowning at her mother. Julia frowned too. What was Scarlett doing? They'd been over the order of events about a dozen times. 'No rings. Just move on to the husband-and-wife bit.'

'No,' Ten said. He reached into his pocket and pulled out two gold rings, placing them in the flat of Scarlett's palm. 'I have rings.'

Poppy blinked up at him. 'You do? But … how?'

He shrugged. 'Where do you think I've been all morning?'

'Oh.'

Ten didn't wait for a prompt from Scarlett as he plucked up the thinner band and raised Poppy's left hand, finding her ring finger and pushing it all the way on. 'Poppy, wedding rings traditionally represent eternity and I couldn't think of anything more fitting for today. On the inside of our rings I've had *come as you are* engraved so that we'll always remember that we never had to be anyone else around each other. That, despite everything, we were us and we fell in love anyway.'

Without saying a word, Poppy picked up the other ring, a wider band and inspected the inside. She looked adoringly at Ten. 'They're perfect,' she said and slid his on.

Julia agreed. Ten had found the sweetest, most perfect way to bring a sense of tradition to Poppy's wedding day. Sure, the words had stayed fairly true to a conventional church wedding, but standing in a mountain village in remote India dressed traditionally and covered in henna, while breathtakingly beautiful, was about as untraditional as a terminally ill white, atheist chick from Australia could get.

But the exchanging of rings? He'd nailed it. More tears welled in Julia's eyes. She was pretty sure snot was also starting to drip out of her nose.

There were a few beats of silence before Scarlett realised Poppy and Ten were looking at her expectantly, and a few more for her to get her emotions in check so that she could finish the ceremony.

'Oh yes ...' she said, dabbing some more at her face. 'By the power vested in me, I pronounce you husband and wife.' Scarlett looked at her daughter. 'You may kiss your husband.'

Poppy beamed at her mother then glanced over her shoulder at Julia, then grinned up her husband before she launched herself into his arms and kissed him like she was dying.

Chapter Fifteen

'Is this what you had in mind? For number twenty?'

Quentin could not remember ever having felt so unsure. And it was crazy. He knew women. He knew what they liked; he knew how to please them. But somehow this was different; this mattered. And Poppy was not the kind of woman you pointed at in the audience and murmured into your microphone, 'This one's for the girl with the brown eyes and killer smile.'

Poppy was no pushover. Poppy required a certain attention to detail. Especially for this, number twenty on her bucket list.

Sleep out under the stars.

It was surprisingly low on detail for his meticulous wife. *Wife.* He grinned as warm satisfaction spread through him. Whatever came next, and they all knew what it was going to be, one way or another, no-one could take this away. She was his wife, and he knew that for the rest of his life he would carry that knowledge like a candle inside him. Maybe a candle that burned your insides a little at the edges.

But regardless, nothing could take it away.

Anyway, this was their honeymoon, after a fashion. And more than anything on God's miserable, unfair earth, he did not want to fuck this up.

Poppy looked out over the scene he had so carefully choreographed, and he followed her gaze, trying to see it through her eyes. He had chosen a spot on top of a reasonable-sized hill. The night was cooling off, but he continued to fret about the possibility of a deepening chill as the sun went down. He had tried to situate their twin swags behind a small stand of trees, but in a spot that still afforded them a view down the valley and out into the sky beyond, where the last slashes of rosy pink were starting to settle into indigo, and a few tiny stars were manfully heralding the onset of night.

The valley sure was pretty. With the last of the light, it was still possible to see the small forest that separated them from the village in the valley below, looking green-black and magical, and the river that oozed like a lazy serpent through the basin. It was only a half-hour walk from the village, but it felt like they were the only people left on earth. The gathering night smelled like cardamon and mango, and the air felt silky against his skin.

It was beautiful, but was it enough? Was it how she had imagined it?

She turned back to him, a warm smile lighting up her heart-shaped face. 'It's perfect,' she said, stepping forward to press herself against him. She felt tiny and insubstantial in his arms, like she was already gone, and he blinked quickly as he breathed in the fruity smell of her skin so she wouldn't see how the thought had affected him.

'And so is this.' She pulled back and indicated the set-up he had prepared – the two swags, made from the thickest, cosiest quilts he had been able to find. He had sprinkled them with rose petals the children had helped him gather, and laid them out close to a healthy fire.

'Great fire,' she said, shivering and stepping closer to it.

He bit his lip to stop himself from asking if she was cold, if she needed another jacket, if they should get into the swags, whether they should go back.

He shrugged. 'What can I say? Boy scout for eight years.' He laughed as he said it, but he was glad she noticed. What the hell was it about being a man that you still drew a certain prehistoric pleasure from knowing you could build a great big hot fire to warm your hearth and protect your family? Screw evolution, screw civilisation. Little in life was more satisfying than stoking a raging bunch of flames from an assembly of sticks and leaves. And this one certainly looked impressive. Spewing from a sturdy tepee of branches and sticks, it leapt wildly but with a certain satisfying symmetry that told him there was no danger of it breaching its confines and swallowing them whole during the night. Or causing a bushfire. But it would last, with some feeding, until morning came, and do its job of warming their skin.

'My hero,' she said, and she looked so perfect caught in the firelight that he could almost forget her frailty, the rings under her eyes, the pallor of her skin. He could just let it all melt away into the orange glow and focus instead on those big brown eyes that saw through him and into him and somehow beyond him, and on the way the curve of her face tugged at his heart, and how the slope of her neck reminded him of some graceful creature you might find out in a forest like this. Out here, away from the harsh light of day and the unforgiving glare of electric lights, he might imagine that Poppy was okay; just a slight, graceful girl. She might just be his new wife; not his terribly sick wife. He might forget.

It took him a second to realise that she was looking at him equally intently. 'Don't think about it,' she said, and her voice was full of command. 'I forbid it.'

He dragged a smirk onto his face, even though it felt prickly and unnatural. 'Think about what?' He wrapped an arm around her waist and pulled her against him, swooping her up into his arms. 'Stop yapping, you,' he murmured into her neck. 'Time to be carried over the threshold.'

He stepped around the fire carefully, to the side of their camping spot that faced away from the valley. She hadn't seen this part of his preparations yet. At the back of the fire, he had laid a neat line of long sticks, and erected a sign that, again, the children had helped him with. It stood atop a neat picket and read, in careful rainbow colours, 'The Threshold'.

He almost lost his focus as he remembered Jonti, Julia's little friend, studying the sign carefully and asking him what it meant. As Quentin had tried to explain both the word and the tradition, Jonti had replied in that precise, serious way of his: 'I know what threshold means; a portal to another state.'

It had seemed weird but cute at the time. Now, suddenly, the words came back to him and the innocent gimmick seemed somehow sinister. Quentin didn't want any portals to any other states, not yet. Since Poppy had become sick he had found himself uncharacteristically, desperately superstitious, and in that moment he wanted to tear up the sign the children had made so lovingly, and stomp it into the ground. He remembered how they had all looked at him so expectantly, eager that he approved of their handiwork.

He swallowed convulsively and remembered what Julia had said about tradition, beating back the black superstition that had taken hold in his heart; the horrible thought from the same prehistoric part of his brain that had revelled in building the fire. But the thought didn't want to go; it wanted to take root and spread, cancer-like, until it was all he could think about. What if there was no turning back, if they crossed this threshold on this night? What if, by crossing it, they were going from being near the end to ushering the next phase, the very end, somehow closer?

Poppy squealed as she saw the clumsy sign. 'Oh my god, oh my god,' she squeaked from the warm safety of his arms. 'Let me down so I can see properly.'

'No,' Quentin snapped, pulling her closer and standing still, unsure if it was because tradition dictated that he carry her across or if it was because he wasn't sure he wanted to go through with it now.

Maybe he could just accidentally on purpose knock the sign over?

Maybe they could skirt it and he could make a joke of it?

The sign suddenly didn't look cute and clever. It looked ominous; a trap into a yawning chasm that might swallow Poppy whole. Cold shivers swept through him and he couldn't move, only cling desperately to the woman in his arms.

Poppy took a deep breath, as if she could somehow divine his fears. 'Getting cold feet?' He could hear the smile in her voice, even though she was pressed against his chest and he was looking at the damn sign. She lifted up her left hand out of the nest of his arms and waggled her ring finger at him. 'Too late, buddy. You bought the wife, you sealed the deal, now you gotta cross the damn threshold.'

She was right, this was ridiculous. There was nothing about stepping over that makeshift line of sticks that could set them on some path they weren't already on. He dragged his body across the line, crunching the sticks mercilessly underfoot as he did so, but he couldn't shake the feeling that his actions had set something in motion. The shivers that skittered up and down his spine took a stronger hold and that prehistoric part of his brain that had somehow been engaged by the building of the fire screamed at him that there was no going back; that something terrible was going to happen here tonight.

He placed Poppy gingerly down on her swag, but as he made to release her she clung on, her hands locked tightly around his neck. 'Don't go,' she whispered, her eyes wide and frightened like she could sense his own bone-deep terror, and it was contagious. 'Lie with me here.'

He smiled, and forced himself out of the funk he was sinking into. This was not the time; this was not the moment to indulge his own maudlin fears, and, worse, infect her with them. This was a moment for celebration; a moment to make memories.

'I'm gonna be right back.' He winked at her before putting her down gently, then vaulting up and going to the pack. He would push through this feeling; it would not take them in this moment. It would not steal their wedding night and Poppy's number twenty. He breathed deeply through his diaphragm like he had learned to do before his very first gigs, when he had still been new and uncertain, and reminded himself that superstition was just that. It belonged in the same place as bottles of dirty holy water. It was a sham, a product of the dark and the fire and Jonti's serious prophesy.

He rifled quickly through the packs and found his prize before hurrying back to Poppy, who had snuggled down into her swag. 'Open up, wife,' he bellowed in what he thought was pretty good caveman. She giggled and flicked the covers open so he could climb in next to her with the goods. Then he sat up slightly.

'Champagne, of course.' He gestured theatrically as he produced two crystal glasses he had tucked into the waistband of his pants.

Poppy gasped. 'Mum's crystal?' Her eyes were wide.

'She never travels without it, apparently,' he said, enjoying the pleasure on her face as he popped the cork and carefully poured two glasses. 'To my beautiful, perfect, singular wife,' he said, handing her one.

She sat up and took it, swallowing visibly. She raised her glass to him and tilted her head. 'To my outrageous, sexy, resourceful husband.'

They clinked and, finally, the demons of superstition that had yowled at him since he had stood poised at that threshold slunk away into the shadows. The tension lifted from his shoulders and he rolled them gratefully.

For now, there was only this: this woman, this moment, this dream of hers, and his, coming true.

Life could be a cruel motherfucker, but it could also give you gifts in ways you never dreamt of, Quentin was learning. And as he looked across at the woman sipping champagne and calling him her husband, he knew that on the balance of all that had happened, he was the luckiest bastard on earth.

'Cheers,' he said, downing the bubbly in one long gulp and hoping its silky potency might send the demons well and truly packing.

'Cheers,' she agreed, doing a similar job on hers. Oh man, he really did like a woman who could drink.

He reached for the bottle where he had propped it beside them, so he could fill their glasses again, but Poppy carefully settled hers on the other side of the swag and then reached back to put a hand on his arm. 'No,' she said, and her pretty face was full of determination.

And something else, something dark and wanton.

'No?' He hesitated. He hadn't thought that this would happen tonight. He hadn't thought about what might happen at all, really. He'd just been glad that they would have some alone time. He knew that Spike would never believe him if he said it, but he hadn't thought for a minute that he might make love to his wife on his wedding night. Poppy had been so unwell the last few days, and sleeping with her had been the last thing on his mind tonight.

'No,' she said firmly, and he left the bottle in its place and slid down into the swag, pulling her close. He buried his face in her neck and breathed in the sweet chocolate and watermelon smells of her. All this time, and he still hadn't managed to work out how her skin smelled that way. She was a mystery to him, and one he never seemed to tire of trying to unravel.

She pulled his head up with her slender hands and kissed him, full and passionately on the mouth. This was no gentle stars-and-moonlight scenario. It wasn't romantic; it wasn't tentative. He could feel it, in the pressure of her lips and the pull of her body. She wanted him, and she wanted him the way they had always taken each other – with joy and pleasure. Abandon. But could he do it? What if he hurt her? She had never been this frail.

She must have felt the hesitation coiled into his muscles as he kissed her back, enjoying the sweetness of her but trying with all his might not to let muscle memory take over and his desire have its head. She pulled away and sat up, commanding him with a swift tug to do the same. Then she gestured over the valley before them, the fire in the foreground, the stars seeming to crowd them as the hill gave way to the valley; the lights of the village far below twinkling like fireflies. 'This is perfect,' she murmured, looking intensely into his eyes. 'You are perfect. And

I want nothing more right now than to make love to you, my husband.'

He hesitated, and she eyeballed him harshly and pulled her trump card from the deck. 'What if it's the last time I can?'

Like a bucket of cold water, her words sobered Quentin in an instant. Of course he wanted to make love to her. It was all he had ever wanted, from the first time he had seen her in that damn line at the cafeteria. This girl and her quirky smile, her young Anjelica Huston vibe; that sexy challenge in her eyes. But could he even do it now, with that dark prediction ringing in his ears? Damn it, did she not know that such pressure could seriously throw a man off his game? And if anything was going to do so, it was going to be the thought that whatever happened now, it might be the last time it ever happened with the woman you loved more than you loved anything – more than you loved your band; more than you loved your favourite Stratocaster; more than you loved your own life.

Oh dear Lord, what if he tried and he couldn't?

He knew it was the worst of all things to think, because down that doubtful path lay an insidious catch-22 trap, but he didn't seem able to contain his thinking tonight.

He wrapped her in his arms and begged his body, which had been his good friend during his whole twenty-two years, not to let him down. He reminded it that it had managed to perform drunk, and high, and shattered to the bone. It had done its thing with groupies and cheerleaders and all manner of questionable women. And he reminded it that it had never met a woman who had been able to turn him on with a single look the way this one did. Less than a look. The sight of this woman's slender back, walking away from him, could set his pulse racing. And now she was his and this was their night and he could not, would not, fuck this up because he was getting cold feet about whether he might be able to perform.

He had to let go and trust in the force, as Obi-Wan would say.

And so he kissed her. He kissed her long and deep and with all the yearning he had felt for this woman from that first moment. He kissed her sweet and wild and hoped that his body would remember, and catch up, and not let him down.

He didn't have to hope for long. As soon as he wrapped her in his arms and let himself go, his body remembered.

And so did hers. As fragile as she was, she responded to him like she always had. She kissed him with a ferocity he had never felt in her, or anyone else, before. Her face was incandescent in the firelight as she rolled on top of him, somehow managing to have divested herself of her clothes.

Naked, and sitting astride him, she was so perfect it hurt his eyes.

The intricate patterns hennaed onto her scalp and forehead lent her an other-worldly gypsy look that exactly suited the way he had always felt about her. She had bewitched him from the start, and now, sitting on top of him, flames playing across the exposed skin of her chest, light playing over the scar she hated so much, her eyes ablaze with love and longing, he knew it. She was a witch, and she had cast a spell on him, and no matter what happened after this, he would never be the same again.

He leaned forward and grabbed her, pulling her down onto him for more kisses, wondering how long he could stand the press of her body against his groin before he slid into her, knowing it was the only thing he wanted to do right now.

Almost.

He pulled back and looked up into her eyes as she sat across him, her shoulders square, her face bright with the knowledge of the desire that pulsed between them.

'I love you,' he whispered, and his voice came out hoarse and low. Not right. 'I love you,' he said again, this time so loud and clear it rang through the clearing. 'You are the love of my life, my beautiful wife.' As he said the words, he felt tears start to well at the back of his eyes at the thought of just how true the statement was. He loved her so much, and this one, perfect instant might be all they ever had. Tears stung his eyes as he tried desperately to blink them away and cursed himself. He should have shut up, left well enough alone. She would hate this; she would hate seeing him sad like this.

But she smiled at him, and put a finger to his lips. 'Shh,' she said, stroking his bottom lip sensuously. 'I know.' Then she slid down onto him and started to move against him in the firelight. 'Can you feel me?'

He nodded, not trusting himself to speak again. He could feel her – her body and her heart and the beautiful perfection of her brain – knowing him, feeling close to him, wanting him.

'Then you know,' she whispered, leaning down and pressing her chest against his as she pushed him deeper into her. Her breath caught as he went deep inside her and he hesitated before she moved harder against him, refusing to let him go carefully with her. 'Then you know how much I love you, too.'

He nodded.

'How much I want you.'

He nodded again, the tears threatening to spill onto his cheeks.

'How you are the best thing that has ever happened to me.'

He put his hands on her hips and pushed himself deeply into her. Nothing he had ever felt had been this intense. It was almost unbearable. He wanted it never to end, and at the same time he wasn't sure if he could take much more.

As he watched her let go, wild and free and full of life, his heart grew so big in his chest he wasn't sure he could endure it.

'I know,' he said, reaching up to cup her face, full of the need to feel her skin and stay connected to her. 'I really know.'

And they let go together, and Quentin was no longer capable of coherent thought. He just dissolved into the sensations of Poppy – her mouth, her skin, and the way she lit him up from the inside in a way that was entirely new to him.

Later, she snuggled against him, and he could almost hear her purring as they both started to drift into sleep.

She turned her head close to him, whispering in his ear, 'There's something else I need to tell you.'

Really? Right now? Quentin wasn't sure he could concentrate on much beyond the feel of her skin and the sensations of his body recovering from the pleasure they'd taken.

She laughed, as though she knew what he was thinking, and tried to move back. He dragged her closer; there was no way she was getting away.

'Shoot.'

'Remember I told you what I was worried about, how I wanted two things from the time at Dharamsala?'

Quentin nodded, his brain racing. 'About your mum?'

She nodded encouragingly. 'And what else?'

Oh no, not that. He didn't want to think about that now. He had thought about it so many times. Couldn't she just leave him this one second, when he didn't have to think about that?

'About the end,' he said, knowing his voice sounded flat and petulant.

She nodded against his shoulder. 'I was worried about what I would think about, when the time came.' Her voice became husky and he cradled her tenderly against him, wanting her to stop, but also glad she was talking to him about it. They never spoke of this stuff.

He waited, but she said nothing. 'And?'

'And now I know,' she said, and she didn't sound sad, or worried. She sounded happy. At peace.

'Do I need to ask?'

'Nope.' She laughed. Then she sat up, allowing him to see her face properly in the firelight. 'That instant.' She swept her hands around the scene. 'This place. You.'

'The best sex of your life,' Quentin said, grinning in a way he hoped was adorable.

'Now don't get ahead of yourself,' she joked back.

He must have looked stricken, because she laughed and snuggled against him once more. 'All of it,' she said, breathing deeply in a way he now knew well; the way she did just before she dropped off to sleep. 'The sex, the moment, the sleeping outdoors.' She paused. 'But most of all, you. Loving me.' She paused again. 'And crying.'

'I was not crying,' he objected.

She laughed again and he could feel her happiness like it was alive. 'Okay, caveman,' she agreed, punching his stomach lightly. 'You didn't cry.' She sighed and settled into him. 'But you sure did look beautiful.'

* * *

Quentin rolled onto his side and felt the first rays of the sun warming his cheek. He nuzzled into Poppy's neck, reflecting that neither of them had slept so well or so long in weeks. As he did, his half-awake brain registered a problem. As he dragged himself out of the deep well of sleep he had fallen into, the dark, nasty feeling from the night before, the one he had felt thinking about Jonti's words, took hold again. *A portal into another state.*

Poppy was cold, and her breathing was shallow.

He sat up and looked at her. She was even paler than she had been yesterday, and she looked like she was barely alive. He shook her roughly. She groaned lightly but didn't rouse.

'Poppy, Poppy.' He started softly, but when she didn't respond he began yelling.

Nothing.

He bundled her into his arms and ran down the hill, his heart racing, kicking the fucking threshold sign over as he went.

Chapter Sixteen

'Oh my god,' Poppy murmured as she looked out over the flat landscape of Paris from the tiny balcony of their shoebox apartment in Montmartre. 'This is so perfect. It's exactly how I pictured it.'

Julia nodded. A clear dusk blanketed grand avenues and tiny cobblestone alleys alike, so crisp Julia felt like she could reach out and crinkle it in her hand like cellophane. The Eiffel Tower rose like a giant erection in the middle of it all – a modern iron phallus out of place amid the subtle majesty of aged sandstone and ancient architecture.

Lights started to wink all the way up its framework and outline the sweeping boulevards. Soon night would claim the city and another page would be ripped from Poppy's life.

From behind them Ten passed Julia a wrap and she threw it around Poppy's shoulders. The evening air held a real nip and thankfully Poppy didn't protest. She just snuggled in, resting her beanie-covered head against Julia's shoulder, as she continued to absorb the grandeur in awed silence. The hilly, haphazard clutter of Montmartre surrounding them was in stark contrast to the wider city fanning out before them.

Julia put her arm around Poppy's shoulders and hugged her closer. The scare she'd given them two days ago in India was still fresh in everyone's minds.

By the time Ten had arrived back at the village, Poppy had revived somewhat, but her weakness had been marked. Ten had been terrified that the end had come and Julia hadn't been that far behind.

Yes, Poppy was dying. But in all of the ways Julia had pictured Poppy's last moments (and that nightmare ran on an almost continuous loop through her head), none of them had been in a mountain village in India far away from world-class medical facilities. India might have had sacred water, but Julia knew they were going to need drugs to get her through the end – the seriously good kind – and a health-care system that was capable of delivering them any damn time they wanted.

Julia had suggested that it was time to go home – it had always been their intention to return to Australia for Poppy's last days. But Poppy had insisted that she was fine, that they go on to Paris. That she *needed* to see Paris. *Had* to see the Eiffel Tower before she died.

So … they'd come to Paris.

'Are you ready for tomorrow?' Julia asked.

'Am I ready to take my clothes off in front of a bunch of strangers and let them draw me? Sure.'

Julia could hear the low hint of amusement in her friend's voice but it didn't stop her from shuddering at the thought. Her internal critic would never let her be so free. Her internal critic would run something like this.

Don't lie like that, Julia, your left side is better. Arms above your head, Julia, makes your giant boobs look perkier. Suck in your belly, Julia. Should have done more sit-ups, Julia. And invested in that hideously expensive cellulite cream. But they test it on animals. Who freaking cares if it works? OMG, why didn't you wax, Julia?

Julia shuddered again. 'You're a braver woman than I am, Poppy Devine.'

Poppy turned her head. 'I'm dying, Julia.' She smiled gently. 'Naked's nothing compared to that.' She looked back at the view. 'It's all just skin.'

Julia blinked back the tears. 'Way to pull the dying card, Pop,' she said, forcing a lightness into her voice.

'Keeping it real right to the end, that's me,' Poppy quipped.

Maybe. But to hear her friend being so matter-of-fact was awful. Poppy seemed to have come to some kind of acceptance, while Julia was still fighting the inevitable.

Not to mention the fact that if their positions had been reversed Julia was pretty damn certain that her vanity wouldn't allow even the approaching spectre of death as an excuse to get her kit off in front of a room full of strangers.

Well, not all strangers. She'd be there. And Ten. And bloody fucking Scarlett.

'About that,' Julia said, seeing an opening she'd been trying to create for the last two days now. 'About the … end.'

Poppy turned to her, one bony hand on the railing near Julia's, the other clutching the edges of the wrap and bunching it together at her throat. 'What about it?'

She looked at Julia with purpose, as if she'd been waiting for this very conversation. A dog barked in the distance and the rattle of nearby traffic wafted up to them. 'Ten mentioned that you … didn't want anybody there with you … at the end.'

Poppy nodded calmly. 'That's right.'

Julia sucked in a breath. She'd been hoping that Poppy would deny it. Or look at her and say, 'It's okay, I've changed my mind.' But she didn't look like she was going to do either anytime soon.

'I don't … understand why you want to be alone,' Julia said. 'I can't bear the thought that you might … that you might be scared or—'

'It's okay.' Poppy lifted her hand off the railing and smoothed it over Julia's. 'I won't be. I know what I'm going to think about in those last moments. It'll be okay.' She squeezed Julia's hand. 'I promise.'

'Poppy … I don't think you've thought this through properly.'

Poppy glanced at her with reproach. She sighed. 'This is my fault. You've always mothered me and I've let you because it was nice to have someone looking out for me for a change, but I'm all grown up now, Juju. And I've been thinking things through properly for a long time. *You're* the one who's been telling me I think things through *too* much.'

Julia nodded. *Guilty as charged.* 'So why suddenly listen to me? Why make such a snap decision without talking to us about it first?'

Julia didn't even realise at first that she'd said *us*. And even if she had realised she wouldn't have retracted it. Since their mountain-top argument she and Ten had been in this together.

'A snap decision?' Poppy laughed. She got that crinkle between her eyes that told Julia she was not pleased, but she laughed anyway.

Just like Poppy to not even get mad when they were discussing her death.

'You don't think I've thought about the fact that I'm going to die and how I want that to happen in great depth?' she asked calmly. 'You don't think I've played out the million and one different incarnations of that in my head?'

Julia shut her eyes. *It did seem very unlike Poppy.* And hell, she'd give her soul to not be having this conversation, but Julia was pretty damn sure she knew why Poppy had made her decision and she couldn't let it go unchallenged. 'I think you're doing this to save *us* the gut-wrenching heartache of watching you take your last breath.'

Even now the back of Julia's eyes burned just mentioning it out loud.

Poppy's gaze didn't waver from hers. 'You think that's wrong of me? You want to watch me die, Julia? *Really?*'

A tear trekked down Julia's cheek, hot against her cool skin. 'No. I'd sooner gouge out my eyes. I want to watch you *live*, Poppy. I want to watch you *grow old*. But we're not going to get that luxury. You think it's going to suck any less sitting outside your door?'

'Yeah … I do.'

Julia blinked back more tears.

How could she really believe that?

'You're wrong.'

'You were the one who told me that no-one could tell me what to do with my life. That I was in charge. Surely that goes for my death, too?'

Julia shook her head back and forth. No, damn it. *No.* 'No.'

'Julia … I thought *you'd* understand that?'

Julia fought the huge welling of emotion in her chest. The kind that brought forth big, ugly, snotty tears. The kind that once you let it out, it didn't stop. The kind that made articulation impossible.

'Part of me does.' Julia struggled with the emotional tornado raging inside her, struggled to find the right words, knowing that she could sway Poppy with sound argument and reasoned debate.

Knowing she could *always* sway Poppy with sound argument and reasoned debate.

'But this is not a normal situation and, like it or not, it doesn't just involve you. This is not a decision you can make without at least talking it over with the people who are most affected.'

There was reproach on Poppy's face again. 'So I don't get to be selfish? Not even in this?'

No. Julia shut her eyes against the censure in Poppy's. *Especially not this.*

'I'm asking you to see this from my side. From Ten's side. From Scarlett's.'

Poppy sighed. 'Tell me why you want to be there.'

'Because I can't bear the thought of you all alone at the end. It's like a knife in my heart. I want you to be surrounded by love. By the people who love you.'

'Oh, Julia,' Poppy murmured, lifting her hand to cradle Julia's cheek. 'You think I'll forget that you guys love me?'

Julia placed her hand over Poppy's, aware of each bone and knuckle, aware of its coolness, its dryness, aware that her friend was slowly slipping away.

'No, I don't think you'll forget. I think you'll be unconscious. In a state where there are no thoughts, where you won't *know* or be able to *articulate* anything. But you just might be able to hear us telling you that we love you and be able to feel us touching you. I want you to *feel* our love pressing around you, pressing in on you when you go wherever the hell people go when they ...'

Julia didn't even know how to phrase it – every word she could think of sounded worse than 'die'. In the end she didn't even try. 'I want our touch, our voices and *our love* to be with you right at the end when nothing else can be.'

Julia watched Poppy's face, saw the tremble of her mouth and the shine of tears in her big brown eyes. Saw a hundred different emotions flit across her face and watched as she blinked the tears away and reined her emotions in. 'That's very sweet, but I'm … asking this of you. Please.'

'Don't. Please don't ask that of me.' *Ask me anything else, just not this.* 'Wasn't Ten enough?' she murmured, desperate for anything to distract Poppy from her request.

Poppy laughed and for a moment Julia thought she might relent, but that determined chin jut was still there when the laughter faded and Julia knew what she had to do next.

'If it's me …' She took a deep, wobbly breath, the mere thought enough to suck every oxygen molecule from her lungs. 'If you don't want *me* there … if you want it to be Ten … that's fine … really.' Julia removed Poppy's hand from her cheek and placed a kiss against her palm before she interlinked their fingers and drew Poppy's hand against her chest. 'Just not alone, Pop, please don't do this alone.'

'Julia, no.' Poppy squeezed her hand. 'This isn't about excluding you. Really, it's not. It's something I need to do alone.'

She took a step forward and lay her head against Julia's chest, her cheek resting near their intertwined hands. Julia wrapped her arm around Poppy's slight shoulders and hugged her close, letting the tears fall unchecked. It wasn't right to feel so much heartbreak in one of the world's most beautiful cities.

'You'll understand … one day – hopefully a long time from now.' Poppy's voice was muffled, but Julia heard every heartbreaking word. 'In the meantime, I hope you can forgive me.'

Julia swallowed against the huge lump of hurt lodged in her throat.

She hoped so, too.

* * *

At ten the following morning, with an easel in front of her, Julia's heart was practically in her mouth as Madam Dubois stood at the front of the life-art class and spoke to her dozen students in French. It had taken Julia days when this trip had first become a reality to find the right studio for Poppy. They were on the second floor of a whitewashed building in the middle of a warren of picture-perfect, narrow cobblestoned alleys, and it had cost her a bomb to convince Madam Dubois that her request was genuine, not some giggle-fest to fill their tourist card.

Poppy was going to get her life-art class and Madam Dubois got an unusual subject for her students to draw. Along with enough money to see her through several long, cold, hard winters should the peasants ever revolt again.

Ten was standing on one side of Julia, drumming his fingers against his thighs, his nervousness rolling off him in waves as he stared at the empty velvet chaise lounge behind Madam Dubois as if it was the rack. Scarlett, on the other side of her, sat perched on her stool, looking as Parisienne as possible in her black pants, blue horizontally striped skivvy and a beret, her charcoal stick poised to go.

In excellent English, Madam Dubois turned to the few non-French artists and said, 'Today we welcome a very special subject to our midst. Pop-pee Dee-vine—'

The accent on Poppy's name made Julia want to smile and say *awww*. It sounded so freaking *French*. Unfortunately, it didn't override her overwhelming desire to throw up.

'Pop-pee has terminal breast cancer and it is one of her last wishes that she sit for a life-art class.'

A gasp, similar to the one that had run around the room a minute earlier, rang out. A muscle jumped in Ten's jaw and he drummed faster.

'So you'll notice that—'

Madam Dubois prattled on about the opportunity to draw a different style of body, a *ravaged* one, and Julia zoned out. She couldn't bear to listen to Poppy being talked about as *a subject*.

Exhibit A – a dying woman, a *ravaged* woman, with one breast.

She knew that's how these classes were approached. That it wasn't about the giggles or drawing naughty pictures, but about the human body as an art form. About muscles and veins and sinews. That the *subject* was looked upon as art. It was only the outside that mattered – not the story of the person beneath.

Behind Madam's head, Julia could make out the Eiffel Tower through the wooden slats of the window shutter just above the chaise. She suddenly wished they were doing that today and not tomorrow. She wasn't sure she was ready for Poppy to strip off her clothes and lie there as *the subject*, while everybody turned their heads from side to side, inspecting her body and the way the light fell across it to find *the art* without knowing what lived and breathed and pulsed behind the art to make *the woman*.

Even though she knew that was *exactly* why Poppy wanted to do it, why she was more determined to do it now than ever. Last night when Ten had asked her (again) if she was sure, had told her none of them would think less of her if she backed out, she'd simply said, 'I want to do it.'

When he'd asked why she'd said, 'Because people look at me and then look away immediately. I feel like I don't exist anymore because people don't know how to cope with me looking like this, with my … mortality hanging over me like a black cloud.

I feel invisible. I want to be *looked* at. I want to be studied not because I'm dying but because I'm *living*. Because the human body is art – even mine. I want somebody to find the beauty left in my body, not just see cancer and death, or some … failed medical experiment.'

Julia had felt about a foot high after that. How often had she looked at Poppy these last months and the cancer had been all she'd been able to see? Her friend – *Poppy* – had got lost amid all the grief and fear.

'If she says *ravaged* one more fucking time I'm going to deck her,' Ten growled, all low and rumbly.

Julia blinked, coming out of her reverie, tuning in to Madam Dubois once again.

'And don't forget – bodies are beautiful. I usually urge my students to remember to see the pain as well as the beauty, the struggle as well as the spoils. But today I am going to remind you all to see the beauty as well as the pain. Okay?'

Everyone nodded and Julia thought Ten was going to break a finger or two; he was drumming so fiercely now it could be practically heard reverberating throughout the small studio area. The drumming made her think about Spike and for a crazy second she wished he was here.

'Pop-pee? Pop-pee Dee-vine? We are ready for you now.' Madam Dubois' accent and girlish lilt gave Poppy's name a musical quality that reminded Julia of the kids in India.

She held her breath as Poppy emerged from another room off to the side, where she'd been waiting for the last fifteen minutes. She was dressed in a silky gown, and although there wasn't the same gasp as when Madam had announced Poppy's terminal cancer status, the reaction around the room to Poppy's bald, tattooed head and slight frame was palpable.

But Poppy didn't seem to notice, or at least she pretended not to as she marched straight up to the chaise and smiled at Madam Dubois.

'Are you ready?'

Poppy nodded. 'I am.'

Madam Dubois nodded briskly, too, obviously approving of Poppy's commitment. 'Take off the gown and lie back on the chaise.'

'How do you want me to lie on it?'

'However you are most comfortable, *ma cherie.* You will need to hold the pose for some time.'

And then with one shrug of her shoulders, Poppy was standing before them all completely naked. 'Fuck,' Ten muttered under his breath, his knuckles whitening as his drumming fingers curled into fists by his side.

Julia knew exactly how he felt. Poppy looked pale and smooth and yes, ravaged, as she arranged herself on the lounge, seemingly oblivious to her audience. Julia wanted to rush down the front, pick up the gown, wrap Poppy up in it and tell everyone to keep their freaking eyes to themselves. She wasn't some exhibit. Some *art.*

She was Poppy and she was theirs.

Madam Dubois opened the shutters behind Poppy, taking care to leave the glass shut – the studio was wonderfully warm but outside the temperature had barely struggled to double figures despite the cloudless day. The last thing Poppy needed was cold air freezing her bits and pieces. Light flooded in, bathing the chaise and Poppy in bright autumn sunshine.

Poppy finally came to rest half on her back, half on her side. Her hips were tilted on the side, her buttocks supported by the back of the chaise. Her top arm lay along the length of her body, her elbow lying in the natural dip of her waist, her hand resting on her hip. Her bottom arm was above her head, bent at the elbow, her palm cupping her nape, her paltry bicep forming a slight pillow for her cheek.

Her right breast, pulled high from her arm position, sat perkily on her chest, the pale mocha nipple erect despite the warmth of the room. The scar where her left breast had been was light pink now.

'Okay, Pop-pee, are you comfortable?'

'Yes. Thank you.'

Madam Dubois nodded approvingly again, then said something in French before saying, 'You may begin,' in English to the non-French speakers.

Scarlett started straightaway, but Julia didn't know if she could. Neither, apparently, did Ten, who just stood there looking at his wife, misery and pride in every line of his body.

'You're beautiful,' he mouthed to her and she shot him a smile that said a thousand things in one slight uplift of the mouth. *I'm fine and I'm alive right now and I love you and* I want this, *so pick up your damn charcoal already.*

That smile would certainly have given the Mona Lisa a run for her money.

So they both did as she had asked. They picked up their charcoal and they started drawing as Madam Dubois did her rounds, stopping to make comments with her students, usually in French.

Despite her flair for style and colour, Julia hadn't been that enamoured with art at school. She'd been quite good at it but had hated being constrained to what the curriculum required and had basically ditched the subject the second she'd been allowed. It was why *paint something* had been one of the few items on her bucket list, because she'd known that she had it in her, that deep down there was an artist ready to bust out. She'd just never really found a subject worth painting before.

Until today.

And if anybody had ever told her that this day would come and she would be engrossed and absorbed in sketching her naked, not-long-for-this-world best friend, she'd have scoffed in that truly cutting way she'd learned at the feet of her mother.

As much as part of her rebelled at being a party to this somewhat macabre last-dying-wish thing, the other part of her, the emerging artist, revelled in the challenge. Maybe it was the way the sunlight transformed Poppy, giving her an ethereal glow, or maybe it was because she wasn't seeing Poppy the subject of a life-art class, or even the cancer; she was seeing Poppy, her best friend stripped bare. All the life and warmth and shared memories stared back at her through Poppy's lovely brown eyes and satisfied, pensive expression.

She could see their first day together at school, their conversations whispered into the night long after lights out.

The holiday at Byron Bay, climbing the lighthouse and dancing on the beach.

The day Julia had lost her virginity – to the gardener's son, who her mother had said would never be any good at anything. She'd been wrong about that: he'd been surprisingly good at some things.

Poppy's first kiss. And then two years and countless compatibility tests later, the day she'd lost her virginity.

The night they'd both got pissed on Julia's mother's bottle of cherry schnapps and they'd drunk-dialled the school pretending to be Scarlett and told the headmistress they were all running away to the circus together.

Poppy walking across the stage at her university graduation.

Even that day all those months ago now when they'd sat on those hard, awful chairs at the hospital in blissful ignorance of what was to come and could laugh about the horrible decor and the orderly who spoke to Julia's breasts.

All of their life experiences – the good, the bad and the *downright freaking ugly* – flowed through Julia's fingers to the paper.

Two hours later, Madam Dubois called everyone to order, urging them to stop, telling them the day's session was over. She thanked Poppy, who pulled on her gown.

'Jules? Are you okay?'

Julia looked at Ten, surprised to find their time was up and that her cheeks were wet. She nodded as she used the back of her hand to wipe away the tears. 'I think it's … catharsis.'

Ten nodded, too, understanding as only he could. 'It's really good,' he said, indicating Julia's easel.

She looked at it then – as a whole. As a picture. Not as an emotional collage of their combined past or a representation of their friendship and love.

As a piece of art.

And Ten was right. It was good. It was really good. It had captured the *essence* of Poppy. The way she was physically now, her thinness, her bald head, her mutilated chest, but also the spirit of the person she was underneath the prominent bones and the murderous disease desolating her body.

She glanced at Poppy, and Poppy gave her a dreamy smile. 'Thank you,' she mouthed at her friend and Poppy nodded, not needing an explanation, as if she knew that Julia had needed this as much as she did.

Julia looked back at the drawing and knew that whatever happened and wherever she went in the world, this would always go with her. Her parents owned a Picasso, but it had nothing on this. This was a work of the heart and it would always be her most prized possession.

Then she looked over at Ten's sketch. It was wildly different but equally compelling. All long, sweeping lines, more soft focus and utterly feminine – capturing Poppy's ethereal quality. A portrait of a lover.

Scarlett's was more about the details. The intricate pattern of henna on Poppy's head, the brilliance of her eyes, the smile so perfect and right. A mother cataloguing her love.

They were all masterpieces, and Julia knew then, as she took them all in, that Poppy had given each of them the most remarkable gift.

* * *

Later that afternoon, they sat around their tiny Montmartre apartment admiring their handiwork while Paris bustled about outside. Tomorrow was another big day – getting to the top of the Eifel Tower – but for now they were happy to rest on their laurels.

'I love them all,' Poppy murmured, beaming at the results as she sat snuggled in Ten's lap on the couch opposite the wall where the sketches had been placed for easy admiration. 'You're all brilliant.'

'We had an easy subject,' Ten teased.

'I'm *so* glad I did this.' Poppy looked at Julia and her mother. 'That *we* did this.'

'So am I,' Julia smiled, reaching out her hand and linking her fingers with Poppy's.

It should have been weird all sitting there with Poppy gazing at nude drawings they'd sketched of her, but it wasn't. Strangely, it seemed like the most natural thing in the world.

Poppy dropped Julia's hand and eased off Ten's lap and wandered over to the charcoal sketches. She strolled back and forth, taking them all in before stopping in front of Julia's and crouching. She picked it up and studied it for the longest time and Julia's heart almost faltered at the constant flicker of emotions across Poppy's face, like a movie reel from the past.

She stood slowly and glanced at Julia. Something shifted in her face. She paused like she was weighing something up. Something big.

'I've changed my mind,' she said, the drawing still in hand. 'I want you there. At the end.' She looked at Ten and her mother. 'I want you all there with all this—' she stared down at the drawing '—love surrounding me.'

Julia's gaze flew to Ten, then back to Poppy. She sat forward. 'Really?'

Poppy nodded, smiling through eyes glistening with tears. 'There is so much love here. How can I not want this around me when I'm going to need it most? I was trying to make it easier for you, but … how can I shut you out of this? From the moment we met we've shared everything. I've shared my whole life with you – it's right here,' she pointed at the drawing, 'in this amazing sketch. And I know it's not going to be easy to share my death, but … I need you there at the end.'

Julia held her breath, and she could feel Ten and Scarlett doing the same as they sat beside her on the couch, too afraid to say anything and somehow bugger up their luck.

'I need you *all* there.'

Julia and Ten were on their feet at exactly the same time. Ten took three paces and crushed Poppy to him. Julia reached them both a second later.

'Thank you,' Ten muttered over and over, putting his arm around Julia as she joined them.

Julia had no words, she just broke down and cried. She'd been invited to witness the most intimate experience of human existence.

An invitation she had craved and demanded.

She hated it already.

* * *

A commotion woke Julia at five the next morning. Her head felt woolly from crying herself to sleep and her body clock being well and truly screwed from multiple time zones in the last few weeks.

'Help! Julia, for fuck's sake, get in here now!'

Julia sat bolt upright at Ten's insistent bellow, stumbling through the dark apartment on automatic pilot to the room next door, Scarlett's sudden loud wail spurring her on. The light stabbed into her eyes as she flew into the room and she squinted against it, but she could still see what the problem was.

Poppy's frail body shuddered and shook, her arms and legs flailing around in grand, rhythmic movements. Saliva frothed out of her mouth, and a wet patch on her silky pyjamas indicated she'd been incontinent. Ten was trying to cradle her head in his lap as tears streamed down his face.

'Please don't die now, baby,' he said. 'We've got the Eiffel Tower to go. You've always wanted to see the tower, remember? Please don't die.'

'I'll call an ambulance,' Scarlett said.

Julia nodded, her heart belting along like a runaway train. She was so frightened she could barely think, but she did know one thing for sure – they wouldn't be going to the Eiffel Tower today.

Or any day.

Poppy was at the end. If she got through this, they were going home.

Chapter Seventeen

Two weeks later and back on home turf, nothing made sense like it should. Her organs are shutting down. What did that even mean?

Things shut down. Things like computers, and shops on public holidays. Not people. Not people who brimmed with life and love and outrage. Not Poppy.

Quentin ran his finger along the crisp white edge of the sheet, caressing the hem between his thumb and forefinger, the rhythmic motion the only sane thing in his world right now. The sheet, and the sound of Poppy's oxygen flowing into her nose. Contrived, but comfortingly regular. One of Poppy's slender, pale hands rested on the edge of the bed near where he was ministering to the sheet. He rubbed his long brown thumb across it, wondering if she could feel the callused scraping. His thumb traced one of the green-blue veins of her wrist and followed it up her arm towards the place it creased delicately in the middle.

As a child, Quentin had hated looking at or thinking about his veins. The idea that his life force rested on those fragile pathways made him nauseous. Even now, he wasn't wild about injections or blood tests. And it wasn't because he was scared of blood; it was because he hated coming face to face with evidence of his own precarious mortality.

But right now those veins looked good to him. They – along with the light pulse that he could feel at Poppy's wrist when he lay his thumb there – were evidence that Poppy continued to live. She was still in the game.

Her organs had not shut down yet. But the thought that they would – that they were doing so – made him want to yell with rage; a brittle bellow that prickled in his stomach and clawed its way up to his throat.

If her organs were shutting down, if the white-coated fuckers knew that, why couldn't they stop it?

They had all those machines. The one that tracked her heart rate. The one that monitored her oxygen saturations. Where was the one they really needed – the stopping-the-organs-from-shutting-down machine? The starting-up-the-organs machine?

Quentin looked at her hand. The palm. The wrist. The arm. Because he couldn't look at her face. It was so thin now, and the nasal prongs that had done their work for her for the last two days seemed monstrous, distorting the heart-shaped outline of her face. He was scared that he wouldn't be able to see her the same way again when they took them off, as they had said they would, at the end. After two days of looking at her with those prongs, he feared he would never be able to picture her face without them again.

He put his face to her palm and breathed in. Even here, in this place of death, she still smelled liked Poppy, somehow magically like chocolate and watermelon, even above all the competing smells of the hospice – disinfectant, medicine, despair.

And he had never known, or loved, anyone like her.

And he never wanted to again.

A soft noise from behind startled him and he pulled his head up from Poppy's palm. The squeeze at his shoulder belonged to Julia; it was her usual brisk touch, part pat, part crippling pinch.

'How's she doing?'

'The same.' His voice was low and flat.

'You been talking to her?'

Quentin had watched Julia through all of her phases of grief over Poppy and he had to admit that her current coping approach was the toughest to take. She was so damn fake-jovial that he wanted to stand up and wring her neck.

'Of course,' he bit out.

'Because you know they said she can hear us. Even though she's slipping in and out of it. So she knows we're here for her.'

'I know,' he snapped. 'I was also there when they said it. Remember?'

'Okay, pet,' Julia soothed him. 'Keep your knickers on.'

Quentin stood and pushed back his chair, hooking his thumb towards the door of the small room. Julia followed him outside, looking over her shoulder at Poppy as she did.

Quentin leaned against the external wall of the room, facing away from Poppy. He still had enough respect for his wife's awesome, almost magical, powers to suspect she may well know, in some subconscious part of her brain, that he was about to blow his lid at Julia. So he wanted to minimise the chances of her somehow knowing what was going on. As he faced up to the tall redhead, his eyes swept the central corridor of the hospice they had been living in for the last two days, since things had become too arduous for Poppy at home. Initially, they had been in one of the rooms in the central grouping. Now they had been moved to one at the other end, with more frequent monitoring.

They all knew what it meant.

Quentin had worked in a hospital for two years, but he had never been in a hospice before this week. It was a place of intense dedication and abject fucking misery. The jury was still out for him as to whether he wanted to punch or kiss the two doctors who worked every twelve-hour shift with such honest precision. All he knew for sure was that he scowled at them a lot. He couldn't help it. His face just seemed to crease into a pissed-off crump every time one of them said something about pain relief, comfort management, progress of the disease, the treatment plan, or Poppy's bloody fucking organs shutting down.

It wasn't rational, it wasn't fair. He could see how seriously the two men took their jobs, and how good they were. But none of that mattered. They spoke, he scowled, and his fingers coiled into a fist, desperate with the urge to beat the shit out of something. Or, at the very least, scream and curse.

Right now, the object of his rage was Julia.

He scowled at her. 'Just stop with the bonhomie crap, okay?'

She frowned at him and pursed her lips. 'Sorry, Sunshine. You tell me how you would have me handle The End. What kind of approach would be acceptable to you? Should I be crying and gnashing my teeth, making sure Poppy knows, all the way through her fucking coma, that she's letting me down so badly by going and dying when that upsets me so terribly?'

It was a long monologue, and Julia delivered it without drawing breath. When she finished, a flush darkened her cheeks and her eyes were bright. Her lips were still pursed and her hands were on her hips.

Quentin ran his hands through his hair. 'No,' he snapped, placing his hands on the cool wall behind him so he wouldn't reach across and strangle her with them. 'I don't give a shit what you do. Just don't act like she's some child who doesn't know she's dying and we're all on some fucking kindergarten picnic and isn't it so damn neat?' His voice was rising and he noticed the nice young nurse who always spoke so gently to Poppy flicked a concerned glance in their direction. He lowered his voice to a hiss. 'And I don't want you to ask me if I'm talking to her, right? Of course I'm fucking talking to her. Just not all the time. I'm not a talker, you know that. I'm not some damn girl.'

He said the last word with such intensity that he realised as he said it that this was part of the issue. He was surrounded by women, had been for so long now.

Poppy, Julia, bloody Scarlett.

Quentin got women, loved them, always had. In all the right and sometimes very wrong ways. And they usually loved him right back. But right now he wanted permission to be himself, not some girly-approved version of the good guy/rocker husband. He wanted to sit and process, and think, and smash shit and just be with her. These fucking women might not get that, but he knew one thing for sure: Poppy would.

'Poppy would understand.' The words were a snarl, poison from his mouth.

It was a low blow.

Julia's face crumpled as he said it, but she wasn't going down without a fight.

'Don't you fucking tell me what Poppy would understand. I know better than anyone what Poppy would understand. I've known her since forever.' Julia advanced on him, one long finger extended, and he just knew it was for the purpose of poking him in the chest to underline her point. 'Sorry I'm too cheerful for you. Sorry I don't want her to be lonely. Sorry I want to make sure you're not sitting there while I'm off getting coffee, self-indulgently brooding about how sad poor little Quentin is going to be when his beloved Poppy is gone.'

She poked him in the chest on the last sentence and it was a bridge too far.

He grasped her finger in his fist and growled at her. 'You have no idea what I'm feeling or how I'm choosing to manage it. Why don't you just fuck off?' He said the last two words like bullets, wanting them to hit their mark right in the centre of the superior redhead's chest, and wound her the way her words had wounded him. Because she was right, damn her. He was feeling self-piteous. He was sitting there, not knowing what to say, not knowing how to feel, being angry with anyone who came near Poppy, wanting to rip the balls from the doctors, wanting to do anything that would mean he wasn't just waiting around for Poppy to die.

He wanted something to happen. He wanted the waiting over.

He wanted them to take those damn nasal prongs out and wake her up so he could talk to her properly. It had happened so fast when she had started slipping in and out of consciousness. She had been crashing and there had been a buzz of activity and panic. There had been no time for 'goodbye' or 'we're here' or anything else. He wanted the prongs gone, the drip gone, and Poppy awake.

But he also didn't.

Because they'd been pretty clear – that would only happen now once she was gone.

As Quentin clocked the hurt in Julia's eyes, he pushed off the wall, released her finger and made for the door.

'Where the fuck do you think you're going?' Julia was a tower of redhead goddess fury, blocking his path. 'Don't you dare leave. Don't you dare.'

He pushed past her. 'Don't you tell me what to do,' he growled, slamming his palms against the swing doors.

* * *

When he got back, he crept quietly to the door of Poppy's room. Julia was talking softly to Poppy, and Scarlett was knitting on the other side of the bed. The creation in her hands was hideous, some kind of scarf being fashioned from multi-coloured vomit. Scarlett sure liked bright things.

'Ten's just gone to get supplies,' Julia was assuring Poppy, and Quentin smiled to himself. Julia was a crap liar and Poppy would be able to discern the bullshit through a hundred layers of coma. But the lie made him feel softer towards Julia, even if he hadn't already been beating himself black and blue over his harshness at her an hour before. Julia was bossy, and a giant pain in his arse, but she was good.

And she loved Poppy as much as he did. Just differently.

He edged into the room.

To her credit, Julia didn't scream at him, or knee him in the balls. Either of which would have been a completely reasonable response to his boorish fury.

But he felt better now. And it was because of the thing he was carrying in his arms. It was time to face the music.

'I'm sorry, Julia,' he said, moving to take a seat and pull it close to Poppy's bed. He turned to his wife. 'I've been a dick, Poppy,' he explained, taking her hand. 'I wanted to be here and I've fucked it all up. I wanted to kill the doctors, and I was a shit to Julia, and then I pissed off for an hour.'

Scarlett looked at him across the bed, nodding approvingly, and he wondered if there was anything he could say that would shock this woman. He supposed if you ran an orphanage in India you'd seen more of the shitty side of life than most.

A thought landed prickly and terrifying in his brain: what if Poppy had died while he'd been gone? It made him breathless, and he rubbed at his chest.

From the chair beside him, Julia picked up his hand and squeezed it. 'He's right, Pop,' she agreed. 'He has been a dick. I really never got what you see in him.'

Then she squeezed Quentin's hand again and smiled at him. He could see the relief and forgiveness in it as Julia turned back to Poppy. 'I don't know how you could have married such a fucking prima donna. Fucking performers. I tell you what. Take some advice from me. In your next life, marry a nice safe lawyer.' She paused, as though pondering. 'Or an accountant.' She paused again, as if wondering how far to push it. 'With a big dick.' She paused a third time and then tapped the guitar in Quentin's arms. 'Someone who doesn't feel the need to make such a show of everything.'

Quentin squeezed Julia's hand in return, and then dropped it so he could focus on what he wanted to do. The moment the thought had formed in his head he had known it was right. All this uncertainty – what to do, how to be. He knew the cure for that. And the moment he had dashed home to pick up Jerry Hall all the uncertainty had faded away. Why hadn't he thought of it before? Why had he been here for two whole days without the other love of his life to keep him company in these darkest hours? It really was a sign of what a complete mess he was in.

He cleared his throat. 'I'm sure it was the man himself who said something about the good thing about music being that when it hits you, you feel no pain.'

Julia wrinkled her nose. 'Who? Which movie is that from?'

Quentin smiled. 'Not a movie. The man himself. Bob Marley.' He frowned. 'I think.'

Julia smiled back at him, and Scarlett put down her knitting and looked at him expectantly as he fiddled experimentally to tune Jerry and then pulled his chair closer to Poppy, brushing his fringe out of his eyes.

He started the familiar, dark and broody chords, and peace flooded through him. He knew it was right. He knew, wherever Poppy was at this instant and whatever she was feeling, it would have the same effect on her. As he played the introductory chords, he had a thought, which was unusual for him. Usually when he focused in on playing, all conscious thought scattered and he became more and less than human, some tuning fork for a message from a more beautiful place. But maybe because of what he was playing, the thought came to him fully formed, perfect. It was about how he had always imagined that monogamy would stifle you, kill the passion that had made you go there. But how instead it had made him more passionate. His devotion to Poppy had been the ultimate turn-on for him.

He loved this woman. And only she could light him up.

Nothing had ever felt as completely sexy as the woman on this bed looking at him like he was the only one she ever wanted, telling him she loved him, that he was her only one.

He wanted her to know, now and forever, wherever forever may take her, that it was the same for him. That she was perfect, just as she was, even in her wasted state, even hovering on the brink between this world and some other place. He would always love her, desire her, wish for one more second with her.

As the introductory chords wound up, he cleared his throat.

And then he sang the sweetest song he knew, words about coming as you are, as someone wants you to be. Even though, as much as he loved them, they burned his throat like acid.

No-one would ever do the unplugged version like Kurt, live in New York, sitting on that stool and croaking the most romantic lyrics Quentin had ever heard. But he was damned if he would not give it a red-hot go, here, in this tiny hospice room, singing to his love.

Into the words he injected all the things this woman had given him – a comfort in his own skin, a sense of something better and more beautiful, an absolute connection he had never imagined possible. He looked at her face, and looked through it to see the woman who'd made him jump out of that damned plane, the woman who had arched above him on his bed making that gurgly squeal that drove him mad, the woman with the stupid list that had taken them halfway around the world. He kept going – singing to her about coming as a friend, like an old memory.

Tears pricked at his eyes and he couldn't look at Julia or Scarlett.

He finished the song and put the guitar gently on the floor, picking up Poppy's hand again. 'I'm here, baby,' he whispered. 'To the end. I'm not going anywhere.'

Just as he said it, one of the doctors appeared at the door. The long, lean one who bore the look of the constantly worried. 'It's time,' he said.

* * *

His name was Jean-Paul, Quentin read now on his name tag. He was sure Jean-Paul had probably told him that at least a dozen times over the last two days, but Quentin had been unable to take it in. Only now could he focus on this doctor as a person; now that he had them huddled in a small consulting area, two sympathetic-looking nurses on standby lest any of them start to froth at the mouth. Yep, this doctor was a person. A tired, overworked person. A person who must, Quentin assumed, go through this same, strange, sorry ritual all the time.

The doctor was tall and thin – elegant, Quentin corrected himself. There was something about his neat moustache and sweet, sad brown eyes that was almost feminine. French-Moroccan, Quentin surmised from his brown skin and his name tag, but he spoke with a very proper English accent as he asked them if they were ready.

Scarlett occupied the chair closest to the doctor. She was pale and seemed to be murmuring to herself. She glanced up at his words. 'Where are you from?'

'Bloody hell,' Julia groaned, scraping her chair across the tiled floor in a way that made them all wince. 'Leave the poor bastard alone, Scarlett, let's get on with it.'

Julia had gone from perky-cheerful to maudlin in one nimble manoeuvre once the doctor had come in to make his announcement. Quentin grasped one of her hands and enfolded it in his. He found Scarlett as irritating as she did, but this was not the time.

'Sorry, Scarlett,' Julia relented.

Scarlett just bowed her head.

'We're ready,' Quentin confirmed.

'Algiers.' The doctor smiled at Scarlett. 'Now.' He opened his palms. 'We've talked about this briefly already, but this is the time to go through it all, explain how it's going to work. I'm going to go as slow as you need me to. Okay?'

They all nodded, and Julia clung to Quentin's hand so tightly it went numb.

'Good,' he said. 'Now, you know Poppy has an Advance Health Directive in place, yes?'

They all nodded again, except Scarlett. 'I never knew,' she said. 'Not until Julia said so a couple of days ago.'

The doctor nodded and made a shape with his mouth that expressed quiet sympathy. 'It can be very surprising, to find out.'

Scarlett shook her head. 'No, I mean, I think it's good, that she did. I just …'

Quentin was sitting between Julia and Scarlett and he reached across and grabbed her hand with his spare one to comfort her.

'Go on,' Scarlett said weakly to the doctor.

'This is not about the three of you making any kind of decision,' the doctor assured them. 'This will always be our call, as the medical team. And …' He paused delicately. 'Poppy's wishes are very clear. That's why she is here, for the end time, and not the hospital.'

He looked around to check they were all following, and Quentin found himself riveted to the man's thin mouth. He didn't want to hurt the guy anymore. He just felt helpless, and mesmerised by the words coming from him.

'At this stage,' the doctor continued, 'there is no remaining medical intervention that can do anything for her. We can offer her pain relief, and make sure she's comfortable. That's what Poppy wanted.'

Quentin knew it. He had heard it from Poppy, over and over, and he had heard it again from the doctors over the last two days. He understood how it worked, and he understood that this conversation was a critical last step on the path Poppy had wanted. It was the path she had chosen, and he would do his best to see that it was honoured.

The three of them murmured unintelligible, horrified agreement.

'Are there any questions any of you have about the treatment options?'

Quentin cleared his throat. 'Maybe we shouldn't assume the worst just yet? Maybe she can come out this slump?'

The doctor shook his head. 'She will not come out of this slump, Mr Carmody. This is Poppy's time. Sometime, in the next day or so, her body will give up.'

This time Quentin felt both Julia and Scarlett squeeze his hands. He felt an unbreakable bond form between the three of them as they sat there, bewildered, terrified, clinging to each other.

'Okay,' he croaked.

The doctor cleared his throat. 'We will give her extra oxygen and pain meds now, and she may have some time where she is more lucid, for a while. There are some drugs we can use to help with that.'

'Will she feel pain?' Julia's voice was small and high.

'No,' Jean-Paul said emphatically. 'Her pain and her anxiety will be completely managed. Even if she rouses a bit more, she will be at peace until she goes.'

'But you don't know?' Scarlett's voice was whiny. 'You don't know if she will wake up, or if she'll just …'

Her voice broke and Julia stepped into the breach. 'If she'll just slip away?'

'No,' Jean-Paul admitted. 'We don't know.'

'So we wait,' Quentin said, wrapping an arm around Julia and another around Scarlett and drawing them close. His breath was hot and ragged in his chest at the thought of more waiting. 'We wait with Poppy.'

* * *

Time stretched, cruel and elastic, as they kept vigil.

Quentin mined a deep well of pessimism as he decided she would never wake up, that any goodbyes they needed to say had already been said.

The three of them filled up the hours around Poppy's bed, telling her things, chatting, patting her hands and her head.

Finally, five hours later, she started to stir.

Her breathing was shallow, and the damn prongs were still there, the gentle whoosh of the oxygen louder than it had been before, but her eyes were bright and she seemed relaxed. 'You're all still here.' She smiled, her voice a reedy whisper.

'I tried to boot them out,' Quentin joked, blinking away the tears that sprang into his eyes as he heard her voice. 'But you know what they're like.'

'I sure do.' Poppy laughed softly. 'Stubborn.'

'Are you in pain?' Scarlett's face was ashen.

'No,' Poppy croaked. 'But I've heard it all.' She stopped, as though exhausted with the effort of talking. 'Everything they've been telling me. I know it's the end.'

They waited.

'Are you okay?' she asked.

Quentin heard the worry for them in her voice. Even now she was thinking about them, worrying if she'd done the right thing.

'Yeah,' Quentin joked, squirming in his chair. 'Back's a bit sore; trust you to get the good spot.'

Poppy smiled weakly.

'They'll come in soon, to talk to you, in case you need them,' Julia said, and Quentin had the feeling she felt small and foolish, like a kid presenting to the class, as she said it.

Everyone was quiet.

A tiny frown creased Poppy's forehead as she considered them all.

No. This should not be on her. She was not responsible for their pain right now.

Quentin took a breath. 'Hey, Pop.'

'Mmmm?' Her voice was dreamy.

'Wanna play a game?'

She paused and closed her eyes, and he worried she had slipped back into unconsciousness. 'Hell yeah,' she agreed finally.

Scarlett whooped and Julia punched the air.

'Queen for a Day?' Poppy asked hopefully.

'I had a different idea,' Quentin said, hoping she would go for it, hoping it was the right thing to do. 'It's called Favourite Memory.'

Poppy sighed, a slippery, sad sound. 'I don't want you all memorialising me already,' she said.

'Hah,' Quentin admonished her. 'That's where you've got it all wrong. It's your memories of us I want to hear.' He hoped he was right. He knew she would need diverting, and he knew the best way, always, with Poppy was to put her focus onto others, onto the people she loved. But then something occurred to him, and he felt suddenly like a clumsy fool. 'If you've got the energy for a game.'

The room seemed to hold its breath.

'Always got the energy for a game,' Poppy sighed.

'Okay.' Quentin smiled, remembering that first night, when she had made him guess what she did for a living.

'Scarlett first. What's your favourite memory of her?'

He crossed his fingers and hoped she could come up with one. He knew there had been some bad times, but surely …?

They all peered intently at Poppy, huddled under the sheets. She screwed her face up as she looked at Scarlett. 'I was four,' she wheezed finally. 'You wanted to do playdough art. Expressive. I wanted to play libraries.' She stopped, and Quentin worried it had been too much, that he had exhausted her. 'You let me,' she said, smiling. 'You catalogued all those books with me. Even helped me make the little cards.'

Tears ran down Scarlett's cheeks. 'I should have let you do that stuff more.'

'No,' Poppy said, her voice stronger. 'We all do what we can. Don't, Mum.'

Scarlett moved her chair closer and wrapped her arms around Poppy.

When she released her, Poppy's eyes were closed again.

They waited.

'Well,' she whispered finally, eyes still closed. 'Who's next?'

'Julia,' Quentin said, even though he wanted with everything in him to say 'me'.

Poppy opened her eyes and beamed at him, then turned to Julia.

'Juju,' she said, sighing again. 'Too easy. Prom night.' Her breathing was becoming laboured. 'That guy, remember? The tiny geeky one who adored you. What was his name?'

'Barry,' Julia offered, her voice low and hoarse. 'I have a history of short men with big ideas about me.'

Poppy coughed and then went on, her voice almost disappearing. 'You went with him because he asked you. Even though you wanted Peter Olsen to ask you.'

'And he would have, too.' Julia scowled.

'You're the kindest person I know,' Poppy breathed.

Julia laughed. 'You're the maddest, to think that. I'm sure you're the only person who does.'

'Except Barry,' Poppy countered, her voice a high whisper.

'That's enough, Poppy,' Quentin intervened. 'You need to rest.'

Poppy turned to him, brown eyes luminous in her pale face.

'I don't need to tell you yours, do I?' Her eyes shone at him from her heart-shaped face. 'You know my memory of you, Q, because I'm thinking about it now, like I told you I would. This is the end and you are in here.' She lifted a hand slowly, painfully, and tapped her temple.

Quentin's skin prickled as he thought about her, remembering their night sleeping out under the stars. He stood up and went to lie on the bed next to her, lifting the covers and nudging in close. He lifted her as gently as he could to make more room, then took off his shirt and snuggled against her under the covers.

Scarlett and Julia each held one of Poppy's hands, and Quentin's chest swelled big and painful as he pressed his dying wife against him, as close as he dared. She was as soft and sweet and wholly his as she had ever been. She smelled, even now, like watermelon and Poppy, and he was glad he was here with these women, cocooned in this bubble of love and peace, waiting for Poppy's last tide.

'We're here, Poppy,' Julia said, her green eyes shining. 'We're all here.'

Chapter Eighteen

'Are you sure you want to walk it?'

Julia turned around and glared at Ten, her feet firmly ensconced on the first of six hundred steps that would take them to the second floor of the Eiffel Tower. She was doing two of her least favourite things (three if you counted the fact they were about to hurl ashen pieces of her best friend off the top of the tower).

One: Physical exertion that *didn't* involve nudity. And two: voluntarily being out in the cold.

This Parisian December morning was teeth-aching, toe-numbing, tits-freezing cold. Minus three degrees apparently. Lapland had been warmer!

'Do I look suddenly feeble to you?' she demanded.

Ten, a fancy earthen urn decorated in Indian motifs and scripture tucked under his arm, held up his hands in surrender. 'Sorry.' Even with Julia's height and the added advantage of the step she still had to look up to him. 'It's just a lot of stairs.'

'Don't think you can manage it?' she demanded.

'I'm good.'

'Same goes for me,' she snapped.

Although she was far, far from good.

But the truth was that now they were here, honouring Poppy in the one way they both thought she'd really appreciate, Julia didn't want to rush it. This would be their final goodbye. Once Poppy was scattered to a Parisian wind, she truly would be gone. Forever.

Not that Julia thought Poppy actually existed in the pile of ashes the crematorium had given them two weeks after the funeral. It was more symbolic than anything, but it was their last connection.

Six weeks down the track Julia still couldn't adjust to not having her around. There was this big void in her life now and she constantly caught herself thinking, *I must remember to tell Poppy that* or *I'll grab an extra doughnut for Poppy.*

Julia wished the stairs would go on endlessly and that the lift that would ferry them right to the top would take an eternity. She wanted to linger over this one last ritual. She wanted it to be a marathon, not a sprint.

But Ten, who shot her an impatient look, clearly wanted to get it over and done with. Or maybe he just wanted to do something other than stand on the spot at the foot of a mammoth, chilly iron structure, freezing his gonads off.

'Come the fuck on, Bridget,' he said with what sounded like a fair degree of forced cheer, sidestepping around her. Julia glared at his back as she trudged up behind him, regretting now that she'd ever made him watch *Bridget Jones's Diary* five times in a row with her because it had been one of her and Poppy's favourite movies. Even Spike, who had been impressively available and unfailingly bulletproof despite her scathing rants at him over the last six weeks, had piked out at the fourth session.

The iron staircases zigzagged up and up and up, looking like switchback roads traversing high mountain passes, and by the time Julia had hit the halfway mark to the first floor her thighs were screaming at her and she was well and truly warmed up. She paused on one of the landings, her eyes roaming over the view as she shrugged out of her long duffel coat and unwound the scarf from around her neck.

She was not taking off her thick turtleneck jumper, no matter how bloody hot she got.

From this vantage point she could see the many famous monuments of Paris rising out of the surrounding sea of architecture. The day was bleak and wintery, with no sun to shine off the gold dome of the Hôtel des Invalides or the many other gold-plated statues that adorned bridges, churches and fountains, but their dull sheen still stood out amid the greyness, as did the bright-green grass of the concourse below.

Someone jostled her as she admired the view, murmuring '*Pardon*' in that delightfully French way. Julia looked behind her to identify who it was. She and Ten had arrived early so they could beat the rush and there were few people taking the stairs at this time of day. Hell, most people took the lifts anyway – even if it meant waiting in line for hours. There was certainly no need for jostling.

The guy, who was halfway up the next flight of stairs, looked over his shoulder and smiled at her. Cute – *very cute* – French boy. Or European anyway – refined, with patrician features. Twinkling his dimples at her and giving her his hey-baby-come-back-to-my-place eyes. And if it had been any other day she may well have taken him up on it. God knows she'd tried some sexual healing these last few weeks, desperate for something – *anything* – to deaden the grief.

And it had worked. To a degree. It just didn't last.

But on this day, flirting, scoring, hooking up seemed wrong. *Icky.*

With Poppy dead in an urn and Ten forging on ahead like he was freaking Scott of the Antarctic, this was not the day to tick off *sex with a Frenchman* from her recently evolving bucket list.

'Jules?'

Ten was frowning down at her from the next landing and she turned away from the open invitation in cute boy's eyes to focus on Ten. 'What's the hold-up?'

'I'm coming,' she said, kicking her protesting legs into action. 'It's not a freaking race. There's no prize for climbing the bloody tower the fastest.'

Ten waited for her, his fingers drumming against his thigh. He'd lost weight. And he wasn't exactly Mr Bulky to start with. As she walked up towards him she could see that his jeans were hanging on him, and now that he'd also removed the bulky scarf from his neck she could see the hollows beneath his prominent cheekbones.

Someone of his height and build couldn't afford to lose pounds. 'You've lost a lot of weight,' she said.

He shrugged. 'Don't feel like eating.' He looked out over his shoulder and she followed his gaze to the heavily populated hill of Montmartre in the distance. 'Food tastes like dust,' he said, looking back at her. He took the urn out from under his arm and looked at it. 'Like ash.'

Considering the man was a talented chef, that was a worry. She wanted to tell him it'd get better. That he had to eat. He had to *go on.* Poppy would have wanted it.

Blah, blah, blah.

But she'd heard enough platitudes to last her a lifetime – she wasn't about to use them on Ten. Her particular favourite had come from one of Poppy's work colleagues, who had approached Julia at the funeral to offer her condolences and said, 'God needed another angel in heaven.'

A mushroom cloud of pissed off had exploded inside Julia's head at the vacuous statement. 'Really?' she'd snapped. 'Don't you think if God's so gosh-darned, awesome-powerful and has the ability, you know, to *create* that he could make his own fucking angels without knocking off perfectly good human beings?'

The woman had gawped like a fish but Julia had been beyond caring.

'I don't feel like playing my guitar.' He looked at her. 'Or singing.'

Julia nodded. *Nothing* was the same as before. 'I don't feel like getting out of bed or going to work, and when I do I don't want to be there or even feel the urge to be polite. A woman the other day at work took forty-eight minutes trying to decide between the silver lamé and the gold lamé trim for her wedding napkins because she wanted to use them afterwards to make a winter coat for her dog. Then she asked me my opinion.'

Ten laughed unexpectedly then stopped as if even that was wrong on this day. 'Did you tell her?'

'I said, "Ma'am, please don't take this the wrong way, but I do not give one fuck about your dog or its coat or any of your first-world problems".'

Ten sucked in a breath. '*Burn!*'

'Yeah well,' Julia shrugged. 'I lost her business and probably the business of everyone she knows.'

Ten put his arm around her shoulder and squeezed. 'Some things are just worth it.'

'Maybe. Or maybe it's the universe's way of telling me I should take some time off work.'

'The universe is pretty damn all-knowing like that.'

Julia nodded. 'Somebody should tell it nobody likes a know-it-all.'

Ten chuckled and kissed her on the cheek. 'Come the fuck on, Bridget.'

By the time Julia got to the first floor her legs were on fire. By the time she'd traversed the next three hundred steps to the second floor, they were like jelly, her muscles dissolved into stringy gelatinous masses.

'Do you want to hang around here for a bit?' Ten asked. 'Get our breath back, check out the view? Buy a key ring or a t-shirt?'

'Unless they have one that says *My friend scattered ashes from the top of the Eiffel Tower and all I got was this lousy t-shirt* I'm not interested.'

Ten laughed. 'I'll get one made up for both of us when we get home.'

Julia didn't doubt it. 'Actually, I think we should head up as quickly as possible. Even though it's winter it'll still be shoulder-to-shoulder up there before too much longer and it'd be kind of nice to be as private as possible.'

He nodded. 'Let's join the queue, then.'

Ten minutes later they were stepping out of the lift on the top level and Julia felt temporarily woozy as she looked out at Paris, all Lego-village-like far below them. She wasn't afraid of heights and she didn't suffer from vertigo, but she grabbed hold of Ten to steady herself. Perhaps it was just the import of what was about to happen, the reason why they were here suddenly slapping her in the face as shockingly as the brisk, cold breeze.

And the fact that it was about ten degrees colder up top when you added in the wind-chill factor.

'You okay?' he asked.

Julia nodded quickly, taking some shallow breaths as the bitter wind whipped strands of her hair across her face and wrapped icy fingers around her exposed neck.

They stood there unmoving, adjusting to the altitude and centring themselves for what was about to come. 'Where do you reckon we should do this?' Julia asked eventually.

Ten shook his head. 'I don't know. Let's just walk around and see what pops.'

Julia figured it was as good a plan as any, so they headed for the edge of the platform, which was already bustling with rugged-up tourists – clearly the ones who had taken the lift from the bottom. The platform was open to the air but caged in with sturdy wire fencing that rose up from the railing and curved over their heads, completely encasing them to prevent people from jumping or, heaven forbid, falling.

They did three revolutions, being jostled from time to time by excitable people, all speaking a jumble of different languages. Julia barely registered them as she sought inspiration for the right spot. In reality she knew it didn't matter. It wasn't like Poppy's ashes were going to hover in the air like a magic carpet in a Disney movie – not with this wind. But it suddenly seemed deadly important. They'd chosen to bring Poppy back to Paris, to scatter her ashes *here* because Poppy had always wanted to stand at the summit of the Eiffel Tower and had so very nearly managed it. It seemed only fitting that they at least try to pick the best vantage spot now they were here.

'What about there?' Ten said, pointing to a section vacated by a bunch of giggling Japanese girls. It looked down on the Seine and its many bridges.

'Yes,' Julia agreed. 'Poppy always liked a water view.'

They moved quickly to the spot before anyone else could claim it. *Man, it was high up here.* She'd been to the summit as a child and didn't remember it being so bloody high.

'How should we do this?' she asked.

He shrugged, looking down at the urn. 'I don't know. Which way is the wind blowing?'

Julia blinked. 'How should I know? Do I look like a meteorologist to you?'

'Well, unless we want a dozen Japanese tourists to get a little bit extra for their Eiffel Tower experience in the form of taking home some of Poppy when the ash blows back *all over them*, I think we need to find out.'

He sucked his finger into his mouth then stuck it out through the large diamond-shaped holes of the wire cage. Julia rolled her eyes. Jesus. This time last year she and Poppy were putting up the Christmas tree and scheming how to get Julia out of the full-on turkey-and-plum-pudding Christmas lunch/guilt trip with her parents. She couldn't believe how much could change in so short a time.

How could she face *Christmas* without her best friend? Every crappy carol in the shops, every house decorated with lights, every glass of mulled wine she drank was going to remind her of Poppy.

It was going to *suck*.

Maybe she'd fly to the Maldives and stay at one of those secluded over-water bungalows and ignore it altogether. Watch tropical fish and get a tan.

She looked at Ten, who was now apparently satisfied with the wind direction. 'What are you doing Christmas Day?' she asked.

'Spike and I usually hang out. Drink beer. Watch the cricket.'

'Come to my place. Drink beer and watch cricket there.'

'Yeah?'

Julia nodded vigorously. *Yeah.* There may have been a time when she'd considered paying a hit man to rub Ten out, but they were bonded now whether he liked it or not. Bonded through grief and tragedy and circumstance. And through love.

Things really *had* changed!

'You like the cricket?'

'Good god, no.' She shuddered. 'But it's a step up from football. And I like beer. And Spike. And it's Christmas.'

She'd never screw Spike again, but she'd always be grateful to him for being there, for letting her use his body, when she'd needed it most.

Her phone beeped at her and she pulled it out of her back pocket. 'Speak of the devil,' she said, looking at the text message.

'Spike?'

Julia nodded. 'Just letting me know he's been and checked on Madam Curie and thrown her some dead baby rodents. It should do her till we get back.'

'I told you Spike'd take good care of her.'

Julia nodded. 'I should employ him to be her primary carer. The thought of having to feed – *having to buy* – packets of those …' She shuddered again.

'I doubt Spike would mind. You seem to have him wrapped around your little finger.'

'Humph,' she said non-committally, ignoring his leading comment. 'I still reckon he's probably taking her to gigs and wearing her around his neck so he looks all Alice Cooper bad boy for your groupies.'

Ten laughed. 'I can't see that somehow.'

Julia laughed too, trying to picture it. 'I can't believe I've got her for maybe two decades … why couldn't Poppy have wanted an animal with a shorter life span?'

Ten gave a fond smile, but Julia could see how much it hurt just thinking about Poppy and she almost bit off her tongue.

'She knew her mind, didn't she?' he murmured.

'Yes,' Julia said, her hand slipping onto his forearm. 'She did.'

'Tell me a memory,' he said. 'Something I haven't heard before.'

Julia swallowed the big ball of emotion trying to lodge itself in her throat. The way the chilly wind buffeted her neck, it was as cold as a block of ice. Ten had asked for this every time he'd seen her since the funeral, and she was more than happy to oblige.

Thinking about Poppy hurt but *not* thinking about her hurt more.

'When we were fifteen we wagged school for the day. We went into the Dendy cinema in the city and watched *Austin Powers: The Spy Who Shagged Me*.'

'Oh *be-have*,' Ten mocked in his best Austin Powers impersonation.

'Yes, we were real rebels. We even ate the popcorn.'

'Oh that is bad. That stuff was renowned for its general crapness.'

Julia smiled at the memory. They'd felt so adult. 'We were fearless that day,' she said quietly, looking down as she became all misty-eyed.

She could see the white of Ten's knuckles as he clutched the urn so hard she was afraid it was going to shatter. 'Easy,' she said with a raspy laugh, taking it off him. 'I'm not sure that urn is at all up to international crematorium standards.'

Ten's laugh was suspiciously husky too. 'Scarlett really outdid herself with that, didn't she? It's possibly the ugliest piece of pottery I've ever seen in my life. It's like a blind, dyslexic, fingerless person made it.'

'It's come from India so that's probably exactly who made it. You know Scarlett, it's all about the journey, not the end result.'

They both stared at the urn's wonky, uneven surface before bursting into laughter. Julia laughed until tears rolled and almost froze down her face, and it felt good to feel something other than overwhelming sadness even if it was just for a short while.

'Well …' she said, sobering. 'It was important to her that Poppy's ashes go into it and I figured it wasn't worth the fight. Not when Poppy had made peace with her and never cared about that superficial crap anyway. Put *my* remains in this ugly sucker on the other hand and I will come back to haunt your sorry arse.'

'Duly noted,' Ten said. He switched his attention to the Seine below as the sun valiantly tried to struggle out from behind the grey curtain of cloud. 'How do you think Scarlett's doing?' he asked.

Julia shrugged. Who knew? 'She's in India. *Her spiritual home.* She finds a peace there that I don't think I'll ever understand even if Poppy tried to really valiantly at the end. I mean, it's beautiful there sure, but … I doubt I'll ever go back again.'

'Is it terrible to admit that I'm pleased she's not here?' he said.

'Nope. You got on with her remarkably well during Poppy's illness and I know that was challenging for you considering you wanted to slap her fifty percent of the time because of how much she'd hurt Poppy in the past. It's *perfectly* fine to admit relief at her not being here. I think Poppy would want it to be only us anyway.'

Ten nodded and neither of them said anything for long moments as they just watched the view. 'I guess we should do this thing,' Quentin said finally.

Julia clutched the urn to her chest protectively. Now that it was actually happening, it seemed wrong somehow to be flinging Poppy off this very tall tower.

'What if it's not even her?' she asked. 'What if we got someone else's ashes and they've got Poppy's and they've spread her all over the local sports field?' She looked at Ten. 'She'd *hate* that. And that kind of shit happens all the time doesn't it, in crematoriums? I've read about it.'

'What? In the fucking *News of the World?*'

Julia ignored his sarcasm, tightening her hold on the urn. 'We should get this DNA tested before we do this, just so we know. For sure.'

He looked at her patiently. 'I'm pretty sure several thousand degrees Celsius destroys *all* DNA, Jules.'

Julia nodded, knowing he was right, knowing it was absurd and preposterous, but … She looked up at him.

'I don't want to let her go, Quentin.'

Julia started to cry and he pulled her into his arms, crushing the ashes between them. 'What's in that god-awful-looking urn is not Poppy, Julia. She's inside us. You and me. And Scarlett. And everybody whose life she ever touched. She always will be. The ashes are just symbolic.'

'I miss her,' Julia sobbed.

'I miss her, too.'

They stood hugging for a long time. Somebody with a camera asked if they'd mind moving slightly to the side and Ten growled, 'Fuck off,' at them.

Eventually, though, Julia felt strong enough to do what they'd come to do and she moved out of his arms.

'Ready?' he asked.

She nodded. 'As I'll ever be.'

Ten wet his finger then stuck it in the air again, and despite the fact that she felt like crumbling in two, Julia found herself smiling at the absolute preposterousness of it all. 'Okay, should be good to go if we open it here.'

Julia removed the dodgy-looking cork stopper on the top and Ten stood behind her, his hand on her shoulder as she lifted it to one of the diamond openings and tipped it up.

The grey ash joined the grey sky, the wind picking it up instantly, swirling it around and around then dispersing it. Julia poured until it was all gone, watching Poppy disappear into the sky.

'Fly, Poppy, fly,' she whispered.

'We love you, Poppy,' Quentin said softly.

They both stood still and watched, long past the time they could see anything at all, the wind snatching Poppy away over the river and rooftops of Paris, claiming her quickly, as if it couldn't wait to know her.

'What are we going to do now?' Julia asked eventually.

Ten shook his head, his arm snaking around her shoulders in a loose hold, his forearm brushing her neck. Neither of them took their eyes off the sky, as if they might catch one last glance of Poppy cavorting in the clouds.

'We'll live,' he said. How could something so simple sound so bloody impossible? 'I'll play in the band and you'll run your events company and I'll come over and cook you dinner every now and then and you'll come and listen to us play when you can and ... we'll live. It'll be tough at first, but we *have* to live. For Poppy. Because she couldn't.'

A hot tear slid down Julia's face. 'And we'll always have this memory.'

He hugged her tighter. 'Yes,' he said. 'We'll always have Paris.'

Julia smiled. And in the distance she swore she could hear Poppy laughing.

Acknowledgements

It seems very odd to say how much fun we had writing this book when it deals with such a serious subject. Few people get through their life without cancer touching them or their family in some way – we know this intimately – and we were very aware of this as the story progressed. But finding the light in the dark is one of the ways we coped, as so many others do, during a very tough time in our lives and it was important for us that our characters reflected our experiences and the gamut of emotions that come with a cancer diagnosis. We also just happen to crack each other up a lot of the time and writing a book with someone you love so dearly and who gets you so completely is fun no matter what the subject matter.

Writing the acknowledgement section of a book is a great honour because there are always a lot of people to thank for getting the book on the shelf and into the hands of readers and, as the author/s, you want to be able to express those thanks publicly. It is also potentially quite fraught as you hope like hell you don't leave anyone out. So, here goes …

To all the team at Mira Australia who have worked on our book in any capacity but particularly to the lovely Sue Brockhoff who acquired *Numbered* and is possibly the sweetest, most savvy and least rufflerable (yes, *not* a word) woman one could ever hope to meet. Also to Annabel Blay for all her general corralling of us and Alex Nahlous whose line editing saved us (and you) from, amongst other things, excessive use of heads nodding/shaking and the word 'just'.

Also, of course, there are our families who deal with mothers and wives who aren't *normal*. Whose brains ponder things like the temperature in Lapland in October, henna tattooing in India and the logistics of sweaty sex with drummers while helping with homework, attending P&C meetings and cooking the evening meal. To Jack, Claire, Saul, Quinn, Neve and Jem, you are the font of and the reason for our creativity. We'd probably still write without you in our lives but then what would be the point? And to Blair and Mark, two ever-loving, ever-patient men who know their lives would be easier with different women but infinitely poorer.

An extra special thanks to Carita Birch who shared some of her experiences regarding the time her dear mum went through intrathecal chemo. And to everyone else (women and men) – be vigilant, check and *know* your breasts/body, listen to your gut and don't take *it'll be fine* for an answer if it's telling you something different.